THE IRISH ADMIRALTY

A STORY OF IRISH NAVAL HEROES OF THE AMERICAN REVOLUTIONARY WAR

AND

LIBERATION OF SOUTH AMERICA

MICHAEL GERARD

Published by Sand Science Books 2025

ISBN: 979-8-9923514-2-2 Hardcover
ISBN: 979-8-9923514-3-9 Paperback

PART ONE

COMMODORE JOHN BARRY
COUNTY WEXFORD
IRELAND
FATHER OF THE AMERICAN NAVY

• • •

PART TWO

ADMIRAL WILLIAM BROWN
COUNTY MAYO
IRELAND
FOUNDER OF THE ARGENTINE NAVY

OTHER BOOKS BY MICHAEL GERARD

• • •

THE KIMBERLEY FILE

• • •

IRELAND'S FINAL REBELLION AND AN AMERICAN DREAM

• • •

THE IRISH MERCHANT OF ALICANTE

Dedicated to the memory of two great Irishmen –
COMMODORE JOHN BARRY
and
ADMIRAL WILLIAM BROWN

To all the countless Irish who were forced to emigrate, who found solace in the four corners of the earth and who assimilated in their adopted countries to create a renowned Irish diaspora for the world –

To Adam for traveling to Argentina for the purpose of research and for photos that have enhanced this book –

To Eoin for his computer and IT skills, his patience and help in this project and in previous books –

To my proofreaders, editors and expert peer reviewers who helped guide me and improve this labor of love –

To family, friends, followers, readers and supporters of Independent Authors and small business publishers –

Thank You All.

TABLE OF CONTENTS

PROLOGUE

Consider a snapshot of Ireland in the early years of the eighteenth-century. In the preceding centuries the Chieftains of Gaelic Ireland had been defeated by ruthless British armies, and the murderous rampage of Oliver Cromwell had finally broken the spirit of the Irish people. With few exceptions, the confiscated land had been doled out in large tracts to loyal Protestant settlers from various parts of Britain. The 'Plantation of Ireland' put this land wealth in the hands of the Irish Protestant Ascendency, in a new land system devised to finally crush all resistance. The typical Irish Catholic family toiled as tenants on a small plot of their once ancestral land, paying high rent to these planted landlords, many of them absentee owners whose local agents did their dirty work. Thoughts of further rebellion were often little more than dreams in the minds of the few brave patriots who strove to keep the ideals of Irish resistance alive. For most of the native population, they had nothing left to cling to except their Catholic faith, their Gaelic language and their close-knit large families. The occupying British Army garrisons, their imbedded spies and their biased judicial system were the organs of control – overseeing the eviction of tenants who did not pay their exorbitant rent on time and snuffing out any attempts by the Irish to resist.

The British Royal Navy ruled the waves, including the seas around the British Isles, and the dominion of Ireland. Catholics were prevented from advancement at every turn and the Penal Laws were strictly enforced to keep it that way for the native Irish unless they renounced their faith. Natives had little or no opportunity to enlist in the Army and were not allowed to join the Royal Navy – a tiny number did circumvent these restrictions with the help of influential insiders.

The island of Ireland has a proud seafaring history that stretches back to earliest times. St. Brendan the Navigator (AD 484–c.577) is one of these revered sailors. He and his companion monks made many sea journeys of discovery to isolated islands in the seas around Ireland, Scotland, Wales, England and Brittany (Celtic Northern France) where they set up monasteries. These voyages and Brendan's famous seven-year voyage further west, searching for the Land of Paradise in the sixth century, are recorded in Annals written in the Irish Gaelic language and in Latin. Many scholars credit St. Brendan for the discovery of North America long before Columbus, sailing there in the 'Irish Currach' – a small simple wooden-framed ship covered with tanned ox hides. In 1977 the explorer Tim Severin proved that this voyage was possible in a 36-foot currach made with the exact materials from St. Brendon's time, sailing a route skirting Iceland and Greenland. Stories such as those of St. Brendan were passed down the generations through the oral 'Seanachie' storytelling tradition of Ireland, sustaining hope among her people during the darkest of times, and fostering a desire among the Irish to keep this seafaring tradition alive.

'THE IRISH ADMIRALTY' recounts the remarkable story of two seafaring heroes born in eighteenth-century Ireland. These two men found a way to rise to prominence in the Navy ranks of two faraway emerging new nations, at a time when The Penal Laws were enforced in their homeland to exclude the Irish from any naval participation.

PART ONE of the book tells the story of Commodore John Barry, born in County Wexford in 1745, who became a master mariner in merchant shipping, and soon thereafter the most accomplished Commander in the fledgling American Continental Navy – a naval force that was instrumental in helping the Colonists to victory in the American Revolutionary War. In due course the Founding Fathers of the United States of America realized that they needed a New American Navy to protect their merchant shipping fleet from pirates and to safeguard the new country's freedom in a world dominated by Navy fleets of the European great powers. Irishman John Barry rose to become their choice to lead this New Navy.

Commodore John Barry is widely acknowledged as being the "Father of the American Navy".

PART TWO of the book recounts the story of Admiral William Brown, born in County Mayo in 1777. Brown honed his master mariner skills in the British Royal Navy, after managing to join as a Cadet with help from an unlikely influential source. After seeing his progress in the Royal Navy stymied by nepotism and prejudice, he transferred to the Merchant Navy, then left the service and sailed South over the equator to settle in Buenos Aires, on the Rio de la Plata estuary of South America.

There, he experienced first-hand the injustices of the Spanish Empire, became a revolutionary and expert navigator of the tricky River Plate estuary waters, and a fearless blockade breaker. His skills attracted the leaders of the fledgling independent Buenos Aires United Provinces who tasked him with forming a Navy. The rest is pure history – he became the "Founder of the Argentine Navy", won the decisive battles that enabled the Portenos (residents of Buenos Aires) to throw off the yoke of the Spanish Empire, and along the way he helped other South American nations to strike out for their own National Freedom.

John Barry and William Brown overcame almost insurmountable odds to achieve their place in history. Both men emigrated from Ireland to their adopted countries to simply ply their trade as merchant seamen. Each man found themselves in a key historical moment of their respective adopted homeland's fight for independence. When circumstances affecting peaceful trade pushed them to fight, they fought fiercely and defeated the oppressors, were quickly recognized as extraordinarily gifted battleship captains and fearless fighters, who went on to win great naval battles for their adopted countries and earn leadership roles.

Both were men of honor, strict adherents to the sacred laws of God and of the sea, and of the rules that apply to naval warfare. Both were wounded in battle and suffered personal family tragedies. Meanwhile they showed great respect for the dignity and safety of their crews, even including their vanquished adversaries – they were universally praised for their treatment of their captives. Despite having to spend most of their best years away at sea, they were devoted family men, and they also maintained a keen interest in Ireland's troubled history, often sending money to aid their 'Irish Family' and to support the Irish fight for freedom.

These Irish heroes are the epitome of what it takes to be included under the title of this book –

'THE IRISH ADMIRALTY'

AUTHOR'S NOTE

My mission in 'The Irish Admiralty' was to place the narrator alongside these two master sailors onboard their ships: to carry the reader along on their extraordinary voyages, and through the fog of cannon smoke during their naval battles. Their deeds are recorded in real history, and I feature these deeds prominently throughout the book, as our heroes interact with the important leaders of their day.

Both men were born into meager circumstances, in a time when record keeping in Ireland did not include details on the downtrodden native Irish – meaning that reliable information on their early years in Ireland is scarce and is clouded. I have evaluated the available information and chosen a narrative for their early years that I think most resembles what they experienced and fits with their own words on the subject. Both men achieved greatness – Commodore Barry in the United States of America and Admiral Brown in Argentina, and both have a special place in the history of their adopted countries, with numerous monuments erected there to honor them.

Thankfully, their exploits have also received some recognition in Ireland. Their stories prove yet again the resourcefulness, talent and spirit that our Irish forefathers possessed, even at a time in their history when they were being oppressed and exploited. I encourage readers to delve more deeply into Irish history – you will find joy in your discoveries, just like I did.

• • •

'The Irish Admiralty' is my fourth book, joining my earlier titles – 'The Kimberley File': 'Ireland's Final Rebellion and An American Dream': and 'The Irish Merchant of Alicante' – all available in print, as e-books and as audio editions.

Go raibh maith agaidh go leir (thank you all very much).
Michael Gerard

www.michaelgerardauthor.com for information and links to purchase my books. I encourage readers to post reviews and share their thoughts with the reading community.

PART ONE

COMMODORE JOHN BARRY

BORN IN WEXFORD
COUNTY WEXFORD

IRELAND
1745

"FATHER OF THE AMERICAN NAVY"

"NOT THE VALUE AND COMMAND OF THE WHOLE BRITISH FLEET CAN SEDUCE ME FROM THE CAUSE OF MY COUNTRY. TELL ADMIRAL HOWE THAT I WILL BE SEEING HIS SHIPS IN BATTLE, AT THE END OF OUR CANNONS."

Captain John Barry's answer to the Loyalist emissary who offered him a bribe of 20,000 guineas and a Royal Navy commission to give up his Continental Navy ship and come over to the British side – September 1777.

Commodore John Barry

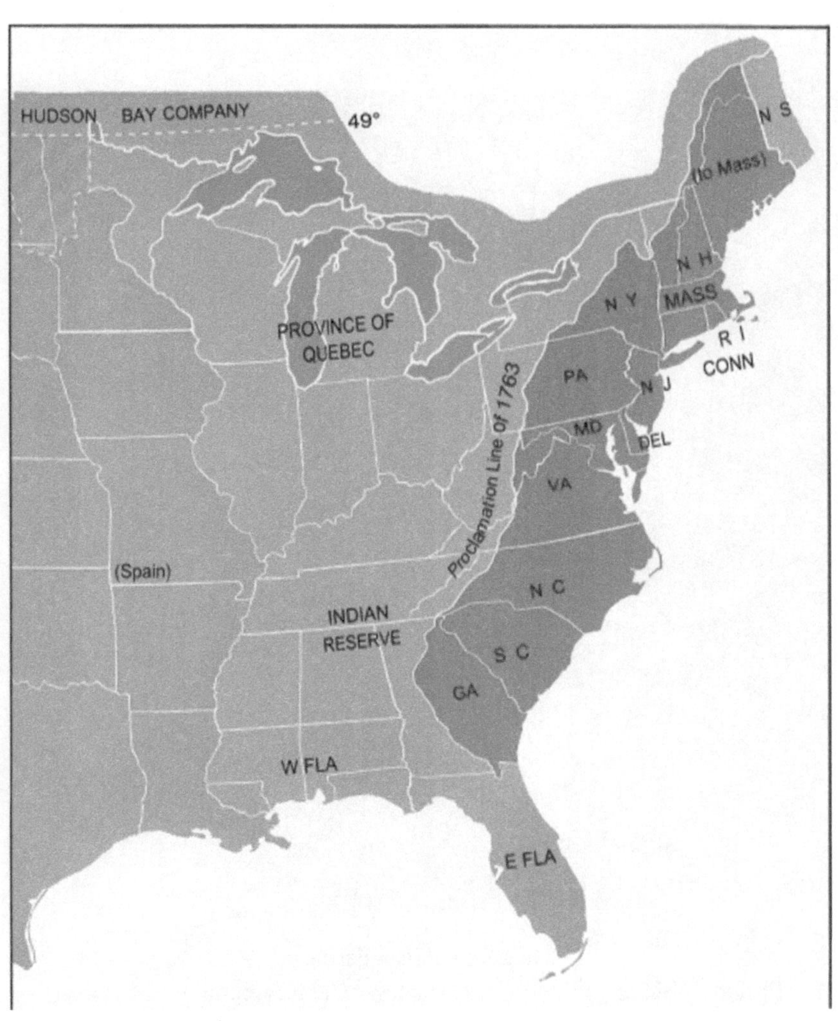

The original 13 American Colonies in 1775 (modern borders overlaid)

Delaware River Estuary
Philadelphia at top and Cape May and Cape Henlopen at bottom

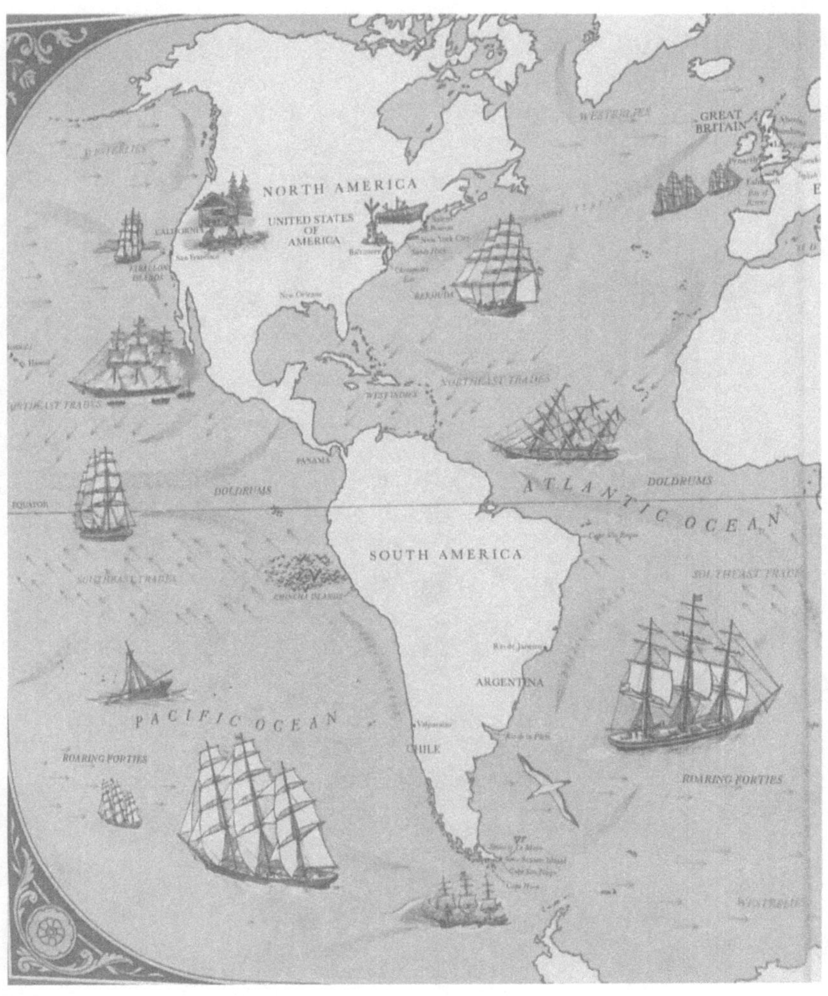

Respect for the prevailing winds in the North Atlantic, the Bay of Biscay and the Caribbean Sea paid dividends in the successful voyages of Commodore Barry

Marker on Merritt Island, Brevard County, Florida

"USS Alliance, commanded by Captain John Barry defeated HMS Sybil, commanded by Captain James Vashon in a one-hour naval battle onslaught off the coast of Cape Canaveral —on March 10, 1783"

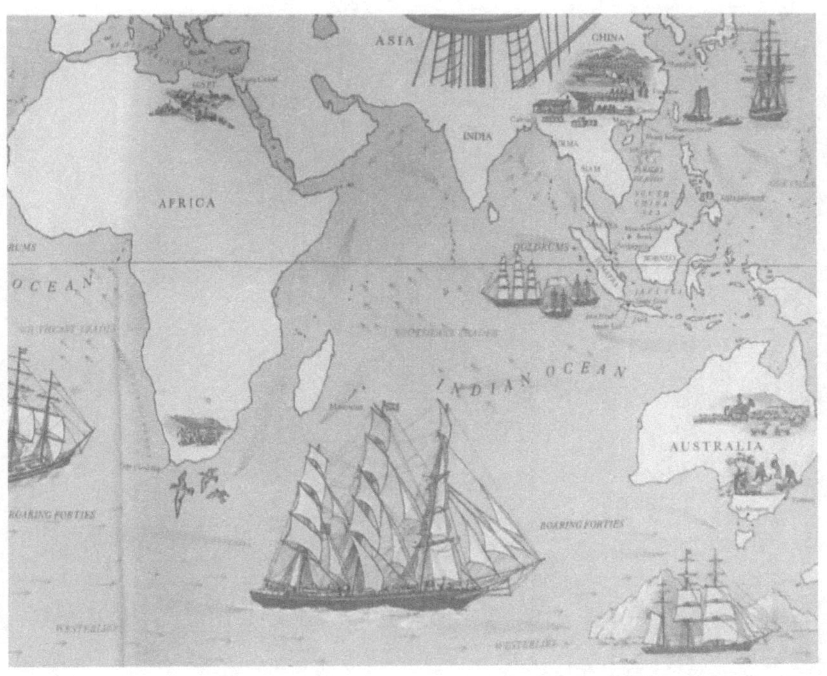

When the Revolutionary War ended, Captain Barry sailed the merchant ship 'Asia' on a mammoth voyage from Philadelphia to Canton, China and back for Robert Morris

Marker on Gascoigne Bluff, St Simons Island, Georgia

"Live Oak timber for the building of USS Constitution (Old Ironsides) and the other ships of our first US Navy were cut on St Simons, under Captain Barry's guidance, and loaded here in 1794 for shipment north where the vessels were built"

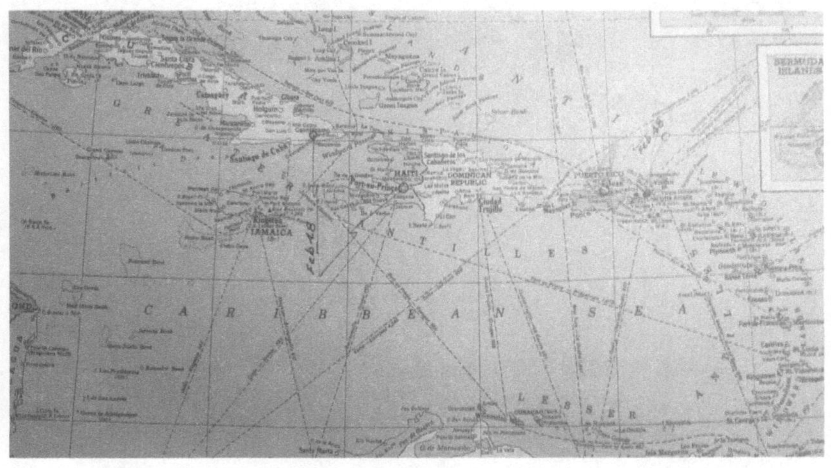

The West Indies and Caribbean, where Captain Barry sailed extensively on merchant ships and as Commodore of the American Navy

Monument to Commodore John Barry in Washington, DC

Monument to Commodore John Barry at the US Naval Academy, Annapolis, Maryland

Monument to Commodore John Barry in Philadelphia, Pennsylvania

President John F Kennedy in 1963, laying a wreath at the monument to Commodore John Barry in Wexford, Ireland, the place of Barry's birth

CHAPTER ONE

FROM WEXFORD TO PHILADELPHIA

John Hancock, the President of the Continental Congress, signed John Barry's commission papers on December 7, 1776, appointing him a Captain in the Continental Navy and captain of the newly acquired brigantine 'Wild Duck'. The Marine Committee, with the full approval of Congress, had acquired the fast merchantman and wanted it hastily converted into a warship – that conversion was to be handled and overseen by John Barry himself. The previous day, John was summoned to meet with Hancock and the head of the Marine Committee, Robert Morris, who informed him that he was being given a command – finally.

Morris had long-known John Barry's reputation as a master sailor, and he apologized for the delay.

"John, in my humble opinion you are the most proven and skillful ship's captain in Philadelphia, or in any of our thirteen colonies for that matter. You have been overlooked too many times as the naval fleet has been assembled. I commend you for your patience and for your recent work leading the outfitting of our fleet to date. I think my esteemed colleagues were concerned about your young age and did not realize sooner that you have immense experience for one so young – I have it in my head that you are still in your twenties. Please note that this is a separate and independent command, directly from the Marine Committee and under the direct authority of the Continental Congress – it is not subject to, or part of the fleet that is under Captain Esek Hopkins."

"Thank you both for this opportunity. Just to clarify, I am past my twenties, soon to be thirty-one. I accept the command and I promise you that I intend to cause as much distress to the enemy as is in my power."

The meeting wasted no more time with banter, setting a tight schedule that sent John straight to work. The 140-ton brigantine 'Wild Duck' was immediately moved to Whartons shipyard in Philadelphia to be thoroughly checked and outfitted for war. Captain Barry began refitting the ship at breakneck speed and accomplished that task in just two weeks. The ship was renamed the 'Lexington' to honor the first action of the Revolutionary War – she carried sixteen four-pounders and twelve swivel guns. A crew of some seventy was quickly gathered, aided in no small measure by the high reputation of her Captain, and by the promise of rich spoils from captured prizes to be shared by every crew member. John Barry and his crew were about to serve under the Articles of War drawn up by the Continental Congress. These American sailors were undeterred by the British promise to treat captured Continental Navy members as pirates and subject them to the same punishment as pirates – hanging from the yard arm.

Thus began the naval service of the County-Wexford-born Irishman, John Barry, as a captain in the Continental Navy of America during the American Revolutionary War, on the side of his adopted country against the most powerful navy in the world, the British Royal Navy.

• • •

The Wexford that John Barry was born into in 1745 was a world away, literally and figuratively.

John was the oldest of five children. His parents, James and Ellen Barry, were lowly farm workers on the estate of a local Wexford squire. They lived in a simple mud hut near Wexford town and near the harbor, close to the rural hamlets of Tacumshane and Ballysampson.

Ireland at that time was firmly under the harsh rule of Britain, and the cruel Penal Laws introduced some 50 years earlier were adding to the misery of the people. When the Gaelic Chieftains were defeated by the new model armies of England in the fifteenth and sixteenth centuries all their land was confiscated, and a master plan was adopted by the British rulers – designed to break the centuries-old Gaelic system.

That plan called for loyal Protestants from England, Wales and Scotland to relocate to Ireland to occupy large tracts of land assigned to them for 'services rendered to the Crown'. History has labelled this plan 'The Plantation of Ireland'. Each Landlord had to subdivide most of their land into multiple small holdings which they rented to the native Irish Catholics at exorbitant rents. The English Parliament figured that these Irish wretches would need to work from dawn to dusk to survive – giving them less time for rebellion and every reason to convert to Protestantism to avail of the incentives that came with conversion.

The Catholic Barry family was on the lowest tier of this system and calling them poor would be an understatement – the only luck the family had was to be living in an area of decent farmland that produced good tillage crops, and to be lucky enough to be near a seaport. The port of Wexford had easy access to the Irish Sea, and it was busy with agricultural exports to Britain and to continental Europe. John's uncle Nicholas was a ship's captain sailing to and from European ports, which gave his family a decent living and much respect from the local community.

Britain had just begun to allow Catholics to get basic schooling, but as always there was a catch – if children wanted to extend that schooling, they had to adopt the Protestant Church of Ireland religion. The Barry brood – John, Patrick, Eleanor, Margaret and Thomas attended school from the age of five or six but like most Catholics they stopped at age ten

– on the 'advice' of the local priest. Learning how to help their families to survive was more important to the poor than attending school, and the Barry's were in that category. Because Wexford was a port the local kids were taught some English at school to go along with their everyday Gaelic Irish. The school master said it would give them better opportunities to earn a few coppers from the visiting sailors, and it was helpful for getting employment on ships.

As the eldest, John didn't have much of a childhood. From the time he could walk he worked on the tiny plot of family land where they grew their own potatoes plus some root vegetables, while his father and mother and some relatives worked the bigger patch to grow grain that had to be sold to cover the rent monies to the squire. John and Patrick ran down to the docks any chance they could, to watch the ships coming and going. They formed the notion that these sailors had a great life visiting foreign places and that life at sea was idyllic. When John was nine years of age, the family was struggling mightily for survival, and they had to borrow money from Uncle Nicholas. John overheard a conversation between his uncle and his father, where he himself was the topic. Afterwards his father told him that there was a place coming available for a cabin boy on Uncle Nicholas' ship.

"I told him you would be able for that job, so I did. I know you are very young, but this is a chance we can't afford to miss, and you will learn more at sea than at school."

"Daddy – Shur don't I know as much already as the master

himself other than fancy English and those foreign words he sometimes comes out with. He calls it Latin; they sound like the words Father Kelly says during Mass. I'll do it Daddy and learn everything I can from Uncle Nick."

"Good. Not a word to anyone now but be ready to walk out of school the minute we get the final word, good lad."

"I will. Go raibh mile maith le Uncil Nich (a thousand thanks to Uncle Nick)."

A week later John was taken out of school and went to sea as a cabin boy on a merchant schooner that plied the local routes between Ireland, England and Holland – on a ship captained by Uncle Nicholas. This 'wooden world' was to change John forever, and sailing was to be his life's passion. He survived early sea sickness to gain his sea legs, then served meals to the captain and did on-deck errands. He was allowed to sleep in a corner of the captain's quarters which was in the calmer aft area of the ship, rather than having to be in the squalor below deck in the bow area, and he got scraps of the captain's leftover food which was better than what the others ate. Regular sailors' rations were biscuits full of worms, rancid salted beef, plus a pint of grog per day (a mix of water, lime juice and rum). John was entitled to a half pint, but he dared not drink it – Uncle Nick made him sup up a little grog every day to get used to it and he explained its importance in keeping away the dreaded scurvy. John was a young child, but he knew immediately what his life goal was – to sail the seas and someday have his own captain's cabin.

The most important thing was that Uncle Nick took John under his wing. Once they had clear sailing, he gave the lad reading and writing lessons, showed him how to write up log reports and how to read sailing charts. Ropes and rigging were the lifeblood of sailing and John learned all aspects of the 'ropes' from this early age – vital knowledge to help him make his way up the maritime ladder. Over the next six years he moved from cabin boy to apprentice sailor to full sailor and moved on from Uncle Nick's ship, with his blessing. All the while the boy was growing tall and lean – he was six foot tall by the age of fifteen and could handle the rigging with the best of them, observing and learning his sailor skills from the experienced 'salts'.

At fifteen he made his first voyage across the Atlantic, to Philadelphia, a two-to-three-month voyage in 1760. The port of Philadelphia, sitting on the Delaware River, some thirty-five miles from Delaware Bay was the busiest port in America. It was also the biggest city in America at that time, with a population of some 30,000 inhabitants that included a significant number of Irish – the city both overawed and intrigued John. He didn't know a lot about the American Colonies, just that there was a dozen or so in the group and that they were also part of the British Empire. It was a minor annoyance to him that leaving Ireland didn't allow him to escape the clutches of the Empire, but his immediate concern was not any of this. America was the land of opportunity where he hoped to prosper and to send money home to help his parents and his siblings in Ireland. When ashore in Philadelphia he had to pay board in a seaman lodge house until he got hired on to a crew and could then live aboard ship.

The London Coffeehouse on First and High Streets was the premier gathering place for the more than 500 merchants doing business in the city, and all life and wealth revolved around the port. The West Indies was the cornerstone of these merchant's trade. Imports from the islands were reshipped to the other twelve American colonies and to England. John managed to find employment soon after arrival – on the ships plying these West Indies routes – Saint Kits, Barbuda and Hispaniola. He was a likeable lad as well as being a good sailor which meant near constant employment from then on, and by the age of nineteen he had risen to the status of ship's Mate. He was by then 6 foot 4 inches tall, towering over most people of Philadelphia and the ports he visited. John was not into the drinking life that most Tars engaged in. He drank very little alcohol outside of his grog and took his mother's instructions seriously – dutifully writing regular letters to her and sending home whatever money he could to Wexford to support the family there. His success in America prompted his siblings to think of following him to sea.

John was ambitious from the start, and he quickly amassed a detailed knowledge of the Caribbean sailing routes, and the important commodities traded there, while his leadership skills aboard ship increased and were noticed by many ship captains who saw his potential as a captain. A select group of merchant firms controlled most of Philadelphia trade at the time and they retained the older experienced captains by giving them equity in the vessels they captained. That made it difficult for a young man like John to break into the top echelons – he had to look outside of this circle if he wanted to become captain of a ship.

He found out about an older merchant named Edward Denny who had done well by brokering cargo through other merchants, and now wanted his own ship and an affordable captain. Denny needed to operate at lower costs to compete with the bigger merchant houses and he was willing to take a chance on a younger captain who would accept less pay. A mutual friend set up a meeting for John with Mr. Denny at the Coffeehouse. John sat and waited nervously at a table until an older man approached him.

"Young man, are you John Barry whom I have come here to meet with?"

"Indeed, I am, Sir, and happy to make your acquaintance," said John, as he stood up to greet Mr. Denny.

"Oh, my word. Joe didn't tell me that you were a giant, or that you are so young, but he did tell me you have a lot of experience in the Caribbean. Tell me about yourself."

"Sir, I have been at sea since I was nine years old, made my first Atlantic crossing as an able seaman at the age of fifteen, which means I have been based here for six years. During that time, I have been a crew member on dozens of voyages with some of the best captains – sailing between Philadelphia and various ports in the West Indies, and further afield. I have worked my way up to First Mate and I am now ready to be your captain – for I know how to handle crewmen and they have confidence in me. I am at your service, Sir."

"I will be taking a big chance on you, John – are you sure you are up to the task?"

"Without a doubt, Sir. I will sail faster and make you more profits than the settled older fat captains. Of this, I am sure."

"Are you able to assemble a crew with haste, and command their respect at such a young age?"

"Yes, to both questions. There are many sailors here at this place tonight that can vouch for me if you have a mind to ask them. Seasoned salts like Joe Roney at the end of that next table have been under my command – I can call him over if you want me to."

"That will not be necessary. John, as I'm sure you know, the Quakers are at the top of the merchant ladder here – they deal in everything except slaves; they leave that trade to us Anglican merchants, and that is fine by me. I have made good profits from slave cargos. With my own ship I want to trade in all commodities, including slaves. Are you fine with that, young man?"

"Cargo is cargo, Sir."

"Then I will put my faith in you, and you must put your faith in me. We will start at 75 percent of the average wages that the old seadogs command, with bonuses to be earned, based on our profits. Those profits you promised me earlier should earn you bonuses to make up for the initial shortfall in wages. Are you ready to shake on this deal?"

"Yes Sir."

They shook hands and raised a toast. Then Denny told him details of the ship he intended to buy – the schooner named 'Pitt'. John knew of it and offered to inspect it. This was done with haste, the ship was purchased for 500 pounds, then renamed 'Barbados' and John Barry was registered as her Captain. John accepted the challenge of working with a skeleton crew of six, to further reduce expenses. Around that same time John had become romantically involved with an Irish girl of his own age who was working as a house servant in Philadelphia – Mary Cleary from County Sligo. Their courtship was cut short when John sailed to the West Indies on 'Barbados' in October, his first voyage as captain.

• • •

The British Empire controlled the American Colonies and during the 1760's and early 1770's their Parliament imposed several coercive laws on the colonists. There was the Sugar Act of 1764, the Stamp Act of 1765, followed by others such as the Townshend Acts of 1767 – which together introduced various forms of restrictions and taxation, leading to growing discontent and resistance among the colonists. Parliament wanted to extract the maximum revenue for their coffers from the American merchants, while protecting the trade of their own merchants. The Navigation Laws and Sugar Act were designed to restrict the profits made by colonial privateers. To circumvent these laws, the American merchants had taken to widespread smuggling as part of their normal business operations.

On his first voyage as Captain, John carried barrel staves, shingles, chains, iron bars, plus other assorted merchandise. He set a course towards Bermuda and then south by east for three weeks, bringing the 'Barbados' into Bridgetown in mid-November. To avoid the North American winter storms the ship then stayed in the islands and sailed local routes all winter, the furthest north being to Savannah, Ga – and they did their share of smuggling, per common practice. In early summer he sailed back to Philadelphia with rum, sugar and molasses. Mr. Denny was happy with the profits and in August the ship made a repeat trip to Bridgetown with similar outbound cargo and headed home with rum and sugar. On that return voyage the ship was caught in a hurricane – John's excellent seamanship steered them through, and he guided the ship safely to Philadelphia in late October. Once ashore he immediately married Mary in a simple ceremony, before sailing again to the West Indies in November; wintering there as before and returning to Philly in May of the following year. John's reputation as a master sailor continued to grow and he was invited to join the Sea Captains Club. He made multiple more successful sailings for Mr. Denny till 1770, when the old man decided to retire – he sold the ship and John was discharged.

John wanted to move up to being a part owner of a better ship and convinced two successful Irish artisans to partner with him to buy a schooner they renamed 'Industry'. After only a year the partners got cold feet because of increased ship repair costs caused by damaging storms. John could not afford to buy them out and it was agreed to sell the ship after her next voyage, which was to Nova Scotia. While there, John found a buyer for 'Industry' and also found a very nice Bermuda schooner named 'Frugality' that was for sale. He inspected the schooner and took an option on it before his return voyage to Philadelphia. He desperately wanted 'Frugality' but couldn't afford it – he needed a merchant with ready cash and the ability to see the potential for this ship, captained of course by himself. By the time he reached home port he had decided who he should pitch his idea to. Reese Meredith, one of Philadelphia's wealthiest merchants was his target and after a short meeting Mr. Meredith agreed to purchase 'Frugality' and appoint John his newest and youngest captain who would command this ship. Once the sale of the 'Industry' was finalized, John sailed it to the new owner in Nova Scotia and returned with 'Frugality', immediately setting about to refit it.

John's next younger brother Patrick Barry had followed him to sea and was also steadily climbing the sailing ranks. He had arrived in Philadelphia several months before as a crew member on a ship – and then found regular work on the

Caribbean routes just like John had done. He now surprised John and Mary by arriving in Philadelphia as shipmaster of the 'Amelia' and showed up at their home unannounced.

"John, how's she cuttin?" Patrick shouted to him in Gaelic, before John even saw him.

"Ceart go leor (great)," he responded, smiling broadly as he turned to greet his brother.

"Maith an fear (good man)."

"And who is this fine Cailin you have in tow?"

"This is Mary Farrell, from Mayo, my fiancée."

"Welcome to ye both, and congratulations."

Inside, over ale and sweet cake, they chatted, and Patrick and Mary filled them in on the details. She was in service at one of Philadelphia's finest homes, a very similar background to Mary Barry herself, before she married John. They wanted to get married right away, before either brother had to set sail again. The wedding ceremony was performed a few days later, with John being his best man and his wife Mary handling the maid of honor duties. Then John got busy refitting his new ship, which was renamed 'Peggy' at registration. His first voyage in the 'Peggy' was to Oranjestad, in Sint Eustatius (part of the Lesser Antilles), known as the 'Golden Rock' of the Caribbean, because it was a free port open to every country, and it was a transit point for all kinds of goods. It was also a hotbed of the lucrative smuggling trade that made the colonial merchant business tick.

• • •

The largest economy in the world at the time was that of Britain, and a mainstay product of their Empire was tea – a commodity that was increasingly traded and was fast becoming a source of major friction between the colonies and the motherland. The East India Company had faded from being one of the main trading companies of Britain and they were close to bankruptcy. Their warehouses held almost twenty million pounds of tea, and they asked for their government's help to trade it and get them out of debt in the process. The British Parliament passed the Tea Act in 1773, giving the East India Company the freedom to deal directly with American merchants. The so-called 'loyal merchants' in Philadelphia and in other American ports petitioned for the handling rights, which would exclude most regular merchants. Delaware river pilots threatened to 'Tar and Feather' any rogue pilot that would guide the newly arrived ship 'Polly', laden with tea, into port. This threat reverberated all the way to London, and the feud intensified when Philadelphia men boarded another tea ship, removed the cargo of tea to shore and destroyed it. In Boston, John Adams and his group, The Sons of Liberty, wanted to show their displeasure with Parliamentary actions, and on December 16 they staged "The Boston Tea Party". Colonists boarded three merchant vessels in Boston Harbor and dumped 342 chests of tea overboard – the ultimate insult to British authority.

These events occurred while John Barry was on his return voyage from the Caribbean. Back on shore, John joined the large boisterous crowds at the State House Yard who proposed and passed many resolutions condemning the British Parliament for their actions – even though he was not interested in the politics of it all and had every reason to expect British power to prevail. Next day John sailed again for Sint Eustatius and did not return until February of 1774. While he was away this time, his wife Mary became very ill with a fever in January and tragically died soon afterwards. His brother, Patrick, happened to be in port at the time – he and his wife handled all the funeral arrangements after doing all they could to save Mary Barry. As John's returning ship was being piloted up the river, Patrick was rowed out to meet John's.

John was pleasantly surprised to have him come aboard and welcomed him with a big hug, then realized that Patrick had a sad look on his face.

"Something is wrong – I can tell. Is there bad news from Wexford?"

"I'm afraid it's closer to home than that. We lost your Mary while you were away."

John was speechless, he felt weak at the knees and had to sit down. He looked away to shore as he teared up – "What happened?"

"She developed a sudden fever and was confined to her bed for two days before my Mary found out. She brought in a doctor immediately. Her condition got steadily worse and he, he couldn't save her – I'm so sorry, John."

"She – she was with child. We were going to surprise you with the news."

"The doctor told me – he said the child died in her womb and that is what brought on the fever that killed her."

The brothers had a long tearful embrace.

"John, this all happened three weeks ago – we had to make funeral decisions. I hope you are alright with that. We had a funeral Mass at St. Mary's for her, and we buried her in a nice grave just behind the church."

"Thank you and thank your Mary from me. I will go visit her grave as soon as I get ashore."

John Barry became a widower at the age of twenty-nine.

While still in mourning for Mary, John received a message from the richest merchant in Philadelphia, Robert Morris, asking him to come to his office to meet with him. John obliged two days later.

Morris stood up from his desk as John entered, a tall, well-built man almost the match of John. He opened the conversation – "Let me first offer you my deepest sympathy on the death of your wife, may she rest in peace. I have watched you mature into a fine sea captain with an honorable reputation to match and I have a proposal for you."

"Thank you for your kind words, Sir."

"John, you remind me of myself in so many ways. I was born in Liverpool, and after my mother died my father took me to Chesapeake, Virginia, where he became a merchant. When he took a mistress, there was no room for me in the house and I was bundled off to Philadelphia as a young teenager, to be an apprentice under Mr. Charles Willing, who traded between England and the West Indies. When Mr. Willing died suddenly, I was in the right place at the right time to work alongside his son, Thomas, who is the same age as me – us two youngsters grew the business a lot, and I was rewarded with a partnership. You are from Wexford, which is not much more than a stone's throw from Liverpool, but of even more importance is the fact that both you and I have left the old countries behind and see our future prosperity and success as being a part of this wonderful young country – America. I'm telling you this because I see great potential in you, and you can do very well for yourself if you take up my offer. As you know, Willing and Morris is now a large merchant business with twenty-four ships in our fleet. I want you on our team and I have two choices to offer you. We have just purchased the brigantine 'Venus' which you can take command of immediately, or you can stay with your current employer for another few months until our new prized 200-ton merchantman 'Prince Edward' is completed, and then take command of her. What do you say?"

"Tell more about the 'Prince Edward', please."

"She is a 200-ton merchantman, 91feet in length with a 26foot beam, designed by John Wharton, and being built locally at his Southwark yard. Along with Willing and Morris, the other owners are Wharton himself, and a countryman of yours, a merchant named John Nixon."

"Very good. I know Mr. Wharton – he is a good ship builder and a man that knows how to finish a ship off to perfection. Mr. Nixon is well known to me also – he is originally from County Wexford, just like myself. All seems excellent, Sir – I would prefer to have this new ship and I do want to give fair notice to my employer of my departure. I have another request, Mr. Morris, if I may – give the command of 'Venus' to my brother Patrick who is also a fine captain."

"Please call me Robert. I like your style, John. Yes, indeed, I have seen mention of Patrick in the newspapers, and I hear from my Coffeehouse contacts that he is a very good captain. I will hire you both – tell him to come and see me about taking command of 'Venus'."

"Great. Can we shake on that, Mr. Robert?"

They did so and John stopped by the clerk's office to sign the papers of employment. Before his next voyage, John told Mr. Meredith that he would be leaving his employment by the autumn – they talked about John's plans and an amicable separation was agreed, as were details of a few last voyages before that time came. Patrick Barry met with Mr. Morris some days later, and after signing up also, he registered the 'Venus' and shortly afterwards captained it to Jamaica on his first voyage with his new employer.

• • •

The high-profile protest action called 'The Boston Tea Party' from the previous December proved to be a red line in the sand for a furious British Parliament, whose members demanded tough action against the American Colonies. They passed the Boston Port Act and by the spring of 1774 British troop reinforcements were arriving in Boston, and then the port of Boston was totally closed. This spelled economic ruin for the entire Boston area. The loyalists, and the peace-loving merchant Quakers were vehemently opposed to the actions that had been taken by the colonists against the Crown and wanted no part in the brewing feud. Events soon began to escalate, and in May 1774 the City Tavern hosted a meeting of Philadelphia's merchants and politicians – a meeting that the Quakers refused to attend. Resolutions were passed that set June 1 as a special 'day of mourning' for the Boston port closing, a committee of correspondence between the two cities was set up and it was agreed to hold a special meeting of the Pennsylvania Assembly. June 1 saw everything stop in Philadelphia – church bells tolled for the entire day, and all shops were closed. Ship captains in port who were sympathetic to the plight of Boston flew their ship's flags at half mast, including John Barry on the 'Peggy'. Mr. Meredith's business partner, George Clymer, was one of the leaders of the growing resistance movement and when he met John at their office he asked him point blank about his stance on the matter.

John answered – "Sir, I am an Irishman, exiled from my country as a direct consequence of the harsh laws that the

British parliament enacted against my people; especially the Penal Laws against us Catholics who comprise the overwhelming majority of the Irish population. You will not find one ounce of sympathy for the British Empire in my body."

"Does that mean that if it comes to a fight – you would fight on the side of the Colonists against the Empire?"

"That is correct, Sir."

John was busy getting 'Peggy' ready for its last voyage under his command. Meanwhile, Meredith, Clymer, and Robert Morris, were part of a meeting at the State House where it was proposed that a Continental Congress be held in September, where delegates from each of the thirteen colonies were expected to be present to debate the issues and find a suitable path forward. John captained 'Peggy' for the last time when he sailed for Montserrat and returned to port on the same day as his brother Patrick returned from a voyage on 'Venus'.

The First Continental Congress was in the third week of its session at this very time. The attendees included individuals that were to play a very prominent role in the future of America – such as George Washington and Patrick Henry from Virginia, plus John Adams and his cousin Samual Adams from Massachusetts. There was much rancor, but they were making progress on a tame letter of protest to the Crown – that is, until the latest news arrived from New England. Citizens of Suffolk County, Massachusetts, passed resolutions that were read out – denouncing the British Laws and ceasing their obedience to the

Crown. That news had a profound change in the mood of the Congress and became the basis for a declaration by the Colonists of their rights – for life, liberty and property. Economic sanctions were imposed on Britain and would remain in place until all the unjust and repressive Acts enacted by the British Parliament against the colonies were repealed. The date of December 1, 1774, was set for when all imports from Britain (including Ireland) would cease; with exports to Britain and the West Indies to cease in September 1775. The First Congress then adjourned, with the date of May 1775 set for the next meeting.

Late autumn had John Barry busy overseeing the finishing details of his brand-new ship, the 'Prince Edward', working hand in hand with John Wharton and Mr. Nixon to have the ship ready to sail by year's end. She was a beauty, a Philadelphia merchantman to be proud of, with a figurehead of a carved knight with his sword and shield.

John confided to Mr. Nixon that he was not entirely happy with the name – "I find the name Prince Edward to be too English. With our Irish backgrounds we shouldn't be promoting names of British Royalty – what do you think?"

"You know, I was thinking the same thing myself. I do know that Morris is keen on the 'Prince' part, so let's look at the possibilities. We could try him on Prince alone, but it has no ring to it. Wasn't Edward known as the Black Prince – I think he would be good with that, would probably prefer it even – what do you say, John?"

"The name 'Black Prince' sounds great and is very apt for the current times. Let's go with that."

Mr. Morris was very happy with the proposed new name and Barry registered the ship as 'Black Prince'. John was told that his first voyage would be to London, England – an odd coincidence considering the growing tensions between the colonies and Britain, but it was a lucrative market at the time and they wanted to get as much out of it as they could. John's second brother, Thomas, arrived in port from Ireland a few days later to take up a job as a clerk, and the three brothers met up at the Tavern for a joyful reunion. John and Patrick wanted to hear all the news from Ireland and peppered Thomas with questions.

"I'm happy to tell you both that Daddy and Mammy are enjoying good health for their advanced age. They want you lads to know that it is the money sent home by you boys that has helped them improve their house and allow them to buy better food, which they are convinced is the reason for their good health. Of course, their big question is – when might you lads come to visit them?"

"We are working on it," John replied, "but it is not easy, especially now, with a big row brewing between our colonies and the British Parliament. How are the girls doing?"

"Eleanor is married to Mick Hayes, and they are blessed with three healthy children, Michael, Patrick and Eleanor. Margaret and her husband Timothy Howlin have three also – Mary, Josephine and Bridget."

"Let's drink a health to them all".

After the toast, Patrick asked Thomas about the overall political conditions in Ireland.

Thomas took a swig before answering – "Shur, it's the same as always. The poor people are all struggling to make ends meet while the tyrant landlords are carrying out widespread evictions with no regard for their tenants' efforts to pay what they can manage. Again, thanks to you two, the Barry's can pay their way, but let me say this – there is no future in Ireland for any of us young people while that landlord system rules the roost – that's why I have come over to join you. I thought I should stay, seeing that I am the last son, but the Muther wouldn't hear of it. They say they have plenty of help and company at home from the girls and their children. What are me chances of getting work here?"

John nodded, "I think we will get you in with Willing and Morris, or one of the other top merchants if they have no openings at present – you'll be just fine in Philadelphia. We will both be soon heading off on new voyages but we will get you fixed up first."

Patrick Barry left port first, setting sail on 'Venus' while John was putting the finishing touches to his new ship, the 'Black Prince'. He began assembling a crew and lining up the cargo they would carry to Bristol, England – wheat, flour, timber boards and wood barrel staves. This was all completed by late December and the 'Black Prince' departed Philadelphia on

December 28, 1774. They were the last ship to leave port that year after a mass exodus during the previous weeks – an exodus caused by growing worries of confrontation with England and concerns that trade would be adversely affected. The weather in the Atlantic was bad – heavy rain squalls and dangerous seas plagued the ship for weeks but could not hold back this great craft and its master seaman captain – they continued to make good time on their eastward journey. They got a brief respite from the weather before more terrible gales struck the ship, at one point forcing Captain Barry to turn the ship around and go in the opposite direction for a while, until better weather prevailed. They were relatively close to the southeast coast of Ireland at one point in the voyage, but John's thoughts of his Wexford home were brief as they battled huge seas. His skill and that of his crew finally won the day and by late January in the new year of 1775, they dropped anchor in Bristol harbor.

• • •

The repercussions of Congress' recent trade decisions soon became apparent when Captain Barry asked for ballast only, instead of trade goods – unsettling news to the Bristol merchants and port managers and it quickly resulted in a retaliatory action against the American ship. The unloading of 'Black Prince' proceeded at a very slow pace and then Barry's shore agents told him that the market would not pay the requested price for their cargo of wheat and flour – the agents eventually managed to find buyers at an agreeable price. It was March 1 before they had enough ballast to sail, and then bad weather delayed their departure for ten more days. He set a course south for the Azores and then westward towards the Carolinas, then northward for home, finally arriving in the Delaware Capes by April 21 to find dense fog that prevented their entrance into the Delaware River and didn't allow them to pick up a pilot for three days.

The same day that the 'Black Prince' was being secured at the Willing and Morris dock, a dispatch rider brought momentous news to Philadelphia – 'musket fire had erupted between the Massachusetts Minute Men and British Lobster-Backs at Lexington and Concord'. The news prompted great fear amongst the merchants of Philadelphia, followed by days of frantic activity on the wharves, with every available ship being loaded with cargo from the local warehouses – everyone wanted to ship their prized wares out of the city as soon as possible. The merchants all claimed to be patriots, but they were regular businessmen first, who wanted to grab one last big payday before their fledgling country, America, became embroiled in a fearful war against Britain – a monumental opponent who was the preeminent world power of the day. On the grounds of the Pennsylvania State House, speeches were made asking for volunteers to enlist and serve the cause of the colonists in the fight that everyone now expected, and loyalists hid in their homes for fear of being attacked.

John Barry's merchant bosses became part of this frantic port activity and ordered John to get the 'Black Prince' refitted and laden to maximum with cargo – all to be done in the utmost haste. Even the return to the Philadelphia waterfront of her favorite son, Benjamin Franklin, arriving from England, did little to slow down the pace of merchant activity at the port. In a record time of only ten days, the 'Black Prince' plus two more ships belonging to Willing and Morris – the 'Nancy', and the 'Aurora', captained by John's good friend Thomas Read, were ready to depart together for London, England – again. The Delaware River was chock-full of ships on that departure day when it seemed that all of Philadelphia was desperately trying to leave.

• • •

Within hours of the departure of the 'Black Prince' on May 11, 1775, the Second Continental Congress went into session.

• • •

Weather plagued the London voyage again, forcing 'Black Prince' to stop and repair torn sails while the other two ships continued to head east. John's speedy ship soon caught up to the others and all three arrived together in the port of London in late June. The news there was dominated by the latest reports of the confrontations in America – rebel militias had captured some significant defense fortifications and gained control of a lot of artillery pieces. The Newspapers carried notices warning that the British were going to use their troops to retain control of all the biggest towns and cities along the American east coast, or they would blockade all the American ports to force a quick end to these hostile acts.

Being that the American sailors were in the 'enemy' capital city, Barry and his fellow captains were so concerned for their safety that they slept on board their ships while their cargo was slowly unloaded – in constant fear that their ships might be seized, and they themselves and their crews imprisoned. By August 8 the empty ships were finally loaded with the requested ballast and set sail for Philadelphia. The return voyage was again plagued with very unhelpful winds and destructive gales that caused severe damage to the 'Black Prince' masts and split up the ships at sea – the 'Black Prince' did not arrive off the Delaware River until early October. Captain Barry's signal for a pilot went unanswered and he sent his mate ashore to find one – he was even tempted to head into the bay without a pilot.

Luckily, he waited, because while Captain Barry was away the colonists had protected the river with several 30-foot wide 'chevaux-de-frise' structures – new man-made shipping hazards constructed from long pointed heavy-duty wooden stakes, that were secured to the bottom of the river with many tons of stone. These monsters sat a few feet below the water surface, designed to rip open the hulls of the enemy ships of the British fleet – ships that were expected to descend on them any day. Only trusted pilots knew the locations of these hazards, and in due course the 'Black Prince' and her sister ships were guided past the obstacles to the Willing and Morris wharf.

The year 1775 was one of momentous happenings, in which John Barry's world in Philadelphia changed during the months he was away – and that was only the beginning.

CHAPTER TWO

ONSET OF THE REVOLUTIONARY WAR

Some months earlier, in April, while the 'Black Prince' was making her way into port, the St. George Society of Philadelphia had been holding its annual banquet at the City Tavern. George Morris, the Society's vice president was proposing a toast when the dispatch rider rushed in with the news that would change the world:

"Musket fire had broken out between Massachusetts Minute Men and British Lobsterbacks."

The place had erupted in a mixture of panic and nervous euphoria and within minutes the hall was empty – the members having rushed off to spread the news and make urgent new plans. This news spawned a rush to convert Philadelphia from a British port of call, into the capital city of the 'United Colonies'. The city fathers now looked to Benjamin Franklin, delegate to the Second Continental Congress, despite him being almost seventy years old, to lead the plans for the city's defense against the might of Britain. He took up the task with zeal, creating a public safety committee to push the defense plans forward at great speed. Forts were built on the approaches to the city, the 'Mud Fort' already under construction on the Delaware River was speeded up, Army recruits were gathered, and the 'chevaux-de-frise' devices were made and set into the water. A local Navy was proposed, consisting of some dozen or more row–galleys that were an updated version of Viking ships, except with guns mounted on their bows. An early warning system was put in place to alert the city of any approaching British warships. Lookouts at the Capes would send dispatch riders via a series of way stations to warn Philadelphia – with a backup plan of cannons at each station to be fired in-series should the rider system be disrupted by the British.

The new Congress granted itself extraordinary powers to move quickly on both the military, political and financial fronts. George Washington of Virginia was named the Commander-in-Chief of their new Army, credit in the amount of two million American dollars was secured, and negotiations were started with Native Indian Tribes to convince them to side with the Colonists. A sense of unity was beginning to emerge between the thirteen colonies, in preparation for the inevitable break with Britain. Everything was progressing well EXCEPT there was no agreement on the formation of a viable

Navy, an incomprehensible omission, because every aspect of life in the colonies was dependent on ships being able to come and go in safety. John Adam's proposal for a Continental Navy had been previously rejected by most of the colonies, due to their lack of understanding of the need for maritime defense.

Rhode Island took the lead in August 1775 and called for the building and equipping of an American Fleet – this resolution was put before the Congress in early October. Much divisive debate was followed by inaction, until General Washington acted on his own authority to re-equip and resupply his Army that was laying siege to the British in Boston. He chartered several local schooners, armed them and sent them out in search of unarmed British merchant supply ships – and he beseeched his Rhode Island comrades to send a ship to Bermuda to acquire gunpowder.

John Adams judged that the time was now right to reintroduce his Navy proposal, and this time he succeeded in getting Congress to create a Naval Committee and to authorize the purchase of several armed ships.

The Continental Navy finally became a reality. The first ship they purchased was 'Black Prince' – the merchant ship that John Barry was captain of at this time. Congress also authorized the establishment of an armed force called the Continental Marines; two Battalions were to be raised to serve as landing forces for the Continental Navy. The Naval Marines were set up under the command of Captain Samuel Nicholas, at a special meeting held at the Tun Tavern in Philadelphia on November 10, 1775.

Strangely, the Naval Committee's seven Congress members included no representative from Pennsylvania – instead it was dominated by New Englanders and more especially by one individual named Stephen Hopkins from Rhode Island. When they drew up a list of Captains for the New Navy that November, John Barry was not considered, even though he was highly experienced, well respected and right there under their nose. The only Philadelphia name on the list was Nicholas Biddle, a minor captain whom John knew quite well. Most of those chosen were closely connected with Stephen Hopkins – his brother Esek Hopkins was appointed leader of the fleet with the honorary title of Commodore.

The 'Black Prince' was renamed 'Alfred': their second acquired ship was named 'Columbus': the third would be 'Cabot': the fourth 'Andrew Doria' and the fifth was to be 'Providence' – none of which were ships of war until they could be totally renovated, outfitted and rerigged. These tasks were handed out as follows – structural strengthening to Joshua Humphreys of Wharton shipyard in Philadelphia: procurement and purchasing to a well-respected merchant named Nathaniel Falconer: outfitting and re-rigging to Captain John Barry of Philadelphia.

John was deeply disappointed that he had been bypassed for a Navy command and it was especially galling that his own ship, the 'Black Prince', the finest in the fleet and now called the 'Alfred'; would not be commanded by him, but by Dudley Saltonstall, a man of questionable naval experience and someone that John knew little about. He swallowed hard and got on with the task assigned to him by the Naval Committee. Large amounts of rope were purchased, and he directed his labor to use tallow and lampblack as they created new rigging. His crew and those of the shipbuilder, Humphreys, worked from dawn till dusk, and the four ships were completely refitted and ready for service by December of 1775. The fifth ship, the 'Providence' was refitted elsewhere and joined the fleet in December also. The speed of the transformation was so amazing that even the British spies were astounded as they sent word of this back to London.

Next, a list comprising twenty names of "persons suitable for naval commands" was drawn up by the Naval Committee – again omitting John Barry's name while favoring those with the right political and family connections. Now that eight more vessels were being considered for addition to the fleet, the Naval Committee was expanded and renamed the Marine Committee, and it included Robert Morris (he would later become known as the chief financier of the American Revolution), a man who held John Barry in very high esteem. Not even Morris's inclusion on the committee could get Barry's name onto this expanded list, causing John more distress and disappointment. The 'Alfred' was chosen as the flagship of the fleet and on December 3, as supplies continued to be loaded aboard, the 'Grand-Union Flag' (thirteen red and white stripes, with the British colors in the top corner), was hoisted on 'Alfred' by its newly appointed Lieutenant, a short and fiery Scotsman named John Paul Jones.

Unfortunately, after all the rush to get ready, the fleet could not go to sea because Esek Hopkins, the new Commodore, was taking care of his own personal business in Rhode Island and was not due in Philadelphia until the beginning of January.

The Continental Fleet finally set sail January 4, 1776, while John Barry could only watch their departure from land. The Delaware River was full of ice by this stage, and it took weeks for the fleet to make its way to the Cape and into ice-free ocean water. Their mission orders were to sail to Chesapeake Bay and destroy all the enemy ships they could find in that region, Chesapeake being under the control of Lord Dunmore, Royal Governor of Virginia with headquarters at Norfolk. Dunmore had foreseen this worsening situation coming and had relocated his gunpowder supplies ahead of a continental militia attack that took place on Williamsburg, led by Paul Henry. Dunmore had declared martial law in November and issued an emancipation proclamation offering freedom to the slaves who were willing to take up arms on the British side. This emancipation only applied to the slaves of the Rebel Colonists, and it didn't apply to the slaves of the Loyalists. Dunmore and his Virginia power base was why Congress ordered Hopkins to attack Chesapeake – and when the American fleet left Philadelphia, Dunmore abandoned Norfolk and had it burned.

Commodore Esek Hopkins had little stomach for a confrontation with Dunmore's ships and found an escape clause in his orders – "follow such courses as your best judgement dictates if you are affected by bad winds or storms". He interpreted this as justification to avoid Dunmore's fleet and instead he set a course for the Bahamas to capture the guns and gunpowder stored at Nassau. This mission he accomplished without a shot being fired but he captured only twenty barrels of gunpowder and a few cannons there – the rest having been relocated before the fleet arrived. Hopkins again avoided confrontation with British ships off the Georgia coast on his voyage north and sailed around them on a course for Rhode Island.

Meanwhile, John Barry, Nathaniel Falconer and Joshua Humphreys were given more ships to outfit. Additionally, a contract was given to the Shurlock Yard to refit a newly acquired warship for Pennsylvania – John Barry being selected as the point man to keep this contract on a fast-track schedule. The new ship was named the 'Montgomery' and this time John Barry's friend, Thomas Read, was appointed the commander. John was beside himself with annoyance as he congratulated his friend –

"I am delighted for you Thomas; this is much deserved."

"Thank you, John. However, you are much more deserving than I am, and I am baffled why the Marine Committee has not been calling you. The men they have picked are generally good men and they mean well, but you are the most accomplished Captain in the Colonies, and I pray that they come to their senses before it's too late."

"The benign elders are all Anglo-Saxon Protestants, and I am a young Irish Catholic – do you think that has anything to do with it?"

"I think it has an awful lot to do with it, John, but let's not let it get under our skin."

"Agreed."

They shook hands and wished each other well.

Barry was next assigned to review the progress on four new ships, followed by a load of clerical work overseeing the payment for the refitting of other ships. He began to worry that he was being so efficient at completing these land-based assignments that he was contributing to his own drydocking.

• • •

The week after Commodore Hopkins had sailed the American fleet away from Philadelphia in January, the British pushed forward with their plans to occupy the rebel capital – they set about finding as much information as possible about the city fortifications and the location of all navigational obstructions near the port, even to the point of offering bribes to river pilots who had knowledge of these. By March the British fleet was cruising along the Virginia coast in search of American merchant ships and military ships to capture as prizes. After capturing one merchantman, the British sloop 'Edward' chased after another prize named the 'Wild Duck', a brigantine bringing an important cargo of gunpowder and arms from Sint Eustatius to Philadelphia for the Rebels. The 'Wild Duck' managed to outrun them and delivered the precious cargo to the port.

Congress immediately purchased the 'Wild Duck' for the Continental Navy and that was when John Barry finally was offered a command – by no less than John Hancock, President of the Congress, and their important Marine Committee financial backer, Robert Morris. John accepted the commission, and immediately brought the ship to Whartons Yard in Philadelphia to refit it for war. She was 86 feet long with a 25-foot beam, already armed with sixteen 4-pounder cannons and twelve swivels. Wharton's workers and John Barry's laborers scraped her hull, re-calked her seams, made a few upgrades on her rigging, and had the ship ready for action in less than two weeks, which astounded everybody. Much of the 'Wild Duck' cargo of arms and gunpowder was used to also supply other ships – John Barry then had the pleasure of renaming the ship the 'Lexington' in honor of the location of the first battle of the American Revolution, and he began actively recruiting a crew. After a week they had seventy men signed on the muster rolls, despite the British making it clear that captured Yankee sailors would be treated the same as pirates and subject to the same fate – the gallows.

The main holdup in final preparations was the arming of the ship's marines, which was being delayed amidst squabbling between the Pennsylvania Committee of Safety and the Marine Committee – even while there were confirmed reports of a British sloop of war and its tender heading up the Delaware River.

Captain Barry raced back and forth repeatedly between the two entities, trying to get approval – it was not until midnight of March 28 that the needed weapons were delivered to the dock and loading began immediately. The 'Lexington' hoisted the Grand Union flag in the middle of the night and along with four row-galleys they set off down the Delaware, with a river pilot guiding the ship past the dangerous 'chevaux-de-frise' navigation obstacles. Barry did not know it at the time, but the British ship reported to be in the river was much bigger than first reports indicated – it was the 44-gun frigate 'HMS Roebuck' under the experienced commander, Captain Andrew Snape Hamond.

Captain Barry ordered his accompanying row galleys to remain at Reedy Island and the 'Lexington' proceeded alone. He knew he had a crew that was inexperienced in naval warfare and all the way down the Delaware River he drilled his men on gunnery practice, so that when he would shout "Clear decks for Action" they would know exactly what to do.

That was followed by practice on the sequence of orders for firing the guns –

- 'cut loose your guns' – the gun barrel was unfastened from the gunport
- 'load your guns' – cannon barrel was set parallel to the deck
- 'take out your tompions' – the stopper was removed from the muzzle
- 'load with cartridge' – a bag of gunpowder and a wad was rammed down the muzzle
- 'shot your guns' – the cannonball was rammed down the muzzle
- 'run out your guns' – muzzle was pushed out the gun port
- 'prime' – gunpowder was put into the touch hole of the cannon
- 'point your guns' – gun was adjusted while a slow match was kept lit
- elevate' – gun aimed on target while the quoin kept the gun in the selected position
- 'FIRE' – the lit match was applied to the touch hole

After firing the cannon, and the recoil of the gun: the order 'sponge your guns' was vitally important – whereby a wet sponge on a long handle was rammed down the muzzle to extinguish any sparks or smoking remains of the cartridge bag.

A good gun crew could do all this in two minutes. The types of projectiles rammed into the muzzle in battle were cannonballs, bar-shot, and chain shot to cut the enemy rigging. At close range, grapeshot was used to great effect. The swivel guns were like high-powered shotguns and also used at close range. The only advantage the 'Lexington' had over the British was her ability to maneuver in much shallower water than the larger enemy frigates like 'Roebuck'. At dawn on March 31 the two vessels sighted each other, and the 'Roebuck' gave chase. Barry sailed into the shallows and escaped up the New Jersey coastline – he knew his ship was no match for the big guns of the British frigate.

After two days of uneventful sailing the 'Lexington' turned south and put in briefly at Little Egg Harbor. After getting some updated reports, Barry's first capture was a sloop from St. Croix on which he put a prize crew and sent her to Philadelphia. Then the 'Lexington' escorted a small group of merchant ships around the 'Roebuck' in poor weather before continuing sailing south, slipping past the 'Roebuck' again and into Lord Dunmore's home waters off Virginia. Later that day 'Lexington' was spotted and chased by the 'Edward', a tender of the enemy frigate 'Liverpool'. Captain Barry was not flying a flag and pretended to be trying to escape – while issuing orders to his crew to load their cannons but keep the gun ports closed. Barry allowed the enemy ship to get close enough for it to fire a warning shot over the bow of 'Lexington'. Lieutenant Boger, the British Captain, ordered Barry's ship to identify herself and to 'heave to' – to turn their ship into the wind and come to a complete stop.

The answer that Boger received was in three parts – the Grand Union flag was raised; Barry announced his ship via trumpet as 'The Continental Brig Lexington' while the gunports were quietly opened; and then he yelled – "FIRE". The first broadside did little damage to 'Edward', but the battle was on and now it was 'Lexington' in pursuit. Exchanges of cannon fire followed for an hour and twenty minutes before 'Lexington' took control of the fight, after her gunners smashed the stern of 'Edward'.

Lieutenant Boger was forced to surrender his ship 'HMS Edward' and his crew of twenty-five. Captain John Barry of 'Lexington' scored the first victory for the Continental Navy over a British warship – it was April 7, 1776.

Barry found American prisoners aboard 'Edward' who had been pressed into service, among whom was Richard Dale of Virginia. He offered young Dale the opportunity to return to American allegiance which Dale accepted, and Barry rewarded him with service on 'Lexington' as Midshipman. A prize crew was placed on board 'Edward', and she was escorted back to Philadelphia, where a crowd that included several Congressmen was on hand at the wharf to celebrate this special event. News of Captain Barry's victory spread quickly in the colonies and beyond. John Adams, never generous with his praise of the Navy, even felt the need to express a few words in celebration, saying "we begin to make some little figure here in the Navy way." The Marine Committee sent a letter to Esek Hopkins, the ceremonial Commodore of the fleet, informing him of the capture and pointing out how significant the loss of a vessel and men would be to the British. He did not issue any letter of congratulations to Captain Barry.

On the other hand, Commander Hamond, the commander of the British frigate 'Roebuck', who had failed to catch 'Lexington' some time earlier, took much more notice of the 'Lexington' success than the Commodore of the American fleet did. Hamond was furious with himself for his failure and wrote to Lord Dunmore that he intended to cut Barry's reign and that of 'Lexington' short.

Congress leaders knew from the start that their Navy force was dwarfed by that of the British Royal Navy. They adopted the centuries-old practice of 'privateering' as a means of leveling the playing field. They wanted to attract the best American ships and ship-captains to fight on their side against the British, and privateering was way of making piracy legal and lucrative. Through 'Letters of Marque' the privateers could seize enemy ships and using a process of 'condemnation and distribution' they could sell these captured ships and the cargos, splitting the proceeds with the Congress. Therefore, Congress issued a proclamation that gave their Navy ships and any privateers acting of their behalf, the right to attack and seize British warships and merchant ships associated with or acting on behalf of Britain. In essence they created a second American Navy with the stroke of a pen.

In Congress – April 3, 1776

Resolved, that blank Commissions for private Ships of War, and Letters of Marque and Reprisal, signed by the President of Congress, be sent to the General Assemblies, Conventions, and Councils or Committees of Safety of the United Colonies, to be by them filled up and delivered to the Persons intending to fit out such private Ships of War for making Captures of British Vessels and Cargoes, who shall apply for the same, and execute the Bonds that shall be sent with the said Commissions, which Bonds shall be returned to the Congress.

By Order of Congress
John Hancock, President

The captured 'Edward' was condemned as a prize of war and sold at auction on May 1, the proceeds were divided between Captain Barry and his crew, after the American government entities took their considerable share. While waiting for 'Lexington' to be refitted, Captain Barry, as the ranking officer in Delaware Bay, was kept busy helping the new continental vessels 'Hornet' and 'Reprisal' complete their action readiness, and overseeing the assembly of a floating gun battery designed to defend the waterway at Fort Island that could help prevent the British from getting to Philadelphia.

Once the 'Lexington' was refitted, Captain Barry put to sea again and within hours she was chased by the frigate 'HMS Solebay' which was part of a seventeen ship British fleet – to no avail, as Barry was able to escape into the shallower waters where the larger frigate could not venture. When 'Lexington' headed for port on May 4 she found three more British warships in the Delaware Bay, including 'Roebuck', who spotted her and gave chase again, on Captain Hamond's orders. Barry kept his ship in the shallows, close to the Jersey shore and escaped from them again. The angry Hamond fired his long gun harmlessly towards 'Lexington' in frustration, and Barry returned the 'salute' with a 4-pounder cannon.

John Barry had received a hero's welcome in Philadelphia and his naval exploits were the banner headlines on the local newspapers. His close friends enticed him to the City Tavern where he was toasted. John was not a man to drink to excess and neither was he a man who craved all this attention – he left the celebrations early and went home to rest up for the battles ahead.

The fleet of Commodore Esek Hopkins had achieved little by this stage – they finally had their big chance when four ships of his fleet chased and caught up with the British frigate 'Glasgow' on April 8. Hopkins ordered them to attack but his lack of experience and nerve cost the Americans dearly. Instead of forming a line of the four ships and overwhelming 'Glasgow', they attacked one at a time and suffered severe damage as the British ship fought each attacker off. Even the 'Alfred' was damaged substantially, and the American ships broke off the attack, allowing 'Glasgow' to escape. Congress eventually saw through Hopkins' questionable report of the incident, and a court of inquiry investigated allegations of incompetence and cowardice. Lieutenant John Paul Jones had accounted himself very well on 'Alfred' during the failed encounter, but he was unable to convince his commander to alter his attack and improve the fighting qualities of the ship. Esek Hopkins' high-level political connections helped him retain his command although he was censured by Congress.

The cat and mouse game between the British Navy and the Continental Navy continued in the Delaware River and in the Bay area beyond. The 'Lexington' and three other ships were ordered to work together to provide escorts at the Capes for arriving merchantmen vessels carrying gunpowder and munitions for the rebel American forces. Barry's 'Lexington' and two other vessels sailed to harass the British frigate 'Liverpool' and draw it away from its guarding position – she took the bait and chased them towards the shallows, almost running aground before recovering just in time to avoid being stuck and captured.

Next, Captain Barry intervened when a Wilmington brig carrying gunpowder and arms to Philadelphia was cornered by the enemy warship 'Kingfisher'. Barry navigated the shallows to arrive at the brig during the afternoon and immediately began transferring the precious cargo to 'Lexington' while the enemy was bearing down on them. By sunset they had transferred the cargo and left the empty ship to be captured, while

'Lexington' carried the much-needed supplies to port. Barry's successful exploits were being noticed by Congress and he was rewarded with the command of one of four new frigates being built for the Navy in Philadelphia. This also brought him into daily contact with the secretary of the Marine Committee, John Brown, a fellow Irishman whom he had known casually for years, as they attended the same Catholic Church. Brown was of similar age and background to John Barry and had worked his way up the ladder of success with the merchant company of Willing and Morris – both men were named John and because of 'B' surnames (Barry and Brown) they were often called JB by their friends and by each other during their friendly chats.

"JB – rumor has it the British are ready to place a bounty on your head, being that you have been causing them so much trouble."

"Thanks, JB, I am getting double the pleasure – by hurting the 'auld enemy' while helping our colonial cause to break loose of the Empire. How is your missus and childer?"

"All well thanks. Are you still a bachelor yourself?"

"My mistress is the sea, and she is good to me, I have no complaints. Now, be a good man and shepherd these four new ships through the system with haste."

"I am on it and will give it my undivided attention. Got to go, goodbye for now, JB."

"The same to you, JB."

Congress rewarded John Barry with the command of the new frigate to be built at Philadelphia – the 'Effingham'. For the immediate future, he had new orders – for 'Lexington' to meet and escort the brig 'Nancy' arriving with 400 barrels of gunpowder from St. Thomas. He spotted 'Nancy' on June 29, already being chased by British warships 'Kingfisher' and 'Orpheus', while her Captain was making for shallow water to try and escape them. Darkness halted the chase and gave the American ships 'Lexington' and 'Wasp' the time to get near 'Nancy'. Captain Barry was determined to save the cargo, and because of shallow water he used the barges from both his ships for his plan – personally leading the action from his 'Lexington' barge, complete with his best gunners. The captain of 'Nancy' was informed of the plan by signals, to cut his anchor and run her as far into the shallows as possible until she ran aground. Barry ordered all the crew to start ferrying the gunpowder to shore using the barges – while his borrowed 'Lexington' gunners boarded and manned the six 3-pounder cannons on 'Nancy'. The British ship 'Kingfisher' got as close as possible and lowered four rowboats to attack the Americans. As the enemy boats got closer Barry had the 3-pounders primed and ready, plus several sailors armed with muskets – all waiting for his order. Once within musket range, he ordered them to open fire with everything – their broadside inflicted terrible damage on the enemy, destroying the two leading boats while the other two turned and rowed back towards the 'Kingfisher'.

Barry then had his gunners fire at the 'Kingfisher' and her

tenders, while his own rowboats continued transferring the gunpowder to the shore. After further bombardment of 'Nancy' the British sent two rowboats from 'Orpheus' plus two from 'Kingfisher' for an all-out attack. Barry's gunners kept firing while he began sending the rest of the' Nancy' crew ashore, ordering the rowboats to then return for his gunners, plus himself and Captain Montgomery of the 'Nancy'. While they waited, they moved thirty of the remaining ninety barrels of gunpowder to the captain's cabin, then made a slow fuse of fifty pounds of powder rolled up in the canvas mainsail and laid it down from the edge of the deck to the cabin, with another trail of powder from the cabin to the hold, where the last of the gunpowder barrels remained. The gunners took down their Grand Union flag and went over the side into the rowboat along with their guns, while Barry dropped two hot coals onto the rolled-up canvas slow fuse, and he was the last man over the side. As they rowed to safety, their comrades already ashore continued to fire muskets at the advancing British boats who were closing in on 'Nancy". Barry, once ashore also, added swivels to the fire directed towards the British. The raiding party reached the stern of 'Nancy' and scrambled triumphantly on board just in time for the slow fuse to have burned its way to the cabin. A massive blast blew 'Nancy' and the British boarding party to smithereens. The Americans had saved most of the precious cargo and lost a few good men, while the British had lost dozens and had nothing to show for their loss.

• • •

Just a few days later, on July 4, 1776, the Continental Congress approved a special document that was drafted by a five-man committee – Franklin, Jefferson, Adams, Livingston and Sherman.

That document became known as –

"THE DECLARATION OF INDEPENDENCE"

A New Country Was Born

"THE UNITED STATES OF AMERICA"

• • •

CHAPTER THREE

SUCCESSES AND FAILURES OF THE CONTINENTAL NAVY

In July of 1776, newspapers in Philadelphia and in cities and towns throughout the thirteen colonies boldly printed important headlines announcing the big news –

"THE CONTINENTAL CONGRESS HAS DECLARED THE UNITED COLONIES TO BE FREE AND INDEPENDENT STATES."

Copies of the Declaration of Independence document began circulating.

The Marine Committee told Captain Barry his new ship would not be ready for quite a while and admitted that the fleet of British ships off the Capes was too strong for the current Continental Navy to go against. Consequently, they gave him permission to take the 'Lexington' away from the Capes for an extended two-month cruise to search for prize captures to enrich himself and his crew, and of course, the committees of government. He took up their offer and sailed east by south to begin his cruise in the waters of Lord Dunmore. Within a few weeks he captured the 'Lady Susan' of Virginia, captained by William Goodrich, part of a wealthy family that were cronies of Lord Dunmore. A prize crew was put on board 'Lady Susan' and they sailed her to Philadelphia to go through the libel and confiscation process. The 'Lexington' continued her cruise and captured another Dunmore sloop a few weeks later – the 'Betsy', which he also sent to Philadelphia. Shortly after that the 'Lexington' was hit by lightning during a bad thunderstorm. Nobody was killed but the lightning strike destroyed most of the ship's rigging and Captain Barry's ship limped back to Philadelphia for much-needed repairs.

On September 28 Barry relinquished command of his beloved 'Lexington'. During his previous cruise Congress had ordered new uniforms for the Navy and the 6-foot 4-inch Captain Barry was now fitted for his uniform. The Naval Captain's uniform was a blue coat with red lapels, a sash cuff, standup collar, yellow buttons, red waistcoat with gold lace, and blue britches – plus a plain cocked hat. After a reorganization of the Navy of the United Colonies, the Marine Committee now published a decree listing the rank of the Navy Captains and their assigned ships.

1. James Nicholson, to the 'Virginia' – 28 guns
2. John Manly, to the 'Hancock' – 32 guns
3. Hector McNeil, to the 'Boston' – 24 guns
4. Dudley Salstonstall, to the 'Trumbull' – 28 guns
5. Nicholas Biddle, to the 'Randolph' – 32 guns
6. Thomas Thompson, to the 'Raleigh' – 32 guns
7. John Barry, to the 'Effingham' – 28-guns

Each Captain would earn the same pay of sixty dollars per month.

This list proved that political connections still took precedent over ability and achievement. James Nicholson of the 'Virginia' was listed as number one, while not yet having served one single day on a Continental Navy vessel. Even strong support from one of the top committee members, Robert Morris, could not elevate John Barry to his rightful position. His close comrades, Captain Read, Captain Robinson and Captain Wickes were even further down the list. Captain John Paul Jones, the little Scotsman who was probably second in the number of battle successes after Captain Barry, was listed at 18 – he was officially disgusted and complained to anybody who would listen. John Barry was more amused than annoyed at the absurdity of the list. He mentioned his bemusement to his close friends but otherwise put it behind him – at least he was lucky enough that a new frigate, the 'Effingham' was being built for him.

Sadly, the Marine Committee's budget was in tatters and the four new frigates were all behind their intended completion dates, with the 'Effingham' being the one that was furthest behind schedule. Two of the four new ships were launched during the summer but did not receive their supply of cannons until November. The other two were launched in the autumn but that was a sham, as there was no timeline for when they would be armed and fully rigged. As the year slipped away, John Barry had no ship to command and could get no answers to tell him when the 'Effingham' would be completed.

• • •

The situation on the land battlefield turned grim for the United States as winter set in. General Washington's Army was routed in New York and had to retreat all the way to Philadelphia, where they were trying to keep the line so that they had the Delaware River between them and the British. Desperate appeals were made for new recruits, as desertions thinned out their ranks and a British attack on the United States capital of Philadelphia seemed imminent. With the Navy ships unable to be of any assistance, John Barry met with four of his fellow Navy Captains to discuss the formation of a sailor brigade, with the idea of bringing the ships' cannons ashore to arm that brigade, and later they made their offer to Congress. After debate within the Marine Committee, it was decided to keep the crew members for the two sea-ready ships on marine duty. The other three captains, including Barry, were reassigned to the land Army. They managed to recruit seventy seamen and mount some cannons on wheel chassis' – then the captains and their volunteers were incorporated into the forces of Colonel Cadwalader. They were mustered to Bristol, Pennsylvania, in early December where Cadwalader added Barry to his staff as his personal aide, while captain Read was asked to form a gun battery with his volunteers and to command that battery. Congress moved its operations and personnel to Baltimore out of an abundance of caution, the only congressman staying behind in Philadelphia was Robert Morris.

The British had a 12,000 strong Army moving south from New York, under the command of General William Howe and General Cornwallis. Included in their army were thousands of German Hessian mercenaries, 1,400 of which were camped in Trenton, NJ. Across the partially frozen Delaware River was the American camp – a much smaller Army than the British one, and very much in disarray. Washington expected the British to cross the frozen river as soon as they deemed the ice to be solid enough.

He knew he had to act before that happened, to have any chance of turning the tables on the enemy. Therefore, he decided to make a difficult and risky river crossing on Christmas night with 2,400 soldiers and make a surprise attack on the 1,400 Hessians at Trenton. Washington's forces completed the crossing and overwhelmed the Hessians, killing dozens of them and taking large numbers of prisoners, then they crossed back over the river after their victory. Cadwalader was thwarted by the ice but eventually got over to New Jersey and began a pursuit of the retreating enemy until he was called back by General Washington.

Captain Read's gun battery was stationed at a strategic bridge, in anticipation of General Cornwallis's attack on Washington's main camp. When it happened, the seamen and their cannons performed very well in helping the American forces hold the line and repel the British attack. Next, Cadwalader and Barry fell in with General Mercer as his forces attacked the British who were marching south to reinforce General Cornwallis. The Pennsylvanians halted the headlong retreat of Mercer's men after a pitch battle in which General Mercer was killed, and they were instrumental in getting Mercer's men to stand and fight – until General Washington arrived with reinforcements and assumed command. A violent and bloody battle at close quarters ensued, with the Americans winning the day as the British broke ranks and retreated. Then Washington pushed on north with his forces before Cornwallis's army arrived at the battle site – too late. Cornwallis quickly realized he had been outwitted by the Americans and retreated to his winter quarters at New Brunswick, NJ.

Shortly after that, in January 1777, the land service 'Army' conjured up by the Navy Captains came to an end. Their seaman troops took back possession of their ship cannons and alongside Barry and Read they marched back to Philadelphia

– just as many of the local population were also returning home, thinking that the danger had passed. Barry met with Robert Morris, who briefed him on the latest Navy news, including the fact that no progress had been made on the 'Effingham'. Captains Barry and Read then spent two months making futile efforts to get 'Effingham' and 'Washington' ready. Even the return of Congress to Philadelphia in March didn't speed up the finishing process of the ships.

• • •

John Barry found other ways to busy himself during this time. He courted a twenty-three-year-old beauty, the wealthy Sarah Austin, whose family owned and operated the Arch Street Ferry between Philadelphia and Camden, NJ. Sarah was also part of a group of women at Gloria Dei Church who ran a sewing circle making flags for the colonist forces and which included the renowned seamstress, Betsy Ross. When Congress adopted the Stars and Stripes as the official flag of the United States of America, the flags chosen were those made by Sarah's sewing circle. John Barry went to her group in search of flags for the Navy and met Sarah during his quest. She already had lots of suitors but was quickly smitten by the tall handsome Irishman in his Continental Navy uniform. He got his flags and also received permission to call on her, then impressed her family, who already knew plenty about his heroic exploits. By the time of the first anniversary of the 'Glorious Fourth' when

Navy ships fired 13-gun salutes, Sarah Austin was John's fiancée, and they attended events together such as the ringing of church bells and a fireworks display.

On July 7,1777, Captain John Barry and Sarah Austin were married, and John became a husband once again. On John's side were his seafaring and Navy friends, Congressman Robert Morris, his brother Thomas Barry and his wife, and Mary Barry, the wife of his brother Patrick who was away at sea at the time. Sarah was a Protestant and John was a Catholic – John received a dispensation from the bishop after he promised him that his new wife would be converting to Catholicism in due course.

• • •

A new Navy Board had been established in February of 1777, and they were to work hand in hand with the Marine Committee to get the ships and commanders in place that would enable Philadelphia to mount a credible defense on the Delaware River. Congress and the Marine Committee dithered on the selection of a commander – the choice was between Captain Barry who was the senior Continental Navy officer in port, and John Hazelwood, the head of the Pennsylvania Navy. Barry was not the type of man to get involved in self-promotion and he left the decision up to Congress. With each passing day there was an increased likelihood of a move on Philadelphia by the British – and just weeks after Barry's wedding a large segment of British General Howe's army left New York harbor aboard 267 transport ships. That caused a major increase in political tension in Philadelphia, resulting in the arrest of prominent loyalists like some of the Quakers, and an overall crisis of authority that Captain Barry had to navigate his way through.

Francis Hopkinson, the de-facto leader of the new Navy Board told Barry that he was authorizing him, and Captain Read to gather enough rigging and sail for the unfinished frigates 'Effingham' and 'Washington', so that the two ships could be sailed further up the river to be anchored in secluded safety. This order was bad news to John Barry's ears – it meant that the two ships would not be ready to take part in the oncoming fight and that the most experienced Captain with the best record of success against the British (meaning Barry himself), was again in danger of being bypassed for the leadership role and would be drydocked. In late August, the British land-army commander, General William Howe, issued a declaration – offering a pardon to all American officers and enlisted men that surrendered themselves to the British forces. General Washington had to counter this with a show of force, and he marched his army through Philadelphia, then marched out to engage General Howe's army in battle at Brandywine Creek – only to be defeated by Howe. As the British reached the outskirts of Philadelphia, Congress was evacuated to Trenton, prompting many well-to-do families to leave also, including the Austin family of John Barry's new wife, Sarah.

The two new ships were sailed upriver in late September by Captains Barry and Read, with a skeleton crew they put together at short notice. George Washington decided that Hazelwood should be made the commander of Philadelphia naval forces, noting that the man had been stationed in the Delaware River for the previous two years and consequently had a better understanding of the river defenses than Barry. Word came that a large British fleet was gathering in the bay, so all the American vessels were ordered to move upriver towards Burlington to clear the river for the upcoming fight. Barry's in-laws, William Austin and Reynold Keen were prominent loyalists and would stop at nothing to help the British. They and other loyalist sympathizers organized to have an emissary rowed out to Barry's ship 'Effingham' as it proceeded up the river. The emissary requested a meeting on board ship with Captain Barry, who obliged, and they met in the captain's cabin.

The emissary began – "Captain Barry, I have been sent here to meet with you, sent by loyalists who have the full backing of Admiral Lord Richard Howe, Commander of the British Fleet (brother of General William Howe, the commander of the land army). If you will come over to the British side with your ship, I am authorized to offer you 20,000 Guineas. You can retain command of your ship under British colors or take command of a British frigate, and you will receive a commission in the King's Service."

Barry was stunned by this blatant bribery offer and his Irish temper was triggered.

"Sir, this is an insult to me, to my birth country and to my adopted country, the United States of America. It is well known that I was born in Ireland, a country that was set upon and conquered by Britain centuries ago. The British and their agents have raped and pillaged Ireland and her people ever since, they have outlawed our Catholic religion, stolen our land, then parceled out that land in large holdings to Protestant planters and forced the Irish to rent back their own land. And if that wasn't enough, they brought in the Penal Laws to try and break our spirit. Those laws forced me and my brothers to flee Ireland, and we found refuge here in America. I am proud to serve America – how dare you come aboard my ship and assume that I would become another Judas and sell my soul for your pieces of silver. If not for my strict adherence to the rules and codes of conduct of the Continental Navy, I would have you thrown overboard.

Sir, leave this ship immediately and go tell your loyalist traitors that this Continental Navy Captain is not for sale. Not the value and command of the whole British fleet can seduce me from the cause of my country.

Tell Admiral Howe that I will be seeing his ships in battle, at the end of our cannons. Go."

• • •

The British soon took control of most of the Delaware River estuary and tried to convince the Americans to capitulate, sending a message to Robert Morris of the Marine Committee –

"General Howe offers to end the War if Congress will renounce the Declaration of Independence."

His offer was ignored.

Hazelwood was appointed the commander for the defense of the Delaware River, with authority over every floating vessel in the port of Philadelphia and he was ordered to defend the river passage with every means possible. The main British forces had halted just outside Philadelphia and General Howe sent General Cornwallis into the city at the head of a substantial force of Grenadiers. There was no resistance, and the welcoming crowd was made up of the families of the loyalist Quakers and Tories. The British immediately began upgrading their fortifications as their main fleet sailed upriver and attacked the river forts that were still occupied by the Americans. Several American Navy ships attempted to bombard the British positions, but the British batteries were too strong and too accurate. In the short battle the American frigate 'Delaware' was captured, the 'Montgomery' was badly damaged, and the others limped away towards Fort Mifflin.

The 'Effingham' and 'Washington' were in Burlington, New Jersey – sidelined far away from the battle, and ordered to stay there by Hopkinson of the Navy Board, much to the annoyance of Captain Barry and Captain Read. General Washington had led a counterattack against the British at Germantown on October 4, and after a see-saw engagement the Americans suffered yet another defeat.

Captain Barry and Captain Read commandeered all the cannons and other arms from nearby sheltering merchant ships and assembled two fighting brigades of some eighty sailors each. Hopkinson refused their request to join the fight and ordered them instead to stay with the anchored ships and prepare to defend them – assuming that the war was about to come their way.

Fort Mifflin scored a brief victory as their guns bombarded the British fleet, when they forced the warship 'HMS Augusta' to run aground. The ship caught fire and exploded. This slowed the British for a short time before they commenced an intensive bombardment of Fort Mifflin, which reduced the fort to rubble and forced the surviving members of the garrison to retreat to nearby Fort Mercer. It then became the focus of the British attack and had to be abandoned by November 20.

The result was that the entire Delaware River basin from Philadelphia to the Capes was then under British control.

• • •

The American Army and Navy forces were reeling from these defeats, while Benjamin Franklin (as minister to France since 1776) was in Paris trying to convince the French to enter an alliance with the fledgling United States. A timely and significant victory by American forces under General Gates had occurred on September 19,1777, in Saratoga, NY – a victory that helped Franklin secure French agreement to a military alliance with America that America so desperately needed.

Meanwhile, Hopkinson received new orders from General Washington, who decided that the two new frigates were of no use to his Navy or Army at this time, while the crew members and weapons on board were desperately needed to reinforce his Land Army. He wanted the ships scuttled rather than allow them to fall into British hands and he ordered that to be done. Hopkinson – a short and irritating man who was convinced of his superior intellect compared to any and all of the commanders and captains around him – thought he knew best how to interpret the orders of his Commander-in-Chief. He did not share details of the orders he had received, nor did he share his own plan with the two captains when he asked them for an immediate inventory list of men, weapons and supplies on board the two ships. Then he ordered the ships to be made lighter so they could be moved into more shallow water near Bordentown. Without telling General Washington, he decided to delay the scuttling of the two ships.

Fresh and urgent orders came from General Washington after he received information that the British were eyeing the two ships for their fleet – he wanted all American ships in the area sunk immediately and in so doing, to block the river channel and prevent the British ships from passage. Captains Barry and Read were ordered to move their ships a few more miles and Barry was summoned to meet with Hopkinson. It was only then that Captain Barry received orders to sink the vessels before sunset that day, and he was furious when he was dismissed from the meeting without any explanation or reasoning for the sinking of the two ships. Read was just as angry when told of the orders – they were disgusted with the entire plan and especially the conduct of Hopkinson for his handling of this sorry affair. They did not have enough labor to remove the weapons, ammunition and supplies from the ships quickly, and decided to return to the Navy Board office to confront Hopkinson – the six-foot-four Barry, bravest and most accomplished captain in the Navy, versus the barely five-foot Hopkinson.

Barry began, "Sir, Captain Read and I have taken great measures to enable us and our crews to defend these two ships. Besides, after all the rain of the past few days the heavy fresh in the river makes it impossible for the enemy ships to come up now. If General Washington knew the full extent of our preparedness, he would not want the ships sunk yet – we can easily and quickly sink them should the situation demand that. I am ready and willing to go immediately to His Excellency and give him my personal report on this."

"Captain – do not dare disobey His Excellency's orders – the Navy Board has already written to him that this is being carried out. He has received information from a lad in Philadelphia that the British are preparing boats, and these two frigates are probably their target."

"You are telling me that all of this is based on the word

of some young lad – that is preposterous. Even if the British boats arrived here, they would not have the ability to board us."

"I will take General Washington's opinion over yours, Captain."

"No doubt you will, but I assure you that I know more about ships than General Washington and the Navy Board put together. Congress issued me orders to command these ships and only the Congress can command me to sink them on purpose."

This remark threw little Hopkinson into a rage, and he screamed his reply.

"You shall obey your orders, Captain."

Captain Read realized that Barry was close to the point of violence, and literally dragged his friend out of the office, saying they needed time to cool off. During the night the last of the guns and ammunition were removed from the ships, and their masts were brought down. The ships needed to be sunk in a very specific and precise way at the peak of high tide, so that they could be recovered later when the danger had passed.

Barry's temper had cooled down overnight and he reluctantly informed Hopkinson that all was ready. Hopkinson arrived a few hours later at the ships, and in a final insult to Barry, had himself rowed out to personally supervise the sinking of 'Effingham'. He asked Barry to stand aside and gave orders to pull the ship towards shore. The Navy Board official did not understand the precision required for this sinking operation and he failed to take account of where they were in relation to the tidal peak – they were on the wrong side of the tide. When the ship struck ground, the little man ordered the carpenters to hammer out the plugs. As the water rushed into 'Effingham' the crew could not heel the ship into the bank – she came very close to capsizing and ended up on her beam ends. Hopkinson did not know nor care whether the procedure was performed incorrectly – he immediately descended the ladder into his boat and ordered it to be rowed ashore. After he left the scene, Captain Read had the 'Washington' sunk in the proper procedure.

The next day Barry informed Hopkinson that both ships were sunk, and that 'Effingham' was in a wretched state, to which statement the little man was unapologetic. Rather than accept the blame, he put it down to misfortune and tasked Captain Barry with finding a way to correct the mistake. He then proceeded to inform General Washington that the ships were in a place where the enemy could not get them, while his people 'had a Secret Gage that would enable them to easily raise the ships when the timing was right'. Barry expended great effort over the following ten days, making three times to raise and stabilize 'Effingham' – alas they were unable to raise it.

• • •

The state of the American Army and Navy were both dire as of December 1777 – Philadelphia and all the Delaware River area was completely under British control. Congress had fled, General Washington's army was nearby but was demoralized, in rags and very short of food; unable to mount any attack to free the city. With a heavy heart General Washington decided to send his Army to Valley Forge to set up a winter encampment.

John Barry had been ordered away from the fight, upriver to Bordentown, then he suffered the indignation of having to watch his ship purposefully sunk by the incompetent Hopkinson of the Navy Board, and John was still stranded far away from his young bride.

Barry was at his wits end during all this idleness – but his brain was still active, and he began hatching a plan in his head – a way to harass the British occupation forces. He asked the Marine Committee for a leave of absence to spend Christmas with his wife and her family in Reading, Pennsylvania. After his leave was granted, he notified Hopkinson of his departure.

Instead of going to Reading, Barry rode to Valley Forge in hopes of meeting personally with General Washington. Upon arrival he was directed to speak with one of Washington's aides, who turned out to be a Frenchman named Lafayette. After some initial language difficulties, the Irishman and the Frenchman bonded as European brothers-in-arms, trading stories of their very different backgrounds and rejoicing in their common cause. Lafayette excused himself and shortly afterwards returned to tell Barry that he had been granted an audience with His Excellency, who already knew much about this sailor's exploits.

Captain Barry shared his new plan with General Washington, a plan that would allow Barry to resume a role as a fighting sailor, and to his delight, Washington was very much in favor of his proposed actions – he called Lafayette into the room, who soon added his enthusiastic endorsement of the plan. Congressman Robert Morris, Barry's friend and former employer also arrived at Valley Forge while John was there, and John was able to warn him to expect distorted complaints that he knew would be made by Hopkinson against him.

After the meetings, John rode on to the Austin family retreat in Reading, Pennsylvania, to spend Christmas with his wife Sarah, where he found more bad news awaiting him. Sarah's half-sister had recently died, leaving eight children to be cared for in the absence of their father Reynold Keen. Keen had thrown in his lot with the loyalists and was now being prosecuted by local officials for this treasonous behavior, and Keen's creditors were demanding payment of his debts from Sarah and her brother, Isaac. Sarah was distraught and embarrassed by the treachery of her family members and John had to take her in his arms to soothe and counsel her.

"My dearest, Irish history is full of treachery – Diarmaid, King of Leinster is forever damned in Ireland for inviting Strongbow to come from England to help him get his kingdom back – the English came and have never left since. Our actions in support of the just American cause are the best means to show William and Reynold the errors of their ways – while you continue to treat them as the family members that they are, despite what they have done."

"Thank you, John, my tower of strength. Please hold me tight." He obliged.

Meanwhile in Philadelphia, the British commanders had settled into the fine mansions that had been abandoned by their former American owners, and they were aided and abetted by the loyalists, including Sarah's family members – William Austin and Reynold Keen. To add to John Barry's woes, on December 30 he was summoned to attend Congress at York, Pennsylvania, where they had relocated, to answer the complaints filed against him by a Navy Board official – his nemesis, Francis Hopkinson. Robert Morris arranged for Barry to have access to John Brown, the secretary of the Marine Committee, who would counsel him for his defense of the allegations.

Congress took up Barry's case on January 10, 1778 – his defense was read into their minutes on January 13, and the case was immediately referred back to the Marine Committee to be resolved. While the committee was deliberating, they were also being briefed on Captain Barry's plan (the one he had outlined to General Washington) to strike back at the British along the Delaware, and they liked it. The plan called for manning the idle boats belonging to the sunken unfinished ships 'Effingham' and 'Washington', using the sailors assigned to those ships and moving these ship's boats to a place on the river below Philadelphia where they could be utilized to harass and even capture Royal Navy supply ships. The river was the only possible route for these supply ships and General Howe's army depended on them.

When Hopkinson became aware of Barry's plan, he tried to undermine it by sending a similar proposal under his own name and nominating one of his supporters to be the commander. Fearing adoption of Captain Barry's plan, he sent word to his allies in Congress to gather votes in favor of his own plan and against Barry's. Eventually those allies forced a vote to try and prevent Barry from being employed to lead the expedition. The vote in York was a tie which meant that Captain Barry kept his leading position, and the Marine Committee used this opening to issue its orders to Captain Barry to go forward with his use of the boats, and to employ any Navy officers not already committed in Active Service. They also directed Hopkinson to furnish Barry with everything he needed to equip his new fleet of rowboats, with a terse statement of support for Barry.

"We have directed Captain Barry to employ the pinnace and boats to harass enemy vessels passing up and down the river. Furthermore, we desire that you deliver to him such warring provisions and supplies as he may think necessary to equip the said boats."

The furious little Hopkinson complied with the orders and shortly afterwards he was reassigned to Baltimore – removing him from any further interference in John Barry's operations.

Barry set off from York on January 30, first visiting with Robert Morris in Manheim before continuing to visit General Washington at Valley Forge, where he persuaded him to issue an order to have personnel from the Pennsylvania Navy assigned to his new mission. He later found that only two of the boats were worthy of consideration for the expedition – he had these overhauled immediately and fitted with 4-pound cannons and swivel guns. Barry made officer positions available to his 'Lexington' veterans – Luke Matthewman and Matthew Clarkson. General recruits were hard to find, due to the bitterly cold weather, but he succeeded in getting a crew of twenty for each boat.

Just over a week later they were ready to depart – Barry took command of one boat, appointing Luke Matthewman to command the other. Despite the risks of capture by the British, Barry decided to head down the Delaware River under cover of darkness, keeping to the Jersey side of the river – having greased the oarlocks and muffled the oars. They reached Philadelphia by midnight where they silently passed houses that they recognized along Dock Street, and even saw the docked Royal Navy frigate, 'Roebuck'. Continuing south they left the river at dawn and hid in the feeder creeks during daylight – resuming their journey after dusk. After passing by Chester, they rowed across the river to where Captain Barry was able to establish contact with the commander of the Continental Army in Wilmington, General Smallwood, who contributed another four boats to the operation.

A few days later General Anthony Wayne of the Continental Army arrived with 300 soldiers, looking to requisition a herd of cattle that could be driven back to Valley Forge to feed the hungry Continental army encamped there. He had secondary orders to destroy any forage found, so depriving the enemy of food for their horses. Barry's boats ferried Wayne's rustling party across the river to New Jersey on February 19 and spent several days helping them complete their mission. They quickly got 500 head of cattle rounded up and a plan was agreed for Wayne's men to do a cattle drive to the north along a riverside road. He needed some action to divert the enemy's attention away from the cattle drive – Barry's boats would perform that diversion by going south and burning all the hay along the shore – carefully noting the names of the farmers and the amount of forage lost, for later compensation. The plumes of smoke were visible in Philadelphia, and it caused confusion and delay among the British. They eventually responded by sending out boats to find and destroy the American arsonists, allowing General Wayne and his 'cattle drovers' to get the herd safely to Valley Forge.

Once Barry had completed his arson attacks, he needed to get to Reedy Island, near the Delaware shore, to escape the redcoats that he expected to descend on the place – and in the darkness of night they rowed in that direction. British galleys spotted them and gave chase until two unidentified ships approached, causing a halt in the pursuit until the ships were proven to be British – precious time that Barry's fleet used to escape and reach the Delaware fishing village of Port Penn.

The next day, February 26, he discharged four of Wayne's men that he had needed for his forage burning escapade and sent them back to Valley Forge with his report to General Washington. Then he proceeded with his original mission to harass enemy supply ships travelling on the Delaware, a river that was fast becoming ice bound. After a week or so the weather relented, and his lookouts spotted two British transports on the river plus an escorting schooner trailing far behind them. Captain Barry ordered his attack boats launched, Matthewman commanding three and Barry commanding three – and in less than one hour they had boarded and captured the two transports: 'Mermaid' and 'Kitty', both full of forage for the enemy horses. The British schooner was closing in on them fast and Barry made the decision to attack it rather than run. Surprisingly, the schooner did not open fire – instead she struck her colors and surrendered immediately when the American boats went straight for her. After boarding the schooner 'Alert' the Americans found that there were three wives of British officers aboard, and the British commander had surrendered rather than risk their safety. As the Americans were securing their prizes a lookout saw several British men-of-war approaching from the south and Barry ordered their boats and their prizes back to Port Penn. There, he decided to parole the British commander and a second officer from the 'Alert', so they could escort the three ladies to Philadelphia in a carriage.

His men then began unloading the 'Alert' cargo, finding engineering supplies and a lot of British mail correspondence, which Barry sent under guard to General Smallwood in Wilmington, along with the rest of the enemy prisoners. The galley of 'Alert' was well stocked, and Barry commandeered a large wheel of cheese plus a jar of pickled oysters, not for himself but he immediately sent them along as a gift to his Commander-in-chief. He included a planning map of the British positions in New York that he had found on the 'Alert' with a note that it might be useful to His Excellency. Next, he rearranged his captured weapons as part of his defense and escape plan – while the enemy ships got closer and closer.

By the following morning, March 8, the enemy ships took shape – the 50-gun ship-of-the-line 'Experiment' under the feared and experienced Captain James Wallace, the frigate 'Brune' with 20 guns, and three sloops-of-war, 'Dispatch', 'George' and 'York'. The draught of 'Experiment' was too large for the shallow water of the area, so Captain Wallace used the smaller ships for his attack that began at 2 p.m., just as a snowstorm with howling winds raged. The American cannons already ashore fired on the approaching enemy sloops and Barry ordered 'Kitty' and 'Mermaid' to be set on fire, while he got the schooner 'Alert' and his boats underway going north – under the cover of the smoke from the burning transports. The boats were able to hug the shore, and Wallace allowed them to escape, knowing that his real quarry was on 'Alert', and he was determined to destroy or capture this rebel captain. The 'Alert' passed Reedy Island, but the enemy ships were gaining on her, and their gunners were getting dialed in and inflicting more damage with their bow-chasers. Once Barry saw that his ship could not escape, he had her guns pushed overboard and ran her aground, got the crew into the schooner's row boats and they all rowed to shore to make a clean escape without losing a man.

Captain Barry had won a moral victory, the news of which was soon the talk of Philadelphia, and the story then spread further afield to Valley Forge. The Marine Committee congratulated Barry on his success and The Pennsylvania Gazette published an article describing how Captain Barry distinguished himself on the Delaware.

General Washington wrote to him also.

"I have received your favor of the ninth and congratulate you on the success that has crowned your gallantry and address in the late attacks on the enemy's ships. Although circumstances have prevented you from reaping the full benefit of your conquests, yet there is ample consolation in the degree of glory which you have acquired. May a suitable recompense always attend your bravery."

According to the accounts of Captain Barry's success, for which he was being lauded – the summary description of the event was startling. Barry, with 27 men, had captured one Major, two Captains, three Lieutenants, ten soldiers plus one hundred seaman and marines – 116 taken by 27. His success won the admiration of friend and foe alike.

• • •

The British were determined not to let the Americans repeat the successes that Captain Barry had enjoyed. Commander Snape Hamond issued new orders from the 'Roebuck' and soon the river was clogged with enemy ships, patrolling the length and breadth of the Delaware. Barry was safe but he was also drydocked. He was instructed to terminate his Delaware operations and send his men back to their respective commanders and regiments. By early May he was back in Bordentown, depressed to see that the place was largely abandoned by the American forces, and he hated to see the exposed hulls of 'Effingham' and 'Washington' in the river.

The good news was that Ben Franklin had negotiated the long-sought alliance with France. On hearing of this development, the British feared that a French fleet and French troops were on the way, and they began preparations to leave Philadelphia for their more secure fortifications in New York.

General William Howe had by this stage been replaced by General Clinton, who wanted to clear the decks before retreating. He sent a force of infantry to Bordentown area – in flat boats, accompanied by row-galleys, a brig and a schooner – to destroy any American boats, barges and supplies they found. Ironically, Captain Barry had gone there at this same time to visit the wife of his fellow captain, Thomas Read, and had been invited to stay overnight, not knowing that a British force was about to descend on the place. A detachment of the British infantry marched towards Read's house first thing the next morning, having been told by an informant that Captain Barry was staying at the residence.

Mrs. Read got wind of the approaching British from her servants and urgently knocked on Barry's bedroom door. She was greeted by Barry who had his face lathered and held a razor in his hand.

"John, John – British troops are marching towards this house and will be here in a very short time. You must leave immediately, or they will arrest you."

"Good morning, Miss Mary, I had a wonderful sleep. Surely they can delay enough to give a man time to complete his morning shave," he said with a wry foamy smile.

"Please hurry, John – I don't think they will appreciate your sense of humor. Jacob is saddling your horse at present."

"Alright then, I'll do the lightning scrape and be on my way. Thank you for your hospitality."

He was used to quick shaves on unsteady ships, and he was not about to waste this lather – he performed a thirty second shave, wiped off, put on his jacket and boots, grabbed his already-packed bag and bounded down the stairs.

Jacob was holding his horse and he pointed out the direction the troops were approaching from. Barry thanked the servant and rode off in the opposite direction, using the house and outbuildings for cover. Mrs. Read waved from the porch and then readied herself for the arrival of the British, who came up the road minutes later and surrounded the house. An officer named Maitland approached the front steps and was greeted by Mrs. Read.

"Madam, I am Major Maitland of the Royal Navy Marines. We have reason to believe that the rebel naval officer Captain John Barry is in this residence, and I regret to inform you that we must search the premises immediately."

"Thank you for your politeness, Major. Captain Barry is not here, he departed yesterday, but you are welcome to search. Give me a moment to gather my keys – I do not want your men smashing down any of the doors of my home."

"Of course, Madam." He turned to his men – "Sergeant, prepare the search party."

She dithered and delayed finding the right keys and made a point of being friendly to the Major.

"You have arrived just as I was about to eat, please do me the honor of joining me for breakfast while your men carry out their duties. They can search wherever they wish."

"Thank you, Madam, I am indeed honored."

Breakfast was served slowly per her instructions, and she engaged the Major in polite conversation. She had some rum sent out to the troops while she prolonged the meal. The search produced nothing and in due course the detachment of troops left empty handed. The British destroyed all weapons found in the Bordentown area and burned the American Naval Stores, plus the homes belonging to several leaders of the rebel American forces but they left the Read residence intact. Over the following days the British burned over fifty American vessels, including the half sunken 'Effingham' and 'Washington'.

Meanwhile Captain Barry had made good his escape and had made his way to Reading to be reunited with his wife, Sarah.

By June of 1778 the British army had evacuated Philadelphia and marched north, while the British Royal Navy escorted three hundred merchant ships to New York with some 3,000 loyalists aboard.

The British had taken over Philadelphia mansions and public buildings during their occupation.

Now, they left these buildings and the entire city in a horrible mess as they departed.

CHAPTER FOUR

USS ALLIANCE AND OTHER SHIPS

The fledging Continental Navy fleet suffered a high proportion of losses during the early years of the War, some of which were embarrassingly close to home shores. The frigate 'Randolph' had been destroyed by a freak explosion during a battle off Barbados, with the loss of all but 4 of its 315 crew: including Barry's close friend Captain Nicholas Biddle. They had also lost 'Reprisal' along with Captain Wickes: the British had captured 'Columbus' and 'Lexington': and the 'Independence' had to be scuttled to prevent capture.

The frigate 'Virginia' was captured in bizarre circumstances when the pilot ran her aground trying to get past British ships blockading the Chesapeake. The commander of 'Virginia' was Captain Nicholson, the top name on the Marine Committee's captains list. He had made several feeble attempts to put to sea – in this latest attempt he abandoned the ship after the pilot mishap, and the British captured her without firing a shot.

• • •

John Barry had only two weeks of R&R in Reading, Pa, with his wife Sarah, before he was summoned to meet with the Marine Committee and Congress, in York, Pennsylvania. He was assigned command of the frigate 'Raleigh' and told to proceed to Boston with papers he was to present to the Eastern Navy Board, who had control of this ship. 'Raleigh's' first commander was Captain Thompson, and his first voyage had been to France along with the 'Alfred' (Barry's old 'Black Prince' before she was renamed) – to pick up 30 cannons to add to the 6 that the Marine Committee had managed to furnish. On the return voyage the slower 'Alfred' was overtaken by two smaller British warships. Thompson attempted to help until he realized that 'Alfred' had been captured, and he then decided to make a run for it and save himself, dumping his guns to lighten the ship. He escaped, but when news hit Boston that he had abandoned 'Alfred' he was suspended by the Eastern Navy Board pending a full inquiry, while the ship was impounded.

Being that the number of Continental Navy ships was so scarce, the 'Raleigh' needed to be in service – and being that Captain Barry was available he was appointed to be her commander. The parochial Bostonian Eastern Navy Board was displeased that this command had been given to an out-of-towner, and they used various tactics to delay handing the ship over to Captain Barry – such as the fact that the ship had no crew, and that court martials were being conducted on the 'Raleigh'. These proceedings dragged on till news came of General Washington's victory over a part of General Clintons British Army at Monmouth Court House at the start of July, 1778.

On July 5 the court martials were moved to another vessel, giving Barry possession of the captain's cabin but he had no men, no cannons and no budget monies. He got some men from the crew of the idle frigate 'Trumbull' and had to make up the critical marine detachment from captured British infantry. More local delays were caused by the arrival of the French fleet and by a lack of ordinance – he finally departed Boston in late September accompanied by a one brig and one sloop, just as word came that there were some 23 British warships in the nearby waters.

During their second day at sea two British cruisers spotted them and began to chase Barry's small fleet. The 'Raleigh' was a fast ship and was able to outpace her pursuers but during the chase she lost sight of her two accompanying American ships – therefore Barry stayed in the area into the next day hoping to link back up with them. Those two ships had been captured by the British during the night, and unbeknownst to Barry the enemy had ascertained his identity and his ship details from the captured officers. Therefore, they kept up the chase – the commander being his old adversary, British Captain Wallace in 'Experiment' who sought revenge for the Delaware incident and was now accompanied by 'Unicorn'. When Captain Barry realized he was still being chased, he and his helmsman decided to make for the safety of Portsmouth, and 'Raleigh' soon showed the pursuers a clean pair of heels. Thinking that 'Raleigh' was then out of danger, Barry changed course to resume his hunt for prizes.

Captain Wallace was a determined and resourceful commander, and he had not given up the chase – he had chosen a course based on what he expected Captain Barry to do. The result was that the next day 'Raleigh' was on a collision course with the two British warships. They were coming fast towards 'Raleigh' when they were spotted, and the British had the controlling wind in their favor. The chase was back on, with 'Raleigh' trying to escape by heading for islands along the Maine coast.

Barry had little knowledge of this coast and none of his crew could help him on this. As he tacked to keep ahead while looking for a harbor, the smaller faster 'Unicorn' got close to them, and it was decision time. He decided to fight, and he ordered a gun fired to leeward – the invitation to battle. His plan was to defeat the smaller ship, then run and escape from the bigger ship. 'Raleigh' and 'Unicorn' exchanged broadsides from a quarter of a mile with little damage to either. A fresh breeze allowed 'Unicorn' to improve her position, and she unleashed a broadside that toppled the fore-to-mast of

'Raleigh': the falling debris and canvas covered the starboard guns, and it also acted as a drag on the ship. Her crew feverishly cut away at the canvas while the 'Unicorn' raked her decks with cannon fire, killing and wounding many. It was getting dark, and Barry knew he couldn't easily escape – he had only two choices, strike his colors and surrender, or attack and board 'Unicorn'. He chose to attack – ordering his ship to turn to windward and go straight towards the enemy, such that his boarding party would have the battle smoke at their backs and the enemy would have it in their faces. With grappling hooks at the ready 'Raleigh' pulled alongside 'Unicorn' while her gunners fired cannon grapeshot and her marines in the fighting tops swept the enemy decks with musket fire. The 'Unicorn' managed to break away before a boarding could be made and the two ships continued firing at each other from close range, while the larger ship 'Experiment' steadily got closer. Captain Barry's 'Raleigh' was winning the battle against 'Unicorn' and her captain fired distress signals asking 'Experiment' to come alongside them to provide immediate assistance.

It was now midnight and Barry decided that his only means of escape was to point his ship directly at the islands they had seen earlier. He fired a broadside of 12-pounders at 'Experiment' as she came alongside, and then 'Raleigh' had to endure several returned broadsides of 18-pounders as she retreated. 'Raleigh' was pulling ahead, and her stern gunners were still firing back at 'Experiment'. She soon ran aground and although now a sitting duck Barry ordered the guns reloaded – surrender was out of the question. After enduring two more broadsides, the 'Raleigh' was ready when 'Experiment' had to make a quick tack, leaving her exposed. Captain Barry roared "Fire" and 'Raleigh' fired broadside after broadside into the two enemy ships, causing them to pull away from the dangerous rocks and anchor out of range of the American guns. The enemy planned to wait for daylight before coming again with broadsides and boarding parties – a strategy Barry anticipated.

In the darkness, Barry ordered their three boats lowered – two were commanded by him and were to row several miles to the mainland with the wounded crew members. He ordered the third boat commander to ferry the rest of the crew to the shore of the desolate rocky island on which they were aground: these crew members were to hide among the rocks and wait for later rescue. That same boat was then to return to 'Raleigh', gather up sufficient materials to set her ablaze – and then row to the mainland under cover of smoke and darkness.

Dawn broke before this third boat had completed its full mission and its crew panicked when they saw the British longboats lowered and coming towards them under a Flag of Truce – they departed their ship without starting the fire. The Lieutenant in command of the boat surrendered shortly afterwards, as did most of the 'Raleigh' crew members who were hiding among the island rocks and all prisoners were taken aboard 'Experiment'. It was later able to pull 'Raleigh' off the rocks and secure the captured ship at anchor before departing. Captain Barry sent his two longboats back to the island after dark the next evening where they rescued thirteen of his 'Raleigh' sailors who had managed to conceal themselves from the enemy, and he brought them back to the mainland. Supplies were purchased at the fishing village they found themselves near, and the badly wounded were left at the village along with the 'Raleigh's' surgeon to continue treating them.

In the darkness of the following night Barry's boats began the long row south along the coastline to Boston – arriving there nine days later. Barry's report and that of his fellow survivors was well received by the Marine Committee despite the loss of 'Raleigh'. He was honorably acquitted at a court of inquiry while being praised for his bravery and leadership. General Washington praised his gallant resistance in a letter. Offers were made by the now-impressed New Englanders to keep Captain Barry in Boston, but he refused and headed home to Philadelphia to see his wife and to wait for new orders.

• • •

The city of Philadelphia, vacated by the retreating British was left in a terrible mess. Nine hundred starving American soldiers were freed from prison, where over a thousand prisoners had lost their lives amid dreadful conditions and were buried in unmarked graves. The city was stinking from open pits full of garbage, dead animals, and body parts from a British

Military hospital. Nice homes and city public buildings had been commandeered by the enemy and used for both humans and for animals – many being defecated and decimated. The new American military governor of the city, Benedict Arnold, faced the enormous task of repairing everything, including the morale of the population – amid spiraling inflation, as prices for all kinds of goods skyrocketed.

This is what John Barry arrived back to find in late October, along with huge family problems caused by the treasonous behavior of Sarah Austin's family members.

The Marine Committee now suggested that Captain Barry lead a flotilla of armed galleys in a land and sea invasion of Florida – his sole compensation being land grants in the Florida swamps. He had to use all his considerable powers of persuasion to convince key congressmen to scrap this foolhardy plan and his arguments were finally successful. He spent Christmas 1778 at home with Sarah, assessing their dire financial circumstances. John's brother, Thomas Barry, offered what financial help he could muster, and the brothers became very close again. They consoled each other over their inability to find the time to visit their aged parents in Ireland – while taking comfort from the knowledge that the monies that they regularly sent home did help the family enormously.

Since there were no Continental Navy ships to take command of, the only seafaring option Captain Barry could see that would produce income for him and his family was Privateering. Barry's friend and former employer, Robert Morris, was a financier of private business as well as an influential congressman, and even though he was on record with his distaste for privateers, he was persuaded to change his stance and view the practice as a necessary evil in this case, because of the precarious financial state of the fledgling United States. The key ingredient needed for privateering was the issuance of a license or 'letter of marque' from Congress which would allow merchant captains to make war on British shipping. This license meant that the seizure of an enemy ship and confiscation of the ship and its cargo was a legal act under international law.

The Irwin brothers were the most successful merchant trading business that had made the transition to wartime privateering, and their success attracted the best captains and sailors. They offered Captain Barry the command of their armed brig 'Delaware', their best ship – he accepted the offer once he secured a leave of absence from the Marine Committee. The respect that he commanded among the seafaring community was evident as he quickly signed his crew of forty-five sailors in a tight market. He and Mr. Irwin registered 'Delaware', got their letter of marque signed by the President of Congress, and John managed to attend the baptism of Thomas Barry's daughter, as godfather to the child.

The 'Delaware' was loaded with cargo while Barry received lessons on the ins and outs of money certificates and currency transactions needed for his new role. She departed on February 16,

1779, a 200-ton brig armed with ten 4-pounders, sailing as a small squadron comprising one other armed brig and three merchantmen, all under Barry's command – bound for Port-au-Prince, Haiti. It was a trouble-free voyage, and he was back home again in three months with sugar, rum and molasses. They performed a quick turnaround and again they put a little squadron together under the command of Captain Barry – already being referred to as 'Commodore' by the other ships. A few days later, on July 16 – the Commodore captured his first privateer prize, the enemy sloop of war 'Harlem'.

Returning to Philadelphia in mid-September, Barry was informed by the pilot that the American Navy vessel 'Confederacy' lay in the Delaware River at Chester and had been 'press ganging' crews of merchant vessels coming up the river. The news alarmed his crew, and many wanted to be put ashore. Barry made an impromptu address to the gathered crew, saying – "M' lads, if you have the spirit of free men, you will not desire to go ashore nor tamely submit against your wills to be taken away, though all the force of all the frigate's boat crews were to attempt to exercise such a species of tyranny." This satisfied them as it gave them his consent to defend themselves.

When they were within hailing distance of 'Confederacy' her commander ordered the brig's main topsail to hove to the mast. Barry answered that he could not do that without getting his vessel ashore, to which the commander responded that the brig should come to anchor. Barry ignored the request – then a gun was fired from the frigate and a boat was lowered from her that came towards the 'Delaware'. Barry directed his men to allow only the officers from the boat to come aboard. The boat came alongside, and two armed officers jumped aboard, ordering the main topsail halyards to be cast off. This order was ignored and Barry wondered whether they were sent to take command of his vessel. These officers tried to intimidate the boatswain by pointing their pistols at him. When that was of no avail the two officers jumped back into their boat and left. When another gun was fired from the 'Confederacy' Barry ordered his guns cleared for action and told his gunners that if any damage was done to his brig, he would give the 'Confederacy' a broadside. A third gun was fired from the frigate and Barry hailed them immediately, asking the name of the commander of the frigate.

The answer was "Lieutenant Gregory."

Barry hailed him – "Lieutenant Gregory, I advise you to desist from firing. This is the brig 'Delaware' from Philadelphia and my name is John Barry."

A long silence followed as the name sank into Gregory's head. 'Delaware' continued her way to port, and no more efforts were made to impede her.

John arrived home to find that Sarah Austin's family troubles had come to a head with mixed results – the sale of Reynold Keen's estate was postponed but the sale of William Austin's estate went ahead to auction. Barry decided to stay home as long as he could and to provide more supportive attention to Sarah, of the type that only a devoted husband could provide.

• • •

Soon afterwards Congress offered Barry the command of the new 74-gun Continental Navy ship 'America' being built at Portsmouth, NH. Yet again, duty won out over profit and Captain Barry reported to the Eastern Navy Board in November. He proceeded to Portsmouth to find that construction of the new ship was very far behind schedule, and he was back in Philadelphia in December to make his report to the new Board of Admiralty. Thus, he was able to spend another Christmas at home and then consumed the early weeks of the new year in fruitless discussions with the Board trying to get funds approved to finish the new ship. Finally, he was told the truth – "there was no money available in the near future to complete the construction of the ship". Therefore, Barry got another leave of absence from the Navy to do more privateering.

Spring of 1780 brought tragic family news – he received confirmation that his brother, Patrick Barry, was confirmed lost at sea the previous August when his ship 'Union' disappeared in the dangerous Bay of Biscay, off the coast of France. John was appointed executor of Patrick's estate with responsibility to see that his widow, Mary, and four-year old daughter were taken care of. Despite this sorrowful event and the ever-present dangers of a sailor's life at sea, John knew that seafaring offered him the best source of income to help cure all his financial woes. Caldwell and Co. offered him command of the 14-gun brig 'American' with a crew of seventy, but the catch was remuneration – he had to find the money to buy a one-sixteenth share of the ship. He was on the verge of refusing the offer until his Irish friend, John Brown of the Admiralty Board, offered to cover half of that investment – Barry was able to scrape the other half together and sailed the ship to Sint. Eustatius with a cargo of tobacco and lumber. He was back in two months and scored a handsome return on his investment.

A second voyage was in the planning when he was called back into Navy Service – to take command of the waiting frigate 'Alliance' in Boston. There was, however, a major complication – first he had to preside over the court martial of the previous commander, Captain Pierre Landais, a Frenchman. That fateful previous voyage was the return of 'Alliance' to America with munitions, uniforms and other supplies for General Washington's army. Landais had improperly retaken the command of the anchored 'Alliance' at L'Orient after being relieved of command for earlier insubordination to Captain John Paul Jones. On the 'Alliance' voyage to America, Landais became demented and ordered the ship to change course away from the American coast. Lieutenant Degge, his second-in-command, in conjunction with an American diplomatic passenger named Arthur Lee, and aided by other officers – took command of the ship away from Landais and sailed the ship to Boston. On arrival, the crew were all promptly arrested on the orders of the deposed captain, who had then remained on board when they anchored in port. The Eastern Navy Board convened an inquiry, while the Board of Admiralty wanted the ship back into service as soon as possible. That's when they called for the available Captain Barry to assume command of 'Alliance' – naming Lieutenant Hoysted Hacker as his second-in-command. After all their recent losses, the Navy had been reduced to only four frigates: 'Alliance': 'Trumbull': 'Deane': and 'Confederacy', plus the sloop of war 'Saratoga' – hence the urgent need to get 'Alliance' back to sea without delay.

Once Barry arrived in Boston, Captain Landais was ordered ashore but refused to leave his cabin. After three days of refusals a force of marines broke the lock on the cabin door and carried Landais ashore, kicking and screaming. The cabin was in a dreadful state when Barry examined it and he put a team to work immediately to make it clean and pristine again. He quickly signed on some officers but struggled to sign any able seamen because of the lure of more profitable work with privateers and the low esteem that 'Alliance' was regarded by Boston sailors.

The court-martial was convened on November 20, 1780, in the captain's cabin of 'Alliance'. Captain Barry was head judge of the four-judge panel. The cabin door was locked and guarded by two marines – nobody was allowed in except the witnesses as they were called. The court continued through Christmas and into early January 1781- at which time the panel of judges met to deliberate. They reached verdicts quickly – Captain Landais was found guilty on all charges and was dismissed from service. Lieutenant Degge was also found guilty and dismissed, even though the mutiny was deemed to have been justified.

Barry could now turn his full attention to getting 'Alliance' back into service and he began to seek able seamen and supplies for her. This was a monumental task as there was no budget and no money available for anything. The finances of the country were in tatters – proof being that a part of General Washington's Army had mutinied after going a year without pay or new uniforms. The wealthy southern states had fallen into British hands, including the port cities of Savannah and Charleston. For many of the top thinkers on the American side the war seemed lost.

Lafayette lamented to Franklin – "We are naked, shabbily naked".

Congress debated what to do and they finally asked France for another loan of 25 million livres. They selected one of General Washington's aides, twenty-six-year-old Colonel Laurens, a fluent French speaker, to go to France immediately with explicit instructions to plead their case – also in the American delegation was the scholar Thomas Paine and Viscount de Noailles, a cousin of Lafayette. Once they arrived in Boston to prepare for the voyage they got a rude awakening from Captain Barry. He had neither enough crew nor the money to outfit the 'Alliance' for a mid-winter voyage across the Atlantic, nor arms enough for the ship to defend themselves against any enemy ships they might encounter. They brainstormed for ways to find a crew, including a suggestion for press-ganging, a practice that Captain Barry loathed for many reasons, including the damage it could do to his good reputation. Reluctantly he agreed to back the press-gang possibility, and the Navy Board petitioned the court for permission, which was denied. That left them trying to source a crew from British prisoners who would be freed on the promise of serving, but they presented a major risk that they would not fight when needed. Barry also worried they might even mutiny when the ship got close to Britain's shores.

Several Bostonians wanted to purchase passage to France on the voyage and they were told that passage was conditional to their serving on the quarterdeck during any encounters. Barry and Laurens approached the commander of troops in Massachusetts, General Lincoln, who gave them permission to talk to recruits and the invalid corps. Laurens asked Governor Hancock for permission to approach volunteers from the castle guard. Both attempts resulted in just a few additional men. Money was raised for munitions and supplies. Then Barry and Laurens asked every merchant captain in port to part with a few seamen, with little success. Laurens sent a new petition to the General Court appealing to patriotism and duty and offering a bounty to raise volunteers – which added enough names to the muster rolls that he thought they were good to go and informed Congress of that fact, wrongly. Barry needed some experienced sailors and after a few were found he was at 236 crew, only 75 percent of what he needed to adequately sail and defend 'Alliance'.

Captain Barry was faced with a dilemma. Their mission was of critical urgency, and because of that fact Barry reluctantly agreed to sail immediately with the crew they had – and 'Alliance' stood down on February 11, 1781. He told Lieutenant Hacker to spread the experienced salts among each watch so that they could teach the raw recruits the ropes. Even on this first day of the voyage Barry lamented to himself –

"The Alliance is the finest ship I have sailed but I have put to sea with the worst crew."

He rejoiced that the winter weather was his ally, knowing that British ships would be in safe harbor till spring, but he had an even greater enemy to worry about – that enemy was ICE. Those fears were justified less than a week later when the captain was awakened in the night by a sharp thudding noise. Bounding up on deck he saw the problem immediately – icebergs dead ahead and all around them. It was a very dark night without any moon – he tried to assess the size of the icebergs, knowing as he did that their size and shape under the water was the real threat. They didn't have a true wind owing to the size of the bergs, so they were at the mercy of the currents – they needed the best of Irish luck to escape this enemy. He ordered a sailor to heave the lead, a weight on the end of a long rope that was used to find the water depth – in this case their best way to find what dangerous underwater ice may be lurking. As the wind increased to a gale, he ordered all sails taken in.

To Thomas Paine's questioning look he answered – "nothing can be done but to lay the ship to and let her take her chance, for she is at the mercy of nature now." Barry and his helmsman guided 'Alliance' between the icebergs surrounding them. He had his sailors place canvas bags of cork outside the rails to act as fenders and to protect the outside of the ship from the ice. Others held gun rammers and anything else of length to parry the ship away from the encroaching icebergs. For hours they all worked to keep the scraping and banging of the icebergs to a minimum, amid loud crunching noises. One sharp outcrop of ice ripped into the gallery cabin of Colonel Laurens, just missing him as he walked out of the cabin. The monster ice rocks continued to float by as the gale raged on through the night until dawn, when 'Alliance' finally found open water after the last of the iceberg field floated away from them. Now it was time to assess the damage and undertake repairs to areas along the sides of the ship, which took the crew a few days. Then they caught better winds and continued their eastern journey.

Unbeknownst to Captain Barry a mutiny was festering as they got closer to England. His own mind was preoccupied at this time with memories from his childhood days growing up in County Wexford, being as they were soon to be passing close to the southern coast of Ireland. One of the ringleaders was the ship quartermaster, an Englishman named John Crawford – the plot involved seizing whatever weapons the mutineers could get, killing all the ships officers except one that would navigate them to a port in Ireland or England. Barry could sense that something was afoot – after discussions with Lieutenant Hacker he put all the officers on notice to be alert for any signs and he ordered the marines to patrol the decks constantly, day and night. Arms were stowed in locked chests and were constantly guarded.

Near the Bay of Biscay two ships were sighted and steadily continued to approach 'Alliance'. Captain Barry hailed them; after receiving no reply he ran up his colors and fired a warning shot – after which both ships 'hove to'. One was the 10-gun privateer 'Alert' from Glasgow and the other was her prize, she had captured a neutral merchantman 'La Buonia Compagnia' from the Republic of Venice. The Alliance boarding party freed the merchantman's captain from irons and after talking with him and examining the ship's papers, Barry determined that the 'Alert' seizure was an act of piracy. He ordered the merchantman released at liberty on March 4 to pursue its voyage – then arrested the 'Alert' captain and his crew, then placed a prize crew aboard and she was brought along with 'Alliance' to France. His passengers, Colonel Laurens and Thomas Paine were pleased and impressed by this act of diplomacy by Captain Barry – they complimented him, saying that his liberation of the neutral ship would bring admiration and goodwill from other nations toward the United States.

A few days later they sighted land as 'Alliance' sailed along the coast of Britany, and after signaling for a pilot they picked one up and he guided them into L 'Orient on March 11, at which time the Alliance rowboat carried Captain Barry and his passengers to shore, leaving Lieutenant Hacker in charge. Word of their arrival was sent to Congress via a letter carried by a ship departing for America that same day. Colonel Laurens delayed his plans to go to Paris when he was informed that the French Minister for Marine was about to arrive in L'Orient – whom he met there, alongside Captain Barry. The minister told them that a French Fleet of 25 ships-of-the-line, plus 90 transports carrying thousands of French troops were headed to the West Indies and thence to America – welcome news indeed.

Captain Barry took Laurens with him to meet their agent, a resourceful Irishman named James Moylan, who informed them that a ship with much-needed supplies for the Continental army would be ready to sail for America in a matter of days. The ship was 'Marquis de La Fayette' and was under charter by Benjamin Franklin's nephew and needed an escort to America from 'Alliance'. Moylan promised to get 'Alliance' refitted quickly and Barry sent a letter to Franklin with Colonel Laurens when he left for Paris – asking for updated orders and Franklin's latest dispatches for Congress.

Most of Barry's first days ashore were spent searching the

port and city for American sailors – finding none. Drunken and offensive behavior committed ashore by members of 'Alliance' crew necessitated disciplinary punishment to be meted out to three seamen with the cat-o'-nine-tails in front of the entire crew – per the regulations, no man received more than12 lashes. Barry hoped that this display of the captain's authority would act as a deterrent to the would-be mutineers. His application for the condemnation of 'Alert' was successful – she was quickly sold, and a share of the prize money distributed among 'Alliance' crew, which lifted their morale. James Moylan speedily got 'Alliance' refitted for departure – as Barry awaited a letter from Benjamin Franklin in Paris with any new orders from Congress. When the letter came it confirmed the instructions to bring the French ship 'Marquis de La Fayette' under his convoy to America, carrying cannons, gun barrels, uniforms and other much-needed supplies for General Washington's Army. He managed to supplement his crew with 'four American seamen from other ships in port and was ready to sail by March 23. A sudden storm delayed their departure, during which time Moylan informed him that he suspected the 'Marquis' was heavier in the water than she should be, because of smuggled goods added to her cargo. Barry deemed it too late to do anything about it during such wind and hailstorms.

Captain de Galatheau of 'Marquis' was problematic from the start, not obeying the prearranged signal to get under way until a personal visit by Barry to his ship forced a resolution of the issue. Barry spoke no French and the Frenchman spoke no English. Barry found a South Carolina sailor on the 'Marquis' who interpreted for him and who agreed to help keep Galatheau abreast of signals, and to quietly keep an eye on him for Captain Barry. After the ships made their way safely through the dangerous Bay of Biscay, an Indian sailor aboard 'Alliance' asked Lieutenant Hacker in the late afternoon for permission to speak privately with Captain Barry. The captain agreed and had the sailor escorted to his cabin.

The man was loyal to his captain and told him the full story of the proposed mutiny, including names of the ringleaders – he was assured of his safety and sent back to his post. A council of war between Barry and his officers soon followed and a plan of action was agreed. Barry ordered the commander of the marines to send an armed detail below the decks to arrest the three ringleaders, who were immediately clapped in irons – then he had armed marines patrol the deck all night. At dawn Captain Barry ordered the ship to turn into the wind and stop, and all hands were piped on deck. The ringleaders were brought out and Crawford was the first to be strung up to the mizzen stay by his thumbs, then he was whipped with the 'cat' while Barry demanded that he divulge the names of his fellow mutineers. He did not reveal any names, but the other ringleaders soon did as their turn came to face the 'cat'. As names were given, those named were brought forward and punished in the same way till they revealed more names – the entire whipping lasted some 7 hours and totaled

25 individuals. Barry decided that the 3 ringleaders would be kept in irons for the entire journey, the rest he made swear a solemn declaration that they had abandoned their plan and would conduct themselves faithfully going forward – they were allowed to return to their duties after the ship's surgeon administered treatment for their flesh wounds.

The 'Alliance' and 'Marquis' then resumed their voyage to America.

Captain Barry knew that a prize capture would lift the morale of his crew and five days later he got his wish. After a chase, and some cowardly broadsides by the enemy that did not meet the proper code of naval warfare adhered to by Captain Barry, 'Alliance' captured two British-flagged privateer brigs – 'Mars' and 'Minerva'. He put an Alliance prize crew on the bigger 'Mars' and reluctantly turned over 'Minerva' to Captain Galatheau of 'Marquis' – giving him strict orders that she and her prize must keep pace with 'Alliance'. A week of good sailing weather was followed by some very heavy squalls and a large sea. Alliance lost a man overboard off the main topsail and 'hove to' but could not recover him. In late April 'Alliance' split her foresail and soon afterwards her four-stay sail, forcing them to slow to a crawl as repairs were made.

Captain de Galatheau used this incident to take 'Marquis' and 'Minerva' off ahead – and neither flag signals nor fired guns had any effect in turning them around. After repairs, Barry tried in vain to find 'Marquis' for two days before assuming that her captain had set a new course back to France

– suspecting that Galatheau wanted to keep the entire prize for himself. Reluctantly, Barry ordered his ship to head home once again, after sending 'Mars' on to Boston under his prize crew. In early May 'Alliance' picked up two more prizes, the brig 'Adventure', accompanied by a 'snow' – which they took with them towards Philadelphia. More bad gales hit them – a lightning strike caused further damage to 'Alliance' and fifteen sailors were badly burned by the strike. In the rain and darkness they lost sight of both prizes, and had to assume that his prize crews would sail them on to Boston as he had instructed them to do if they became separated.

With over 50 crew members on the sick list, mutineers in chains and 44 more sent off to sail the two prizes, 'Alliance' had less than 150 able-bodied seamen left to sail a ship that needed twice as many sailors. Two British merchantmen were sighted but not pursued because of this manpower shortage. In late May off Novia Scotia, Captain Barry's ship fell in with two British sloops of war. Because of a lack of wind and the damage already suffered to her sails, the 'Alliance' was unable to quickly move away from these enemy ships. The enemy stalked 'Alliance' for two days, then they closed in ready for battle. The two ships were the 20-gun 'Atalanta' under the experienced Captain Edwards, and the 14-gun 'Trepassey' under Captain Smyth – both smaller than the 32-gun 'Alliance' but the enemy captains decided that as a pair working together, they could defeat her. Once the British hoisted their colors and beat their drums, Captain Barry did the same, and his crew manned their battle stations. There was very little wind, and it took until noon the next day for the two attackers to position themselves on either side of 'Alliance'. Barry hailed the nearest ship, 'Atalanta', asking who they were. Edwards replied, identifying "Atalanta, sloop of war belonging to His Britannic Majesty."

Barry responded – "This is the Continental Frigate Alliance, John Barry – I advise you to haul down your colors."

Edwards tried to prolong the conversation to give 'Trepassey' time to get into a better position before commencing the battle. Barry was not fooled by this tactic and broke the silence with his loud command – "Fire".

A broadside hit 'Atalanta' which damaged her rigging and injuring several, including one of her officers – and the battle was on. The enemy ships had one major advantage on their side this calm day – they had oars, while 'Alliance' had to rely totally on the wind, which was unfortunately absent. The 'Trepassey' crew were rowing to get into prime position and 'Atalanta' held her fire waiting on them, while also manning their oars. The enemy pair miscalculated, and 'Trepassey' approached too fast as she got abreast of her partner and then she began to glide past 'Alliance'. Barry slammed two broadsides into 'Trepassey' which smashed her rigging to bits and killed several, including her commander, Captain Smyth, who suffered a direct hit from a cannonball. Lieutenant King, second in command, ordered the men to keep rowing to try and get his ship away from the 'Alliance' guns. Captain Edwards bravely ordered the 'Atalanta' crew to row his ship between 'Alliance' and 'Trepassey', to save his sister ship, and she took another broadside which damaged her masts. The damaged 'Atalanta' was still able to maneuver into a better attacking position and the becalmed 'Alliance' was soon caught in the crossfire where the combined fifteen 6-pounders of the two enemy sloops were able to unleash all their guns on her. Captain Barry ordered some of his 9-pounders to be moved from their normal places, relocating them to positions that allowed his gunners to return fire.

Without any wind 'Alliance' could not get close enough to the enemy to board them – the calm conditions also meant that all this action was enveloped in thick smoke which had reduced visibility to near zero from the first minutes of battle. The position of 'Alliance' relative to the enemy ships reduced her usable guns to less than half of their normal firepower, and they were suffering substantial damage with many casualties. Officer Kessler was wounded, and Pritchard was killed by a 6-pound cannonball, while Barry stood on the quarterdeck directing his defense amid all these projectiles and wood splinters flying about. Some men were impaled by the wood splinters and surgeon Kendall's people worked feverishly below decks to treat the wounded so they could return to the fray.

As the battle raged on past three o'clock in the afternoon Captain Barry was hit in the left shoulder with a grapeshot ball, which knocked him to the deck. He struggled to his feet, blood streaming from his wound and he waved away help from Lieutenant Hacker – while he continued to lead his defense. Bleeding heavily, he became faint, and he finally agreed to be helped below for treatment – passing the command of the ship to Lieutenant Hacker. The ship's surgeon, Kendall, gave priority to his captain despite being overwhelmed by casualties. With the help of some laudanum and several men to hold Captain Barry down, he worked feverishly to remove the grape ball from his shoulder, then cleaned the wound as the captain fell unconscious.

Up on deck more broadsides hit 'Alliance' and Lieutenant Hacker narrowly avoided being hit by a cannonball, but all the while the Americans continued to return fire. A British cannon blast knocked down the 'Alliance's' colors while her gunners were reloading. Amid confusion about whether it was a surrender, the British let up – 'Alliance' then fired a broadside at them, and the enemy continued their onslaught. Hacker surveyed the devastation from the quarterdeck – the deck was covered in casualties, blood and debris, the rigging was in tatters and the sails mostly shredded. He conferred with his surviving officers and summoned the courage to go below and tell Captain Barry what they suggested as the next course of action. Barry was sitting up by this time, being bandaged by the surgeon.

He immediately said, "Lieutenant, why are you not at your post"?

"Sir, the ship is in tatters and we have a lot of casualties. I have conferred with the officers – should the colors be struck, Sir"?

Barry's Irish temper flared as he roared his reply –

"No, No, No – if the ship cannot fight without me then I will be carried on deck to direct our defense. Get back to your post, Lieutenant. Surgeon, get me dressed immediately so I can go back on deck."

Hacker went back on deck and told the officers and crew that Captain Barry had ordered everyone to keep fighting. They all accepted these orders and continued with their desperate defense duties. As if on cue, the wind also responded, and a small breeze came on – as if in answer to the sailor's belief that "he who sails without oars stays on good terms with the wind." Lieutenant Hacker shouted orders to the helmsman, the ship moved a little and she slowly got into a better position to enable her to fight back. Almost immediately, a broadside from the 'Alliance' fourteen starboard 12-pounders slammed into 'Atalanta' – shredding her rigging and badly damaging the masts. Then the 'Alliance' portside guns did the same to 'Trepassey'. This finished off 'Trepassey' and Lieutenant King, the stand-in commander, struck his colors. Captain Edwards of 'Atalanta' tried to break off the engagement and attempted to sail his ship out of danger – but her masts were not up to the task, and they immediately tumbled onto the deck. 'Alliance' cannons were primed ready again and on Hacker's order they fired another broadside into 'Atalanta' – that was the end for them, and Captain Edwards now struck his colors also – after five hours of battle.

This final fusillade happened as Barry was being helped up the stairs to the deck, where his exhausted crew greeted him with loud shouts of jubilation. Barry acknowledged them and then ordered that he be brought to his cabin. Minutes later Lieutenant Hacker joined him there.

Barry was full of praise – "Well done, Lieutenant, that was a hell of a fight you put up while I was incapacitated. I am indebted to you, and your actions will be dutifully recorded."

"Thank you, Captain, for making us continue the fight, Sir. It's as if the wind responded to your orders."

"Aye, I have deep respect for the wind gods and maybe they have some respect for me. Send Kessler off in the pinnace to ferry the defeated British commanders back to 'Alliance' to discuss terms of surrender."

"Aye Captain."

The boat bypassed the 'Trepassey' on being told that Captain Smyth was dead and proceeded to the 'Atalanta' for Edwards. He asked them to collect Lieutenant King from the 'Trepassey' as they passed it on the return. Both commanders then climbed the 'Alliance' gangplank and were escorted to Captain Barry's cabin.

Captain Edwards presented his sword to Captain Barry. He took it, looked at it, and with his good arm he handed it right back to the British officer, saying –

"I return it to you Sir. You fought well – you deserve a better ship from your King. My cabin is at your service; use it as your own."

"Thank you for your courtesy, Captain – you fought even better. I was confident that we could subdue your ship, when the disadvantages under which 'Alliance' labored were considered."

"Ah, yes – our disadvantages. We Americans are blessed with being able to turn the tables on disadvantages. What is the state of your ships and your casualties?"

"Six killed and twenty wounded out of 125 on 'Atalanta': seven killed, including Captain Smyth, and eighteen wounded out of 80 on 'Trepassey'."

Captain Barry tallied up these numbers in his head. Part of his 'disadvantages' were that 'Alliance' already had many prisoners locked away below decks. He added the new lot to his current 126 prisoners, bringing him close to 300 total – too many for 'Alliance' to hold and to feed. He quickly came up with a solution to this problem.

"Sir, I had some prisoners already aboard before our encounter. If I allow one of your ships to sail to Halifax as a cartel with all the British prisoners aboard, will the British Admiral in charge there free a similar number of American prisoners in exchange?"

Captain Edwards responded – "Thank you, Captain, for your generous offer. The Admiral in question is my uncle and I can assure you, Sir, that we will honor that fair exchange."

"Good – that's agreed. It's late in the day now. Both of you commanders, plus your other officers and your wounded will stay on 'Alliance' tonight. I want both of you to make use of my trumpet here and now, to convey these terms to your crews and get their assurance of orderly behavior during the night – we will handle the details come morning and get your ship on its way."

"That is agreeable to us, Captain," they responded. Both officers duly made the required announcements across the water.

The preparations for the cartel ship began at dawn, but not before the remainder of Atalanta's mast cracked and fell on her deck. The Trepassey's guns were tossed overboard, and her military stores were transferred to the 'Alliance'. Then the sloop was loaded with all the British prisoners from both captured ships plus those previously held on Alliance – the exceptions being Captain Edwards and the other officers. Captain Barry placed 'Trepassey' under the command of her sailing master and allowed her to set off for Halifax that evening after repairs.

The 'Atalanta' repairs took two more days, and she was then sent to the nearest safe port, Boston, under the command of her prize captain, Hezekiah Welch. The 'Alliance' casualties were noted as five killed and twenty-five wounded, three of whom died soon afterwards. The ship needed even more repairs before she could sail, and Captain Barry didn't think she could make it all the way to Philadelphia. Therefore, he decided that 'Alliance' would instead sail slowly for Boston, where she arrived on June 6, 1781, after avoiding the British blockade. The battered and barely recognizable 'Alliance' was greeted warmly by crowds along the waterfront, some seventy days after departing L'Orient.

Captain Barry was stretchered off 'Alliance' and he set up accommodation at a waterfront house where he later dictated letters to his clerk, Fitch Pool. One letter was to Congress, and one to the Admiralty Board – recounting details of his voyages to France and back. He withheld details of his heroic role in the ferocious battle, as was the style of this very unassuming man. He specifically requested that the 'Alliance' hull be sheathed in copper, he praised the bravery of Lieutenants Hacker and Kessler, and that of his entire crew, making a side mention of the fact that he was one of the wounded – adding that he would be fit for duty by the time his ship was ready to sail.

His letter to his wife Sarah was brief and in it he played down his injuries, while asking her to accompany his courier, John Kessler, back to Boston to be with him during his recovery.

Accounting for the captured prizes that he had sent ahead earlier – 'Adventure' and the 'snow' made safe harbor, but his prize 'HMS Atalanta' was recaptured by British blockade ships as she struggled into Boston. It was quite some time later before Captain Barry found out that his accompanying ship the 'Marquis', who had sailed away on him when his masts had been damaged by storms, had been captured by British ships, along with her prize, 'Minerva'.

• • •

Before long, the news of Captain Barry's latest adventures, his bravery and the story of his capture of two enemy ships appeared in the Boston Continental Journal and then quickly spread to newspapers around the United States and to Europe. Congress passed a resolution applauding Captain Barry's brave service and his naval successes. Lieutenant Kessler sang his captain's praises in an interview with the Philadelphia Press. General Washington sent a letter of congratulations to Captain Barry and offered best wishes for a speedy recovery. John Brown, his Irish friend and the Secretary of the Admiralty, praised him in a letter and confirmed to him that the Warren shipyard would be commissioned immediately to sheath the 'Alliance' hull with copper as Barry had requested. Sheathing with copper protected the wood from damage caused by marine life such as barnacles and shipworms, because copper has a natural toxic effect on marine organisms – the process improved the performance of the ship and extended its lifespan. Barry knew that a rolling mill near Boston could provide thin sheets of copper for this purpose, which were nailed with copper nails in an overlapping pattern on the hull below the waterline.

The news of Captain Barry's noble act – namely the liberation of the captured neutral Venetian merchantman – also made the newspapers in Europe. Even Benjamin Franklin in Paris, felt it necessary to add his voice in praise of Captain Barry's noble diplomatic act on behalf of the United States of America.

Meanwhile the noble Captain was laid low with a serious shoulder wound.

CHAPTER FIVE

THE CONTINUING WAR AFTER YORKTOWN

Mrs. Sarah Barry arrived in Boston in late June, escorted by Lieutenant Kessler of the 'Alliance'. John had not included a lot of details in his letter to her about the severity of his wound and Kessler avoided discussion about it as much as possible on their journey from Philadelphia. She was shocked to see her husband mostly confined to bed and in much worse condition than she had been led to believe. The shock was short-lived and had to be pushed to one side as she assumed control of his care and recovery – her very presence gave an immediate uplift to his spirits. They had been married almost four years and during that time they had spent very little total time together, such was the extent of his sailing duties and long voyages. Now she had his undivided attention and company, and she was determined to make the most of it while she nursed him back to health.

Captain Barry already had a substantial amount of paperwork to deal with, too much in Sarah's opinion, but she couldn't convince him of that. The court-martial of the mutineers was about to start, and John was completing his testimony. It was an open and shut case – the three ringleaders were found guilty and had to be made an example of. McEllany was sentenced to be hanged from the 'Alliance' yard arm; Sheridan got 300 whip lashes and Crawford received 80 lashes. Once that was behind them, John took Sarah to view the Celebration of America on the Fourth of July in Boston, at which time they also celebrated their wedding anniversary being that the dates were so close.

Barry spent this downtime reviewing the sorry state of the Continental Navy. The 'Deane' was the only American warship to survive the disastrous April convoy when 'Confederacy', 'Deane' and 'Saratoga' set off to escort 36 merchantmen from the Caribbean to Philadelphia. A storm separated the warships – 'Saratoga' went down in the storm with the loss of John's friend, Captain Young, and all hands. The 'Confederacy' was surprised by two British frigates – 'Orpheus' and the infamous 'Roebuck' under Snape Hamond; and Captain Harding surrendered his ship to them without a shot being fired. The British Navy were happy to have this nice vessel for their own fleet and renamed her 'Confederate'. 'Deane' made her way to Boston after the storm without incident and all but four of the merchantmen made port safely. After that, Captain Nicholson's 'Trumbull' was captured by two British ships off the Delaware estuary – the salt in the wound being that these two ships were originally the Continental vessels 'General Washington' and 'Hancock'.

By the end of July 1781, Captain Barry was well enough to go back to work – he put pressure on the Admiralty Board to finish the copper sheathing of the 'Alliance' hull and to provide the money for masts, rigging and canvas. The 'Trepassey' arrived from Halifax with 130 freed American prisoners – part of the surrender terms agreed between Captain Barry and British Captain Edward of the 'Atalanta' after his capture of the two British ships. Barry was able to begin the condemnation and distribution process for 'Trepassey' and get her sold quickly – the proceeds being split between Congress, the 'Alliance' crew, and Barry himself as Captain, which improved his personal financial state. When his other prize 'Mars' was sold, Barry bought a one-sixteenth share in her as part of a group of investors, as she became the 'Wexford' – as a nod to him and the Irish County of his birth. On her first voyage for the group, she was captured by the British in the St. Georges Channel area between Ireland and England – all the investors lost heavily, including John Barry.

The arrival into Boston of the French frigate 'La Resolute' on August 25 ignited a greater celebration than a victory on the battlefield – Colonel Laurens and John Paine were aboard, plus tons of supplies for Washington's army and two-and-a half million silver livres to help the money-strapped Congress. Captain Barry was as elated as anyone because he knew that Washington's Army had been hanging on by a thread. Both the Army and the Navy had been suffering in much the same way – from a serious lack of money for weapons and even for supplies as basic as uniforms. Added to that was the confusion, incompetence, internal fighting and nepotism that burdened the fledgling United States – as the country struggled to stay afloat and stay the course in her war against the country with the strongest Army and best Navy in the world – the mighty British Empire.

Barry was disheartened by the American predicament and saw many good men walk away from service to their country – he himself had to fight constantly to keep from being pulled into the political and financial quagmire. He was owed a lot of backpay by the Navy and he had been squeezed out of substantial prize rewards – he could have become rich if he stuck to privateering, but he chose duty over money.

While he was musing over his troubles, Barry had an unexpected visitor to Boston – none other than Captain John Paul Jones. Jones was on his way to Portsmouth to try to speed up the completion of his new command, the frigate 'America' – the ship that Barry had been assigned to oversee until he found that there was no money available to finish it at that time. Jones had tried unsuccessfully to meet Washington at the Army encampment at White Plains. The General was too busy planning a new campaign with French General Rochambeau, which coincided with the entry of the French Naval Fleet into the war on the American side. The two John's had not seen each other for almost five years, while both Captains had risen to become by far the two most successful and decorated Continental Navy Commanders, and the irony of it was that neither of them was American born. Jones was Scottish, a man who was vertically challenged but made up for it with a very large ego – a constant talker and self-promoter who already thought of himself worthy to be named the first Admiral of the Navy.

Jones' first command in the Continental Navy was as Lieutenant on 'Alfred' in 1775 (John Barry's old ship 'Black Prince' before Congress purchased and renamed it), where he served under the cowardly Captain Esek Hopkins – by all accounts Jones had performed well despite serving under such a weak leader. Next, he was made Captain of the sloop 'Providence' and after that he commanded the 18-gun sloop 'Ranger' with which he made a name for himself. He prowled the waters near Britain's coast and was a thorn in the side of the Royal Navy as he destroyed many of their ships and threatened their trade. In 1778 through1779 he was Captain of 'Bonhomme Richard' when the combined Franco-American Navy defeated the Royal Navy in the Battle of Flamborough Head, in the North Sea. Jones's ship defeated and captured the much larger 44-gun 'HMS Serapis' in one of the bloodiest naval engagements in history.

Captain Barry was a very different individual than Jones, a 6-foot 4-inch Irishman with broad shoulders, also a fierce fighter warrior, but a modest man who shied away from the limelight – and strangely they had developed a good friendship. They ate breakfast together the next day in Boston and talked for a few hours – creating a stir for those who spotted them as both still possessed the brogues of their native countries. Their discussions were for the most part about their respective ships, 'Alliance' and 'America', and the state of the war. Both had lost many good friends – they mourned those losses and consoled each other over the Continental Navy ships that had been captured by the British. The common trait that both possessed was their fighting spirit, their strong desire to get their next ship command seaworthy: to get back into the war and do their utmost to help General Washington turn the Revolutionary War around. This need was especially urgent now that America was about to get the long-awaited help from their French ally – aided by a fleet of warships and thousands of French soldiers.

As expected, Jones did most of the talking during their meeting and he made mention of the derogatory letters that were circulating about him. Barry parried those inquiries away and never admitted that he also had received letters on that subject. Next morning Captain Jones departed for Portsmouth. The visit served to highlight the frustrations they were both experiencing due to the exceedingly slow progress of getting their ships completed – all either of them wanted was to get to sea and to win back naval control of the sea for America. It pained Captain Barry so much to see the only two ships that remained of the Continental Navy – 'Alliance' and 'Deane'- both sitting idle. The 'Alliance' now had her hull sheathed in copper, but she was still lacking some masts and was without any new canvas.

Barry decided to leave Boston and escort Sarah home to Philadelphia via coach – where he intended to plead his case with Congress. When they arrived home in early October there was good news from General Washington's camp at last, and there were expectations of even better news to come from Virginia. The terrible days of cold, hunger and disease of the Valley Forge encampment were behind them. New supplies had arrived along with a French fleet of warships who carried over 5,000 French troops to reinforce the American army. General Rochambeau commanded the French, and through the interpretations and intercessions of General Washington's aide, the Marquis de Lafayette, the two generals struck up a strong relationship from the start, and the two armies were quickly aligned to form a formidable force. That combined Franco-American Army then quietly marched south to rendezvous with the French fleet, and in the process, they had trapped Lord Cornwallis and his British army on the Yorktown peninsula.

The French fleet under Admiral Francois Joseph Paul de Grasse had relocated from the West Indies to Chesapeake Bay, just as he promised Washington he would do in a July letter. The French fleet reached Chesapeake on September 1, with 24 ships-of-the-line, 1,700 guns and 19,000 sailors. The British fleet under Admiral Graves arrived five days later – 19 Warships, 1,400 guns and 13,000 sailors. The battle of the fleets began at 4.30 p.m. in the September afternoon and continued until sunset. The British came off worst with 314 killed and many ships badly damaged. Next morning, Admiral Graves determined that his fleet had suffered too much damage to engage the French again – he ordered his ships to break away and they sailed for New York.

That left the French in control of Chesapeake Bay, and their presence prevented any British reinforcements from getting to Yorktown – which in turn would secure the entrapment of the British forces.

• • •

Congress had finally faced up to the reality that the Marine Committee and its replacement, the Admiralty Board, had both outlived their usefulness – having been dogged by infighting, indecision and lack of funds to get and keep any meaningful Navy in place. Captain Barry and Captain Jones had numerous battle victories and prizes to their names, while many of the other captains had failures that dragged down these successes. Robert Morris had been a member of the Committee and the Board; he and John Brown were the only personalities that had won the respect of the Navy Captains and the respect of members of Congress.

A new approach was called for and Robert Morris was given supreme control over financial matters as they related to the Navy – with the new title 'Agent of Marine'. He immediately dispatched John Brown to Boston with orders and authority for Captain Barry to get 'Alliance' and 'Deane' completed and seaworthy with great haste. The coaches of John Brown and John Barry passed each other on the road without either of them knowing it. Upon arrival in Philadelphia Barry surprised Morris in his office, and after pleasantries, Morris summarized the details of the letters that Brown was carrying to Boston. Barry would have one week of home leave and then assume command of a joint cruise of 'Alliance' and 'Deane', as soon as they were made ready to go to sea.

During that week Barry did what little he could to help Sarah and her brother Isaac – trying to save what was left of the Austin family fortune. Within days, a letter came from Secretary Brown in Boston that 'Alliance' would be finished before 'Deane', which necessitated a change in orders for Captain Barry. He would take 'Alliance' to sea on her own as soon as the ship was ready – John said his goodbyes to Sarah again and set off for Boston.

While he was on his carriage ride to Boston the "Big News" became public.

"BRITISH GENERAL LORD CORNWALLIS HAD SURRENDERED TO GENERAL GEORGE WASHINGTON IN YORKTOWN, VIRGINIA ON OCTOBER 19, 1781."

Barry arrived in Boston on October 27 to find the city in the throes of celebration – the happy news having beaten him to town by one day. John Brown had more good news to share – he had secured a wealthy benefactor named Thomas Russell who would advance to the Navy the money needed to complete and refit Barry's ship 'Alliance'.

Captain Barry immediately started on the difficult task of putting together a quality crew including officers, in Boston, a city that did not know him very well. Lieutenant Hacker had gone privateering, both the surgeon and the chaplain declined to return to serve on 'Alliance'. At a brainstorming session he decided to make use of the local paper – The Continental Journal ran a front-page picture of 'Alliance', adding an advertisement to attract sailors with promises of incentives and the chance to make extra prize monies from captures of enemy warships and merchantmen. Despite the adverts and additional offers of an insurance policy, they failed to get many to sign the muster rolls. He got some returns for his officer rolls, such as Parke, Welch, Fletcher and Gardner – completing the officer roster by December 1, but his overall crew number was insufficient.

• • •

Then, America's favorite Frenchman, The Marquis de Lafayette, arrived in Boston on December 10, carrying orders to Captain Barry from Robert Morris. The 'Alliance' was to make an urgent voyage to France, carrying Lafayette himself on "most important business for America."

Captain Barry was pleased to be reacquainted with the jovial Frenchman who told him how happy he was to be a passenger on 'Alliance' returning to France. His entourage included Vicomte de Noailles, General Du Portail, Colonel Gouvion, Major La Combe and some aides.

Gilbert du Motier, aka the Marquis de Lafayette, was born into wealth and privilege in France in 1757, with close family connections to the French throne. Due to some untimely family deaths, he inherited enormous wealth while still a young teenager. He was pressed into a strategic marriage alliance at the age of fourteen with the powerful De Noailles family who had much influence with King Louis, and he was given the rank of Sous-Lieutenant in the Musketeers. After the couple were married when he turned eighteen, he was made a Captain in the Dragoons. He developed an early fascination with the colonial conflict brewing in America. When he expressed a desire to go and fight with the colonists his father-in-law persuaded the King to issue a decree forbidding French officers from serving in the Colonial Army.

He was so desperate to serve in the American Revolution that he purchased the ship 'Victoire' and despite delays and setbacks he set sail from Paullaic on March 25 of 1777. On route, the ship picked up 5,000 rifles and crates of ammunition in Pasaia on the Basque coast, and arrived in Georgetown,

South Carolina on June13. From there he journeyed to Philadelphia and through his Masonic membership connections and his offer to serve without pay, he was commissioned as Major General by the Continental Congress. When he met George Washington, his enthusiasm impressed His Excellency, and he then became a member of the General's staff. His first combat was at the Battle of Brandywine, where he was wounded during the American retreat while being cited by Washington for 'bravery and military ardor'. He spent the harsh winter of 1777-78 at Valley Forge with the American Army, where he built up a close companionship with General Washington. It was in Valley Forge that Captain Barry first met Lafayette when the Frenchman facilitated Barry's meeting with His Excellency there. By the autumn of 1781 Lafayette found himself at the center of the action at Yorktown where he commanded a force that surrounded and held the British at bay until General Washington arrived with reinforcements to initiate the siege that eventually led to the British surrender. Now, Lafayette was going to France on urgent diplomatic business for the Congress and Captain Barry was chosen as the man who could get him there quickly and safely.

• • •

Despite the Yorktown victory the war was far from over. Washington knew this, as did his fellow leaders in Congress, and so did John Barry. The British still had two substantial armies in the field – one in New York and one in South Carolina, plus a large and powerful Navy fleet. The commanding Admiral of the French fleet had decided to sail his fleet south till the northern winter had passed – an understandable action but one which greatly reduced General Washington's military offensive options. Washington reluctantly had to halt his campaign and so he marched his Army to a camp in New Jersey, from where they could keep an eye on the British Army in New York, commanded by his old foe, General Clinton.

There was still much diplomacy going on between America and France – Franklin was in Paris playing the diplomat cards, and Lafayette's mission to France was deemed to be of the utmost importance. The latest orders from Robert Morris told Captain Barry to take Lafayette and his entourage safely to a French port as quickly as possible "on business of vital interest to America." Hence, Morris directed Captain Nicholson of 'Deane' to give up some of his crew to Captain Barry to complete the 'Alliance' muster rolls and let her depart as soon as possible. Morris told Barry to avoid all vessels on the voyage to France, telling him – "your sole object is to make a quiet and safe passage to France" – an order that voided the promises that Barry had made to prospective crew members when he told them that they would be in line to share rich prizes.

Morris also had advice on what extra stores Barry should carry for the comfort of the French gentlemen –

"Let it be done with discretion; remember we are not rich enough to be extravagant nor so poor as to act meanly."

After delivery of his aristocratic passengers to France, Barry was given permission to 'go on a cruise' for enemy prizes for a month, then return to France for new orders. At this time Barry was owed some $5,200 in pay from the Continental Navy and now he was further handicapped by being forbidden to capture any enemy ships on his voyage to France – he was not happy about it. Still short of enough crew members, Barry ordered Captain Nicholson to send over 40 sailors from the 'Deane' crew to top off the 'Alliance' crew – an order that was reluctantly obeyed but it only yielded a fraction of that number. Lafayette was impatient to leave and used his influence to get 37 crew from the French ships in port – a motley group that consisted of their castoffs. This got the 'Alliance' crew up to 255 and Barry told Morris that he would shortly depart. As he was getting the last of their supplies loaded, he wrote to Sarah lamenting his predicament and wishing Lafayette was already in France. The 'Alliance' stood down on December 23, 1781.

The North Atlantic Ocean in winter was always a bleak lonely place and it was days before they spotted another vessel. The crew looked at Barry anxiously, hoping for the order 'Beat to Quarters' but instead the order was to change course and avoid contact. The 'Alliance' made full speed in the skillful hands of her captain and arrived at L'Orient, France, on January 18, 1782, just 26 days after departure – the only reward Barry received was having spirited conversation with his French guests over dinner. Lafayette was full of compliments for Barry's ship, his seamanship and the speed of the voyage – he called it one of his happiest voyages and promised to help find some American sailors for 'Alliance' once ashore.

The duty-bound Captain Barry returned his French sailors to French command and was forced to search for more crew members before he could sail again. His orders allowed him to go on a cruise until March, then return to L'Orient for Franklin's dispatches. Through his Irish friend, deputy consul Moylan, he got nine American sailors from French privateers, then attempted to get more from French and neutral ships while he waited in hopes of more help in that regard from Lafayette. No help came and Barry put to sea with what he had on February 10. They sailed the shipping lanes between Portugal and England for weeks but found only neutral ships – no enemy prizes – and so they returned to L'Orient. A spat with Franklin then followed – the diplomat wanted 'Alliance' to go to Brest to take aboard 'unexplained goods' for him and a supply of gunpowder. Barry had no interest in going to Brest and stuck to his orders, which were to wait a few more weeks for dispatches before sailing for America.

Franklin's dispatches eventually arrived – 'Alliance' departed March 16 and soon ran into very powerful storms that destroyed two longboats and did damage to her rigging. The storm forced them to head southeast and by late April they were near the Leeward Islands, where they sighted a large fleet of sail – Barry changed course till the fleet was out of sight. Sickness then spread among the crew and nine of them died before they caught favorable winds that carried them northward to Cape Henlopen. Their luck ran out on their arrival, as they sighted the 64-gun enemy ship, 'Chatham' with its tender, the sloop-of-war 'Speedwell'. Barry had to reverse course as they were chased down the Delaware coast where Barry's knowledge and ability to sail 'Alliance' into shallower water paid dividends – the enemy ships could not follow him there. After they gave up the chase, Barry reversed course again but still could not enter Delaware Bay because of the presence of enemy ships. 'Alliance' continued north and was forced to flee from large enemy warships once more, eventually reaching the port of New London, Connecticut on May 13 – the voyage home from France had taken 60 days, compared to 26 days going to France.

Once in port he wrote to John Brown, Secretary of the Board of Admiralty, telling him of his arrival and more – "Not a prize this trip, hard luck indeed! Mr. Morris has sent me orders to join the French frigates at Rhode Island and be under the command of a French officer there. He must be unacquainted with the Frenchman's rank, or he must think me a droll kind of fellow to be commanded by a midshipman. I assure you I don't feel myself so low a commander as to brook such orders. I suppose he will be much offended. I assure you that although I serve the country for nothing, my rank being all I have earned during this time – I am determined no midshipman shall command me, let him be a chevalier or what he will."

Even though New London was a 'friendly' port, Barry was unable to make progress with the uncooperative local agent to get ship supplies, needing two rowboats to replace the ones lost in the storms – and to make matters worse, his crew were asking for their pay and for shore leave.

Barry wrote again to Brown – "I never was in such damn country in my life. You never was in so miserable a place. All the people here live five miles from home, and yet, not a house have I been in but the tavern and the house of one Irishman. The tavern is kept by this Irishman, Thomas Allen, who came here from the island of Antigua, and whose antipathy to the British borders on abnormal."

The captain didn't have money to pay the crew and fearing mass desertion if they went ashore, he refused leave – and then decided to go himself to Philadelphia to get Robert Morris to authorize pay and refitting supplies. That meant leaving Lieutenant Welch in command, a weak stand-in, but he felt he had no better choice. A mutinous uprising quickly followed, and Welch barely held control of the ship, locking the hatchway to confine the troublemakers below deck, while he sent a rider to go after Captain Barry. The rider caught up to Barry's coach and the captain was back aboard by dusk. The big man was very angry and immediately ordered the locked hatchway opened, and with his booming voice he called out the crew one at a time. He questioned each as they came forward – eventually arresting sixteen men and clapping them in irons. Without enough officers for a court-martial, he held a one-man inquiry in his cabin – questioning all officers and crew one at a time. Three ringleaders were identified, and they were transferred to the harbor guard ship – the rest were allowed to return to duty after a stern lecture and a demand that they swear allegiance to their Captain and to the Navy.

Adding to his woes, Barry found out that his turncoat brother-in-law, William Austin was now a prisoner of the Continental Army. Austin had been given command of an armed enemy vessel which he used to participate in a Chesapeake expedition with the traitor, Benedict Arnold. They had destroyed much of Virginia and then Austin had become part of the British defenses at Yorktown. After Cornwallis's surrender Austin was captured and imprisoned. Barry had no personal sympathy for Austin, but for Sarah's sake, he offered to help gain Austin's freedom. He wrote a letter to General Washington asking him for a special favor. In his letter he paid his respects and provided an update on British naval activities, before getting to the real purpose of writing –

"I am indeed aware that no person is exchanged without permission from Your Excellency, and I have a favor to ask in that regard – that you will suffer a captain by the name of William Austin to be exchanged or to go on parole. He is an old friend of mine. If Your Excellency will be pleased to grant this favor, I shall ever esteem it as a mark of your friendship."

Washington granted his wish and Austin was set free.

The morass of incompetence and untrustworthiness continued to plague Captain Barry as he navigated his way around the French command structure and tried to deal with the unhelpful New London shore agent named Mumford – finding only his friend John Brown to be honest enough to tell him what was preventing 'Alliance' from being refitted for sea. Knowing that there was one place where he could be confident of raising a crew, Barry got permission to travel to Philadelphia in mid-June. There, after a joyful reunion with Sarah, he met with Morris to iron out the problems with supplies and crew. Morris sent explicit instructions to the New England maritime agents of the Navy "to provide Captain Barry with such supplies as he found necessary to have."

Within two weeks he had was able to head back overland to Connecticut with 50 experienced sailors. His wagons passed near to Washington's encampment along the Hudson, and he paid a courtesy visit to His Excellency – at which time they both appraised each other of the status of the war on land and on sea. Barry finally arrived back to his drydocked ship at New London on July 20. Many letters awaited him there, including more sad family news – this time it was about his Irish family in County Wexford. Both of his parents were now deceased and his two sisters, Eleanor and Margaret, were destitute along with their families. Despite his own precarious financial situation, he wanted to help them and immediately arranged for money to be sent to them via London agents.

With Robert Morris's authority he could now force the hand of the local agent and made quick progress in getting 'Alliance' seaworthy. A court-martial for the three ringleaders of the mutiny was held – they were found guilty, and each sentenced to lashes ranging from 20 to 90. After the whipping was carried out the following day on 'Alliance', Barry allowed two of them to return to duty and sent the third one back to an army regiment. To complete his crew, he took on several slaves locally, whose owners were promised prize shares when 'Alliance' returned from her cruise. The ship finally left New London on August 4,1782, with a happy and high-quality crew – a crew who appreciated the fact that they had a master sailor and the best captain in the fleet as their Commander. Within days they had their first prize, an enemy brig; and a few days later captured the schooner 'Polly', bound from Bermuda to Halifax with a cargo of molasses, sugar and lime – sending both to Boston with prize crews aboard.

At this time Bermuda was a haven for loyalist privateers who regularly dropped off American captives there. Barry decided on a bold plan – he sent Captain Tufts of 'Polly' with a message to the local governor demanding the release all American prisoners to him immediately, or 'Alliance' would prevent ships from leaving or arriving. It took a full day for the governor to comply, who then sent a slow boat with some prisoners towards 'Alliance' just as Barry's lookout spotted two sail to the west. Regretfully, Barry could not wait for the prisoners and the 'Alliance' departed to chase these prizes. The two ships were neutrals, but they told Barry of 88 merchantmen recently departed from Jamaica – the famous 'Jamaica fleet'.

Captain Barry knew their regular route – north to Newfoundland and from there on to England. He also knew they would be protected by the Royal Navy – several ships-of-the-line and frigates. That didn't faze him – he could keep his distance and snatch a few merchantmen – and so he ordered 'Alliance' to sail north to intercept them at the Newfoundland Bank – capturing another prize on his way, a whaling brig bound for New York. Shortly after that, 'Alliance' was hit by the tail end of a hurricane, but they came through mostly unscathed and captured their first brig from the Jamaica fleet on September 18. The brig's captain told them the fleet had been hit by a very strong hurricane which destroyed many of the Royal Navy protection ships, including the 74-gun 'Ramilie', as well as sinking over a dozen of the merchantmen – the surviving ships were now scattered all over the ocean. Within a week 'Alliance' had snatched several more merchantmen prizes and one enemy frigate, to the point of being overburdened from putting prize crews aboard them, and by the number of prisoners they had to feed. Barry decided to head to France with his total of nine prizes, reaching L'Orient on October 17. All prisoners who had not agreed to enter into American service were sent ashore and he immediately set about the legal disbursement of the prizes. The ships were loaded with rum, sugar, coffee and liquors. Half the proceeds went to the American government and half to 'Alliance' officers and crew, Captain Barry being entitled to six shares.

• • •

There were rumors in France that major progress had been made in the peace negotiations between America and Britain. Barry wrote to Lafayette to find out the true status of the negotiations. The American ship 'General Washington' of the Continental Navy arrived in L'Orient with secret dispatches for Franklin, and Barry sent along his own letter to him with the express rider, suggesting to Franklin that 'Alliance' and 'General Washington' should go on a joint cruise. Before a reply came, Barry was invited by Lafayette to come to Paris. He had to decline because he was struck down with a bilious fever, which laid him low for a week and then left him in a weakened state for several more weeks.

Six of the 'Alliance' officers demanded payment of their owed wages before sailing again – many of them had not been paid their wages by the Navy for years and demanded payment now. Barry's answer was that he did not have the power to pay their wages but promised to do all he could to get them paid once 'Alliance' was back in America. He was trying to get them their share of the prize money for all nine prizes before they sailed, and he told them they were taking advantage of his sick condition. When he got them their prize monies they left the ship, refusing to report back for duty because of the wages dispute. Barry told them they were under arrest, but he didn't send his marine detail to physically arrest them – instead he marooned them ashore and got 'Alliance' ready to sail – only to have his orders changed again, making him wait for Franklin's latest peace negotiation dispatches so they could be brought back to Philadelphia.

Those dispatches came December 6.

The word was that "Peace between America and England was NOT concluded."

Captain Barry was eager to get in one last cruise before peace was finalized and he departed on December 9 to run down the coast of Guinea before returning to America via Martinique. They battled a northeast gale for a few days before being able to head south to Africa, then changing course at Madeira and headed west towards Martinique and America. No prizes were found – a large enemy two decker warship gave chase, but the superior speed of 'Alliance' allowed them to escape easily.

In Martinique there was a dispatch from Robert Morris waiting for Captain Barry – he was ordered to proceed to Havana, Cuba. First though, 'Alliance' needed some repairs including a new top mast plus some supplies, especially drinking water. January 18, 1783, had them in Sint. Eustatius, the Golden Rock where Barry had spent a lot of time in his early career as merchant captain and where he was welcomed with a night of feasting. Off Hispaniola, Lord Hood's 17 ship British fleet gave chase, but 'Alliance' was too speedy for them. Next stop was Cap Francois in Haiti where Barry went ashore while supplies were being loaded, and where he met Seth Harding who had once captained 'Confederacy'. Over dinner, Harding asked for a voyage home as a passenger, and he helped Barry sign six experienced American salts to his muster rolls.

They departed January 22 with two smaller ships going

along for protection from 'Alliance' – reaching Havana's harbor on January 29.

The Spanish West Indies fleet was anchored in the harbor – Barry fired a gun salute which was returned – then he went ashore wearing his smartest uniform.

• • •

Shortly after 'Alliance' had departed L'Orient, and unknown to Barry, the terms of the peace agreement between America and England were finalized in Versailles, which also included Articles of Peace between France, Spain and Great Britain.

The American diplomats had their own agendas and didn't fully understand the problems besetting the Continental Army and Navy – especially their inability to pay their troops and sailors. Congress was frozen by their lack of finance and left it to the wizard financier Robert Morris to find a solution – part of that solution was sending Captain Barry to Havana. America had succeeded in getting a loan from Holland – Robert Morris arranged for Benjamin Franklin to sell the Bills of Exchange in Paris for specie (gold and silver coins), through a Spanish company that had offices in Havana. Captain Barry was to pick up that money – 72,000 Spanish dollar coins and 500,000-dollar equivalents in American paper money. As extra cover and in case 'Alliance' didn't make it to Havana, Morris had ordered the 'Duc de Lauzun' to sail to Havana under Captain John Green and even sent

John Brown along as a passenger on that ship to oversee the government interests.

In Havana the 'Alliance' spacious cabin hosted a dinner for the dignitaries – Governor of Cuba, Don Luis Vizaga; Admiral of the Spanish Fleet, Don Josef Solano; American Registrar in Havana, James Seagrove; American 'fixer', John Brown; Captain Green and Captain Barry. Don Josef told Barry that the port was closed for security reasons – until the Spanish fleet was ready to depart and join the French fleet for an invasion of England's richest island – Jamaica.

Barry used this delay to put his crew to work overhauling the 'Alliance' – careening (heaving down) the ship so that the exposed hull could be scraped clean and then caulked with oakum that was made there and then by all hands. It took three long arduous days to complete these tasks and then all the cannons, ballast and stores were reloaded back onto the ship. On February 13 Barry requested permission from the Governor for 'Alliance' and some merchantmen to leave port – permission was denied. Barry now ordered Green to careen his ship also, while he had his 'Alliance' crew perform cannon and small arms practice firing exercises every day, hoping the constant noise would help change the governor's mind – it did not. On March 5 the Spanish fleet got ready to leave and departed several hours later. The next day 'Alliance' and 'Duc de Lauzun', both loaded with their cargo of money, finally got under way, along with six merchantmen they were escorting. Their mission was to deliver the money to Philadelphia, or proceed to Providence, Rhode Island, if that was the better option.

The course that Captain Barry set had the ships headed for the Gulf of Florida and they sighted the Martyrs Rocks (Florida Keys) by midafternoon. They were then spotted and pursued by two British frigates – 'Alarm' under Captain Cotton and 'Sybil' under Captain Vashon. Barry watched anxiously as the British kept up the chase, worried that the 'Duc' was too heavy in the water and was slowing down the 'Alliance'. He purposefully slowed 'Alliance' so that 'Duc' could catch up and by midnight he ordered decks cleared for action as 'Alliance' prepared to defend 'Duc'.

Calling it his Irish Luck, they then sighted what they all believed were the lanterns of the Spanish fleet – which prompted the British ships to break off the chase. Barry kept company with the 'Spaniards' all night and in the light of morning the 'fleet' was found to be 10 fishing sloops – but, as Barry remarked to his officers, 'they answered our ends.'

Seeing no sign of the British ships, Barry made the best of his way and continued northward between Florida and Grand Bahama Island. The 'Duc de Lauzun' continued to labor and slow down their progress – so Captain Barry brought Captain Green, two of his officers and John Brown aboard 'Alliance' to discuss ways to speed up 'Duc'. Barry decided to transfer most of the specie from 'Duc' to his 'Alliance', against Green's wishes, which caused Barry to suspect that Green had something else besides the money in his hold. The transfer was completed in a few hours, leaving some of the money cargo on 'Duc' to appease Green – the weight reduction allowing them to make better speed, and by the next morning they were located off Cape Canaveral, Florida.

On March 9 they were spotted and pursued again by the same British ships, 'Alarm' and 'Sybil', now joined by the sloop of war 'Tobago' – the three together were too strong for the Americans to mess with. Captain Barry signaled 'Duc' to make all sail and follow 'Alliance', just as he spotted another large ship farther away that he also kept an eye on. He changed course and sailed south towards where he assumed the Spanish fleet to be – giving themselves the best chance of survival. He had already decided that he might have to abandon 'Duc', as the 'Alliance' now had most of the money aboard – and that money cargo needed to be saved at all costs. Captain Green in 'Duc' was still not able to keep up, and the 'Alarm' was gaining on her.

Both American ships hoisted their colors and prepared for battle – then Green signaled that he wanted to speak with Captain Barry. 'Alliance' shortened sail and turned back towards 'Duc', scaring the first approaching British ship into slowing down also. Barry spoke via trumpet to Green while ordering his crew to clear the decks for action. Green stated that he thought the other ships were privateers – a statement that shocked Barry and angered him. He told Green the 'Alarm' was obviously a 32-gun Royal Navy frigate and said the 'Alliance' could not stay with 'Duc' any longer. He told him to lighten his ship by dumping most of his cannons and to try to outrun the British. The mystery ship seen earlier had now moved closer to them and Captain Barry, thinking it had to be French or Spanish, took a calculated bold approach – he ordered signals run up asking for assistance from the mystery ship and decided to go to the rescue of 'Duc'.

Just as Captain Vashon brought 'Sybil' closer to 'Duc' in preparation for an attack, the other two British ships, 'Alarm' and 'Tobago', broke away – when Commander Cotton of the 'Alarm' realized that the mystery ship was 'Le Triton', a large French ship-of-the-line. Barry changed course quickly to put 'Alliance' between 'Sybil' and the almost defenseless 'Duc' – who then slowly began to move out of harm's way. Barry went from gun to gun on the main deck to steady his gunners, reminding them not to fire until the enemy was completely abreast. They waited over the starboard cannons as 'Sybil' got closer, even though they assumed that her Captain must surely have noticed that the 'Alarm' and 'Tobago' had abandoned the attack. 'Sybil' fired a Bow Gun which did some damage to the 'Alliance' cabin, and then she tacked, but fired her broadside too early and missed 'Alliance' completely.

'Sybil' was by now gliding past the 'Alliance' starboard guns. Barry shouted out an order – 'main topsail hove to the mast' – which slowed his ship. Just as the 'Sybil' entire port side was exposed he gave the order – "Fire". Their broadside destroyed most of the 'Sybil' rigging which fell onto the deck. 'Alliance' marines raked the enemy decks with musket fire from aloft as both ships reloaded. 'Alliance' swivel guns sprayed musket balls across 'Sybil', but she did manage to fire another broadside – doing little damage to 'Alliance'. Barry's next broadside brought down the fore topmast and studding sails of 'Sybil', killing and wounding many of her crew. Captain Vashon continued to sail 'Sybil' alongside 'Alliance' while Barry's 12-pounders shot holes in her hull. Another broadside struck 'Sybil' as she hoisted a signal of distress – all she got from her commanding ship was a signal to break off the engagement, as the 'Alarm' continued to move away.

Captain Barry knew that he had won the battle and 'Sybil' was dead in the water. However, he decided not to pursue her because of his own precious cargo and the need to protect 'Duc'. This point was not lost on the commander of 'Sybil', Captain Vashon, who knew he was there for the taking if not for Captain Barry's disengagement. He later spoke about the battle with glowing praise for Barry.

"I had never seen a ship so ably fought as the 'Alliance' and I have never received such a drubbing. The coolness and intrepidity no less than the skill and fertility in expedients which Captain Barry displayed on this occasion are described in naval annals as truly wonderful; every quality of a great commander was brought out with extraordinary brilliance."

'Alliance' proceeded instead towards the 60-gun French ship, 'Le Triton'. When they were close to her, Captain Barry hailed the captain of 'Triton', asking why he had not joined the fight. The reply he got was that the French ship was carrying a lot of money for the French islands and her captain thought the two American ships were already captured prizes being used to trick 'Le Triton' – and he didn't want to risk her capture by the British. Barry didn't believe the explanation but decided to keep his cool. Then, the French ship offered to accompany the Americans and they all gave chase to the British – they did this rather half-heartedly and allowed the British to escape. After that the French ship broke off and bid them Bon Voyage.

Captain Barry was still fuming and got Green and Brown over to 'Alliance' for talks. He accepted John Brown's praises for the way 'Alliance' had defeated the British ship and thanked him – then he assailed Green for his conduct since leaving Havana. Barry blamed Green for getting them into the situation with the British ships, blamed him for the damage and casualties suffered by 'Alliance' in the battle and especially the death of master's mate Shubal Gardener from his wounds, whom they had to bury at sea that very day.

He now insisted that the portion of the money cargo still on 'Duc' be transferred to 'Alliance', and he also took eighteen sailors from 'Duc' to cover for his casualties in the battle. After that they had good sailing winds through to Cape Hatteras, other than captain Green did not make all sail as instructed and fell way behind 'Alliance' again. Barry had enough of Green's slow sailing by this stage and pressed ahead, making it to Cape Henlopen in two more days.

There was thick fog at the Cape which hid their approach, but it also hid the enemy. 'Alliance' fell in with two British warships and was able to sail away from that danger, but later found their way into the Delaware Bay blocked by two other enemy ships and 'Alliance' had to bear away again. The British ships chased her in vain and this chase opened an entry corridor for 'Duc' when she finally arrived at Delaware Bay – she was able to proceed up the Delaware to Philadelphia unhindered. 'Alliance' had to continue north to escape, and she went instead to Newport, Rhode Island. Barry put a man ashore with orders to carry a letter to Robert Morris in Philadelphia containing a report of his voyage, a request to get the money cargo removed from his ship with all haste, and reminding Morris that the crew needed to be fully paid immediately. While he waited for a reply, 'Duc' had arrived safely in Philadelphia on March 21, with John Brown thankfully aboard and ready to correct Green's inaccuracies in his account of the voyage.

On March 23, 1783, a French sloop arrived in Delaware Bay and a dispatch rider who was put ashore in Chester brought the 'BIG NEWS' to Philadelphia –

"THE TREATY OF PARIS HAS BEEN SIGNED.
THE WAR IS OVER."

Captain John Barry had commanded the first Continental Navy cruiser to defeat a British warship when his 'Lexington' captured 'HMS Edward'.

Now, as commander of the 'Alliance' he won the last naval

battle of the American Revolutionary War with his triumph over 'HMS Sybil' on March 10, 1783 – while being unaware of the signed Treaty ending the war.

• • •

The Provisional Articles of Peace had been signed in Paris by John Adams the previous November 1782. Then the Preliminary Articles for Restoring Peace had been signed at Versailles on January 20, 1783; and later still the Ratification of the Preliminary Articles was signed on February 3, 1783, by the Ministers of the United States, France and Great Britain – by which a cessation of hostilities was agreed upon.

All these peace agreements were being concluded while Captain John Barry was masterfully sailing 'Alliance' across the Atlantic, fighting the fight for America, defeating enemy ships and capturing enemy vessels as prizes. On top of that he was bringing to Congress a cargo of desperately needed money to help the country survive.

CHAPTER SIX

TREATY OF PARIS ENDS THE NAVY MISSION

The news of the Treaty had not yet reached Newport when Captain Barry anchored there. Being worried about enemy ships, Barry took the 'Alliance' further upriver to Providence. That's where he heard the Big News and he sent off letters to Robert Morris, and to his wife Sarah, asking her to come to Providence. Morris sent a letter back congratulating Captain Barry on his great victory over 'Sybil' and offering him his old merchant captain's job back – but he didn't tell him how or when the cargo of money was going to be removed from the hold of 'Alliance'. Morris asked that 'Alliance' be refitted quickly and to then sail to Virginia where a cargo of tobacco would be taken on, bound for Holland.

These letters ushered in a protracted run of bad luck for the brave and triumphant Captain Barry. The surgeon, Dr. Kendall, who had treated Barry's shoulder wound during the battle against 'Atalanta' and 'Trepassey', and had later deserted his ship, was successful in a lawsuit over a disputed payment – winning the suit and costing Barry 180 pounds. Another lawsuit against Barry's agents was filed by the owners of the 'Fortune', an American ship prize that Barry had recaptured from the British the previous summer. A shore agent had sold the ship without going through the legal process of condemnation. There was another problem to do with wages and shares of prizes for the owners of the slaves that had served on 'Alliance'. Barry had given one slave shore leave, thinking the man did not have a master, when it turned out later that he had – and that master was a congressman. Morris also notified Barry that each crew member would be paid off by giving them a certificate showing that he belonged to that ship, and it could be cashed in later.

Mrs. Sarah Barry arrived in Providence in the company of another young lady, her teenage cousin, with a letter from John Brown advising the captain that all trade was at a standstill and that Captain Barry's prizes in Havana and L'Orient had not sold. Yet again there were no instructions included for the removal of the desperately needed money from the 'Alliance'. Barry left the two ladies in comfortable accommodations and rode to Philadelphia to talk face-to-face with Robert Morris, arriving there on May 31. He found the city to be in disarray – inflation was rampant, prices for everything had gone up and some items were up as much as 100 times what they had cost just five years earlier. His meetings with Morris went on for days – reviewing his voyage reports and documentation with promises of full payment after the auditor checked them. Arrangements were made for removal of the Spanish coins and other monies from the 'Alliance' hold, and a place was designated to where they would be safely moved – thus making room for the next cargo to be loaded on the soon-to-be merchantman 'Alliance'.

The legal suit of the marooned officers against Captain Barry went Barry's way, and each was found guilty of dereliction of duty. John Paul Jones was back in the city also, too unwell with tuberculosis to travel to Boston for the court martial of two other Navy captains. Jones had worked diligently to get his new ship 'America' rigged and launched, only to have Congress and Robert Morris give the new ship to France in gratitude for all their support, and to get the ship costs off their books. Jones met briefly with Captain Barry before Barry headed back to Providence, Rhode Island – while Jones headed to a local sanatorium for treatment.

In Providence, the 'Alliance' was being converted back to being a merchantman and Barry supervised the transfer of the money to shore. Afterwards 'Alliance' departed Providence for Virginia, with a pilot on board plus two important passengers – Sarah and her cousin, alongside her proud captain. Then, the unimaginable happened – the pilot ran the ship into a large, submerged rock, stopping her dead in the water. For hours the ship lay there while carpenters assessed the situation. They reported no serious damage, the ship was floated off the rock with the high tide and they continued the voyage. The weather turned bad for the four-day trip to Virginia, during which time the two ladies were in the grip of severe sea sickness.

It took six weeks for the unprepared Virginia agent to get the ship's hold filled with tobacco. Finally, 'Alliance' sailed for Holland while the two ladies boarded a coach for the long ride to Philadelphia – they had enough of sailing already. Within hours of departing, 'Alliance' began to take on water, while the ship was still off Delaware Bay. Pumps were barely able to keep up and Barry decided to go up the Delaware river to the Willing and Morris wharf in Philadelphia, to lessen further seawater damage to the tobacco cargo.

Meanwhile, joy and relief spread throughout the land and Philadelphia was again open to the commerce of the world. One of the first merchant ships to arrive was the 'Hibernia' from Dublin, but Barry was not in the mood to celebrate with the Irish sailors on board. At the wharf, 'Alliance' was thoroughly inspected, and it was decided to unload the cargo after realizing that significant repairs were needed. Morris was very upset with their misfortune, and he discharged the crew, save a few hands and Captain Barry – then he ordered a survey to be conducted, to estimate the full repair costs. While the repair estimates were being worked on, Barry went home to his house on Spruce Street. He was there to greet Sarah when her carriage finally arrived back in the city – she was very surprised to see him and sad to hear about the damage to his ship.

Captain Barry's bad news continued – there was no likelihood of any monies coming to him from the sale of his prizes in France and Havana because of the downturn in the market for goods. That meant that the state of the Barry family finances became perilous. As part of his ongoing efforts to get discharged Navy crews paid, John learned that veteran Army Officers were to get half-pay and land grants, but Navy Officers were not included – Captain Barry and his fellow officers petitioned for similar treatment for their service. There was sympathy but no results, and Morris's promise on the cash value of the certificates for 'Alliance' Navy crew members turned out to be hollow – there was no timeline on when that paper would be redeemable for money.

Simply put – Congress was insolvent.

Barry was aboard 'Alliance' every day despite not being paid and he had constant visits from his discharged crew members asking for their prize money – later begging for it as they became destitute. It was a constant pain and embarrassment for Captain Barry to see his men in such condition, just months after they were hailed for their seamanship and courage. He joined forces with his friend John Brown to borrow money from the bank so they could purchase some wage warrants from the neediest sailors, at deep discounts. It was the only way they could provide some assistance, and they did not know when or if they would be able to redeem these warrants for cash themselves. Adding to everyone's misery, the winter of 1783 was one of the coldest in memory.

Captain Barry presented his report to Congress on the cost of the repairs needed on 'Alliance' – a sum of $5,900. No decision was made because there was no money to cover it. He himself was almost out of money by March 1784 and even wrote letters to some of his military comrades seeking assistance – people like Anthony Wayne (whom he had helped rustle cattle along the Delaware to feed General Washington's army in Valley Forge some years earlier) – all to no avail.

• • •

Robert Morris began to think that there was no alternative but to terminate the Navy – it was more of a luxury than a necessity for now: until the American public realized they must have a Navy and began calling for its restoration. Congress decided to sell the 'Alliance' and the 'Washington' – until James Madison convinced Congressmen to sell only the 'Washington' and keep the 'Alliance'

"For the honor and glory of the flag of the United States".

The Continental Marines were disbanded at this time also.

After all this attrition, Captain Barry was then the ONLY naval officer retained on the employment rolls by Congress – at a pay rate of sixty dollars per month.

By May, some money came in for prize warrants allowing Barry and Brown to split 900 livres between them, while

Barry kept up his attempts to collect his own eight months of back wages owed to him by Congress. He continued to be bombarded with correspondence from former naval crew members and officers – inquiries and questions and recommendations, and rants about their unfair treatment.

Robert Morris resigned his position in November 1784, which pushed every claim even further back in the line – being that Congress then had neither a Department of Marine nor an Agent of Marine.

• • •

Morris went back to fulltime private commerce and his focus was on the new market of China. He had always been irked by the unfair British prohibition on colonial Americans from participating in the China trade, which ironically included the 'Tea' that had been instrumental in provoking the Americans in Boston. Months before, he had stated publicly – "I am sending some ships to China to encourage others in the adventurous pursuit of commerce": without admitting his profit motives. He acquired a ship for his China trade and named her 'Empress of China'.

John Barry was not offered the position of captain because of his ongoing employment by Congress, and Morris was probably still a bit sore about the 'Alliance' pilot fiasco at Providence, where repair work on the ship had just commenced. The captain's job for 'Empress of China' went to

John Green. Fat John was not high on Captain Barry's list of the better captains, but he ignored it as he had lots of personal, and family financial problems to resolve.

It soon became apparent that of the many entities that owed money to John Barry, they either couldn't or wouldn't pay him. He also had to get involved in trying to help Sarah's family win back possession of the Austin Ferry business. Sarah's brother Isaac eventually won control of the business, and everyone knew it was very much due to the help and influence provided by his brother-in-law, John Barry.

Congress approved half-pay to widows of Army Officers but denied those benefits to Naval Officers, ruling that naval duty was less arduous and claiming that Navy personnel were able to win substantial riches through sharing of prize money for captured vessels. Barry was disgusted, being that he and numerous other members of the naval service were unable to get payment of their prize monies owed, and their back wages claims were now several years in the pleading stages. As this sorry situation continued to drag on into the following year – John Barry's only regular income was the sixty dollars per month he earned from the Navy.

• • •

Ireland provided Barry's next slate of bad news. His sister Eleanor had died, leaving three young children under the care of her invalid husband. Margaret, his other sister, was widowed and living in poverty. John sent money to both families plus assurances that he would make a special effort to help the children. Numerous other letters poured in from distant acquaintances and from strangers in Ireland, asking for assistance in getting a foothold in America for penniless emigrants. Young people even turned up on his doorstep with letters on this subject, all assuming that "John Barry, the War Hero" was rolling in money and power. Some months later a young man showed up at John's door bearing a letter from his Uncle Nicholas, his hero and mentor from his youth, informing Barry that Eleanor's husband was now also deceased- leaving three orphaned children, and asking when he could send the three youngsters to John in Philadelphia. To add to the sadness, Nicholas informed him that there was no headstone, no memorial to his parents at Rosslare Churchyard where they were buried.

• • •

When Captain Green returned triumphantly from his very profitable voyage to China, the promised repairs to 'Alliance' were not even close to being completed, even though the need for her was obvious. As proof of this, several American ships had been captured by the Barbary Pirates around the Atlantic and Mediterranean coasts of Africa. A collection of North African States known as the Barbary States – Morocco, Algiers, Tunis and Tripoli – had for centuries practiced state-supported piracy. Apprehended people were sold into the slavery trade, and the captured ships were held for ransom, which later led to a system of extracting money tributes from countries not strong enough to confront them. Prior to independence, the American colonists had the protection of the British Royal Navy.

After the United States declared independence, British diplomats soon informed the Barbary States that U.S. ships were open to attack – and in 1785 Dey Muhammad of Algiers declared war on the United States and began capturing American ships. Congress knew that the United States needed a Navy protection force, but it had no money to fund it – nor did they have the money to pay the tribute to protect their merchant ships. They managed to negotiate with Morocco in 1786 but failed in their efforts to sign one with Algiers. Luck was on their side in that Portugal was at war with Algiers and they blocked Algerian ships from leaving the Mediterranean at Gibraltar – thus giving American ships in the Atlantic some temporary relief (the problem with the Barbary States eventually led to America having to go to war and defeat them in selective naval engagements between 1801 and 1816. The French conquest of Algeria in 1830 finally their piracy practices).

In another shortsighted move Congress had decided to put 'Alliance' up for sale. On August 1, 1785, she was sold at auction to a consortium for only $7,700 – a day of great personal sadness for Captain John Barry. Investors led by Coburn & Whitehead were the purchasers – who planned to finish the repairs and use her as a merchantman. The new President of Congress at the time was Richard Henry Lee. Captain Barry, together with his close friend Captain Thomas Read tried again to get help for themselves and fellow Navy veterans, hoping Mr. Lee would be sympathetic. They delivered a joint memorial to Congress, petitioning to be placed on a similar footing to their brother officers in the Army – for half pay, commutation and lands. Their plea never got past the committee stage.

John and Sarah Barry had soured of city life by this stage – they sold their Spruce Street home and bought a 62-acre farm property a few miles north, named 'Strawberry Hill'. This move was also made for health reasons. John was only forty years old, but he had been in harm's way for almost all those years, and many of them included being in the smoke and gunpowder fumes of naval battles for long spells – breathing in all that nasty air. His shoulder wound had never fully healed and on top of that he often had trouble breathing – soon he was diagnosed with asthma. He began receiving treatment from one of the top doctors in this new field of medicine, his friend Doctor Rush, who treated him with medicated vapor. Sarah was convinced that the country air at their new farm would act like a sanatorium and help control his asthma.

Captain Barry, Captain John Paul Jones and other naval commanders and comrades were recognized by the Society of the Cincinnati, for their naval service. George Washington was the society's first President – it was an honorary membership group that allowed officers to meet for reunions and they each received a medal which Barry was proud of – especially being that the society emblem was the bald eagle.

In 1786, three years after the end of the war, Barry's monetary claims and those of other naval veterans were still unpaid and were largely being ignored. The veterans were now past the stage of worrying about it, they quietly put it out of their minds and got on with their lives as best they could. For the Barry family, their most important day in a long time came in early 1787 when the ship 'Rising Sun' docked in Philadelphia after a voyage from Wexford, Ireland. The children of Eleanor, John's deceased sister: eighteen-year-old Michael Hayes and his sixteen-year-old brother Patrick walked down the gangplank into the welcoming arms of their uncle, John Barry, and their aunt Sarah. The boy's sister, young Eleanor, had decided to remain in Ireland as she was about to be married to a local Wexford lad. Michael was already a career seaman and he soon left on a voyage to Jamaica aboard 'Rising Sun'. Young Patrick was to be the son that would fill the void for Sarah and John, who had no children of their own.

John's old ship 'Alliance' now came back onto the scene again. Robert Morris bought her when the former owners floundered, and he added her to his fleet under the captaincy of James Read, who soon took her on a voyage to China. The next big addition to the Morris fleet was to be a new purpose-built ship for the China trade named 'Asia', and Morris's co-owners wanted John Barry to serve as captain. He was offered a generous package that included shares that would make him wealthy if he could make the venture successful. Barry accepted, knowing that it would be a two-year stint away from home and he got straight to work selecting a crew. Sarah was already resigned to the long absences of her husband during the Revolutionary War, and this China voyage was very similar, except much longer. She was happy for John because returning to the sea was all he ever wanted, and it was something he had missed so much. It would be a lonely two-year absence for her, made all the worse by John's decision to bring young Patrick Hayes with him to China.

• • •

While John Barry waited for the completion of his new 400-ton ship 'Asia', he continued to be very much interested in the ongoing debate about what type of government would best suit the emerging country of the United States of America onto the world stage. Philadelphia had hosted the meetings that led to the drafting of the Declaration of Independence, and it was the Capital of the 'United States'. In the year of 1787 a Federal Convention was planned for Philadelphia to formulate a constitution – "by which the 13 States could form a more perfect Union" and replace the Confederation that was deemed to be unsuitable for the future government of the country.

The most powerful men in America had long thought that the only way that the fledgling United States could survive and grow, was by having a stronger government – the moment to achieve this was at hand and these men spent that summer engaged on this task. Other than Thomas Jefferson and John Adams who were in Europe, the country's best and brightest were gathered in the Hall of Assembly in Philadelphia, debating and compromising on ways to come up with a better union. George Washington served as president of the convention and the sickly eighty-one-year-old Benjamin Franklin was carried in every day in a sedan chair. Having taken four years to write the Articles of Confederation, it now took only four months to draw up the Constitution.

On September 17 the Convention unanimously adopted this Constitution.

It was going to be a much more difficult task to get the States to ratify the new document – favored for the most part by the more numerous city dwellers and opposed by their rural counterparts. The Pennsylvania members of the Convention notified the Pennsylvania Assembly that they were ready to report to them immediately, being that they were already in session. Franklin led the delegates before the Assembly the next day where they made their report and presented the new Constitution. John

Barry was a regular attendee in the public gallery to watch the assembly debating the issues – he and his Navy comrades believed their best chance of getting their long-owed wages from the government was via the adoption of this Constitution by Pennsylvania and by a majority of the thirteen original states. Speaker Mifflin read the entire document, which was well received by Barry and the rest of the public gallery, to judge by their applause. Supporters of the Constitution in the Assembly were speaker Mifflin, George Clymer and Thomas Fitzsimons, with the opposition being led by James McCalmont, James Barr and Jacob Miley. The Constitution adoption supporters tried to push the ratification through quickly, but the anti-Federalists opposed and stymied their attempts at every turn.

When they reassembled on day three after two days of heated debate, Speaker Mifflin called the assembly to order and moved for Ratification of the Constitution. There were motions for amendment and motions for postponement – both failed. A motion was made to select delegates that would resolve the issue immediately – it was passed on a vote of 43 to 19, but no date was set. A motion by the opposition to recess till 4 p.m. was passed, the understanding being that a date for the State convention would be set at that time. When 4 p.m. came, all nineteen anti-Federalists were missing and therefore there was no quorum. The sergeant-at-arms was sent to find them, returning to announce that he had found seventeen of them at a local boarding house – who all refused his order to return. Speaker Mifflin called a recess until 9.30 a.m. the next morning.

John Barry sized up the situation and that evening he formulated his plan of action. He was at the waterfront early next morning and gathered a group of tough sailor types with him who then joined the crowd waiting outside the State House. When the doors opened, Barry and his group muscled their way up the stairs to the public gallery. Speaker Mifflin called the session to order, and the resolution was read aloud – which asked for each state to hold a convention on the new constitution, and he asked for an early date for the state of Pennsylvania to do so. Again, the opposition were not present and there was no quorum. The sergeant-at-arms and a clerk, carrying a copy of the resolution, were sent off to the local boarding house to fetch the missing assemblymen – returning quickly with bad news. Only the two leaders of the anti-federalists, McCalmont and Miley, were to be found at the boarding house and they refused to come to the State House. While Mifflin and the others discussed what to do without a quorum, Barry and his group stood up and noisily left the gallery. This was noticed by Speaker Mifflin, who then left his chair, which had the effect of delaying any adjournment of the assembly.

John Barry's group went straight to the boarding house and an ultimatum was issued by Barry to the two holdouts.

"Walk with us to the State House now, or we will carry you there."

McCalmont was almost as tall as Barry and he confronted him nose to nose.

"We will not go there, and you cannot make us go, you pathetic Irish sailor."

"Take Them", Barry ordered in his loud Ship's Captain voice.

A scuffle ensued and despite putting up a stiff resistance, the two assemblymen were manhandled all the way to the State House and were pushed over the rail from the public gallery into the chamber room. With their presence, Mifflin now had a quorum and immediately called a roll. When their names were called the two disheveled gentlemen did not answer, but their fellow assemblymen answered 'Here' for them. The quorum was complete, and the assembly was called into session. McCalmont protested his forced entry but was overruled by Mifflin – "it does not matter how you got here, all that matters is that you are here".

"I demand that the rules be read," McCalmont then said.

"If they are read – will you abide by them, Sir"?

"Yes".

When the clerk read the part that announced a five-shilling fine for premeditated absence, McCalmont pulled his purse from his pocket and put the money down on the desk.

"Here is your fine, now I am leaving."

Barry's group stood up immediately and McCalmont hesitated. Mifflin looked around at the assembly before addressing McCalmont.

"Your assembly colleague, Mr. Smith, is assigned to collect all fees, and he is not present. The fine cannot be accepted in his absence – the quorum stands complete".

A motion was then made that the state convention would be held on the first Tuesday of November 1787. The members voted and the motion was passed by 44 to 2.

Mifflin addressed the assembly – "The motion is approved. There is no other business to attend to, so I adjourn the assembly. All assemblymen are free to leave the chamber".

The crowd erupted in loud cheering. Barry and his group quietly left the scene to avoid any further confrontation with the two disgraced assemblymen.

McCalmont presented a complaint to the Supreme Executive Council that he and assemblyman Miley had been insulted and mistreated – asking that Captain John Barry be prosecuted. The Council agreed to direct the Attorney General to commence an investigation. Barry was upset that his friends, Benjamin Franklin, the Council President, and councilman Charles Biddle, both cast a yes vote. Biddle assured him that there was method in this madness – that the Attorney General would take a long time to gather this evidence, and the system would work in John's favor.

On December 12, 1787, the Pennsylvania Assembly ratified the Constitution by a vote of 46 to 23 and was the second state to do so.

• • •

The 'Asia', commanded by John Barry and the 'Canton' commanded by William Truxton departed for China on December 8. Truxton was making his second trip to China and Barry was able to pick his brain on what to expect. It would be an approximate two-year voyage for Barry and his young nephew Patrick Hayes, who was one of two cabin boys aboard. It was indeed going to be a long and dangerous voyage and Barry prepared for the likelihood of pirate trouble by having four 6-pounder cannons stowed aboard – with a plan to place them at the ready when they traversed the pirate infested waters off western Africa and later again in the South China Sea.

First, they sailed across the Atlantic towards the coast of Senegal in West Africa, then down through the South Atlantic to the Dutch port city of Cape Town at the southern tip of Africa, where they traded some cargo and got resupplied – leaving Cape Town in mid-April. From there they continued due East to the far distant and desolate island of St. Paul in the Southern Indian Ocean, then sailed Northeast across the Indian Ocean to Java Head and past the massive volcanic mountain of Krakatoa. They sailed between the islands of Java and Sumatra, and on through the South China Sea to the island of Macao – which was the gateway to China. Other than several bad storms and some unfavorable winds that slowed their progress, the voyage was kept smooth and on course by the two experienced captains. They were armed and ready for any encounter with pirates but did not have to use this power.

In Macao they had to apply for a "chop" or permit to proceed, and then take on a pilot to guide them up the Pearl River towards Canton, China. The 'Asia' anchored at their Whampoa Reach destination in July 1788 – after an 18,000-mile voyage lasting 195 days. Patrick Hayes marveled at this round-the-world experience where they crossed the Equator twice and Tropic of Capricorn twice – he wrote copious notes in his journal every day. In China they had to go through the laborious Chinese customs process, where all foreign trade went through the monopoly system managed by the group of Chinese merchants known as 'Hongs'. China didn't have any compelling interest in trading with the outside world – they even had several edicts in place that were scornful of dealing with foreigners. Years earlier, Emperor Ch'ien Lung of China had stated their position in a letter he sent to the British King, George III.

"The Celestial Empire has no need to import the manufactures of outside barbarians. Being that our products of tea, silk and porcelain are absolute necessities to several European nations and to yourselves, we have permitted, as a signal mark of favor, that foreign Hongs should be established at Canton, so that your wants might be supplied, and your country thus participate in our beneficence."

Patrick noted in his journal that the little settlements along the river were overcrowded with desperately poor people and were filthy – the river itself being chock full of the local small boats called 'Sampans' that were each a veritable floating household. At night the bamboo shrines on these boats were lit up by candles, giving the appearance of thousands of points of light.

When the 'Asia' finally arrived at her mooring, Barry ordered a gun salute from his cannons, which was returned by the several other foreign ships in the anchorage. China officially regarded all foreigners as 'barbarians', and as inferior people to the Chinese. They had been trading for many years with Europeans, and the Americans were at first regarded as part of the English. To help clarify that situation the Americans were called 'The New People' or the 'Flowery-Flag Devils' because the Chinese referred to the American flag as the 'flowery flag'. The 'barbarians' were forbidden to sail any further upriver than Whampoa, or to enter the city of Canton itself, and had to conduct their business on a narrow strip of land on the riverbank where all business had to be transacted in warehouse structures named 'factories' that were provided by the collective of Chinese merchants called 'CoHong'.

This was as close as John Barry could get to Canton, and he had to pay exorbitant rent for one of these structures for the several months they planned to be there. He and his chosen handful of crew member traders (supercargoes), plus his Chinese comprador (merchant go-between) and his linguist, all lived on the second and third floors of this 'factory' with their servants – they even had western style furnishings at a cost – while the ground floor was used as the ship's godown (warehouse). This is where the cargo they brought on 'Asia' to trade with China was held until it was sold, and then the space was reused to store the Chinese products as they were purchased, prior to moving them to the hold of 'Asia'. The new cargo of exotic goods being purchased included a long list of personal wants for friends and clients in Philadelphia. Most of the crew had to remain on board the ship, with limited access to onshore strips of land named 'French's Island' and 'Dane's Island' – provided they conducted themselves with good behavior.

Before the Americans could commence trading, a ceremonial visit to their ship had to take place, conducted by the chief customs official called the 'Hoppo' with his entourage and guards. A ritual then ensued whereby western gifts like perfume (smellum water) and clocks were presented to the Chinese, and the 'Hoppo' was toasted with glasses of fine wine. Chinese servants measured the ship 'Asia' in their unique way to calculate steep customs fees that amounted to almost three thousand dollars, plus another fee for the privilege of having Chinese mandarin soldiers stationed on the ship. Once Barry paid it all, the Hoppo informed him that the 'Celestial Emperor' would permit him to commence trading – then he gave him two live bulls, eight sacks of flour and a few bottles of a strong Chinese wine called Samshu, before departing. Barry was not impressed with all these rituals and expenses but had little choice about it. The bulls were indeed welcome for a crew that had not eaten fresh meat during the previous year.

Months of trading then began – the Chinese wanted sea-otter pelts and sandalwood (from Hawaii), and some ginseng root to supplement their own supplies. Americans wanted tea, silk, nankeen (Chinese cotton), porcelain, spices and miscellaneous artifacts. The tedium of dealing with the Chinese was relieved by the substantial amount of socializing that took place amongst the visiting foreigners. Despite the recent war, the American and British seamen were on good terms with each other – Captain Barry was well received by his British counterparts, and he dined frequently with them during his extended stay.

Once trading was completed and the holds of the two American ships were full, both ships prepared to depart China in early January 1789, after a display of fireworks by their Chinese hosts calculated to curry favor from the Gods. Captain Barry and Captain Truxton had to endure another visit by the 'Hoppo' who reviewed all papers and certified that all duties had been paid. Then they received their 'Chop' pass and sailed downriver to Macao where they dropped off their pilots and compradors. They delayed a few days in Macao where Barry and Truxton allowed their sailors shore leave, to enjoy the delights on offer there – such as opium, prostitutes and gambling. The two ships had a relatively uneventful return voyage – some severe storms, thankfully no pirate trouble, and despite getting separated by bad weather, both ships arrived off the Delaware Capes in June, within one day of each other.

• • •

While Captain Barry was away on the very long China voyage, the infant United States continued to search for a resolution to its financial issues and to refine its political status. Just in time for the July Fourth Celebrations of 1788, New Hampshire had become the ninth state to ratify the Constitution – meaning that it then became the Law of the Land. The investigation into John Barry's role in 'moving' McCalmont and Miley to the State House had been quietly dropped, just as Biddle had promised it would. George Washington had been elected the First President of the United States – Barry wrote to congratulate him and told him of his spectacular voyage to China.

While he was on this long journey, direct communication from Barry to home and family was not possible. The time-honored method of 'up to date news' was via the Newspapers who relied on reports from arriving sea captains that were then published for people to read the latest news on ships at sea. The only news Sarah Barry had read in The Pennsylvania Gazette was in July of the previous year. A captain arriving from Madeira had passed on the news relayed to him by a captain from Guinea, who in turn had spoken via trumpet with 'Captain Barry of the Asia' in February 1788 – bound for Canton and all was well. This lack of up-to-date news was very stressful for Sarah, adding to the isolation she experienced in the rural location of her home at Strawberry Hill Farm. Now that John Barry was home the full impact of his trip hit them both. The China voyage would net John Barry a lot of money and would put his finances back on a sound footing, but he vowed to Sarah that he would not sail to China again.

As soon as the ship docked in Pennsylvania, John Barry and Patrick Hayes rode home to Strawberry Hill for a tearful reunion with Sarah and all their extended family members. The return of 'Asia' was front page news in Philadelphia, with long articles about all the exotic Chinese goods being sold. Captain Barry took a well-earned rest and spent money on new furnishings and improvements to his home. His friends at the Sea Captains Club and the Hibernian Fire Company were eager for his resumption of activities and he regaled them with his adventures in the Far East. Patrick Hayes soon took a shine to Betsy Keen, before embarking on new voyages to the Caribbean; his brother Michael remained a crew member on the 'Rising Sun'; William Austin was living far away in England by this stage. Christmas 1789 was a very pleasant time for the Barry's and their extended family, followed by a very cold winter which brought back some of John's breathing problems. His old ship 'Alliance' came back into the picture but not in a good way. Robert Morris owned her, she had sailed to China and back, then to Spain – returning from that trip in very poor condition. He decided to scrap the ship, and after stripping all valuable copper and iron work off her, the hulk was then run aground purposefully along Petty's Island. This was unfortunately a place that gave John Barry a full view of the hulk from his home on Strawberry Hill, especially in winter when the trees were bare.

• • •

In the spring of 1790, the American people were saddened by the news of Benjamin Franklin's death – the grandfather of the American Revolution died April 17, at the ripe old age of eighty-four. His funeral was a major event for Philadelphia and for the country.

• • •

John Barry took his political cue from General Washington, and he did not join any political party – remaining an 'Independent' despite his friendship with members across the political spectrum. He was still only in his mid-forties but Barry's long years at sea were taking their toll, with his asthma and other ailments plaguing him. He fought them off and enjoyed some restful times with family, away from the decks of ships, while remaining very close to his seafaring friends, who made visits to see him and wrote to him of their voyages and their ports of call.

Fellow Revolutionary War veteran, Captain John Paul Jones, had been plagued by misfortune since his last parting with John Barry. In Europe he had thrown in with the Russian Navy of Catherine the Great – that relationship later soured badly, and he ended his days in Paris almost penniless and in very poor health. The American Minister to Paris visited him when he received news that he was dying from his ailments, and he oversaw Jones's burial after his untimely death. He sent Jones's gold sword to Robert Morris to pass on to John Barry, to whom Jones had bequeathed it.

Captain Barry continued to financially help his extended Irish family in Wexford, Ireland, but turned down offers to travel there – he had no desire to visit a land that was still in the clutches of his erstwhile enemy and where the people were forced to live in poverty.

"Everything that one's heart could wish for is here in America," was Barry's response to a gentleman who thought that he would benefit from a visit to Ireland and to Wexford.

For his own personal reasons, he did not want to go back to Wexford, but he actively helped to find housing for newly arrived Irish immigrants, and he personally assisted many Irish individuals who were fresh off the docks. He also helped to advance the seafaring careers of both his Irish nephews, Michael and Patrick Hayes.

CHAPTER SEVEN

A NEW AMERICAN NAVY IS BORN

The French Revolution of 1789 was a massive event that sent shock waves throughout Europe and America. The Revolution itself and the subsequent Reign of Terror, tested the delicate connections between France and the fledgling United States of America and drove a wedge between factions within President Washington's cabinet. The tyranny of the mob took its toll among French people who were friends of America. The King and Queen were beheaded, and the Duc de la Rochefoucauld was killed. These cataclysmic events ushered in a new era that had a destabilizing effect on the relations between France and other countries, including America.

Coinciding with these cataclysmic events Captain John Barry was drydocked at his farm –

"Retired to a handsome competency", per his own words

– enjoying his time with family and keeping up with his seafaring friends via letters and personal visits. Captain Truxton voyaged to India, and on a later visit to Barry at Strawberry Hill, he told him stories of his trip and of meeting Lord Cornwallis there – he who had surrendered at Yorktown and who was at that time in his first of two stints as the British Governor General of India. Cornwallis was later to be Lord Lieutenant of Ireland during the time of the 1798 Rebellion which impacted John Barry's Wexford severely, when he presided over the slaughter of thousands of Irish rebels and civilians.

William Austin (Sarah's brother), and John Barry had developed quite a close friendship despite Austin's loyalist past, and they corresponded via frequent letters. One of Barry's favorite officers, Richard Dale, was a regular visitor to Strawberry Hill, where he met and later married Dorothy Crawthorne, a member of Sarah Austin Barry's family – adding another sailor into John Barry's extended family group. The city of Philadelphia had entered a period of sustained prosperity with the construction of many large homes by its wealthy residents, and an improved road system that included the Lancaster Turnpike. President Washington held weekly dinners at the President's Mansion, where John and Sarah Barry were regular attendees. In March 1793 George Washington was inaugurated as President for his second term, and the Barry's attended the joyous event.

After war broke out between France and Britain, President

Washington's policy of "Proclamation of Neutrality" spurred a huge increase in trade between America and the French West Indies; only to cause a backlash from Britain, who responded with two "Orders of Council". Under these orders, Britain would not trade with neutrals who were trading with the enemy, and British ships could seize American vessels carrying French goods. The orders even allowed the British to press-gang American sailors into the Royal Navy.

Britain had brokered a truce between Portugal and Algiers, which ended Portugal's Mediterranean blockade, and that allowed the Barbary Pirates to start preying once again on merchant shipping in the Mediterranean and nearby parts of the Atlantic. Before long, twelve American ships had been captured by these corsairs and the captured crews were subjected to hard labor. David Humphreys, the Commissioner, reported to President Washington that in his opinion an American Naval Force seemed to have become necessary again. The adoption of the Constitution in 1789 conferred on the American government the power to levy taxes and the authority to raise and maintain armed forces – the time was now ripe for the Congress to authorize the creation of a new American Navy.

France's new ambassador to America in April 1793 was Edmond Charles Genet, a commoner who had worked his way up the diplomatic ladder but who possessed no discretion for such a post. He had lots of money to splash about as an incentive to American sea captains to get them to join the

French cause as privateers against British shipping. Summer that year brought another yellow fever epidemic which turned Philadelphia into a ghost town. John Barry was stricken with it but recovered after treatment from Dr. Rush and the family sequestered themselves at Strawberry Hill – shunning all visitors. President Washington was determined to stay in the city until concerns for the health of his wife, Martha, changed his mind and the family moved out to Mount Vernon. As with previous epidemics, the situation did not improve until the first frosts of October. People gradually returned, including most congressmen. Washington wanted to personally reassure the people that all was well and on November 10, the President rode alone on horseback into Philadelphia, so that he could be seen by the public and that event restored confidence to the population.

French Ambassador, Genet, finally outstepped his authority with a flagrant violation of American law. He was recalled to France but refused to obey the command, expecting that he would surely be guillotined there – he was generously granted asylum by President Washington and remained in America. By the spring of 1794 hundreds of American ships had been captured by Britain under their Orders of Council, adding to those taken by the pirates. Barry's nephew, Patrick, who had risen to be captain of the brig 'Florida', was captured in the Bahamas – the cargo was seized, and he and his crew were imprisoned by the British. Through Uncle John Barry's influence, he was released with his ship but had to forfeit his cargo.

In President Washington's annual message to Congress that year, he said –

"If we desire to avoid insult, it must be known that we are at all times ready for war."

• • •

None of the major world naval powers regarded the United States as a serious naval threat to them at that time -- it therefore became obvious to American leaders that it was finally time –

"TO CREATE AN AMERICAN NAVY."

After the commissioner's report had sunken in, Captain Barry's friend and Congressman, Thomas Fitzsimons travelled immediately to visit him at Strawberry Hill, asking for his advice and input on the country's predicament. He wanted information on the cost of a Navy and the estimated time it would take to build ships for Congress. Barry knew that the shipbuilder who had built the continental frigate 'Randolph' years earlier was the genius they needed – Joshua Humphreys. Joshua believed that the large ships-of-the-line were unsuitable for American coasts and harbors – he wanted to build a bigger and better frigate, built with the best American wood available – Live Oak and Red Cedar – and he had pitched this idea some time earlier in a letter to the still-influential Robert Morris. These new ships would be the largest, fastest and the most powerful frigates ever built. Morris had shared this letter with Barry – now Barry shared it with Fitzsimons and, through him, with President Washington.

The President delegated Secretary of War, Henry Knox, to take up the plans – who then began a series of meetings with Barry and Fitzsimons, plus Joshua Humphreys and the other two best local ship builders. Fitzsimons' committee recommended the building of four 44-gun frigates and two 24-gun frigates – at a cost of $600,000. Congress was leaning towards rejecting the proposal until Washington informed them that further losses of ships were sinking his government bonds, and that American merchants were demanding protection by an American Navy. After more heated debate, the Bill was passed by a vote of 50 to 39. Joshua Humphreys, the ship builder, immediately presented his designs to Congress and followed that with a half-model of a stronger, faster and bigger frigate than any possessed by other countries – having 147-foot keel, 43 -foot beam, and 30 guns on the main deck.

Captain Barry was on board from the start, literally, as he could not imagine a New Navy without him.

He wrote to President Washington – March 19, 1794.

"Sir: – Finding that the government have partly determined to fit out some ships of war for the protection of our trade against the Algerines, I beg leave to offer myself for the command of the squadron, conceiving myself to be competent, thereto assuring Your Excellency that I should be honored with your approbation, my utmost abilities and most unremitting attention should be exerted for the good of my country and also to approve myself worthy of the high honor shown by Your Excellency.

Your Obedient, Humble Servant
John Barry

President Washington signed the Bill into law one week later, when he declared –

"The depredations of the Algerine Corsairs on the commerce of the United States has rendered it necessary that a naval force should be provided for its protection."

Congress ordered the building and equipping of three frigates with forty-four guns, and three of smaller weight with thirty-six guns. Captain Barry was soon inundated with letters from naval officers trying to curry favor from him, after it was rumored that he would be instrumental in organizing the New Navy. John Barry and John Paul Jones had been the top two captains of the previous Continental Navy. Sadly, Jones was deceased, so there was no other captain who could rival Captain Barry in bravery or the number of captures of enemy ships. For months, President Washington, Secretary Knox and Captain Barry reviewed the applications that would yield a list of six captains. In a message to Congress in June, Secretary Knox presented Washington's six choices, who were approved without delay. A messenger then delivered a letter to Captain Barry from the War Department.

War Department, June 5, 1794
To Captain John Barry.

Sir: The President of the United States, by and with the advice and consent of the Senate, has appointed you to be a Captain of one of the ships being provided, in pursuance of the Act to provide a naval armament, herein enclosed. It has been decided that the Naval Captains will be ranked in the following order:

John Barry
Samuel Nicholson
Silas Talbot
Joshua Barney
Richard Dale
Thomas Truxton

Please inform me as soon as convenient whether you will accept or decline the appointment.

I am, Sir,
Henry Knox,
Secretary of War.

That same day a public announcement was made of the appointment of the six captains to superintend the construction and to take command of the vessels ordered.

Captain Barry responded to his letter the very same day it was received.

Strawberry Hill, June 6, 1794
"The honor done to me in appointing me Commander in the Navy of the United States is gratefully acknowledged and accepted by,
Your Most Obedient, Humble Servant,
John Barry

Sarah knew this was coming and she was happy about the news on John's behalf, even though it increased the likelihood of more long absences because of his Navy duty.

John Barry was only thirty years old when he was first commissioned into the Continental Navy for the Revolutionary War. Now at forty-nine years old, he was one of six surviving captains from that war and the only one who was not American born.

Per 'Cooper's History of the Navy' –

"He was not born in America, but he had passed nearly all his life there and was thoroughly identified with his adopted countrymen in interest and feeling. He had often distinguished himself during the Revolution and, perhaps, of all the Naval Captains that remained, he was the one who possessed the greatest reputation for experience, conduct and skill. His appointment met with general approbation. Nor did anything ever occur to give the Government reason to regret its selection."

The County Wexford-born Irish Catholic was now the Commander-in-Chief of the new American Navy, the Commodore, appointed by President George Washington, who was universally accepted as 'Father of the United States'. John Barry thus became 'The Father of the American Navy' and testament to that are the many seamen who were trained under Captain Barry and served with great distinction in later years.

His commission read –

"To take rank from the fourth day of June, one thousand seven hundred and ninety-four."

On July First, 1794, John Barry "swore true allegiance to the United States of America and to serve them honestly and faithfully against all their enemies or opposers whomsoever."

His salary as Commander of the Navy was $75 per month.

• • •

President Washington had put the project of building the first ships for the new Navy in the hands of his Secretary of War, Henry Knox, from its inception. During the following months Knox met repeatedly with Captain Barry and the ship builder, Joshua Humphreys, as they honed their ideas and recommendations – bringing in other shipbuilders like Wharton and Hackett for their input. Congress was already well versed in the spreading of patronage, and the building of the six frigates was spread over six American ports. The 44-gun ships went to Boston, New York, Philadelphia and Norfolk; the 36-gun ships went to Portsmouth and Baltimore. Captain Barry was appointed Superintendent of the 44-gun frigate to be built on the Delaware River at the port of Philadelphia – the flag ship of the fleet that was to be named the 'United States'. He immersed himself fully in this complex and arduous task, working closely with 'Constructor Humphreys', Henry Knox – Secretary of War, and a multitude of other people and entities involved in the project. Philadelphia had plenty of quality tradesmen available to hire – what it did not have was suitable wood for the ship, and the same problem hung over the other cities chosen to build the fleet of ships.

Humphreys and Barry believed that the ship had to be constructed from Live Oak, the densest and hardest American wood that copes best with salt water, some of the most durable wood in the world. The heavy curved branches of the live oak were exactly what shipwrights wanted. The best live oaks were to be found in the Southeastern states where trees reached heights of seventy feet and had trunks measuring over twenty feet around. As early as the previous June, the Boston shipwright, John Morgan, had been recruited and sent to Savannah, Georgia, to seek out the landowners with the best live oaks, plus red cedar, white oak, yellow pine and locust. He found that St. Simons Island, in Southeast Georgia, was the most promising source for the large quantity of live oak trees required. The problem was that the location was lowland and swampy, and seriously under water during the rainy season – in his own words he said, "this Yankee shipwright needs help from Hercules to harvest wood from this place."

By October, no wood had arrived from Mr. Morgan. Despite the huge workload already on Captain Barry's shoulders, he was directed by the Commissioner of Revenues, Tench Coxe, to go to Georgia and find out what was happening. The brig 'Schuylkill' carried Barry to Savannah, Georgia, along with teams of oxen and horses to move the cut timber to the wharf. Barry made his way to Gascoigne's Bluff on St. Simon's Island, where he surveyed Morgan's operations. Upon arrival he found that Morgan was laid low with illness for the umptieth time, and his camp was nothing more than a primitive sawmill surrounded by the trees they needed, but "not a stick of wood was cut." Captain Barry took charge of the operation immediately; he sent to Savannah for wood cutting equipment and ordered Morgan to find some local help to make an access road to the stands of trees they wanted to harvest – their estimate was that they would need about 2,000 trees. Between Morgan and Barry together, they requisitioned sixteen slaves from local plantations and began the road work.

Eighty-one craftsmen from New London, Connecticut, arrived shortly afterwards and were put to work – making simple cabins for men to sleep in, and covered areas to work – transforming the place into a real working camp. As soon as the camp was completed, Barry sent the wood cutters out to begin felling the trees, while he went back to Savannah to contract ships for transporting the timber northwards, and to enlist more men for Morgan. Shortly afterwards Barry sailed to Philadelphia with a substantial quantity of rough-cut live oak. He presented Congress with a very optimistic report that he expected the necessary live oak timber would be cut within a few months and even predicted that some ships could be built inside one year. He believed that this entire exercise would function efficiently this time around and everyone would work together for the common good of the country. Little did he know then that the project would be plagued with rival political agendas, favoritism, infighting, gross inefficiency and incompetence – all of which would cause delays and try his patience and his reputation.

The wood unloaded from the 'Schuylkill' and in a follow-up ship name 'Anna' was pronounced by Humphreys as the best wood that ever came to his shipyard. Workers were finally able to start the construction and by late December the stem of the frigate was already raised when President Washington made his first visit to "An American Navy Yard".

Christmas was festive for the Barry family – other than hearing Morgan's continued bad news from Georgia where his fever ills continued. Most of the New Englanders had deserted his St. Simons camp, most of the oxen had died, and the rain continued to pour down on them. Despite this, the early months of 1795 saw much progress at the Southwark Shipyard – the frigate continued to take shape until they ran out of wood in late spring, which brought the work to a virtual standstill. Other yards were faring worse, some getting double shipments and some getting none at all. The newly appointed Captains, unaware of the slow progress, pestered Captain Barry for their uniforms and their commissions – wanting their pay and rations to begin.

The names of the other ships were chosen to follow Barry's flag ship 'UNITED STATES' – they were 'CONSTITUTION': 'PRESIDENT': 'CONGRESS': 'CONSTELLATION': 'CHESAPEAKE'.

On the Barry family front – his Irish nephew Patrick Hayes married Betsy Keen in April 1795, with his brother Michael Hayes as his best man. Strawberry Hill hosted the reception for the guests, including all their seafaring friends who happened to be ashore at the time. Afterwards, Barry's asthma issues laid him low for several weeks, requiring constant treatment from Doctor Rush. A less than satisfactory treaty was agreed between the United States and Britain – its terms caused riots when made public – and most Americans professed to have greater sympathies for France than for Britain.

It was July before Barry was well enough to perform his duties at the shipyard. Further delays in timber deliveries from Georgia caused Secretary Pickering to close four of the yards – leaving only Philadelphia and Baltimore open. President Washington was trying to navigate his way between the three potential sources of war – Britain, France and Algiers. When peace was made with Algiers in December 1795, a clause in the March Act of 1794 was activated – namely that work on the frigates would cease in the event of such a peace agreement. The French had overseen the Algerine negotiations – promising large sums of tribute money to the Barbary Pirates to not plunder American ships, and France promised the Dey (the rulers of the Regency of Algiers) that America would gift them a new armed schooner built by Humphreys – very bad news for the new American Navy waiting on their own ships.

President Washington wanted the ship building work to continue but his hands were tied from a combination of resignations and deaths among his government cabinet members. Congress eventually agreed to use the unexpended monies that had been allocated but ordered work after that to be discontinued. In his annual President's Message to Congress, Washington declared –

"To secure respect for a neutral flag requires a naval force organized and ready to vindicate our country from insult or aggression. Our trade to the Mediterranean will always be insecure without a protecting force. Will it not then be advisable to begin without delay to lay up materials for the building and equipping of ships of war and to proceed with the work by degrees, in proportion to our resources, and without inconvenience, so that a future war of Europe may not find our commerce in the unprotected state which it was found by the present."

The President moved Secretary Pickering to Secretary of State and appointed a new Secretary of War, a friend named

James McHenry, who naively assured Congress that two ships would be ready by November 1796. In a compromise it was agreed between President Washington and Congress that two 44-gun frigates and one 36-gun frigate would be completed, which added Boston back into the yards to stay open.

Captain Barry was sent to check on the progress of casting the cannons – at Cecil Furnace, Maryland. Their contract from Congress didn't call for proving the guns, it had no delivery timetable and no penalties for late delivery – unforgivable issues in Barry's estimation that had to be resolved immediately. Barry demanded that the guns would have to be proved – otherwise men would be more afraid of their own guns than they would be of their enemies.

By the summer, the Southwark yard had progressed so much that the hull of the large new frigate dwarfed the yard and the surrounding neighborhood. Strawberry Hill had good news in July 1796 when Betsy Hayes gave birth to a son whom she and Patrick named John Barry Hayes – which pleased the Commodore very much. In September, Barry's progress report on the frigate called for an estimate of the cost for fitting out his new ship with officers and crew – coming in at $7,285. The vessel was 175 feet long, had a 44-foot beam and a weight of 1,576 tons – (the completed construction cost for the frigate 'United States' would later be figured at $299,336).

• • •

President Washington's final term was nearing an end, and in the fall of 1796 the young country was about to witness its first presidential election campaign between John Adams and Thomas Jefferson. Barry kept his political leanings to himself, but he preferred Adams simply because he was pro-Navy; the electors would not announce the result before February of 1797.

While Humphreys continued working to complete the ship during late autumn and into winter, including all the rigging, John Barry was able to enjoy Christmas at Strawberry Hill and then to stay home during the terrible cold weather of January. The election results were announced in February – John Adams defeated Thomas Jefferson by three electoral votes.

During President Washington's final days in office a special event was held to coincide with his sixty-fifth birthday in February 1797; an event to which John Barry and his wife Sarah were special invitees. At that event the President issued the following naval commission –

"Commission Number One to Captain John Barry, appointing him Commander of the new frigate called United States; Commander of the Navy of the United States – to take rank from the Fourth of June 1794."

It was purposefully backdated by the President himself to honor Captain Barry and show the high esteem in which he was held by President Washington. Through this action President Washington anointed John Barry as the founding

Commander of the United States Navy and backdated his commission was to reflect that.

More celebrations of President Washington's birthday continued during the following weeks – and on March 4, 1797, John Adams was sworn in as the new President of the United States.

By late spring the finishing touches to the frigate 'United States' were being completed and some workers began construction of the launching rail frame that would soon send the ship into the water. Barry announced May 10 as the launching date, when the great ship would slide into the Delaware River – weather permitting. The weather did not co-operate and strong winds effecting the tides threatened to delay the event, but the winds died down just in time. Thousands of Philadelphians came out for the launch, waiting all day as the excitement continued to build.

Captain Barry went aboard the ship along with a carefully picked crew, while Joshua Humphreys waited for the right moment to begin removing the restraints – he gave the order, and 56 mallets were swung in unison. After a brief and stressful delay, the cables were cut and the 'United States' plunged down the rail and into the Delaware River. Hours of festivities followed. Next day it was back to the work of getting the new ship ready for sea and for her mission.

• • •

President Adams reported to Congress on the continuing escalation of their problems with France, while he strove to avoid a war with them. In the wake of the 1789 French Revolution that overthrew the monarchy, the new French government altered their interpretation of the longstanding Treaties of Alliance and Commerce that had been forged with the previous French government. The new Republique destabilized the European status quo and in the process reignited a war in 1792 with Britain and a coalition of European nations. America was steadily establishing global trading relationships, while prospering from having peace with Britain – and declared its neutrality. They still had many lingering unresolved issues with Britain from the Treaty of Paris that ended the Revolutionary War, such as trade barriers with Britain's colonies in the Caribbean – negotiations began on the Jay Treaty to resolve those issues in 1794.

France did not accept the American neutrality position, nor their assertion that the revolution negated America's obligation to side with France against Britain – if American merchants were going to trade with France's enemies, then the Americans also became enemies in their eyes. There was no formal declaration of war and there were just a few scattered incidents of French naval warships in direct combat with American ships. Instead, France directed its privateers to attack and seize U.S. merchant ships in the Caribbean and the three-year conflict became known as the Quasi-War with France. These privateers began capturing American merchantmen trading with

Britain and its colonies, throughout the Caribbean and even in American waters along the Eastern Seaboard – taking hundreds of ships from late 1796 through the summer of 1797. In response to this, America suspended payments of their war debt to France and the countries drifted closer towards war. Then France refused at first to receive Charles Pinckney as America's new ambassador, only accepting him after intense pressure from the government. President Adams proposed, and Congress agreed, to send three envoys to France to negotiate an amicable resolution of America's grievances.

• • •

Preparations continued getting the new American Navy ships ready for service – Captain Barry went back to Cecil Furnace to prove their guns before taking delivery of them, finding that "there was not a gun there that was fit for a Ship of War". The masts and spars were being finished and Barry informed Congress that gun issues were turning out to be the hold up. He began selecting his officers as the summer approached and he and Sarah celebrated their twentieth wedding anniversary as part of the July Fourth festivities. Another yellow fever epidemic hit Philadelphia, closing the government and shutting down most work at the shipyard. Thomas Barry, John's youngest brother who had chosen a shore career as a shipping clerk succumbed during this epidemic. John avoided the fever but instead he went down with gout, which forced him to sit at home resting until his feet and legs recovered enough to allow him to walk again. The sister ships of the new fleet, 'Constitution' and 'Constellation' were launched at their respective ports and preparations continued to get them fitted out for service.

It was not until the arrival of the cold weather of autumn that the yellow fever outbreak abated. Barry then sent Doctor Gillasspy, the ship's surgeon, home to New York to recover his own health after a summer of feverish medical work had worn him to the bone. This proved to be a lucky break for Captain Barry as the good doctor found some sixty "smooth and handsome 18 and 24-pounder guns" sitting and available in the New York area. Barry kept this information hush-hush while he worked to convince the listless Secretary of War to give him permission to inspect and acquire these proven guns.

• • •

Increased attacks on American merchant ships by French privateers resulted in a flood of letters to the Secretary of State that forced President Adams to make his first in-person address to Congress. It was a mediocre speech whose only statement of conviction was to exhort the members "to protect our commerce and to place our country in a suitable position of defense".

The American envoys sent to France were not well received by their hosts, who demanded a loan of 10 million dollars and insisted that America should pay for the damages inflicted on French privateers while they were in the act of seizing American merchantmen. The delegation returned empty handed and the recently appointed US ambassador to France, Charles Pinckney, answered the French demands thus –

"We will pay millions for defense but not one cent as a tribute".

• • •

Secretary McHenry's lackluster performance and obvious foot dragging on the urgent issue of acquiring the New York guns brought out Barry's temper and his criticism. When he was asked by the Committee on Naval Affairs for his assessment, he responded thus –

"I believe that you will agree with me that it has been but indifferently managed hitherto; that there might be some allowance made for young beginners. The Secretary is indeed a fine man, but his administrative skills leave a lot to be desired. The department ought to be placed by itself and have three men skilled in Naval matters running it. There should be three commissioners under the President: one a Commander, one a Merchant, and one a Ship Builder. There should be three freshwater river anchorages for the Warships to rendezvous – places that are safe from enemies in the event of war breaking out. These places should be near large seaport towns where it will be easier to raise crews."

Barry's suggestions later became the backbone of the Navy's policy for a hundred years.

Meanwhile the American peace mission to Paris was a failure. The report from Mr. Marshall was handed to President Adams in early March,1798. He waited two weeks before he informed Congress, weighing the implications for America before ordering that the country should prepare for war – while withholding the actual documents. He was accused by the opposition of being a warmonger. His release of the report with redacted names of the French officials brought public opinion to the side of the President, in what became dubbed as the XYZ Affair, and the entire episode was a tremendous boost for the creation of the New Navy.

McHenry's delays in deciding on the New York guns continued through the autumn, while he bowed to local merchant's complaints about the position of the unfinished Navy ship in the river – he ordered Barry to move the 'United States' to where the river channel was wider.

Captain Barry had to go back to the foundry in Maryland when they sent word that they had 23 guns ready to prove – this time bringing Mr. Hughes, the foundry owner, with him to the testing range. Six of the first eight guns they tested blew apart, and testing was postponed until the following day. Three more days of testing followed and only twelve guns passed out of the forty-four tested. Barry was furious with Mr. Hughes and told him he would not take any of his cannons.

This incident finally convinced Secretary McHenry to give Captain Barry permission to go and inspect the guns in New York. Once again, he had to personally make the trip and he tested twenty-five guns at one location when he approved twenty-three of them, and dozens more at another location passed also. The moment he arrived home he presented his report to McHenry, who had only to send an official request to Governor Jay in New York to secure the guns. Again, the Secretary continued to waste time rather than send the request. Congress had by this stage approved an additional one million dollars for added Navy expenditures such as the purchase of several merchantmen for hasty conversion into ships of war – including the 'Ganges' and the 'Delaware'.

Barry's midshipmen were sworn in – a May 5, 1798, dispatch from McHenry ordered him to go on board the 'United States' with all haste and complete her muster rolls, reminding him –

"It is the President's express order that you employ the most vigorous exertion to accomplish the several objectives."

Barry sent his second-in-command to New York to enlist sailors while he and an assistant did the same in Philadelphia – advertising went up everywhere, appealing for "all able-bodied and patriotic seamen who are willing to serve their country for one year at the pay of $17 per month."

The strong response pleased Captain Barry – "I am apprehensive of having more seamen than our compliment" – and he passed the extras on to his other captains. The next delay was getting the regular supplies needed for a cruise and getting carriages for the 24-pounder guns. Uniforms for the crews were finally ready, and Barry passed them along to his waiting captains, no longer concerned about whether his own ship was the first to depart or not.

It was Captain Richard Dale who had the 'Ganges' refitted and ready first, and on May 23, Barry complied with Secretary McHenry's request to come on board that ship with him.

They presented Captain Dale with his orders –

"To protect the jurisdiction of the United States on our coast, and to cruise between the Capes of Virginia and Long Island."

A salute was fired before the 'Ganges' weighed anchor and proceeded to her cruising station. Captain Barry decided to move the 'United States' downstream into deeper waters while waiting for her final supplies to come aboard and elected to make do with whatever gun carriages were available.

• • •

Captain Dale's sendoff was McHenry's last official act before he was replaced by Benjamin Stoddert, in the newly created post of Secretary of the Navy. Stoddert came from a merchant and land purchase background, as well as being a veteran of the army during the Revolutionary War. His first day on the job was June 19 and Captain Barry was one of his first visitors, where he found an engaging middle-aged man of average height. When Barry broached the subject of the faulty cannons and the need to acquire the proven guns from New York, Stoddert agreed with him and immediately made the decision to have the guns shipped to the Delaware River by a fast-sailing vessel. Stoddert was the total opposite of McHenry, and Barry was suitably impressed. Within days the guns arrived, and all defective gun carriages were replaced immediately, so that all guns were safely mounted and ready in record time. The brig 'Delaware' proceeded to sea on June 26 under Captain Decatur Senior, and in Virginia the 'Constellation' under Captain Truxton was almost ready to head to sea.

On July 3, 1798, Captain Barry received his official orders and was told to sail with the first favorable wind. Fittingly, on the Glorious Fourth, Commodore John Barry, resplendent in his blue and buff uniform, was escorted out his front door by his proud wife, Sarah, and was taken by carriage to the waterfront. He wore the decorated sword of John Paul Jones, which he had inherited from Jones in his will. Then he boarded a longboat to be carried down the river to his new frigate – amid the Fourth of July celebrations.

The Commodore's boat arrived alongside the frigate at 4 p.m. and he climbed onto the 'United States' to the cheers of his crew in their full-dress uniforms. He still found time for some final simulated gun practice while they waited for the purser to get a small herd of live beef on board the ship, the last items on the provisions list. On July 7, gun salutes were fired as the largest ship to date to be built in America sailed down the river towards the Capes. Next morning they met the 'Delaware' coming in with the first prize of the 'war', a French privateer. The crew of 'United States' gave 'Delaware' a rousing cheer.

Fresh orders from Stoddert via a pilot boat followed the Commodore's departure down the Delaware – to stay off the Capes and await further orders. Congress had decided to give "letters of marque" to American privateers, and in 1798 they passed the important "Act to re-establish the Marine Corps" – who had been disbanded in March of 1783 after the Revolutionary War ended. The next group of orders given to Barry from the long-winded Stoddert was to go to Boston with the 'Delaware' and there to add two smaller ships to his squadron.

Per Stoddert's letter –

"The French have considerable force in the West Indies, it is thought that a small squadron under the command of an officer of your intelligence, experience and bravery might render essential service and animate your country to enterprise by picking up a few prizes on a short cruise of these islands. Also, pay a visit to St. Johns (later to be San Juan), the principal harbor of Puerto Rico, and after two or three weeks of cruising return to the continent. It is time we should establish an American character. Let that character be love of country and a jealousy of its honor. This idea comprehends everything that ought to be impressed upon the minds of all our citizens, but more especially the minds of those citizens who are seamen and soldiers."

Stoddert added yet another letter telling Barry that Congress was still deliberating over a declaration of war against France. He informed his Commodore that Mrs. Barry was well and that he expected Barry's ships back on the American coast in two months.

Barry and his crew were enthralled with the handling and speed of their new frigate, 'United States', and the Commodore was quick to brag about the ship –

"She was built for fighting, but first and foremost she was built for sailing, and she answers her helm better than any ship ever put to sea."

He had to slow his ship down to allow 'Delaware' to catch up. In Boston, thousands of people crowded the waterfront to see the new ship, 'United States'. Guns saluted her arrival; Barry returned the salute with a blast from his guns to the delight of the crowd. The ships he had come to Boston to hook up with – the 'Herald' under Captain Sever and a revenue cutter, were not ready – and so the 'United States' and 'Delaware' departed for the West Indies without them. They made Barbados on August 21, now flying the Commodore blue pennant on top of the main mast – a triumphant return to the island for John Barry since his quiet first-arrival there in a little schooner thirty-two years earlier. After inquiries about French activity in the area they departed for Martinique.

Next morning they captured their first French prize, the schooner 'Sans Pareil' from Guadeloupe with 87 crew.

Commodore Barry sent 'Delaware' with the prize to St. Bartholomew and continued to hunt for more French ships. His hunting route took him past Sint. Eustatius, then past the top French stronghold of Guadeloupe, and on to Dominica – having not sighted any enemy ships he proceeded to St. Barts to join up with 'Delaware' and they took on supplies there. The two American ships plus their prize continued to Puerto Rico, capturing the French sloop, 'Le Jaleux', on the way. No more French activity was encountered and the two warships plus their two prizes headed home in September ahead of the hurricane season, as Barry did not want to expose the new ship to tropical storms immediately. They arrived safely at Cape Henlopen on September 18 and proceeded into the Delaware River where Barry disembarked, while the ship continued upriver.

Barry rode home by coach to reunite with Sarah. She told him of the latest yellow fever outbreak which had again forced government officials to leave Philadelphia for Trenton. That's where he found Stoddert the next day and got a surprisingly cool reception. The Secretary seemed a little annoyed at the squadron's early return, especially when Barry's report did not include the capture of a major prize like a French warship, despite having captured two privateers. The Secretary conveniently forgot that the Commodore had followed his orders to the letter, those same orders that were issued by Stoddert himself. The truth was that Stoddert needed some spectacular results from the cruises to boost public support for the

'Quasi-War' and keep the opposition in Congress at bay, but he failed to understand that the French fleet were deployed in European waters against the British and that the French plan was to use their privateers in the Caribbean during this 'Quasi-War'. Privately, Stoddert complained to President Adams about Barry's early return, saying that the "the first cruise by 'United States' fell far short of my hopes."

In contrast, the local newspapers were totally excited to have the 'United States' back in port, making a big story of Commodore Barry's return and his capture of the two French privateers – stoking the patriotic sentiment of the public. The other captains trickled back in, and their lack of success made Barry's two prizes look excellent, but Stoddert seemed determined to make little of Barry's success. He wanted 'United States' back on patrol immediately so he facilitated Barry in his efforts to get refitted quickly, and on October 1 he ordered the ship to proceed to sea – "to protect the trade from Delaware to New Hampshire" – telling him that the hurricanes were now past and there was no need for delay. As soon as the frigate departed, she was hit by a terrible storm that forced the ship towards the Virginia Capes and battered the rigging and masts so badly that they had to make for Cape Henlopen for repairs, where their pilot even ran the ship aground briefly. Barry brought shipbuilder Joshua Humphreys to Chester to see the damage to the new ship up close for himself and asked him to organize the necessary repairs.

At that same time General Washington unexpectedly

arrived in the area leading his troops – he had been coaxed back from retirement to lead the Army again during this 'undeclared war' or 'proxy war' against France. Barry ordered a fifteen-gun salute fired from the 'United States' in General Washington's honor.

• • •

Stoddert continued adding more ships of varied sizes to the fleet – by late 1798 the fleet had increased to fourteen, with even more on the way. Captain Barry chose this time to make overtures for his own promotion, addressing Stoddert on the matter.

"Mr. Secretary, the rank of Commodore is a courtesy title that all the squadron commanders utilize. Being that I am the Navy Commander, I think it is now time to acknowledge that fact with the title of Admiral."

"Commodore Barry, I am not a man for titles. My information is that there are about 150 armed French privateers operating out of Guadeloupe at present and our American merchants are clamoring for protection – especially now that we are being told that there are two larger enemy predators out there – the 'Insurgente' with 50 guns and the 'Volontaire' with 44 guns. They are rumored to have captured Captain Bainbridge's 'Retaliation'. I want American warships to rule the Caribbean. Accomplish that for me and I shall see what I can do about the Admiral rank."

"We will rule the Caribbean," Barry replied.

The 'United States' was quickly repaired and went on with its mission to protect trade from Delaware to New Hampshire, while the 'Delaware' did the same from New York to the Chesapeake. Barry was unable to get any home leave so he wrote to Sarah – "my reason for going to sea so soon is that some American merchant ships are expected any day from Europe and should any of them be taken while I am lying in the harbor, the merchants may blame me and no other, although it would not be my fault."

He returned home in mid-November; then was directed to make a report on a new and better system of governing the Navy – on which he consulted with Captains Dale, Truxton and Tingsley. Before the Secretary of the Navy position had been created, the War Department had directed all naval affairs. Back then Barry had recommended the establishment of several Navy Yards and the setting up of a separate and independent Navy Department – something that was finally coming together.

• • •

When President Adams addressed Congress in December 1798, he declared that France's threat to seize neutral ships carrying cargo that originated in Britain, was an act of war on the commerce of the nation it attacks –

"Whether we negotiate with France or not, a vigorous preparation for war will be alike indispensable."

He urged an increase of the Navy and in February 1799 Congress agreed to add six 74-gun ships and six 18-gun ships to the fleet – making the naval appropriation for that year $4,594,677. Back in December, Commodore Barry had been placed in command of the entire fleet. Barry's squadron included the following – the frigates 'United States' under Barry himself: 'Constitution' under Samuel Nicholson: 'Merrimac' under Moses Brown: 'George Washington' under Patrick Fletcher – plus six smaller vessels – 'Portsmouth' under Daniel McNeill: 'Pickering' under Edward Preble: 'Eagle' under Hugh George Campbell: 'Herald' under Charles Russell: 'Scammel' under Jay Adams: and 'Diligence' under J Brown.

This squadron was to be employed in the West Indies and based in Dominica -

"For the protection of our commerce and for the capture or destruction of French armed vessels from St. Christopher's as far as Barbados and Tobago; with attention also to Cayenne and Curacao, and La Guayra (La Guaira, Venezuela) on the Spanish Main (the northern coast of South America) – to which places our citizens carry on considerable trade."

Commodore Barry assigned groups of two or three ships to different parts of the area "to rid those seas of French armed vessels and also the pirates which infest them." Barry utilized these operations to continue his unique training system of young officers – many of whom would achieve later fame – such as Charles Stewart, Stephen Decatur Jnr and Jacob Jones.

Three months later the 'Constellation' squadron under

Captain Truxton captured the 50-gun 'Insurgente', a capture which endeared Truxton to President Adams and Secretary Stoddert, at the expense of Commodore Barry. Stoddert wanted constant correspondence from his commanders and Barry did not fit that mold – he wrote upon arrivals and departures only, and that put him in Stoddert's bad books, compared to Truxton who wrote much more often.

At one stage Barry's 'United States' exchanged a few salvos with a very large 74-gun French warship, then withdrew due to the superior size of the French ship. In February, while chasing a French privateer, his gunner put a 24-pound cannonball through the hull of the fleeing ship. The vessel 'Amour de la Patrie' quickly began to settle and fill with water. Barry's ship saved all 70 of her crew. Then he captured 'Tartufe' with 8 guns and 60 men, plus he saved the captured American sloop prize that the privateer had. Having so many prisoners, Barry sailed into Guadeloupe under a flag of truce, hoping to exchange the prisoners for Americans imprisoned there. As soon as he was fired on by the French batteries, he hauled down his flag of truce and returned fire so effectively that he battered their walls to pulp. During this entire campaign Barry was quite unwell, but the resilient sailor fought through his illness and performed his tasks to perfection. Eight other vessel captures were made by Barry's squadron.

April 8, 1799, found Commodore Barry at Bridgetown, Barbados, a place with a lot of personal memories for him as it was where he had voyaged at the age of twenty-one when he commanded his first vessel. Over the years he had come to be regarded as a favorite son of the island and on his arrival this time he was celebrated as the commanding officer, Commodore of the American Navy. The local newspaper declared – "Whatever good fortune attends Commodore Barry will but increase the public esteem which he already possesses, as to see merit rewarded is the generous wish of every British bosom."

Barry accepted this well-intended praise, but with a heavy heart – he had received news of the failed 1798 Irish Rebellion of the previous year, in which his native county of Wexford had been one place that saw much fighting and bloodshed – a rebellion that had been brutally put down by British forces with much loss of innocent Irish lives, including some people that were related to him.

On April 15, the 'United States' was recalled, and she departed St. Rupert's Bay for home on April 17, accompanied by 'Constitution' and over thirty merchantmen – leaving Captain Truxton in command of the rest of the squadron to continue operations. Arriving in Delaware Bay in early May, Captain Barry was allowed to disembark and ride to Philadelphia by coach, while the rest of the crew were quarantined until they got the all-clear for yellow fever. Barry met with Stoddert first, to report on the successful cruise, and was told of the plan to refit quickly for the next mission – then he went home to see his wife, Sarah.

Stoddert was running a timetable that had too many vessels in port at the same time, and to cover for himself with President Adams he blamed Commodore Barry, saying "he came home too soon and ordered the return of those under his command, too soon."

The French privateers were actively harassing merchantmen along the United States Southeast Coast, which was deemed "to be making the public mind very uneasy." Consequently, on June 20, Barry sailed under orders to cruise south along the coast to Charleston, remaining there long enough to let the citizens know that US ships were in their vicinity. Then he proceeded south along the Georgia coast (past St. Simon's Island where all the live oak timber for the ships had been harvested) – going as far as the St. Mary's River before returning to Hampton Roads by mid-July. The plan after that was to be joined by the 'Constitution' for a cruise to the Western Isles and possibly include the Canary Islands and areas close to the coasts of Spain and France.

This plan was scrapped because of President Adams' concern about America's coast, when he said – "The protection of our local commerce is the great object of the naval armament."

Stoddert told Barry that "the frigate United States has to remain on our coast for our protection at home", and that the frigate 'Constitution' was to be employed in the same manner. Therefore, the 'United States' sailed on August 1, to cruise the Southeast coast again from the Florida state line through to the coast of New England.

Commodore Barry stayed on this beat until mid-September without capturing any prizes – he noted ruefully that "the coast had been protected."

Captain Truxton had resigned at this stage to avoid falling beneath the rank of Captain Talbot, per the earlier ranking list that Truxton disagreed with. Talbot was returning to service to command a ship – a development that gave Barry's top position in the Navy more security despite Stoddert's efforts to undermine him.

Returning to port, Barry's ship was unable to enter New York as planned, due to the sandbar – so he sailed the 'United States' to Newport, Rhode Island, instead.

CHAPTER EIGHT

NEW THREATS ASSURE FUTURE OF AMERICAN NAVY

President Adams and Congress were eager to end this 'Quasi-War' with France. To do so they needed to send envoys to France for peace negotiations, but Stoddert didn't want to waste American frigates on diplomatic missions. Barry wanted to take leave to go home and spend time with his wife Sarah, who had been reduced to what John referred to as a 'sea widow' – but he was gruffly directed by Stoddert to stay in Newport to await orders.

In due course Stoddert submitted to the will of his President, who had declared that -

"This diplomatic mission is one of the most critical, important and interesting moments that ever occurred in American History".

Stoddert informed President Adams that the frigate

'United States' had excellent accommodations for passengers and that Commodore Barry was the man for such a mission. Barry was told to get ready for a November 1 departure for France, stopping at Lisbon before continuing to L'Orient – all under a flag of truce, which meant that Barry could not engage with or capture any other vessel on the voyage, a policy sure to be resented by his crew.

Stoddert threw in an incentive that he knew would please Commodore Barry –

"I hope to salute you an Admiral on your home arrival."

The 'United States' left Newport amid cheering crowds and gun salutes on November 3, 1799, bound for France with two US envoys on board – Chief Justice John Ellsworth and W.R. Davie, the former governor of North Carolina. Barry had recently promoted young John Barron to Captain and second-in-command. This allowed him to pass the day-to-day sailing duties to Barron and spend his own time taking care of his guests. After a smooth and quick voyage, they arrived in Lisbon on November 25 and lay at anchor in the Tagus River for weeks, waiting for news from France.

There had been a 'coup d'etat' in France, and it was unclear how and when they could proceed with negotiations – the new leader was reported to be a Corsican – Napoleon Bonaparte. Barry and his guests were treated to several lavish dinners by William Smith, the American consul stationed in Lisbon, who was also the point man on news from France. They got clearance to proceed to L'Orient on December 21 and then ran into atrocious weather in the dreaded Bay of Biscay. The storm ignited John Barry's memories of his lost brother Patrick, whose ship had disappeared there. Ironically, the 'United States' was pushed so far off course during the storm that she was close to Cape Clear in Ireland at one point – the nearest John Barry had been to his Wexford homeland since he had emigrated to America. His envoy passengers were so seasick that they begged to be put ashore anywhere. Barry complied by landing them at Coruna in Northwest Spain on January 11, 1800, after another mishap – an unforeseen problem with their primary anchor which forced them to use their spare one. The envoys were eventually rowed ashore to a fishing village and then had to set off on the long overland winter journey to Paris.

When the storm abated, Captain Barry docked the 'United States' at Coruna and went ashore to inquire about help with repairs. That's when he found out that General Washington had died on December 14. He was devastated and emotional as he shared the news with his officers and crew, saying to his second-in-command, John Barron –

"I felt Washington's death with uncommon anguish."

The ship's colors were lowered to half-mast, and he ordered his officers to wear crape on their left arm below the elbow.

They began extensive repairs to the ship which continued until mid-February. The envoys engaged in long negotiations with the new French government and after a dispatch arrived from them addressed to Secretary of State Pickering, Barry weighed anchor and headed home, arriving at the Delaware River on April 2, 1800. Barry didn't know it, but the envoy's letters had not given him any credit for his efforts during the fateful storm and instead complained about the 'overland ordeal' they endured – which did further harm to Commodore Barry's reputation in the eyes of Stoddert and President Adams.

Stoddert had made a less than sterling case before Congress to raise several Navy Captains to the rank of Admiral, Commodore Barry included. Congress refused to act on the request and President Adams made no efforts on behalf of his officers – so the matter was dropped.

When Stoddert saw how battered the frigate 'United States' was, he decided that his easiest route to escape his failure to gain the Admiral promotion for Commodore Barry was to put blame for the ships damage and delayed return on the back of Barry himself – this way he avoided his own failure and never brought up the case to Congress again for Barry's elevation to the rank of Admiral. During Barry's meeting with Stoddert to report on the voyage, the Secretary told him with glee about the Navy's successes in the Caribbean, especially those of Captain Truxton who had come back from retirement to command the 'Constellation'.

John Barry went home to find that his wife Sarah was discontented also – she was tired of the loneliness of Strawberry Hill in winter, during the long absences of her husband and those of her nephews. They decided that they would look for a house in the city and use the farm as a summer residence.

The shipbuilder, Joshua Humphreys, was shocked at the damage incurred by his frigate 'United States' and he decided that he would have to dismantle the ship substantially to perform the extensive repairs needed – repairs that would take months. Then, President Adams fired both Secretary of State Pickering and Secretary of War McHenry, asking Stoddert to take over the War Department in addition to his Navy duties. Because Barry's ship would be out of action for repairs, Stoddert began discharging her crew and reassigning the junior officers to other vessels.

The overworked Captain Barry had also been working for quite some time on a new signal book for the Navy and he now gave that manuscript to his second-in-command, John Barron, asking him to review it, and once satisfied with the contents, to get it printed and distributed to the active fleet. This new book later became an essential manual for his Navy commanders and was used for many years by the entire American Navy. Meanwhile, the drydocked Commodore spent his time overseeing improvements to the old farm – Sarah and he took a three-week vacation to the New Jersey shore before he returned to duty.

The US envoys' negotiations in France continued, with virtually no progress being reported – that lack of progress meant that President Adams would likely lose his bid for reelection. Newspaper headlines declared that the privateers of Guadeloupe were making many captures of American merchantmen – something that had not happened on Barry's watch and was pointed out to Stoddert by supporters of Commodore Barry. The repairs to 'United States' progressed slower than expected and Joshua Humphreys got the ship finished by early October that year. Stoddert told Barry to enlist a crew and get officers signed up. Personally, Stoddert wanted Talbot to get command of the largest Caribbean squadron, but he could not bypass Barry's seniority and his popularity – he solved this dilemma by sending Barry to command 'the Guadeloupe Station'.

Barry signed up his crew and waited patiently for final orders – while news of the agreement on a "Treaty of Peace, Commerce and Navigation" with First Consul Bonaparte of France was finally made public.

The 'United States' stood down in December with conditional orders –

"Treat the armed vessels of France, public and private, exactly as you find they treat our trading vessels."

Despite suffering a last-minute asthma attack, Commodore Barry got the ship underway on December 14 and sighted two 'sail' on New Years Day, 1801. They chased and captured the American brig 'Sally', only to find a prize crew of eight Frenchmen aboard and her captain clapped in irons below deck. Sally's captain told Barry that he had been captured by the French schooner 'Diamaid' the day before. Barry detained the French crew, freed 'Sally' and then sailed in search of the French schooner for eight hours, caught sight of her briefly before losing her in poor light – but his crafty hunch was correct, and he found her again a few hours later. This time there was no escape for the French ship, and she was captured in the early morning hours – her captain and crew were detained, and a prize crew was put aboard.

One week later Barry made rendezvous with the 44-gun American frigate 'President' at St. Kitts, commanded by Captain Truxton, who immediately ceded rank to Barry by hauling down his blue commodore pennant. He informed Barry that Governor Davie had arrived in America with the finalized peace treaty and that Thomas Jefferson, the Republican, had been elected President. Both captains agreed that this result would usher in a period of uncertainty for the Navy. Truxton handed over the Guadeloupe station command to Barry and departed for home with his squadron.

Guadeloupe had always frustrated Barry in the past, and he was anxious to see what reception he would receive on this occasion. As the frigate 'United States' approached the harbor, the French guns were run out, but this time it was to fire a salute and to receive "The Commodore".

For the next two months Barry's squadron did their usual cruises and convoy escorts without incident. Thomas Jefferson was inaugurated as President on March 4,1801, and things began to change quickly for the US Navy. Re-supply ships arrived April 12, carrying new orders from Stoddert – Commodore Barry was to send his squadron back to port immediately and he was to make his way home to Philadelphia. He enjoyed his return voyage as he pushed the ship to her sailing limits and made it to Delaware Bay by April 21, took on a pilot there and was almost immediately greeted by springtime thunder and lightning. That slowed his progress upriver to a crawl and Barry decided to disembark a few days later in Chester while the ship continued to port in Philadelphia.

He took a carriage home to surprise Sarah, but it was he who was surprised. Strawberry Hill was in mourning for his nephew, Michael Hayes, who had been lost at sea. The ladies – Sarah Barry, Michael's widow, and the wife of Michael's brother Patrick's were all grief stricken – Patrick was away at sea and unaware of the tragedy. John did all he could to comfort his family and in due course he got Michael's estate sorted out.

• • •

The American Navy that Commodore John Barry had nurtured and loved so much soon began moving in the wrong direction. Ahead of Jefferson's inauguration in March, Stoddert had resigned rather suddenly as Secretary of the Navy, citing health issues. He agreed to stay on until his successor was named, and President Jefferson had trouble finding anyone to take the post, it being widely known that the department was to be downgraded in his new administration – one which was fully expected to be vehemently Anti-Navy.

The New American Navy that was proudly established by the Act of 1794, was soon to be reduced to almost nothing. All the ships except 13 frigates were to be sold, reducing the muster rolls, and only 28 Navy Captains were to be retained. The new Congress controlled by Jefferson ordered the cessation of work on the 74-gun frigates and total yearly naval expenditures were to be reduced to a paltry $250,000. Before leaving his post, Stoddert used the money saved from abandoning the building of the seventy-fours, to buy land that would house Navy yards – in Washington, Norfolk, Boston, Philadelphia, Portsmouth and New York. This decision was in accordance with the recommendations that Commodore Barry had made in 1798 – a parting 'gift' from Stoddert, a man who had thwarted Barry at every turn during his tenure as Secretary of the Navy.

The frigate 'United States' was in the Delaware River by the end of April, and on May 1 the acting Secretary of the Navy, General Dearborn, ordered Commodore Barry to bring her to Washington, "where it is intended that she shall be laid up." Barry was annoyed by this order but followed his orders as always, and he sailed her up the Potomac River to Washington – with difficulty because of the inherent dangers of shallow water, reporting his arrival there on May 23. He made his way to the office of the Secretary of the Navy in the sprawl that was the 'New Capital', and he handed over his report and his inventory list.

Barry then returned to the cabin of his ship and sat there

in quiet contemplation for more than half an hour. When he finally exited the cabin the sailors stood to attention, the bosun's whistle blew, and second-in-command, Richard Sommers, ordered the broad blue pennant lowered. When it was folded, Barry saluted, climbed down the gangway and took his carriage home.

"The flagship frigate of the New Navy was made to cease operations, was put at rest – not because her usefulness was at an end and she might no more be serviceable, not because there would never be occasion for her power as a protector of American commerce – but because the political policy of the Party in Power did not sanction the possession of a Navy."

Having fulfilled the Navy's mission, and the commanding Commodore of the Navy having obeyed orders and brought the first ship of the Navy to the New Capital of the New Nation – Commodore John Barry received a terse notification on June 6, 1801, whereby he himself was put on the shelf at the age of 56 –

"You have permission to retire to your place of residence and there remain until the government again requires your services."

On June 11,1801, President Jefferson put the Navy on a "Peace Establishment".

The retained personnel – 28 Captains, 36 Lieutenants and

150 Midshipmen were all to be put on half-pay from July 1, 1801.

• • •

More tragedy struck the Barry family shortly afterwards – Sarah's brother Isaac became very ill. They moved him from the city to the country setting of Strawberry Hill and Doctor Rush attended to him but could not save him – he died on June 15, at the young age of forty-nine. Sarah was in shock and mourning – after his burial, John took her and their two servants to the New Jersey shore at Long Branch for a week. The vacation certainly helped to invigorate John Barry's health and Betsy Hayes sent a good-news letter to her husband Patrick at sea – "our good old uncle is much improved since his trip to Jersey."

• • •

A letter arrived soon afterwards informing Commodore Barry that the number of retained captains was being further reduced to nine, himself being one of those nine. He also received news of brewing trouble with the Barbary States. American Navy Captain Bainbridge had delivered the latest tribute payment to Algiers, at which time his frigate 'General Washington' was commandeered by 'The Dey' to carry their ambassador and his entourage to Constantinople, while flying the Algerian flag instead of the American flag.

This incident served to convince President Jefferson to re-evaluate the importance of the Navy, and he offered Captain Truxton the command of a Mediterranean squadron. Truxton asked that his rank be placed above Talbot and when President Jefferson refused, he declined the assignment. It was an assignment that Commodore Barry would have loved but instead it went to his friend, Captain Richard Dale.

The good news as far as the Commodore was concerned was that the frigate 'United States' was going to be refitted for service and by August 1801, a letter of inquiry came to Barry –

"President Jefferson is contemplating sending another squadron to the Mediterranean, and inquires whether you are determined to command 'United States' yourself or to surrender your old favorite to be enjoyed and commanded by another?"

Barry replied immediately "If I am called upon and my health will admit, I shall as a good citizen feel myself bound to come forward and do my might to subdue any enemy of my country."

There was no hurried response from President Jefferson to Barry's letter, and John went ahead with the purchase of a house in town at 126 Spruce Street, to fulfill his promise to Sarah. The Secretary of the Navy next required input about the 'false keel' of his old frigate, the 'United States'. John again replied promptly – "I never discovered any deficiency in her, her bottom is in perfect order. Give her a bower anchor along with cables and sails, and she will be ready. Pray tell me when I can start rounding up officers and a crew."

He received no reply.

With winter approaching, the next letter from the Secretary asked Barry to go with Alexander Murray to prove some guns – a request that coincided with Barry suffering a spate of severe asthma attacks, and he was too unwell to accompany Murray. This did not go down well with the Secretary and there was no more correspondence during the winter. The refitting of the 'United States' continued but at a slower pace than expected, and nothing prevented the Barry's from spending Christmas at their new house in Philadelphia.

Barry received a letter from his niece in Ireland, Eleanor Hayes, informing him that she had not received her share of the estate of her deceased brother Michael – she detailed the sad plight of her extended family who were suffering repercussions from the defeat of the momentous 1798 Irish Rebellion in which County Wexford had featured so prominently. It upset John to hear that the Lord Lieutenant of Ireland who oversaw the brutal defeat of the Irish rebels was none other than General Cornwallis (he who had surrendered to General Washington at Yorktown). John sent money immediately to help Eleanor and her extended family.

Spring of 1802 brought more asthma attacks and Doctor Rush sent John to a spa in rural Pennsylvania which helped him tremendously. Summer came and went – he made a short trip to Jersey to prove guns and was the sponsor for the newborn fourth child of his nephew Patrick Hayes and his wife Betsy – all the while Barry was fighting off asthma attacks that Doctor Rush was struggling to treat and contain. Barry was appointed to a board along with Captain Dale and Captain Bainbridge – to examine applicants for admission to the Navy.

There was still no sign of the orders for the second Mediterranean squadron.

Congress was divided as to whether the country needed a more vigorous Navy, or whether to continue paying tribute money to the Algerines – finally they came around to the idea of using their Navy instead of paying what amounted to ransom to Algeria's rulers, The Dey.

On December 22,1802, the new Secretary of the Navy sent a notification to Commodore Barry –

"We shall have occasion to keep a small force in the Mediterranean and we shall expect your services on that station."

Unfortunately, Commodore Barry was becoming more and more enfeebled from a life of overwork, stress and the affliction of asthma, and he struggled to admit to himself that he was no longer well enough to go to sea. All through Christmas he prayed for a spell of good health and sought Sarah's counsel on the matter.

"My dearest, I have been wanting this Mediterranean appointment for over a year, my chance to achieve the rank of Admiral, and now it has finally come at a time when my asthma is giving me much trouble. What is your advice?"

Sarah took his hands in hers and looked into his eyes.

"John, I have been a sea widow all our married life. I know you love the sea and I know you feel a duty to serve. However, nothing and nobody lasts forever. You have served America well, you have given her your best years and won great sea battles for her Navy – you have trained some exceptional junior officers during those times. It is time for you to let it go now, let those young men take on the responsibilities that you trained them for. I have never asked you not to go to sea, but I am asking you now – I want you here with me, where I can nurse you and love you and not be thousands of miles away when the next asthma attack comes. You richly deserved the rank of Admiral, and it is the fault of others that you did not attain it – you are indeed my Admiral, and it is time now for Admiral Barry to stay in drydock."

They had a long and tearful embrace.

On January 2, 1803, he wrote the painful letter that he hated to write but knew he must –

> To the Secretary of the Navy,
>
> "Sir – The honor of being named to command the Mediterranean squadron is greatly appreciated. It is with deep regret that I inform you that I must decline the post due to health reasons.
>
> I am, Sir.
> John Barry

• • •

Doctor Rush had already confided to John that there was little more he could do to keep his asthma at bay, and that time was getting short. Barry took the advice bravely and began putting his affairs in order – selling some investments and gathering his papers.

On February 27, he made his last will and testament – naming his wife Sarah Barry and his nephew Patrick Hayes as his executors. By early summer the attacks became more frequent, and Barry asked that he be moved to his beloved Strawberry Hill farm, where he wanted to spend his final days.

• • •

The squadron that he had hoped to lead to the Mediterranean departed in July – led by Captain Edward Preble and it included many of the officers that had been trained in Commodore Barry's 'academy' – such as Charles Stewart, Stephen Decatur Jnr, Richard Sommers. It made Commodore Barry very proud to know that these fine young Navy officers would fly the colors of the United States, and he received letters from them on the progress of their mission. Betsy Hayes read him her husband Patrick's letter from far away China where he had sailed to conduct trade in Canton.

By early September John's treatment was upgraded to laudanum to relax his attack spasms, and he began drifting in and out of consciousness. All that could be done was to make him as comfortable as possible.

• • •

At his Strawberry Hill farm in the early morning of September 13, 1803, surrounded by family members, his breathing became shallower, and Commodore John Barry died peacefully – he was fifty-eight years old.

• • •

The notice of his death was printed in the afternoon edition of the Pennsylvania Gazette – news that stunned the city of Philadelphia.

On September 14, members of the Society of the Cincinnati led Mrs. Sarah Barry, her family and a throng of Philadelphians to St. Mary's Catholic Church. Bishop Kenrick celebrated the Requiem Mass and during his oration to the congregation he reminded them of Barry's faith –

"Commodore Barry consistently attended Mass in this church when in Philadelphia."

The church was filled with sailors, landsmen, dock hands and merchants – Republicans and Federalists. After the service the crowd walked silently to the graveyard at the rear of the church where Commodore John Barry was laid to rest.

News of Commodore Barry's death spread around the country, and much was written about his patriotic service to his adopted country and on the scope of his character. The Massachusetts Spy headline was an example – "At Philadelphia, Commodore John Barry, to his valor was owed much the honor acquired on the seas during the American Revolution."

His will provided for Sarah Barry and all his extended family and friends. He left his silver-hilted sword to his nephew Patrick, and John Paul Jones's sword (bequeathed to him by Jones) to his close friend, Richard Dale.

Two more close friends, one of his officers, John Kessler, and his Irish friend from the Marine Committee, John Brown, summed up his life in words that rang true for all that knew John –

"The first of patriots and the best of men."

Doctor Rush, his long-time doctor and close friend, offered to write an Epitaph for his tomb, which Sarah Barry gladly accepted.

The Original Epitaph

Let the Patriot, the Soldier and the Christian
Who visits these mansions of the dead
View this monument with respect.
Beneath it are interred the remains of John Barry.

He was born in the County of Wexford in Ireland
But America was the object of his patriotism
And the theatre of his usefulness.
In the Revolutionary War which established the
Independence of the United States
He bore an early and an active part as a Captain in their
Navy
and after became its Commander-in-Chief.
He fought often and once bled in the cause of Freedom.
His habits of war did not lessen his
Virtues as a Man nor his piety as a Christian.
He was gentle, just and kind in private life,
was not less beloved by his family and friends than by
his Grateful Country.
The number and objects of his charities will be
known only at that time when his dust
shall be reanimated and when He who sees in secret
shall reward openly.
In the full belief in the doctrines of the Gospel
he peacefully resigned his soul into the arms of his Redeemer
on September 13,1803, in the 59th year of his age.
His affectionate widow hath caused this marble to be
erected to perpetuate his name after the hearts of his
fellow-citizens have ceased to be
the living Record of his Public and Private Virtues.

• • •

A monument to John Barry was erected in Fairmount Park, Philadelphia, in 1876, on the Centennial of Independence. The inscriptions on three sides of the monument are recorded below.

East side –
John Barry
First Commodore of the United States Navy.
Born in 1745
in Wexford County, Ireland.
Died September 13, 1803
at Philadelphia.
West side –
During the Revolutionary War he distinguished himself greatly.
He filled the various commands entrusted to him with skill and gallantry.
When unable to fight on the ocean he obtained command of a Company of Volunteeeers
and fought against the enemy on land.
Among his exploits was the capture,
Upon May 29, 1781, of two British vessels of war,
the HMS Atalanta and the HMS Trepassey,
after a hotly contested action with his own ship, USS Alliance.

North –
In January 1776, he commanded the brig Lexington,
The first regular cruiser that got to sea under the authority of

The Continental Congress, and the vessel that first carried The American Flag upon the ocean.

• • •

The Hibernian Society for the relief of Irish emigrants (later the Friendly Sons of St. Patrick) presented a copy of Gilbert Stuart's portrait of Commodore Barry, to the City of Philadelphia on March 18,1895 – to be placed at Independence Hall. It was presented to the Mayor by General St. Clair Mulholland, who declared Commodore Barry to have been –

"One of the most illustrious of Ireland's sons, a brilliant child of the wind and waves, a heroic warrior of the sea who never knew defeat, the Father and Founder of the Navy of the United States, the Navy that from its beginning has been the admiration and model of all nations of the earth."

• • •

In 1906 a Bill was passed by both Houses of Congress and signed by President Roosevelt – to erect a monument in Washington in honor of Commodore John Barry. After the usual governmental delays an eight-foot bronze statue of Barry was unveiled at Franklin Square, Washington D.C in 1914, with the inscription –

JOHN BARRY

The Father of the American Navy

• • •

The US Government gifted and delivered (via the USS Charles S. Sperry) a statue of John Barry to the Irish people in 1956. It was erected on Wexford's Cresent Quay facing the harbor and dedicated on September 16 of that year.

President John F Kennedy, whose forefathers came from County Wexford, proudly displayed Commodore Barry's sword in the Oval Office during his Presidency. On his historic visit to Ireland, President Kennedy laid a wreath at the Wexford monument to John Barry on June 27, 1963.

• • •

In 1981 President Ronald Reagan designated the date of September 13 as Commodore John Barry Day, as a "tribute to one of the earliest and greatest American Patriots."

• • •

Congressman Peter King introduced a resolution in Congress on St. Patrick's Day, March 17, 2005 – which became law on December 22, 2005.

It officially recognizes Commodore John Barry as the First Flag Officer of the U.S. Navy.

• • •

On May 9, 2011, a memorial to Commodore Barry was erected at the U.S. Naval Academy in Annapolis, Maryland.

• • •

Four ships of the United States Navy have been named in honor of Commodore John Barry –

USS Barry, a Bainbridge-class destroyer in 1902

USS Barry, a Clemson-class destroyer in 1920

USS Barry, a Forrest Sherman-class destroyer in 1956

USS Barry, an Arleigh Burke-class guided missile destroyer in 1992

• • •

Much has been said about the friendship of the two greatest naval warriors of the American Revolutionary War – John Paul Jones and John Barry. Even though Jones talked up his credentials and wanted Admiral status for himself, he knew he was hiding a questionable past and he accepted that John Barry was head and shoulders above him both physically and in the qualities that defined leadership of the American Navy. When Jones' remains were discovered in a Paris cemetery in 1905, they were returned to America and buried under the Naval Academy Chapel in Annapolis, Maryland.

Jones' gold sword is there now; bequeathed to Barry, who left it to his great friend Richard Dale after his own death and it was later bequeathed to the Naval Academy.

Up on the Chapel alter is the Holy Bible that once belonged to Commodore John Barry.

Requiescat in Pace

EPILOGUE

Sarah Barry was the perfect widow and never remarried. She continued to foster the tradition of the 'naval family' that she and Commodore Barry had built around her nephews, Patrick Hayes and Michael Hayes, and their offspring. US Navy Captains, Richard Dale and Richard Sommers, had married into the family of John and Sarah Barry. She sold Strawberry Hill in 1805 and lived the rest of her life in Philadelphia. Sarah was a willing and successful investor in ships, cargo and merchant captains. Naval officers flocked to visit her and pay their respect when in port and seek her advice and good counsel. Sarah Barry died in 1831 at the age of seventy-seven and was buried at St. Mary's Church with her husband John and his first wife, Mary.

John's surviving nephew, Patrick Hayes, always regretted not being at his uncle's bedside when he died – he was far away in China at the time and did not return until 1804. Later in life, he accumulated a fleet of merchant ships that plied the Caribbean routes, and his large family maintained very close ties with Sarah Barry. At forty-two years old he was turned down as being too old for naval command, during the 1812 war with Britain. Instead, he went on to serve terms as harbor master and maritime warden of Philadelphia. He died in 1856 at the ripe old age of eighty-six, and he and his wife Betsy are buried alongside the Commodore.

Barry's friend Richard Dale continued his naval service for many years and remained active in the Sea Captain's Club. He died in 1826. The young officers from 'Commodore Barry's Academy' – Stephen Decatur in the 'United Stares': Richard Sommers in the 'Intrepid': Charles Stewart in the 'Constitution' (Old Ironsides) – all served the United States Navy with distinction in the War of 1812. John Kessler and John Brown remained close confidants of Sarah Barry, and they promoted the life achievements of Commodore Barry in magazine articles until their deaths in 1840 and 1833 respectively. Joshua Humphreys built many more ships for the United States Navy and even for Czar Alexander's Russian Navy. He died in 1824 at eighty-six years old. Doctor Rush continued to defend the Commodore's legacy in letter correspondence with the cantankerous ex-President, John Adams, and he remained Sarah's doctor until his death in 1813.

Commodore Barry's uniforms, weapons, logs and such, were auctioned by his heirs in 1939 and most of the collections went to important museums and the Library of Congress. His sword hung in the oval office of President John F. Kennedy from 1961 to 1963, when this descendant of County Wexford, Ireland, navigated the U.S. Navy through a crucial episode of the Cold War. The signal book that Commodore Barry compiled became a standard in the United States Navy.

Commodore John Barry never forgot his humble Irish roots. It is said that he fought for his adopted country with relish against the British Royal Navy, in honor of the countless Irish heroes who had fought in vain to free Ireland.

That freedom was finally won in 1921 when the Irish Free State emerged after 700 years of rebellion.

It happened 118 years after the death of one of the 'Boys of Wexford' – Commodore John Barry.

• • •

** Go to the author's website www.michaelgerardauthor.com for current information on all titles and links to purchase – print, e-Book and audio formats available.

PART TWO

THE IRISH ADMIRALTY

ADMIRAL WILLIAM BROWN
(ALMIRANTE DON GUILLERMO BROWN)

BORN IN FOXFORD
COUNTY MAYO

IRELAND
1777

FOUNDER OF THE ARGENTINE NAVY

"IRISHMEN ARE NOT GOING TO ALLOW ANYBODY TO STOP THEM ON SAINT PATRICK'S DAY. PLAY 'ST. PATRICK'S DAY IN THE MORNING' AS LOUD AS YOU CAN – NOW!

– Admiral William Brown's orders to his pipe and drum players, when he used the music to urge his pinned-down troops to storm gun batteries on Martin Garcia Island, in the River Plate estuary on March 15, 1814 – a battle that eventually led to his great naval victory over the Spanish fleet in the May 14 Battle of Montevideo.

Admiral William Brown

South America showing Plate Estuary inset – Buenos Aires, Colonia, Montevideo and Juncal Island. Martin Garcia Island is SW of Colonia.

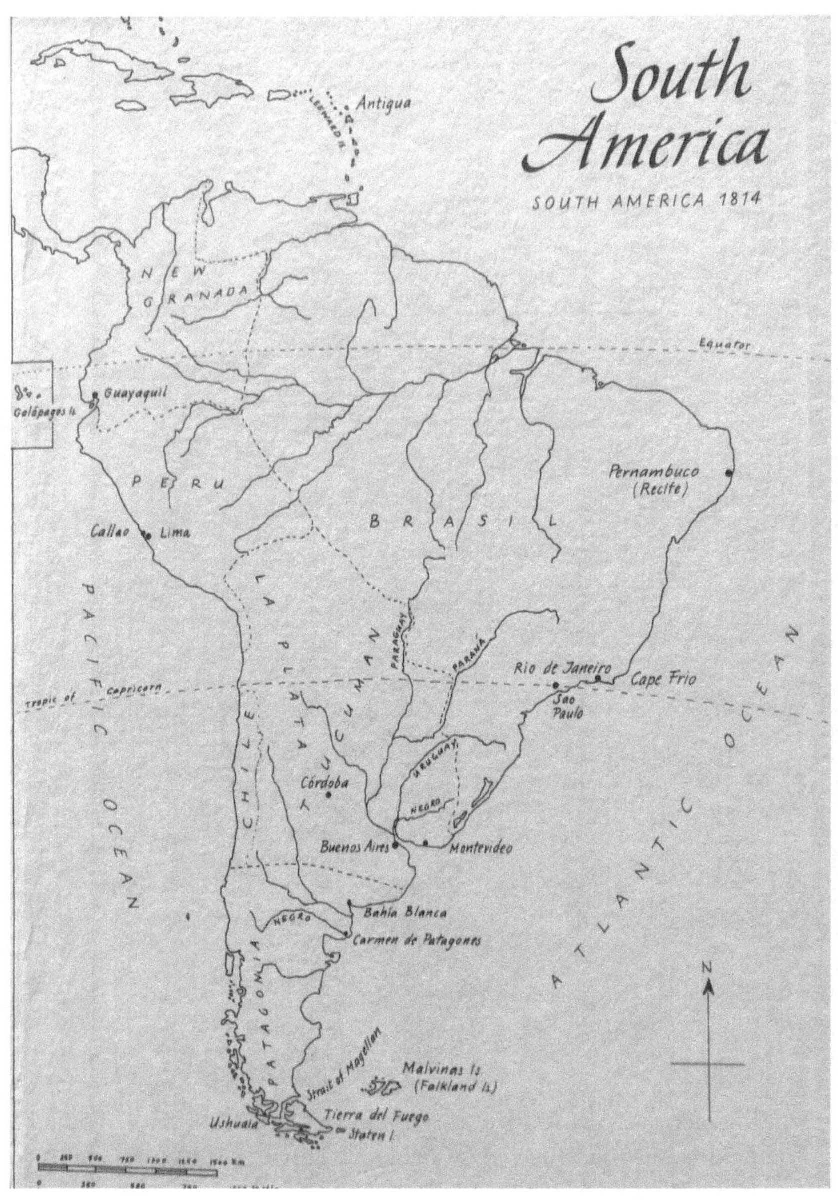

1814 map of South America showing the East and West ports visited by Admiral Brown, Cape Horn and the navigable rivers near Buenos Aires.

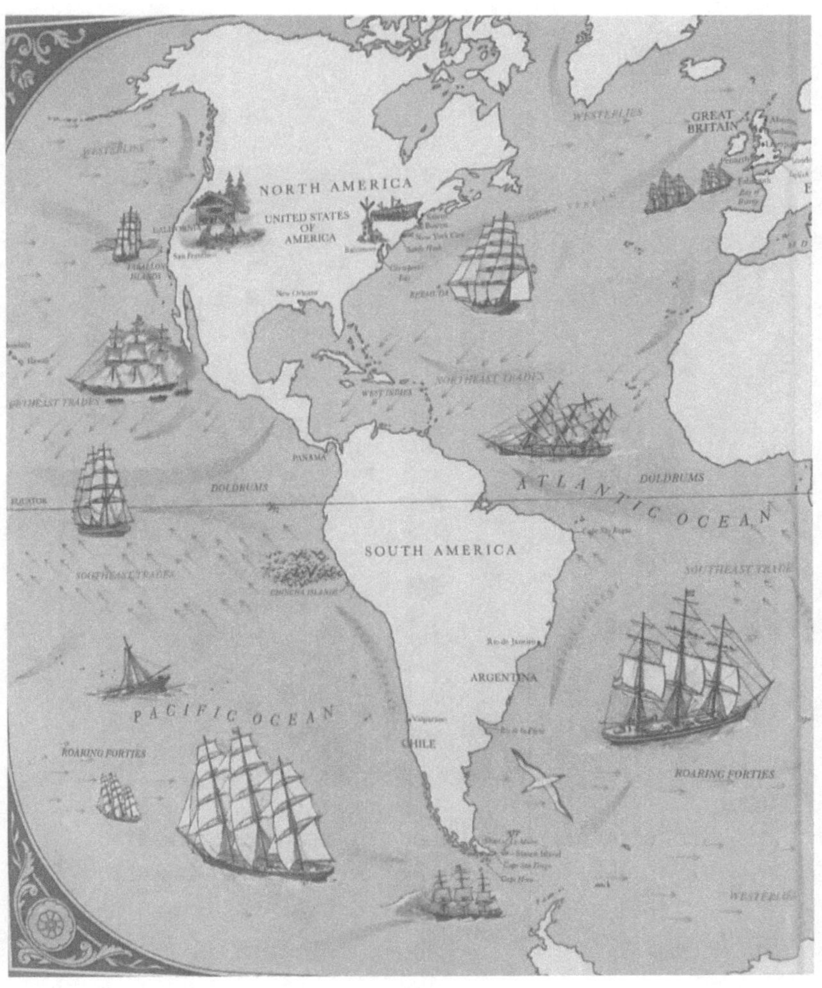

The prevailing winds and currents affecting Admiral Brown's voyages.

Replica of Casa Amarilla, home of Almirante William Brown in Buenos Aires – Argentinian Naval Museum

ACADEMIA NACIONAL DE LA HISTORIA

MEMORIAS
DEL
ALMIRANTE BROWN

PUBLICACION
DE LA COMISION NACIONAL DE HOMENAJE AL
ALMIRANTE GUILLERMO BROWN
EN EL CENTENARIO DE SU MUERTE

BUENOS AIRES
1957

Admiral William Brown wrote his original memoirs in 1857

Ornate grave (green monument) of Almirante Don Guillermo Brown in Recoletta Cemetery, Buenos Aires. Designated a National Monument.

Admiral Brown is revered throughout the region – this monument to him is in Montevideo

Monument to Admiral William Brown in Dublin, Ireland

One of the numerous monuments to Admiral Brown around Argentina

Monument to Admiral William Brown beside the River Moy in his birthplace of Foxford, Co Mayo, Ireland.

CHAPTER ONE

COUNTY MAYO BEGINNINGS

1774 – Foxford (Beal Easa), Co Mayo, Ireland.

The little town of Foxford straddling the mighty River Moy (An Mhuaidh) was a gathering of small stone buildings on either side of the river, many of them being small shops where the shop owners lived on the premises. The Anglican Church of Ireland rectory and chapel dominated the place, along with the barracks for the constabulary and a small contingent of British troops. Foxford was the poor neighbor of Ballina, the big and important river town closer to the Moy Estuary and to Killala Bay, which itself was the gateway to the Atlantic Ocean. The river was navigable to Ballina for smaller ships, the town had docks and warehouses and kept any wealth local to the town. What did move down the river to Foxford were salmon, lots of them, and Foxford had a good fishing reputation among the leisure fishermen of the upper classes.

It was a pleasant May afternoon with a fresh breeze coming off the Ox Mountains, as a pretty peasant girl, Maire O'Breoin, walked alongside the river on her way home with the meager food items her family could afford at the shop. Her long red hair flowed in the breeze, and she stopped to adjust her head scarf. A few 'gentlemen' were fishing, having waded out to their knees into the river to access the important riffles – casting long thin rods whose thinner fishing line made a whooshing sound in the air as they cast. She knew it was the famous Mayfly season, a popular few weeks for the gentry who could indulge in such activities, being that they lived a life of comfort and of plenty. Maire's poor family only ate once a day and her stomach rattled from hunger as she walked. One of the fishermen hooked a fish as she was passing, so she stopped again, this time to watch him work his line in and out as the fish battled to get free. The fight lasted almost ten minutes – the man was able to lead the tiring fish to the shallows and get it into a net that his servant guide had ready. It was a fine big Brown Trout (Breac Donn) and she lingered, as the man struggled to remove the hook. He looked up at her and smiled – "good afternoon to you, pretty Cailin. Would you like a nice brown trout to take home for dinner?"

"Yes please, Sir."

"Well, here you go then." He chopped the flailing trout on the back of the head with his hand and it stopped moving, then he retrieved some old newspapers from his pouch which he used to wrap up the fish and handed it to her. That's a nice two pounder for you."

"Go raibh maith agat" she blurted out in Irish, then remembered herself, "thank you, kind Sir."

Maire skipped her way home with her prize catch. Mother was delighted, and immediately set about cleaning the fish while Maire took advantage of the afternoon breeze to put out the washing to dry on the hedges behind the house. Daddy was always hungry when he came home from the quarry, and he would have a lovely trout dinner this evening. She paid little attention to the donkey cart she saw in the distance coming down the boreen (laneway). When the cart got closer, she noticed that in addition to the driver there was a second man sitting inside the bed of the cart. She still thought little of it as she whistled a jig in her head and thought about the crossroads dance coming up on Saturday night, where she would meet up with Packie Kelly, who was sweet on her. Next thing she knew, the cart stopped in front of their house, so she set the washing basket down and headed to see who the visitors were. A man was shouting in Irish for Mrs. O'Breoin and as Maire rounded the gable she saw her mother at the cart – in obvious distress.

"Oh, Michael, Michael," her mother began to wail.

Her husband Michael was lying prone and deathly pale in the bed of the cart, with white bloodstained bandages wrapped around both of his arms. He was being lifted out of the cart by the two men as the girl arrived, and she knew immediately that he was badly injured. The men were now carrying her father from the cart towards the open cottage door.

The man called out to her in Irish – "Cailin, make a place ready for him on the bed, please."

She rushed into the cabin and threw back the blanket from the bed near the fire so they could set him down quickly. As they laid him down, she saw that her Daddy was indeed alive, and she blessed herself and thanked God. She noticed that he was without his jacket and hat, as she pulled the blanket over him. Mother had composed herself to some degree by now and they were both at his bedside when the leader of the cart men spoke.

"Ma'am, I'm sorry to have to tell you this but Michael had an accident at the quarry earlier. His arms got trapped under a slab of rock when a lifting rope broke. Mr. Mangan's doctor treated him almost immediately after we freed him. He has lost a lot of blood, and both his arms are severely damaged. I'm very sorry, and Mr. Mangan asked me to convey his great sorrow as well."

"Oh, Mother of God," exclaimed mother and daughter – young Maire grasped her mother in time to prevent her from fainting. With the big man's help they got her to a chair where she burst into floods of tears.

The man spoke again as Maire got a wet cloth to mop her mother's brow – "Doctor Walsh was able to stop the bleeding, he applied these bandages, and he gave him some medicine to ease the pain which will make him sleepy. His instructions are to let Micheal rest while supporting his arms as high as you can. Make sure he drinks some water when he is awake. The doctor will come here tomorrow to change the bandages and check on him."

Maire nodded her head in acknowledgement as her mother called out for her Rosary beads. The men began to move towards the door and Maire followed them to the cart.

"We have his hat here, and his jacket too if you want it, but it is all mangled."

"I'd better take it all – oh, Sweet Jesus, look at the arms of the jacket, I'll hide it from my mother. What did the doctor say about his recovery – will he get the use of his arms back?"

"He didn't say. Michael is a tough bird and he'll be right as rein before you know it. We had better be heading back to the quarry now."

Maire hid the jacket behind the reek of turf and went back into the house with the hat. Mother had recovered her composure and was tending to her sleeping husband. She turned as Maire entered and asked about his jacket.

"In their haste they left it at the quarry – they will put it to one side, and I will collect it in the next few days."

"A Ghra (my love) – let us say a decade of the Rosary over your father now."

• • •

The O'Breoin's were a poor family in one of the poorest counties of poor Ireland – where a population that was 85%

Catholic was under the iron fist of the Protestant minority who were agents of the oppressor, Britain. The family's one-room thatched cottage was better than most of their neighbors, being that it sat on two thirds of an acre of decent land that supported one cow, one pig, a few chickens, a small meadow and a garden where they grew potatoes and other vegetables to sustain themselves. The anchor of their life was Michael's job at the quarry – a job that made it possible to pay the high rent to Captain White, the estate manager for the absentee landowner in England. Neither Mary O'Breoin nor her daughter Maire said it out loud, but they both knew that their life was about to change for the worst, as Michael would not be able to earn any wages for a long time. They sat by his bedside till late evening, mostly in silent prayer as he slept, and watched him moan in pain as he tried to move his bandaged arms. They wet his lips with some spring water while their own appetites disappeared – they drank strong tea and fasted alongside Michael. The family bread winner was a crumpled heap on the bed, with bandages covering what was left of his arms.

After a long silence Mrs. O'Breoin spoke to the girl – "What are we going to say to your sister Nora, and her with her own sick child?"

"I will walk over to Baillur to visit her tomorrow or the next day, after the doctor has visited and we know more about the extent of Daddy's injuries. James and Nora are barely managing to feed themselves and their two young children, they cannot help us – we will have to figure how to get by till Daddy is able to work again."

"A Stor, go to bed now, I will sit up with Michael. You can take over when you wake up."

"First I'll take in the clothes that should be dry by now, we will probably have rain overnight."

Maire's cot in the corner of the room gave her no respite – she tossed and turned for several hours till she got up to relieve her mother while it was still dark. Daddy was by now struggling even more with the pain as the effects of the medicine wore off. He was awake enough that they became concerned with his attempts to move his arms – young Maire had to tell him about his accident and plead with him to keep his injured arms still. Despite the pain that was visible on his face he indicated that he understood and was remarkably calm under the circumstances. They managed to get him to sip a few spoonsful of warm tea and then some chicken soup. His eyes were full of worry and full of questions. They assured him that he was doing well and that the doctor was coming to check on him the next day. Morning broke while her mother was asleep in the corner and Maire slipped out quietly to care for the livestock and collect a few eggs. She boiled one that she mixed in a cup with a little butter and salt, which she was feeding to Daddy when her mother got up. They made idle meaningless conversation for Michael's benefit, to show him that everything was normal, while their minds raced in all directions.

Doctor Walsh arrived in his horse and trap about 11a.m., a short middle-aged man with glasses perched on the end of his nose and he carried his doctor's leather satchel to Michael's bedside. The women stood off to the side, silently clutching their rosary beads, awaiting his instructions. They had a boiling kettle sitting on the hob and had a basin of hot water and two clean towels in front of the doctor moments after he asked for them. When he unwrapped the bandages, Maire had to be strong for her mother's sake, as she became visibly weak at the sight of the Michael's black and blue mangled arms. The doctor added some liquid to the basin and gently dabbed the arms with a hot cloth to clean the wounds while Michael moaned in obvious pain during the cleaning process. Then the doctor gently took one damaged arm at a time and used both of his own hands to feel along the arm – obviously assessing the damage as he moved along. He then placed two wooden splints on each arm from wrist to elbow, bandaged them quite tightly in turn and gave Michael two spoonsful of some dark liquid out of a bottle. Motioning Mrs. O'Breoin to follow, he exited the cottage followed by mother and daughter, and strode to his trap, laying his open bag on the step.

"Mrs. O'Breoin, your husband is lucky to be alive and lucky not to have lost his limbs. He has broken bones in the wrist and forearm of both arms. They will take a long time to heal, hopefully the bones will stay in alignment and will heal completely – these splints must stay in place for at least six weeks. Take this bottle and give him two spoonsful about this same time every day – it will keep him mildly sedated, but you must also convince him to keep his arms very still for the next few weeks. The more rigid the arms the better the likelihood that the bones will stay aligned and heal that way. I cannot be sure how much use of his arms he will regain but they will never be the same again. I must tell you that he will not be able to return to the work he was doing – maybe Mr. Mangan can give him a different job when his arms are healed. I will suggest this to him in my report and ask that he finds him something. I will come back in a week and gradually come at longer intervals after that until he is on the mend. Mr. Mangan is paying for my services – do not worry about that part. Again, please accept my heartfelt sorrow but it could have been much worse. Do you have any questions before I go?"

Mother looked like she hadn't understood what she had just been told, so Maire answered.

"Thank you, Doctor, for all you have done for my father so far. I understand everything you said, and I will explain it in more detail to my parents later – we will follow your instructions. This accident has deprived us of the family bread winner, and it will cause us terrible hardship – but we are tough, and we will survive. Thank you for your promise to come back to treat him during the coming weeks."

With that he said goodbye and drove away.

The next few days were very hard on the three of them while Michael was confined to bed. Mother took over the duties of helping him constantly and Maire did everything else – caring for the animals, carrying in turf from the reek, walking into the town for the few items they could afford to buy – she did quite a lot of the cooking and cleaning also. She retrieved the jacket and cut off the mangled bloody sheeves above the elbows before washing it – she wanted to throw it away, but they had so little clothes she dared not. Her sister had heard the news of the accident by the time Maire was able to visit her – she assured Nora that they had everything under control and told her to concentrate on taking care of her own family. James promised to come over with his scythe and cut the little field of hay when Maire decided it was ready. By the fourth day Michael was able to leave the bed and sit at the fire with pillows supporting his bandaged arms. He was in a lot of pain despite the medicine and was upset that he would not be able to work for a long time – they had no savings to fall back on. The quarry owner, Mr. Mangan, arrived on that fourth day, after Michael was up out of bed. He seemed to understand how the accident was decimating the family and even though he was not obliged to do anything, he showed his generous side. He handed over a full month's wages for Michael and promised to find a suitable job for him when his health allowed. Maire spoke up and said she wanted to find some work to help the family – he said there was no suitable work for her at the quarry and suggested that she might be able to get some housekeeping work. He promised to help find her a position – even mentioned that he thought one of the local Church of Ireland ministers was looking for someone – he would inquire and put in a word for her.

After he departed, the women were more optimistic for the future – at least they now had enough money to get by for one to two months and Maire fully expected that with Mr. Mangan's help she would get a position locally that would bring in some extra money.

True to his word, a messenger brought a letter from Mr. Mangan two days later. Maire opened it excitedly to find that a housekeeper/cook job was available at Vicar Smith's house, subject to a satisfactory interview with the vicar's wife. She was to go there on Monday morning, ready and prepared to go to work. Maire decided immediately that she would still go to the Saturday night crossroads dance, but she would have to have a serious talk to Packie about their future.

As usual, she was one of the most popular girls there and easily the prettiest. The weather was good and there was a fiddle player, concertina player and a lad on the bodhran. She danced jigs and reels with many different lads but finished off the evening doing a two-handed reel with Packie. As he walked her home in the moonlight, she reminded him that they needed to have a heart-to-heart talk, being that her life had now been turned upside down by her father's accident. They stopped at the holy well where there was a nice stone seat. Packie could sense that bad news was coming and wanted to get the first word in.

"I understand that your situation has changed – but shur – we're young and have plenty of time – I'll wait for you."

"You're very sweet Packie but it is not that simple. Daddy will never be able to work again and that means that I must become the breadwinner for our family – there is only me, as Nora has her own struggles and mother must spend most of her time looking after Daddy. You are the third son in your family, and you will not get the land – it is too small to sub-divide."

"But –," – she put her finger over his lips and told him to hush until she was finished.

"We talked about this before, remember – about us immigrating to Amerikay, away from this troubled land where we have no future, especially with these cursed Penal Laws that are making life for all of us Catholics even more miserable. I cannot leave home now, I must abandon my plans, our plans – marriage is out of the picture for me – I must take care of my parents. Because of that, I release you from all promises made and I ask you to release me from those promises also."

Packie was speechless and began to sob.

"Packie, you should still go to Amerikay and find a better life – but you will have to do it without me. Go on your own or find someone else to go with – I'm fine with that, I'm sorry, but that is the only way forward. I am starting a housekeeping job on Monday at the Vicar's home. Between the job and all the work that I must do at home I will not be coming to the Saturday night dances anymore."

He was still sobbing as they embraced, and they sobbed together. Several minutes passed, she had to explain it all again to him before it finally sunk in.

"I need to get home, Packie – I'll be alright on my own."

"No, I will walk with you – it's such a beautiful night that one would never think there was so much trouble in our lives and in our country."

When they arrived at her house they had a last embrace. She stood waving as he walked down the boreen, then he turned around – "I'll see you at Mass, won't I?"

"Definitely."

Maire O'Breoin's life plan is altered by her father's accident, but being a pretty girl gives her an ace card that she can and will use to her advantage.

CHAPTER TWO

LOSING HER SURNAME AND HER VIRTUE

Maire was neatly dressed and on time on Monday morning when she knocked on the door of the Vicarage. An older lady opened the door, one of the Kellys from out the Swinford road, she thought.

"Come in a Stor (my love). I am Margaret Kelly, and I will tell Her Ladyship you are here, you're Maire, right? Let me say first that we are all praying night and day for your father's speedy recovery. Follow me into the drawing room – wait here and Her Ladyship will be right with you."

"Yes, I am Maire. Thanks for your prayers, I will tell him."

Mrs. Smith came bustling in a few minutes later, a younger woman dressed in nice clothes. When she spoke, her accent was not an Irish one – she sounded like some Scottish people Maire had heard speak in town. She spoke to Maire in English.

"My, you are a pretty girl, probably too pretty for this kind of work. Mr. Mangan told us the story of your father's unfortunate accident. I hope he is progressing well and on the road to recovery."

"Thank you, Ma'am, he is doing better but it will be a long road."

"Firstly, we must do something about your name. I cannot pronounce your name. With the help of Margaret Kelly, we have come up with an English version that I think my children will be happier with – Mary Brune – good. Now that we have got a pronounceable name, and with you having a decent command of English, I can tell you that I do need a governess to care for my two young children, and to help Mrs. Kelly whom you already met. There is not much governess material around this poor unfortunate area of Mayo and Mr. Mangan speaks highly of your family. Your main attributes are being young and pretty, you can speak English, and you have a nice smile. How much education do you have, my dear?"

"I went to school until I was twelve – then the Penal Laws forced me to leave. I loved school and I learned how to read English – I read books any chance I get. I don't speak English as well as my native Irish, but I will improve as I get to speak it more."

"Ah yes, the Penal laws. Those of us in the ministry of the Lord are in favor of easing those laws, I want you to know, but as loyal subjects we must wait for government enlightenment.

Do you think you can cope with a ten-year-old girl and a seven-year-old boy?"

"I do indeed Ma'am, and I am happy to help Mrs. Kelly with household work. I am ready to start work immediately if that is your wish."

"I will start you on a trial basis, eight o'clock to six o'clock every day except Sunday. Go to the kitchen and help Mrs. Kelly till the children return from riding lessons. We have two other servants, an upstairs maid and a chamber maid, so you will not have to do any of that work. You will address me as Lady Smith or Your Ladyship. I will call you when the children return and introduce you to them. That will be all."

"Yes, Your Ladyship."

Maire wasn't happy about her name being changed but she knew she had to accept it. She had no idea what a governess was supposed to do but she was ready for the challenge. The children returned two hours later and Lady Smith called her in to meet them. The girl looked her up and down while their mother explained the duties. Much of the detail was over Mary's head but she realized immediately that the first and best step was to get the children to like her – especially the older girl who acted quite grown up. Maire paid compliments on Miss Lilly's hair and dress, and on Master George's height.

Over the following months Mary formed a bond with the children. She asked them to help her with her English and in return she would teach them about Irish legends and take them to fairy forts and other archaeological sites nearby.

Mary's English improved greatly, and she learned the words and expressions that were popular with the ruling class. Thankfully her Ladyship was open minded and had an interest in Irish culture – she wasn't like many of the ruling class that regarded the Irish as ignorant heathens. Mary was given some hand me down clothes that allowed her to improve her wardrobe, and the family sometimes took her along to their social events nearby – picnics along the Moy River where the men fished and smoked, while she supervised games among the children. On many occasions she heard Her Ladyship singing her praises to other ladies.

Of course, she saw the opulent life that the upper classes enjoyed, something Mary could never aspire to. Mrs. Kelly often let her take quality leftover food home that she shared with her parents. Michael continued to make slow progress and Doctor Walsh replaced the heavy splints with lighter ones. After eight months the damaged arms finally started to resemble normal arms again. Her father's biggest problem was with his fingers – they did not recover the range of motion that was hoped for. Michael could only grasp things by using his two hands together to lift small items and food – Dr. Walsh devised some exercises for Micheal to perform every day in an effort to continue the healing process. Mary viewed them as a way to keep Michael's spirits up rather than any real improvement – they all prayed fervently for a miracle. Young Mary went to early Mass and rarely saw Packie. Eventually he accepted the obvious fact that she was lost to him, and he found a girl in another village to fulfill his dream of going to Amerikay. The pair sailed out of Ballina for Liverpool, where they boarded a bigger ship to the New World.

By the one-year anniversary of Daddy's accident, Mary accepted the inevitable – that her father would never work again and that she was to be a spinster, looking after her aging parents. It came as a shock to her when Her Ladyship announced that Lilly would soon be going to some type of finishing school in England, and Mary knew that the boy, Charles, would soon follow her. While she was digesting this information, Her Ladyship hit her with a broadside. The Vicar had accepted a post in England that was near the schools that Miss Lilly and Master Charles were going to attend.

"Don't worry my dear, it will not happen yet for a few months. Our replacement here will probably have children also, and I will personally recommend that they continue to employ you."

One evening that autumn Mary overheard the vicar telling his wife that his replacement was to be someone from Dublin who was bringing their own governess with them. They wondered out loud how and when they would tell Mary – she was devastated. She was already wracking her brains trying to think what she would do, when a week later Her Ladyship officially told her that she would soon be out of a job. That evening she told her parents the sad news.

Her mother tried to put on an optimistic face. "A Stor

– God is good. Something will turn up, I'm sure. Let us pray tonight to the Lord and ask Him to deliver us."

Mary was fine about praying but she knew that she had to do something to help herself. Mr. Mangan had come by their house a few times and saw plainly that Michael could never again work any job at the quarry. He inquired about Mary and told her parents that his door was always open. Mary decided that she would put his generosity to the test again. She was granted time off to visit him at the quarry office on the pretext that there was inside work there for a woman. The day she went there Mr. Mangan was meeting with a very official looking man, and she turned away to wait outside. He saw her and gestured to her to come in.

"Hello Mary, how are your parents? You are sporting an unusual sad face today – what is wrong, pray tell?"

She blurted out her predicament amid tears. She asked if there was any suitable work there for her. He stroked his beard and said he would think about it – but that quarry work was hard and heavy and not suited for a refined girl like Mary.

The other gentleman spoke up. "Young lady, I am a collector of revenue for the government, and I am here with Mr. Mangan on official business. Most of my work is in County Mayo and I recently decided to rent a house here in Foxford. I am a keen fisherman, and the River Moy is my favorite river in all of Ireland. My house is in a wonderful spot, right on the river – but I confess that I am already tired of looking after myself and I need a housekeeper. Would you be interested in that job?"

"I need work to afford care for my parents and there are very few jobs around here suitable for a woman – as you just heard Mr. Mangan say. I am indeed willing to be your housekeeper."

"Excellent. Can you come round to visit me on Sunday afternoon – I assume you are off Sunday. I will write the address on this piece of paper – do you know where that is?"

"Yes indeed. It's a grand stretch of river along there – is it the house with the entrance between two tall hedges?"

"That's it – I call it Moy House now – come about 4 o'clock – my name is Mr. Browne."

Mr. Mangan was delighted – "Mary, Mr. Browne will be able to pay you well – with all the tax money he takes from me."

"Please don't scare her off, Mr. Mangan. Mary, I'm so glad you dropped in today while I was here, and I commend you for the courage to come in here asking for work."

• • •

On Sunday afternoon Mary knocked at the door of Moy House and Mr. Browne immediately opened it and invited her in.

"I knew you would be punctual, and I was listening out for you. Welcome to my humble abode."

It was a stone house, not large by the usual standards of the gentry but magnificent compared to the hovels that Mary and all her relatives lived in. He gave her a quick tour of the downstairs – drawing room, dining room, kitchen and small sitting room with big windows that offered a view of the river. They finished up in that sitting room and he motioned her to a chair.

"Allow me to apologize for the unkempt state of my house. Do you like it overall and could you work here?"

"It's lovely – there is nothing that a woman's touch could not put right. I love the view and I love all the paintings – are they family portraits?"

"They are family members of the owner of this house, not my family. He has moved to a warmer climate because of his health. I love the view also – just sitting here watching the river, and when the weather is good it's even nicer to sit outside close to the water. I'm watching the fish, and the fish are watching me. The Browne family, my greater family, re-located to the Mayo-Galway area from England in the 1600's and are now scattered over quite a bit of the country. It may surprise you to know that we were Catholic back then. The Penal Laws affected us in much the same way as they have affected you – my forefathers were forced to convert to the Protestant Church of Ireland faith if they wanted to hold onto their property."

"I had no idea that any of the families in the big houses were ever Catholic, please excuse my ignorance. Mr. Browne, I would be happy to be your housekeeper, and I should be able to start very soon. Her Ladyship is keeping me on for the present but has said that I can leave with a week's notice if I find something else – so I could start a week tomorrow."

"Excellent. To begin with I will pay you what you earn now – until I see how it all goes. Food and other provisions will be in place for Monday, and I am open to any suggestions you may have that will make the house more comfortable. I like to eat breakfast at 9 a.m., lunch at 1.30 p.m. when I am not away, and dinner at 6.30 p.m. I release most of the trout I catch but I like to feast on the odd one."

"Please understand, Sir, I am not a fancy cook – and I have never cooked some trout on my own."

"Don't worry Mary, I like plain and simple food and I will show you how to cook trout."

With that Mary took her leave. Next day she gave her one week's notice at the vicarage and on the following Saturday she said her goodbyes to the Smith family. The children both gave her a hug and she was given a few shillings as a going away present. Mary had waited until after her interview to tell her parents about her new job. Her mother had been frantic with worry about their future and immediately gave all the credit to God.

"Didn't I say that the Lord would take care of us. Michael, haven't I been praying night, noon and morning for a miracle and it has happened – praise be to God."

"You have certainly been praying loud, to be sure," he chimed.

"Mother, I have been doing my share to help God on this. Daddy, I went to see Mr. Mangan at the quarry to ask his help in getting a job – he was asking about you and sends you his best wishes. Anyway, this other man was there visiting him at the time who took a back seat for a few minutes while Mr. Mangan invited me inside. The man heard me asking about any job prospects, and shur, didn't he pipe up that he had recently moved to Foxford from Athlone and was looking for a housekeeper. Before I knew it, he asked me to come work for him – he lives in that nice stone house right on the river near the weir – the one with the hedges at the gate."

"Yes, I know it – a doctor who was here before Doctor Walsh lived there for many years. What does this new gentleman do?"

"He's some kind of government official who goes round to visit businesses like the quarry. He decided to move here from Athlone because he loves fishing on the Moy."

"What's his name, does he have children that you have to take care of?"

"His name is Mr. Browne, and he is in his forties I would say. There is just him – he wants me to look after him and his house, and he's paying me the same wages that the vicar paid."

"Maith an Cailin (Good Girl)."

• • •

Mary was up bright and early Monday morning. Before heading off to her new job she decided to pop some fresh soda bread, butter, and a few freshly laid eggs in her basket – just in case. She arrived at Moy House a little after eight to find no sign of life. After a few knocks, a sleepy head appeared through the open upstairs window.

"Mary, I'm frightfully sorry I overslept – the front door is open. Let yourself in and start wherever you think best – I will be down presently."

The house was in disarray and Mr. Browne had not brought in any fresh food. She concentrated on the kitchen area and was able to get the fire started quickly from the hot raked coals in the ash hole. Dirty dishes were moved to one side so that she could clean the table and make space for what she already knew would be his breakfast – her boiled eggs, soda bread and hot tea. By the time he ambled into the kitchen she had a pot of tea made, sliced the soda bread, and she was ready to boil two eggs. Amongst profound apologies for his mess, he complimented her on her immediate progress.

"I failed to complete my tasks and you have bailed me out – thank you Mary."

"Shur, I have some bachelor uncles myself and I know what they are like. I assume you have egg cups – do you want me to set up your breakfast place in the dining room, Sir?"

"No, I prefer to eat at the small table in the room facing the river – I call it the breakfast room. I will get the egg cups, salt, some plates and cutlery if you can start the eggs. This is wonderful."

Before long Mr. Browne was sipping his tea and munching on soda bread while waiting for the eggs. He was as happy as a lark. While he was eating, Mary got the boiling kettle and washed up all the accumulated dirty dishes, then used the hot water to scald the kitchen surfaces, following up with the dresser where plates and such lived. By the time he came back into the kitchen to speak with her, the room was looking much better.

"I almost turned around, thinking I was in the wrong room. The woman's touch you mentioned has hit this kitchen with a vengeance – what an amazing difference. Breakfast was delightful – it was so thoughtful of you and sensible to figure that I would be unprepared. I was reading Greek classics till very late last night and you rescued me – please tell your chickens how much I liked their eggs."

Mary blushed but knew he was genuinely pleased with the first meal she provided him. "Can you show me what the sideboards and presses hold – and where utensils and cooking pots are kept. Then please show me where the well is and the washing tub, the yard layout, turf and woodshed. What do you want me to work at today, Sir?"

"Clean all you can downstairs. Shortly I will be going up the street to my stable boy for my horse and I will be away all day – back in time for dinner. Here is three shillings – go and get whatever provisions you need for the house, and I leave it up to you to buy something for my dinner. Please do not overtax yourself trying to do too much – it took quite a while to make all this mess and it will take some time to get it right again."

They did a detailed tour of the lower floor and the outside

– the spring water well, sheds, the clothesline and even the 'privy' – what Mary called the cesspit, near the river's edge. Then he departed and Mary could feel more relaxed – she made herself a mug of tea and walked out to the riverbank, where she sat for several minutes watching the mighty river rolling by and listening to the birds. After that it was back to work, and she was happy that nobody was around to bother her. In the early afternoon she walked into the town with money in her purse. She was careful not to arouse any gossip with her spending, spreading her custom over a few shops and limiting herself to what she could easily carry home. Then she did a lot of dusting and wiping before she hung a pot over the fire containing a slow cooking stew of mutton and vegetables, which wafted a great smell around the house as the late afternoon wore on. Mr. Browne returned at 5.30p.m. and heaped praise on her for how much she had improved the look of the downstairs in just one day – and he had to lift the lid of the pot to see for himself what was giving out such a wonderful smell. He asked her to note in a ledger what items were bought and how much was spent – telling her to store the change in a jar for ongoing expenses.

While he ate, she continued with her cleaning until he called her in.

"Mary, I must compliment you for two wonderful meals today. There is more food here than I can eat and I will be away again tomorrow and each day until Friday. Please take the rest of this great stew home to share with your family.

Tonight, I will attempt to tidy the upstairs area enough to save my embarrassment when I show you around that area tomorrow."

After breakfast the next day Mary got the upstairs tour. His bedroom was the largest room and had a dressing room off to one side where his washing basin sat with his shaving tools at the ready, plus a kettle stand for his hot water. It was still a bit of a mess, but he had made the effort to remove bedclothes from his bed and had them plus pillowcases in a pile for washing. The second bedroom was smaller and had a small bed plus a chair and table. The third room was a small empty room. All the rooms needed dusting and sweeping – all the furniture needed wiping and polishing. He then set off to get his horse, leaving Mary in charge of the house.

• • •

Over the following months Mary Brune settled comfortably into her new job. She got to know Mr. Browne's habits, the food he preferred, and he began to tell her more about himself – she was now addressing him as Mr. George. He told her about the titles that some of his relatives had, the Big Houses they lived in and all the land they owned. His ancestors had intermarried with the native Irish in County Mayo, and according to him they would have remained Catholic if they hadn't been forced to convert. She was overawed by all this information

– she chose not to share it with her parents. Her father was steadily slipping into worse health and hardly left his bed. Her mother was worn out caring for him and worrying about him – her sister had sickly children and was barely able to manage her own family. That left Mary working herself to death trying to keep the family going from the wages she earned.

She took Mr. Browne into her confidence and told him of the worsening home situation. He seemed keen to engage her in conversation and he started talking about how the families of the gentry forced their children into marriages of convenience – disregarding the wishes of the bride and groom.

"Why didn't that happen to you Mr. George?"

"Oh, it did. I was forced into a match with an older woman from another family because it suited my father's purposes. It has made me very unhappy, but I'm trapped in the system. My family has a lot of influence with the government and if I do not conform to their wishes, I will lose this job. Leasing this house in Foxford has become my escape."

Mary had assumed that he was a bachelor and was shocked by this news but concealed her shock.

"Did you have any children with your wife?"

"No – we have led very separate lives. In the public eyes and in the eyes of my family we are married, and that is all that matters to them."

Mr. George kept reminding Mary how pretty she was and how much he enjoyed her company. She was also young and naive, and she allowed her loneliness to cloud her better judgement. The Irish gentry or aristocracy were in a separate and higher class than peasants like Mary. The usual contact between the two classes was as servant and master – and Mary knew this rule. Gradually though, he was winning her heart with all this revealing talk about his personal life, and his compliments. When bad weather hit that winter, he offered that she could stay overnight in the spare room, and she accepted. This slippery slope led to her becoming intimate with him shortly afterwards. In January of 1776 Mary's father's health took a turn for the worst, and he died in February. Her mother was a lost soul without Michael, and she followed him to the grave a month later. Mr. George helped Mary through this traumatic time both financially and emotionally. She stayed more frequently at his house during this time and their relationship deepened, despite her reservations about the barriers that society had placed between them. He suggested that she end the lease of the family small holding, and instead move to Moy House – she accepted.

By Christmas of 1776 she was pregnant with his child.

"Mr. George, I cannot go to Mass and face all the stares, the questions, and especially the Priest. When do you think we might be able to get married?"

"Mary, you know I cannot divorce my wife. We will have to maintain our current situation until my circumstances change. I will organize for a midwife to come from another town when it is time."

When Mary gave birth in June to a son they called him William. She wanted the boy's surname to be Browne, knowing that his life prospects would be better with the name of his father. George said his family would never allow that and he suggested a compromise.

"Let's settle on something between this Brune name and the Browne name – let's drop the 'e' and call him William Brown. Later, when my family situation allows it, we will only have to add back the 'e' on the end of his name."

Mary accepted the compromise, and Mr. George was agreeable to her raising the child as a Catholic.

She had lost her Gaelic name and now she had lost the chance to give her son the aristocratic family name of his father. Mary had given her love to this man who was not prepared to fully repay that love to her, or indeed to acknowledge his own flesh and blood in name – yet she was willing to continue being his concubine in the hope that her son would somehow earn a reprieve and be able to make something out of his life.

CHAPTER THREE

A FAMILY ADOPTION OF SORTS

Ireland was in a period of relative calm during the 1770's and 1780's – there were no active Rebellions against the British authorities going on. That was probably due the fact that the Penal Laws had broken the spirit of the people. Mayo was one of the poorest and most backward counties in the country – where keeping fed and staying alive took precedence over worrying about sexual liaisons between the peasants and the gentry. Most peasants never travelled past the boundaries of their own village and even the privileged classes were severely restricted by the dreadful state of the roads and the dangers of attack by highwaymen. Mary's sister Nora and her family had been evicted from their home and had moved twenty miles away to live with a relative of her husband. This situation helped insulate Mary from prying eyes and questions. Mr. George continued with his revenue collection work and was frequently away, but she knew little of where he went. She assumed that he had to put in regular appearances in Athlone, where he said his wife lived – a distant place in Mary's world.

Life was relatively good for her and in nineteen months she had a second son, Michael, followed by a daughter named Mary a little over a year later. By early 1782 she was the mother of three children under the age of five. Mr. George went away as usual on a Tuesday morning in April, saying he had to go to Dublin for special revenue meetings and would be gone for a week. That week stretched into two and then three – Mary began to get worried that he may have deserted them or that he had fallen ill. As the clock ticked away the weeks, the situation at Moy House began to get desperate – Mary had rummaged through Mr. George's desk and found some coins that helped the family to buy food.

A month to the day that Mr. George had departed, a man on horseback arrived at the house. He was peasant Irish like her but well dressed and able to converse in both Irish and English. He identified himself as Joe Roney, the steward for Mr. George's relatives, and he had come from Westport to speak to Mary on an important family matter. She invited him into the house, and they went to Mr. George's favorite place, the river room, where he asked her to sit down before addressing the reason for his visit.

"Ma'am, I have been sent here to report to you on important Browne family matters and assess your situation. Mr. George Browne was hit with a bilious fever some weeks ago while in Dublin and is gravely ill. His extended family in Westport recently became aware of your existence and that of your children, fathered by him and living here in Foxford with you, their mother. I trust the children are well?"

"Yes Sir, they are well – hungry but well. I heard what you said – is Mr. George alright and will he recover?"

"Sadly, I must confirm that Mr. George is deceased – I am sorry to tell you this. The Browne family recognizes that they have a duty to his children and to yourself as their mother, but it is a delicate situation. I assume that he told you that he was already married – is that correct?"

Mary had been expecting bad news and accepted it without emotion. She nodded and he continued – "His wife, now his widow, did not know of this second family in Foxford and she wants nothing to do with you or your children. However, his cousin, the head of the Browne family clan, wants to do the right thing on behalf of the family. The lease for this house was not renewed and it must be vacated within two weeks. The family wants to relocate you to a cottage nearer to Westport where you will continue to care for the children. Once you are settled there, we will commence discussions on their future and your future. Is this agreeable to you?"

"Sir, as you can see, I am about to be destitute, without a home and unable to care for my children. I have no choice but to accept your offer to secure both the children's wellbeing and my own. I plead on their behalf that you, and the Browne family that you represent, are earnest in their representations."

"I can assure you that is the case, Ma'am. Furthermore, I shall go into the village and return with provisions to sustain you and the children while you await this relocation. The family wish to accomplish this move with quiet discretion and I beseech you to do the same."

• • •

A little over a week later a nice carriage plus a second horse and cart arrived at Moy House, accompanied by four laborers, and by Joe, the steward, on horseback. Mary, her three children and her meager possessions were transported to the Westport area. Mr. George's possessions were put into a separate crate and carried away at the same time – that crate stayed in the cart when Mary was deposited at her new home. She was provided with a temporary servant girl to help her with housework and the children – the house was already stocked with food. Her new cottage was small but comfortable and the children made the transition with ease. While still grieving for Mr. George, Mary was glad to be in a place where nobody knew her story and her shame. Every waking hour was consumed looking after the children and she wanted to keep as low a profile as she could – knowing that there were very serious issues at stake for the children's future.

It was two weeks before Joe Roney came back to visit Mary at the cottage and to check on the children. Measurements were taken to establish the clothing needs of mother and children – and Joe came back again two weeks later with a trunk full of nice clothes. At that time, he shared more details with Mary of what was to happen going forward. Lady Browne of Westport had decided to take the children under her wing and make sure they would be raised in a manner that was acceptable to the Browne family. She wanted to meet the children, and a date was set for a carriage to collect them all for that meeting. On the appointed day the carriage took them to a very large house, and they were deposited on the front lawn. William and Michael were encouraged to run about with some other little boys while Mary cared for her young daughter. Twenty minutes later Mary and the children were ushered into the front room where they were met by a nurse and a doctor.

William was examined first – they poked and prodded him, examined his features, his hair and his teeth. Once he was examined, a woman brought him forward to meet Lady Catherine Browne, who spoke some words to him. She was shocked that the boy had just a few words of English and they were forced to proceed in Irish, with the servant translating. The examination process was repeated with his younger brother, Michael. Finally, Mary herself and her daughter were told to approach the seated Lady, who first inquired whether she could speak English. When Mary said yes, the Lady addressed her.

"Miss Brown, the circumstances we all find ourselves in are unfortunate. The behavior that you and Mr. George

Browne engaged in is deplorable – I will say no more than that. However, you seem to have two fine healthy boys here and by all accounts your daughter is also healthy. The boy's features are in keeping with the Browne male features, even if diluted with peasant blood and red hair, but we will do our duty to turn them into loyal citizens of the realm. That is why we have rescued you from the clutches of poverty and ignorance. I am shocked that the boys are only able to speak their native Irish tongue, and this must be corrected before they are deemed fit to attend suitable schooling. Starting immediately, I will have a tutor sent to your cottage three times a week to instruct them in English and in proper etiquette. Your girl child will get the same instruction when old enough. A carriage will take you home now and my steward, Joe Roney, will continue to be your point of contact. In due course he will have further instructions for you, and papers to sign that will constitute a legal record of our dealings. Good day to you."

Mary was not invited to speak and was dismissed at that point.

In the months that followed, the material needs of Mary and her family were satisfied but she was kept in the dark about long-term plans. Tutors did come to the cottage as promised and began instruction in the English language. The boys were intelligent and by the time William was six and a half and Michael was five – they had enough English to carry on a conversation. That was when another meeting was organized whereby the family met again with her Ladyship, and this time the two boys were also introduced to her Ladyship's father – an older gentleman who was visiting from England. He peppered them with questions and told them stories about the tall ships of the Royal Navy. Even to Mary, who was kept at a distance during the encounter, the old man seemed to take a liking to the boys, especially to William, who engaged the man in lengthy conversation. Several months later they were taken again to meet the same old gentleman – this time he was dressed in a very ornate uniform, and they were told that he was an Admiral in the Royal Navy. William was wide-eyed and told the Admiral that he wanted to wear a uniform like that someday.

• • •

The old man was Admiral Lord Richard Howe, born in 1726, who entered the Royal Navy in 1740 and quickly rose through the ranks. He took part in the 1759 Battle of Quiberon Bay as a captain, where victory ended the prospect of a French invasion of Britain or Ireland. In 1763 he was appointed to the Board of Admiralty as Senior Naval Lord, Commander of the mediterranean fleet in 1770 and Commander-in-Chief of the North American Station in 1776, as Vice-Admiral. His fleet provided support to the Redcoat land army commanded by his younger brother, General William Howe, when the

British captured the Colonist capital of Philadelphia in 1777 during the American Revolutionary War.

From 1778 to 1782 he was out of the service because of disagreements with Prime Minister Lord North's government, returning as Viscount Howe to command the Channel Fleet in 1782 – at which time he was promoted to a full Admiral. After commanding the Relief of Gibraltar, he became First Lord of the Admiralty in 1783, resigning again in 1788 during Pitt's government. A major dispute with Spain brought him back into the service to command the Royal Navy in 1790, followed by command of the Channel Fleet in 1793 during the French Revolutionary Wars. This command culminated in victory over the French fleet at the battle named the Glorious First of June, in 1794, after which he was promoted to Admiral of the Fleet in 1796.

His marriage produced three daughters and no sons. His second daughter, Catherine, became Lady Altamont when she married John Browne, Third Earl of Altamont, Westport, Co. Mayo, and this brought the Admiral regularly to Ireland, where Catherine introduced him to young William Brown and his brother Michael: the illegitimate children of Mr. George Browne, a cousin of her husband.

• • •

After their interactions with Admiral Howe, the Brown brothers were ferried back to the cottage and their daily life continued as before. Shortly after that, Joe Roney came by to tell Mary that it was time to proceed with discussions about the children's future, and she used this occasion to ask him more about the Admiral who gave so much attention to her boys.

"That is Admiral Lord Howe, first Lord of the Admiralty – the most important man in the Royal Navy. Lady Catherine, or should I say Lady Altamont, is his daughter, and it is Her Ladyship who enticed the Admiral to meet your boys. I can tell you that he likes them both and his influence can get them a career in the Royal Navy. The Lord Admiral is the father of three daughters and has no son, no male heir. I think that is why he was so taken by your boys."

On Joe's next visit he was accompanied by another gentleman, an attorney who carried papers in a leather satchel. The language in the papers was legal stuff that Mary struggled to understand – so she asked them to explain the details to her in simple terms, which the attorney complied with.

"Ma'am, the Browne family want to send the two boys to a proper boarding school that is far above the level of your Irish hedge school. They will get an education there that will allow them to enter the Royal Navy as Cadets by the age of twelve – something that is only possible for boys like them if they have a personal recommendation from someone of the stature of Admiral Howe. From there they will hopefully progress to become midshipmen, which is the route to becoming an officer of the Royal Navy. This is only possible if the boys are wards of the Browne family – which is the paperwork I have here for you to sign – it is the opportunity of a lifetime for these boys."

"Does this mean that I will never see my boys again?"

"It doesn't mean that at all. You will continue to live at the cottage, and they will be home regularly on leave."

"What does that mean for their sister, young Mary?"

"She will get tutorage in English and she will attend a suitable school later. That schooling will also open opportunities for her that you never had."

Mary was worried and decided to ask the advice of Joe, the steward she had now met many times.

"Mr. Roney, do you think I should sign these documents?"

"Yes Ma'am, I do. I remember young William saying to Lord Howe that he wanted to wear an Admiral's uniform someday – that is entirely possible, but only if this opportunity is taken up."

Mary stalled for a few minutes before replying to the attorney – "There is something important that must be included in this document. I am Catholic and my children are Catholic – it must be written in that they are to be sent to a Catholic school."

The attorney huffed and went outside with Joe for a few minutes. When he came back, he removed the documents from his satchel and proceeded to make the relevant amendment that Mary asked for – "Ma'am, neither of us know if there is a suitable school in Ireland that is Roman Catholic, but we do know of a few in England. With your permission I will write that the chosen Roman Catholic school shall be located either in Ireland or in England. Is that agreeable to you?"

"Yes, and I ask God's Blessing for us all."

Three copies of the amended document were signed by the attorney on behalf of the Browne family, and then by Mary Brown – the 'e' on the end was left out and was not negotiable.

• • •

Young William Brown learns quickly how to fend for himself as a child. He is an early walker and talker, a friendly and trusting boy who is not cowed by strangers. Irish Gaelic is his everyday spoken language and the one his Mammy speaks to him, and in which she sings him to sleep with a suantrai (lullaby). He has only vague memories of a visiting gentleman whom he is told later to have been his father, but he has fond memories of the big house where he and his siblings are taken on regular visits, and the old seanathair (grandfather) figure who talks to him in an English accent that the boy has some difficulty understanding. On their way home in the carriage from one of the Big House visits, Mammy tells him that he must be very nice to this Sasanach (Englishman) because he is an important gentleman who will help him and his brother as they grow up. He especially remembers the old man in his colorful 'Admiral' uniform who gives the boys a lot of attention.

William is packed off to a school near Dublin at the age of seven and a half – a place where he is scolded on his very first day for speaking his native language. The school is run by Priests, who can speak Irish when they want to, but they tell William gruffly he must speak the new everyday language – English. All students are forbidden from speaking Irish except at Mass where the Latin prayers and Irish prayers are mixed – something William finds confusing. His brother Michael joins him at the school eighteen months later. They have two short breaks each year, Christmas and July, when they are allowed to spend several days with their mother and get to make a trip to the Big House.

Their school classes are geared very much to the Royal Navy requirements, and every student there knows that a life at sea is their destiny. The Brown brothers are bright boys, in the top tiers of their classes. In 1789 William leaves the school at the age of twelve to join the Royal Navy as a Cadet trainee. He has a good relationship with his 'English Grandfather' by this time, he knows that he is Admiral Lord Howe and is indeed a very important man in the Royal Navy. The Admiral tells him stories of great battles that he has won on the high seas against Britain's enemies – France, Spain and America. William conjures up images of a wonderful life in the Royal Navy and sailing to exotic places – he tells Admiral Howe that one day he intends to be an Admiral also.

"Sure, you will, my boy," the old man beams.

The Admiral has a private meeting with William before he joins his first ship – HMS Vigilant, in Bristol.

"William, this ship is a converted merchantman and was part of my own command during the American Revolutionary War. I have done my part to make sure you have been accepted into the best Navy in the world. Now it is up to you to prove your metal and take your career to the highest level. God Speed. You must never mention your family connections to me, trust me in that."

With that he shakes the boy's hand firmly. William salutes him, thanks him for his patronage and promises to make him proud. The Admiral is briefly choked with emotion as his daughter, Lady Catherine looks on.

Young William possesses great self-confidence, to the point of cockiness, and is blessed with the gift of a wonderful memory for details. At school he was not intimidated by the mocking of his accent, or the bragging of boys who came from wealth and privilege. Now, he sees this tall ship full of strangers as a place that presents opportunities for him to excel as a Cadet. The moment he is introduced to his assigned officer, Lieutenant Jones, he studies every feature of the Welsh officer as they have their first encounter, particularly his accent.

"Cadet Brown – from where do you hail?"

"From Ireland, Sir: a town named Westport in County Mayo."

"That's a port on the west coast, I think I've been there

– it's dominated by a mountain and has lots of islands scattered about the bay, I cannot remember what it is called. I see you've got the Irish red hair, and probably the temper to match."

"It's called Clew Bay, Sir. The red hair runs in our family, Sir."

"Ah, yes, Clew Bay, a fine body of water. No doubt your red headed father was in the Navy ahead of you?"

"No Sir, he died when I was very young, but I think I have distant relatives in the Royal Navy, Sir."

"Did they achieve rank?"

"I, er, don't know, Sir."

"Here is a list of your expected duties. We muster at 1500 hours. You are dismissed."

William's basic duties are simple – running errands for Lieutenant Jones to the captain and to other officers on the ship; serving some meals to him and holding instruments or charts for him – but William wants to do more and especially wants to learn much more about how ships like this function. Their ship is part of the Channel Fleet that is assigned to protect merchant ships sailing between the Caribbean and ports along the southern coast of Ireland and as far as the southwest coast of England. The young Irish boy has a passion for details and is extremely observant. Lieutenant Jones is very helpful and very patient with William from their first meeting and begins the training of the boy that very evening, as HMS

'Vigilant' makes her way to the open sea – explaining what tasks the sailors are seen performing up in there in the rigging, and Willian begins his detailed journal entries.

These journals will prove to be of immense value to William as his seafaring life unfolds.

CHAPTER FOUR

FROM ROYAL NAVY TO PRIVATEER TO BUENOS AIRES

In 1792, at the age of fifteen, after three years of training as a Cadet, William Brown becomes a Midshipman on HMS Dryad. Proudly he dons the uniform that is like that of commissioned officers, but with his badge of rank – a white patch of cloth with a gold button and a twist of white cord on each side of the coat collar. He quickly finds his feet in this new environment and continues his determined path to becoming a commissioned officer in the Royal Navy – he observes, he listens, he writes notes, he does all the hands-on work. In three more years and he will have the required six years at sea, will have learned everything he needs to know to be eligible to take the examination for Lieutenant – he will know how to rig sails and all other duties of an able seaman, will have learned all aspects of seamanship and navigation including the keeping of detailed navigational logs. Unlike his previous ship where he was a Cadet, he now experiences a less welcoming atmosphere – is it the competition for commissions or something more sinister?

His red hair earns him the nickname of Red Willie. He takes it in his stride and powers ahead with renewed determination, achieving higher levels of skill than the other midshipmen on board. HMS Dryad is burdened with numerous challenges from storm damage and from several engagements with enemy navy ships once the war with France begins in 1793. William excels at supervising gun batteries, commanding small boats for boarding parties, he even commands a sub-division of a ship's company under the supervision of Lieutenant Bond.

The time arrives for him to take the formal Lieutenant examination in 1795, and William is summoned before a board of three captains who question him about discipline, seamanship and navigation. One asks him about a hypothetical engagement with a powerful enemy warship. William is in his element in this battle format, and he elicits high praise from the board for his detailed descriptive answer. He knows he has passed with flying colors, but he also knows that promotion to Lieutenant is not automatic. Within a few weeks he is informed that he has passed the examination and has become what is called a 'Passed Midshipman'. Shortly afterwards his worst fears are realized – others who barely scraped through the exam are promoted and commissioned while William is left waiting. He knows what is going on – senior serving officers and government officials are exercising their influence to get their sons through, peerage and landed gentry are doing the same. This is happening at a time when the Royal Navy is desperately trying to increase its numerical strength, and he hopes that such a need will push him through. What William experiences firsthand is discrimination against him as an Irish-born midshipman – it is a big barrier blocking his way in the commissioning process. He is unable to contact Admiral Howe for that extra push – all he can do is to hope that the Admiral remembers to follow up on the boy's career progress, like he promised he would.

William joins the Freemasons group on board, in hopes of increasing his chance of a commission, without success. As time goes by, he knows his opportunity for a commission is slipping away – especially when he gets transferred to HMS Standard. That is when he hears that Britain has seized several French colonies and he makes his decision to become a master's mate – a petty officer who assists the master and does other duties like serving on watch. It means an increase in pay and conversely it also reduces his chances of a commission, but that doesn't matter anymore because William is already refocusing on his future. With that plan in mind, he soon makes the decision that he will leave the Royal Navy at the first opportunity, and move to the ranks of the British Merchant Navy, the collective name for British civilian merchant ships and associated crews.

A few months later, HMS Standard stops in Folkstone for repairs and supplies. William manages to get shore leave and in keeping with the sailor's reputation, he ends up in the local tavern but leaves in despair. His mission is not to get drunk: he wants to make contacts in merchant shipping. At the local Freemason Hall, he falls in with a friendly young man named Walter Chitty, from the nearby port of Deal, in Kent – who is bragging about his shipping family – "Our family have been ships pilots for years, we sell lots of ship supplies and we have our own ships – merchantmen and luggers. I am here delivering supplies that will end up on your Navy ship."

"I don't know the town of Deal – tell me about it."

"I've got a better idea, mate. I'm headed back there shortly for another load of supplies and will be coming straight back here with them. You said you have several days off – come with me and I'll show you what Deal is like."

William takes up the offer and rides with him in his wagon to Deal. On the way, Walter gives him a history lesson. He explains the importance of the sheltered anchorage known as The Downs, which lies between the town shoreline and the dangerous Goodwin Sands – 'the ship swallower'. "Hundreds of ships anchor in The Downs, often for weeks at a time and Deal has grown rich from supplying provisions to those ships. It was granted a Royal Charter in the 12th century as part of the confederation of five great ports of England – along with Sandwich, Portsmouth, Plymouth and Rochester."

"That's great but tell me about what your family does there."

"As well as providing pilots to guide ships through to the English Channel and to the North Sea, we have our own ships, merchant ships and luggers. In case you don't know, luggers are small two masted boats under thirty tons. They were designed and built here to be launched from Deal's steep shingle banks – strong, fast and seaworthy."

"Are you willing to employ someone like me, once I get out of the service?"

"My father and my uncles are always looking for captains and mates and able seamen – we are all just one big family. That's why I am bringing you to see the town and see our place for yourself."

"Is there anything else I need to know?"

"Well, we do some privateering. The streets run parallel to the beach, and we have several closed storage yards and sheds around the town. It is said that Deal does its share of smuggling, but you didn't hear that from me."

"Interesting."

The town fascinates William even before he sees it, and more so once he lays eyes on it. As they trundle through the town, Walter points out the many features he has mentioned earlier, including the artillery fortress built by Henry VIII. William sees immediately that the family has a thriving business, and he is graciously received by Mr. Thomas Chitty senior. It is that night, while he is eating supper with Walter and other family members, that he first sees Eliza Chitty, Walter's sister. He makes sure that she sees him too, and the next day while supplies are being loaded onto the wagon for Folkstone, he manages to see her again.

He is talking to Mr. Chitty at the time, about how this nice man will use his influence on securing William's move from Royal Navy to Merchant Navy. The father notices his interest in the girl and comments – "I see that your attention to me is waning, in favor of my Eliza – the apple of my eye."

"I'm very sorry Sir. I've been at sea a long time and your daughter is very pretty – please forgive me."

"Eliza is also very good with numbers and is a great help to me here. I will be very sad to lose her when she marries."

"Oh, she is about to get married?"

"I hope not, and I should be the first to know. Calm down, young man – Eliza is way too young to be thinking about marriage. Now, let us get back to the details of the names of your commanders aboard HMS Standard and your personal details. I have your age and a description of you – Irish, red hair and 5 foot 9 inches. You say your service renewal is due in three months and at that time you wish to leave and become a mate on one of my ships – is that correct? What if they give you a commission in the meantime?"

"That's not going to happen, especially now that I'm a master's mate – I'm labelled as working class once I took that position. The system is rotten and is being exploited by influence peddling. It's no wonder that the tiny American Continental Navy was able to inflict such damage on the Royal Navy, and dare I say that their naval success against our Navy led to their overall victory. The officers coming up through our ranks at present have no stomach for battle. Give me a similar ship to any under Royal Navy command and I am confident that I would triumph over them in a sea battle. Yes, Sir – I would be obliged if you could use your good offices with the Admiralty to secure my honorable discharge."

"So, you think you could defeat a Royal Navy ship – those are fighting words, young man. I like your spirit and your enthusiasm. The real money to be made legally on the high seas is in privateering and once you come on board with us and get some merchant navy experience, you will get your chance at proving yourself in that role."

"Thank you, Mr. Chitty, I am already looking forward to privateering."

• • •

In the summer of 1797, at the age of twenty-one, William Brown is discharged from the Royal Navy and makes the move to merchant shipping – becoming mate on the Chitty merchantman 'Union' under Captain Smyth. He is in Deal for only two days before setting off on his first merchant voyage to the West Indies – time enough to put eyes on Eliza again and to have Walter introduce her to him.

"You're Irish, aren't you," was all she said when they met first.

"Was it my accent that gave me away, or maybe it was my red hair?"

"Neither. My father told me you are Irish."

"Is that bad or good?"

"I don't know, I've never met anybody Irish before. We don't send ships to Ireland, only to the West Indies and to other places in the Caribbean, and to the Mediterranean Sea ports."

"That's fine with me."

"I would like to see the West Indies – I like warm weather."

"Me too."

• • •

William Brown embarks on a new chapter of his life. He is first mate on a ship that is one of a convoy being escorted by a Royal Navy squadron for part of the journey. He revels in the open ocean once they leave the squadron behind, and they have an uneventful voyage other than some weather issues. They return to Deal in August with a cargo of molasses and rum. He has minor contact with Eliza before his next voyage. Captain Smyth is pleased with the performance of his young mate, and he sings his praises to the boss. Mr. Chitty knows the autumn hurricane patterns and he prefers to avoid the Caribbean during the upcoming hurricane season – they sail several shorter voyages instead – to Cadiz, Seville, Gibraltar and Alicante.

William is learning fast and sets his sights on becoming a captain. Even better is the fact that he is more frequently at Deal and continues to have some chance encounters with Eliza – she is responding to his attempts to engage her in conversation, at least to some degree, and he is encouraged.

In December of 1798, he returns from a Caribbean voyage to be told the news of a serious rebellion in Ireland that happened during the summer while he was away. Thankfully, his brother Michael is by this stage in the Royal Navy and is away from the country – William thinks Michael's ship is part of a squadron that is guarding the Irish coast against a French invasion. His sister Mary is in school somewhere near Dublin and his mother is in Mayo, to the best of his knowledge. He sends off letters to all three as he gets ready for his next voyage. News filters back later that his brother and sister survived the upheaval of the rebellion, but the news of his mother is bad – she has perished in the rebellion according to his most up-to-date information.

County Mayo had been the site of a French naval force landing during the rebellion, who were then joined by rebel forces. The combined army had a few successive victories that resulted in casualties among the rural population, including his mother. The Big Houses at Westport and Claremorris belonging to the Browne's, the relatives of William's father – had been ransacked and burned by the marauding rebel armies. British forces later defeated the Franco-Irish army in County Longford with great slaughter. Following the defeat, cruel retribution was being exacted on the native population of County Mayo and would continue for the foreseeable future.

In this moment of William's sadness and loss, Eliza's heart softens.

"I am very sorry to hear of the trouble occurring in Ireland. We are all hoping and praying for your family. Father says you are welcome to join us at church tomorrow at St. John's for 10 a.m. service when we will offer prayers for your family in Ireland."

"Thank you, I will do that."

William is wondering why he said yes – he is Catholic, and the Chitty's are Anglican. He knows why he accepted the invitation – he didn't want to miss the opportunity to be close to Eliza and he's good with that decision for now. Catholics aren't supposed to be in the Royal Navy, so he has played this hand before at Anglican services while at sea. On Sunday everybody is very welcoming, and the minister sympathizes with William over his loss, the small crowd sings several hymns, and everyone shuffles over to the adjoining hall where food is laid out. He avoids further conversation with the minister in case he is found out as a Catholic, and he uses the occasion to talk more to Eliza, despite interruptions by her brother Walter. Later that day, Mr. Chitty is surprised and taken aback when William asks him for permission to court Eliza.

"William, you are very direct, and it unnerves me sometimes. She is too young and so are you. Besides, you still have much to learn about merchant shipping – it is very different than the Royal Navy. Keep working and improving, young man – my permission is denied for now."

William suppresses his anger at this rejection – obviously he is deemed unworthy, again. If he cannot prove his worthiness to the Chitty's here in Deal, then he must leave and prove it through other means. In January he puts out some feelers at the Tavern Club where sailors congregate ashore – asking which privateers are capturing the most prizes. His own reputation as a sailor is good and word of his battle experience with gun batteries in the Royal Navy has gotten around. An intermediary brings him an invitation to meet a Captain Maxwell, one of the most successful British privateers. They meet on his biggest ship, an East Indiaman named 'Aeolus', where William is escorted to the captain's cabin.

"Fine ship you have here, Captain Maxwell, interesting name you picked – 'Aeolus' is the Greek God of wind, if I remember rightly."

"Aye, you are correct. She's a beauty, a dangerous beauty."

"I counted twenty gunports as your longboat carried me to the anchorage – that seems almost too much weight."

"You're a sharp lad, sure enough. There's a reason for that – enemy beware."

"What do you mean by that?"

"Well, some of them gunports be only painted, and some are real. To many an enemy spyglass we look too dangerous to mess with. We have less guns than the twenty gunports you counted but we have enough to fight almost any ship on the high seas, and we are much faster in the water than we look – as many a captured enemy ship learned to their cost. We have captured more French merchant prizes than any other British ship over the last few years – and you know what that means – big prize money."

"Why are you looking for a mate?"

"Old George Crabtree has come down with the gollywogs and has taken himself off to a sanitorium in search of a cure. I hear you're a good sailor and gunner – we sail very soon for Saint-Lucia and Martinique in the Indies – with some cargo, and on a quest for rich prizes. Are you with us, Lad?"

"Yes, but I need a few days to settle affairs of business and of love."

"Let's shake a paw on that."

The following day William goes to see Mr. Chitty and tells him he is going privateering with Maxwell.

"You will get your chance to be a privateer here in due course, like I told you – you don't need to throw in with a dangerous man like him. You are upset because of our discussion about Eliza, aren't you?"

"Not at all, Sir. You are right, Mr. Chitty: I need to learn a lot more to become a master mariner – I also need money to support Eliza, and to set up my own merchant enterprise. Walter and the others will take over from you, and rightly so. I must forge my own way. Merchant trade is booming between Britain and the Indies since we booted the French out of many of the islands there, and French ships still travel through that region all the time. That presents great pickings for an aggressive privateer like Maxwell – prizes galore."

"There is much danger to go along with that – it is safer here."

"There is plenty of danger here as well – a storm in the Bay of Biscay could take me down anytime. I am young, I am an experienced sailor, I am well tested with gun batteries – my mind is made up and I need to do this. Can I have two requests."

"What are they?"

"Can I speak to Eliza before I leave, to explain? And will you have me back when I return – older, wiser and richer?"

"Agreed on both requests. Here, shake my hand and let us part as friends."

• • •

Eliza reads his face as he approaches her.

"You're leaving, aren't you? Why?"

"Your father says we must wait till we are older to be together, and he is probably right. I need to get more navigation experience in the Caribbean waters where most of the merchant shipping is happening, and I need to improve my finances. I intend to accomplish both goals in the next few years by privateering in the Caribbean with Captain Maxwell. Will you wait for me?"

"Of course. Will you remember to come back for me?"

"Absolutely, and I'll write as often as I can."

They hold hands for a long time and then have a parting kiss. William goes to his quarters to pack up his possessions and sets off on foot for the dock area near where the 'Aeolus' is anchored.

Captain Maxwell is both pleased and relieved to see William. He tells him they will weigh anchor within hours and sail to London – "it is better for us to use London for cargo exports and imports, and better for money transfers. Whatever ports we bring prizes into, they can figure a way to get our prize money sent to our representatives in London, and quickly into our pockets."

• • •

In London they load cargo that is nonperishable and that will sell anywhere – barrel staves, nails, lumber and other hardware supplies that are always in demand. Then they add as many armaments as they can safely carry, they get an updated letter of marque, and depart London in good weather in late January. Once in the open Atlantic, William presents a new idea – to fly the Royal Navy ensign at the top of the mast and he unfolds one then and there – to the consternation of Captain Maxwell.

"Now why would we be wanting to fly this?"

"Same reason that you painted some fake gunports. When the spyglasses of enemies, friends or merchant targets are trained on us from afar they will see that ensign. It will make enemies think twice about approaching a ship that might be part of the Royal Navy, it should keep regular Royal Navy ships at a safe distance and might entice merchant prey to us seeking protection."

"I like the way you think, me lad."

On their first voyage they capture a French merchant ship, and a six-gun French privateer who had a British merchant prize under her control. The French ship tries to outrun the 'Aeolus' until she shows her speed and fires a bow cannon, after which they strike their colors. William's crews bring the captured ships to Jamaica and 'Aeolus' stays in the area for a month while the crew members enjoy spending some of their spoils. Captain Maxwell establishes their Caribbean base there and William uses the reliable British postal service to keep in correspondence with Eliza.

He finds out by chance through a ship's pilot that there is a Jamaican connection to the Howe-Browne family, when the harbor pilot mentions Admiral Lord Howe in conversation. Further questions establishes that the Admiral has recently died in London, but it also leads William to a man named Joseph Moore, the local manager of the Howe plantation.

Joseph brags about the Howe family's influence with the island governor when they meet, even going so far as to say that he could use this influence to help a distant relative like William if need be. The 'Aeolus', under Captain Maxwell, continues to ply the waters between the Caribbean and Britain, a feared ship whose captured prizes help William to salt away a sizeable amount of money.

He manages only one trip to Deal during this time, during which he and Eliza renew their promises to each other. The declaration of war on Britain by Spain in 1805 complicates their privateering enterprise but "Aeolus' is able to alter her sailing routes and continue capturing prizes. Storms take their toll on the ship and then they are grounded for extensive repairs after they are blown onto rocks in a hurricane. They get the damage repaired, and not long after that William must enlist help from Joseph Moore at the Howe plantation, when their ship is impounded by the authorities of the island of Jamaica for unpaid fees – Joseph comes through for him.

• • •

By 1807 William realizes he cannot stay too long away from Eliza, or he might lose her. He decides it is time to move on from 'Aeolus' and begins asking about opportunities in the new nation of the United States of America, in particular the Southeast coast and on the USA land frontier that is already extending westward. Then he hears about an attack by a British expeditionary force on the wealth center of Spain's South American empire that had occurred the previous year – an attack led by Commodore Home Riggs Popham, targeting the River Plate estuary and the city of Buenos Aires.

The expedition had a decidedly Irish flavor to it – Popham being from an Anglo-Irish family from County Cork, and the 1,770 soldiers he ferried ashore were mostly Irish, led by Brigadier General William Carr Beresford, the illegitimate son of the marquess of Waterford. Through paid informers, the adventurers became aware that there was a large consignment of gold bullion and specie at Buenos Aires awaiting shipment to Spain, and that the River Plate area was largely devoid of defenses. Their daring expedition seized this treasure and carried it back to London, to enrich themselves and the British government, who had secretly sanctioned the affair. In the story that William hears, the 40,000 residents of Buenos Aires (known locally as Portenos) were so disgusted with the way their Spanish governor surrendered the city and the treasure, that they formed militias and began a rebellion that targeted both the invaders and the Spanish authorities. That part of the story didn't faze William, and a new plan takes shape in his brain – he begins to think that South America could be a source of immense wealth for him, it could be the new place that he had been searching for.

The 'Aeolus' sails to London with cargo and to collect their accumulated prize monies there. Once the ship is unloaded and the profit monies are shared out, William tells Maxwell he is retiring.

"And why would a young man like you leave such a profitable life behind?"

"Love – it's all about love, Captain."

"Humbug – with your money you can buy all the love you want."

"What you are talking about is lust. Captain Maxwell, you don't understand love. I'm going back to Deal and I'm going to marry Mr. Chitty's daughter, Eliza."

• • •

The Chitty family welcomes William Brown back to Deal with open arms – they are indeed good people, and it warms his heart. Not only is Eliza thrilled to have him home, but Mr. Chitty seems happy too.

"You're welcome back, William, and you have my full permission to court Eliza – her heart has been pining for you these few years. By all accounts you are now a master mariner and a man of financial means."

"Did I not tell you that I would return after sailing the seven seas. I am going to rest my sea legs awhile and spend time with beautiful Eliza before I move onto the next chapter of life."

Eliza Chitty has grown up in the meantime and has matured into a beautiful woman. It is obvious to William that she could have jilted him for another suitor, if the stories that her brother Walter tell him are true. The pair of love birds spend their time walking and talking, and she takes him on picnic rides to see her favorite places – including to the white cliffs at Dover. William speaks to her in his usual direct style, proposing marriage to Eliza that very day.

"Of course I will marry you, that's what I've been wanting for a long time. We shall have to go through the formalities of you asking my father for permission, but he knows now what to expect from you and he knows how direct you are."

"Eliza, do you know that I am Catholic – will that present any problems?"

"I somehow thought you might be, even though you never mentioned it before. I want to get married in our local Anglican Church, and I am sure father will want that also. What do you suggest?"

"I am happy to marry you in your preferred church. The compromise I suggest is that our boy children are raised Catholic, and our girl children are raised Anglican."

"That seems fair, and I think father can be persuaded to accept that. Why do you want to bring up such a subject so early?"

"Because I have big plans for us. Remember I told you I wanted to set up my own merchant business."

"Father is hoping you will captain one of his ships and settle here in Deal as part of the family."

"I am happy to do that for a little while, until I finalize plans for our future."

"Can you tell me what they are – these plans?"

"Sure, but you must not tell anyone – they must be our secret for now."

She nods.

"South America is the new land of opportunity. I have studied it and now is the time to act, just as Spain is losing her grip in that region. The wealth center of the Spanish empire in South America is in the area on either side of a vast river estuary named The River Plate – with the city of Buenos Aires on one bank and the city of Montevideo on the other bank of this freshwater sea. The region may stay in the Spanish empire, but my guess is that it will become a group of independent states or countries – either way there is great opportunity for merchants trading there and I intend to exploit this opportunity."

"But William, it is so far away – at the other end of the world, I think. I've never been that far away from home – I'm scared, and I know father will try to persuade you to stay here."

"That is why you must say nothing for now. First, I will captain some of your father's ships and earn him more profit, while you and I concentrate on getting his blessing for our marriage. Agreed?"

"Agreed."

William offers his services to Mr. Chitty, who gladly accepts him as his newest Captain.

"My boy, I have a ship that I know you will like, the 'Effort'. She is almost ready to sail – will you take command of her, Captain Brown, and take her to Grenada in the West Indies? "

"The title of Captain Brown has a nice ring to it. I'll be honored to do it, Sir, but I have an important request first. I ask for your permission to take the hand of your daughter Eliza in marriage – not immediately, mind."

"You have it, and I'm glad you have the sense not to rush. Earn some more money on a few voyages while Eliza figures out the wedding details."

"I have another request, Sir. My contacts have provided me with evidence that South America is the next great trading destination for British merchant ships. While I am away in Grenada, I implore you to plan a voyage and cargo for me to take to Buenos Aires, the largest port on the River Plate."

"I will check into it while you are away, I promise."

True to his word, Mr. Chitty does just that. William returns in time for Christmas and is overjoyed that a plan is taking shape for a voyage to South America. During leisure time with Eliza, she tells him of her desire to have her wedding in the new year – "I will be past twenty-one years old by then, and it is time for me to be married. Father has agreed to your request that our sons be brought up Catholic and our daughters will be Anglican."

"Excellent my dear, you think of everything. Your father

wants us to take our time, and I would prefer to wait one more year – so I have the chance to make one exploratory voyage to the River Plate in South America to confirm what opportunities exist there."

• • •

After Christmas, William completes a profitable voyage from Deal to Cadiz in the 'Effort' – shoring up his finances, and more importantly, keeping Mr. Chitty happy and on track for the South America exploratory voyage.

Then, in the spring of 1808, William sets sail in Mr. Chitty's 'Maryann', bound for South America – his voyage of exploration to the River Plate (El Rio de la Plata) is finally happening. There are rumors of an uprising against the Spanish, and that a Spanish blockade may prevent him from getting all the way to Buenos Aires (Pleasant Airs). William knows how vast the estuary is, and he is confident that no blockade is tight enough to prevent him from getting through. The only prior information he has found about the River Plate navigation is that the waterway has many navigation hazards – shallows, sandbanks, unusual tidal swings and erratic winds.

On arrival he sees lots of small ships crowded in certain areas of the estuary, many of which he is unfamiliar with – his river pilot, Pedro, tells him they are shallow-draft vessels such as small coasters, feluccas, lugs, sloops, pinnaces and smacks. During their upriver trip to Buenos Aires, William bombards the pilot with questions about this fickle river – he makes copious notations on his charts and writes extensive notes in his logbooks. His time ashore is brief but he still wants to make inquiries about the fateful Popham expedition that he had been told about. The money that was 'stolen' by the British expedition is still a delicate subject, and the incident has had the effect of galvanizing together several factions of the local independence movement. The Spanish forces that were supposed to protect the city had crumpled and they surrendered in the face of a small force of invaders. Now, with increased unity among the 'Portenos', there is a belief that they can shake off the yoke of Spain, and citizens' militia units have sprung up all over the province.

In the port, William strikes up a conversation with William Guillermo Pio White, who told him he came to the River Plate many years before from America, speaks Spanish fluently and is a wealth of information. Pio, in his high-pitched voice, recounts how the local militias defeated the Popham invaders and forced them to surrender. He tells him that hundreds of the defeated soldiers were Irishmen like William and chose to stay behind – they have since been forgiven, and according to Pio they are doing well in their newly adopted homeland. Everything William hears from Pio convinces him that this is where he and Eliza should settle, a place where he can become a successful merchant.

He tells Pio about his plan to return – they swap addresses for correspondence and Pio promises that he will help William to get set up when he comes back to settle. With Pio's help he gets a decent price for his ship's cargo, and he takes on a cargo of animal hides plus exotic wood for the return voyage to Deal. The same pilot, Pedro, guides 'Maryann' back downstream towards the ocean and William uses the trip as another navigation lesson: he knows that he will have to master this river if he is to succeed. They get hit by the 'Pamperos'- sudden fierce winds that Pedro says come off the interior plains – and William learns another valuable lesson in local navigation.

An uneventful return voyage has 'Maryann' back in Deal by early December. The cargo sells quickly, and Mr. Chitty is well satisfied with the profits. They all have a pleasant family Christmas – Eliza and William decide on a July wedding and she begins planning in earnest. Mr. Chitty and William continue to work very well together, and they concentrate on shorter voyages to the Mediterranean during the run up to the wedding. William keeps the subject of South America alive but at the same time he senses that Mr. Chitty is wavering and is trying to steer him towards a life in Deal. With the wedding fast approaching and Eliza reaching high levels of excitement, William decides to bide his time until after July.

• • •

The wedding of Elizabeth Chitty to William Brown takes place on July 29, 1809, at St. Johns Anglican Church in Deal, Kent. The Minister blesses their union, and in his sermon, he invokes the sun-filled day as a sign from the Lord that their lives will be filled with sunshine – very apt in William's mind since he hopes and expects them to live in the warm sunny climate of Buenos Aires. The event is very much a Chitty family affair as William has no attendees from Ireland. His mother had died during the turmoil of the1798 Rebellion, which also destroyed much of the property of his 'relatives' – the Browne family. The rebellion aftermath severs William's contact with his sister Mary and that severance ruins any prospects of further contact with Lady Altamont and the Howe-Browne side of the family – taking with it the potentially important 'e' to put at the end of Brown. That leaves his brother Michael as his only contactable relative and he retains hope until the last minute that he can attend, but that doesn't happen as Michael is away at sea with the Royal Navy.

William is formally welcomed into the Chitty family – Mrs. Chitty and some older ladies cry and then Eliza cries. The guests enjoy a luncheon at the Parish Hall, and they raise a toast to the happy couple. Mr. Chitty surprises them with the keys to a stone cottage at the edge of town – a very nice gift but also one that puts more pressure on William to stay close to home. After a few passionate restful days as man and wife, it is back to work, and William sets sail in 'Effort' for Gibraltar. In his head he is 'half a world away' and he makes his mind up to have the overdue conversation with Mr. Chitty. His opportunity comes in late September when they are talking about ship repairs and whether to sell some of the older ships.

"Sir, everything is great in my life, and I thank the Lord every day for the Chitty family. However, I cannot get the River Plate, Buenos Aires, and South America out of my mind – going back there is something I must do. It seems to be my destiny – I hope you understand."

"William, you are a master mariner now, and we are proud to have you in our family. Being that you are married you have new responsibilities, and you must take all of that into consideration. I had no experience with Irish people prior to you coming into our lives, but I know that your people have suffered hardships for centuries at the hands our Kings, our parliament and our armies. That situation has forced thousands of your people to leave the land of their birth, with many becoming wanderers: but the future is surely looking better now that Britain and Ireland are one United Kingdom, don't you think? I had hoped that your restless spirit would find peace here in our quaint village of Deal. If you feel that you must go back to South America, I will do my best to support you and to support Eliza in that endeavor – I'm assuming that you would first go alone and establish yourself there."

"Yes, Sir, I would go first, and she could follow me later. My next big quest is to find the right ship – something bigger than 'Maryann' would be better for the voyage and allow me to carry more cargo. Once there I need to acquire a small shallow-draft coaster which is best for coping with the thousands of shallow channels and shifting sandbanks that I observed on my first visit. Mr. Chitty, I have reason to believe that the British government wants to promote the independence movement in that region – to help weaken Spain's South American empire and to solidify a British presence there which will put Britain in the best position to trade with these independent states as they get established. Can you speak to your contacts in the government halls of British trade – I have a gut feeling that the government might be willing to sponsor my trip there."

"William, that may prove to be too much for my low level of contacts, but I will make some inquiries next time I'm in London. I am already on the short list of preferred buyers for ships that the Royal Navy captures as prizes of war. If we bide our time we will find a bargain vessel."

• • •

That November a notorious French privateer responsible for the seizure of many British merchant vessels is chased by a Royal Navy warship off Folkstone. The 'Grand Napoleon' is heavily armed, and her captain decides to engage the British frigate in a battle that lasts for five hours. The privateer is de-masted in the battle and the captain is killed, then his first mate finally strikes her colors. The heavily damaged sloop is dispatched to The Downs anchorage near Deal to await condemnation and sale, after her crew are arrested.

Mr. Chitty is informed of the capture because of his presence on the preferred buyer list and he is invited to inspect the ship as a potential buyer. He asks William to accompany him on the inspection. The moment William sees this ship he is in a state of giddy excitement. She needs a lot of repairs – mostly masts, rigging and upper deck repair: luckily, she has not been damaged below the water line. Other than that, she meets all the criteria that William wants for his ship to carry him back to Buenos Aires and to the River Plate.

As they are being rowed back to shore, William turns to Mr. Chitty and gestures towards the sloop – "I want this ship, she has no serious damage that we cannot fix, and she is the ideal size for my voyage – I have already named her in my head: Eliza."

Mr. Chitty smiles and is cheered up by William's enthusiasm.

"Young William, I hate to think of you and Eliza being so far away, but I bow to your confidence and to your infectious enthusiasm. Let us play the poor mouth with the ministry and see what we can 'steal' her for."

William spends time before and through Christmas overseeing repairs to Chitty's fleet of merchant ships while he dreams of sailing south over the equator. Mr. Chitty goes to London and upon his return he tells William great news.

"The 'Grand Napoleon' will soon be ours for 4,000 pounds, along with promises of some free supplies and rigging from the Navy Stores to help us fix her and make her seaworthy. It will take several weeks before the papers are stamped and arrive here – only then can we take possession and bring the ship to Deal for detailed inspection before commencing the repairs and refitting. We cannot drop any of our regular work for this – plan on taking a year or more to get 'Eliza' ready for the high seas. We will have plenty of time to figure out an ownership arrangement between us."

"I understand, Sir, and thank you."

"My contacts are going to talk to their people in the upper echelons of government about your planned voyage, and they will come back to us in due course about any interest the government might have in participating. Don't hold your breath waiting for the government – now, where are we on our own ship repairs?"

"We will have the repairs on 'Effort' completed in two weeks – ready for her Caribbean voyage, then start on the next ship in line."

That Caribbean voyage in 'Effort' is captained by William, and it reminds him of the southern hemisphere latitudes that he craves to return to.

CHAPTER FIVE

REVOLUTION AND LEADERSHIP OF NAVAL WAR AGAINST SPAIN

The imminent purchase of 'Grand Napoleon' boosts William's morale to great heights. It gives him a renewed purpose and he begins subconsciously counting down the days to when his new life in South America will begin.

The bureaucracy of the Royal Navy and the government are prone to lengthy delays, and this is the case with Mr. Chitty's purchase of the condemned 'Grand Napoleon'. William has no choice but to be patient and continue his work. Mr. Chitty's merchant ships are voyaging to the Caribbean, Bermuda, Southeast ports in America and the Mediterranean – William spends most of his time at sea during 1810. He and his wife welcome their first child in October, a baby girl they name Eliza, after her mother. To coincide with that happy event the legal wrangling over the condemned sloop is resolved and by early November the 'Grand Napoleon' is at the Chitty dock, where William's first task is to remove the old name and get ready for her new name – 'Eliza'. The winter is a harsh one and progress on repairs is slow after they enter the new year of 1811.

A letter arrives from Pio White in Buenos Aires. William reads it in private and rereads it several times to absorb all the details. He is already aware that on the European battlefield Spain has been in a struggle with the French armies of Napoleon, but until now he did not know if or how that struggle was affecting South America. Pio tells him that on May 25, 1810, the city of Buenos Aires and the province declared the Spanish Viceroy's powers to be null and void and proceeded to replace him with a local independent government – "United Provinces of the Rio de la Plata". It is a revolution by the criollo population according to Pio's words, and the cry on everyone's lips continues to be 'Libertad'. He tells him that Montevideo continues to be under Spanish control and their fleet is attempting to blockade the port of Buenos Aires to force the rebels back under Spanish control. Spain will not be successful according to Pio, and he encourages William to come as soon as possible, telling him there will be even more commercial merchant opportunities in the new political landscape.

William decides to keep the contents of the letter to himself. A few days later his brother Michael arrives unexpectedly in Deal. Michael's Royal Navy ship has put in at Folkstone for repairs, he is on shore leave and makes a surprise visit to see William and the Chitty's. The brothers have not seen each other for years and they enjoy a tearful reunion.

William takes his brother to see his new ship and they have a long talk while sitting aboard.

"There is much to do, Michael, as you can see, but I expect to be ready to put to sea later this year."

"Tell me about your plans and about South America."

"Well, the River Plate Estuary on the east coast of the continent is where I visited in 1808 and that whole area is beautiful. The river is so wide it is like a sea, but it is difficult to navigate because of shallows, shifting sandbanks, erratic winds, tides and currents. On the southern bank and quite a distance from the open ocean is the biggest city, named Buenos Aires, and on the northern bank are two smaller cities – one opposite Buenos Aires named Colonia, and the other a bit further to the east is Montevideo. As in most of South America, this area is part of the Spanish Empire, but Portugal does control a huge land area to the north of the estuary – it is named Brazil."

"What is the political climate there at present?"

"Spain is losing its grip on South America as we speak, and it is my opinion that the area will eventually split into several independent countries. Regardless of how it plays out, there is huge potential for merchants like us to move cargo around locally – heck, there is not even a packet service across the estuary connecting these main port cities that I just named.

The vast interior lands are full of wild cattle and forests waiting to be exploited for beef, timber, silver and gold – there is huge potential for merchant shipping. Yes, there will be some difficulties as the various independent forces square off against the colonial powers, but there is no reason why I cannot benefit financially amid all this confusion. I am sailing there as soon as possible, with Eliza to follow me later. Young Walter Chitty is already expressing interest in going, and you should also think about it. There is limited opportunity here in Britain for people like us because of how the old aristocratic families and government insiders' control everything – and they stifle the progress of the Irish every chance they get. In South America we are all new immigrants together, starting out on the same level, and there are few barriers preventing us from rising to the top and becoming wealthy – just like my American friend Pio White did."

"Wow – I like the sound of it. Realistically, when are you hoping to set sail, William?"

"It will take at least six months to fix and refit this ship, but I fully intend to be settled there before next Christmas."

"You must send me regular letters on your progress, and I will definitely give some consideration to going there – the sunny climate and merchant opportunities appeal to me."

Michael stays a few days and is very well treated by William's new family, the Chitty's. The weather improves and William's crew of shipwrights and carpenters make steady progress on the repairs and upgrades to the ship. Masts and rigging materials arrive in spring from the Royal Navy Stores as promised to Mr. Chitty, and the progress on refitting the ship continues at speed. They are caulking the hull one day when a delegation from the government arrives, asking to meet with Mr. Chitty and William Brown. After a brief inspection of the ship, they convene in Mr. Chitty's office for a meeting.

A man named Mr. Smith identifies himself as spokesman for the delegation and addresses them –

"The situation in what has become known as the United Provinces area surrounding Buenos Aires has been under review by Britain as conditions on the ground there have evolved. Britain supports the independence movement against the Spanish colonial power and wants to help the local population achieve self-rule: our interest is purely compassion and to expand free trade that will benefit the inhabitants. The British merchant fleet will also benefit, and our citizens in Britain will have access to the imported products coming from that region. The independent government there is sorely in need of weapons and munitions to help them in their fight against Spain. Mr. Brown, your Royal Navy record and your mariner skills are both excellent. Mr. Chitty, your extensive record of co-operation with the British government is exemplary. We propose to send a military cargo to Buenos Aires on 'Eliza' – unofficially, that is. The outline plan is that we provide the undocumented cargo to you, Mr. Brown at no charge. Your part is to get the cargo there safely: the independent government in Buenos Aires will purchase the cargo from you and these monies will compensate you handsomely for undertaking the voyage. After that, you proceed with your plans to set up a merchant business and nobody is any the wiser, if you see what I mean."

Both William and Mr. Chitty were speechless for several minutes as they absorbed the details.

William finally pipes up – "I had been mulling in my head what cargo to bring with me – I don't have to worry about that under this plan. The Spanish are in control of the ports of Colonia and Montevideo as I understand it, and they have a sizeable naval fleet that they are using to blockade the mouth of the river and choke off supplies to Buenos Aires – I assume I will have to get through the blockade to ensure I bring my cargo to the independent government. Is that independent government aware that a shipment is coming, and have they agreed to pay the captain for the cargo? Will these monies be enough to buy a few small coasters there?"

"They are aware of the eminent arrival of this important cargo and agreed to have a very substantial sum of money ready to pay to the ship's captain for that cargo – those details will be shared with you in due course. We are still months from this happening, and though we do not see the situation on the ground changing much this year we cannot guarantee it, and of course we continue to monitor everything in the region. Yes, you will make a very large profit that should easily cover the cost of buying up a few local smaller craft and we will have other resources in the area to help you in case anything unexpected happens. We urge you to be ready to sail this summer and arrive there before year's end."

Mr. Chitty speaks – "This could be a dangerous mission for an unarmed ship."

"We are not disputing that, Sir. An escort can be arranged for part of the voyage, and we envisage a few discreetly mounted cannons for defensive purposes."

"Mr. Smith, please allow us some time to mull this over while we are continuing the work of preparing the ship. Leave us your contact address – we will be in touch very soon."

After the delegation leaves, Mr. Chitty expresses some reservations, while William likes the idea of a guaranteed sale that brings in big profits. He knows there may be unforeseen problems and expenses to overcome, but getting a head start like this seems to be worth the risk, in his mind. They agree to proceed with their ongoing work plans while letting the full implications of the government offer sink in.

A month later the ship's refitting is nearing completion, her name 'Eliza' is proudly painted on her stern and a crew is being assembled. William's desire to accept the government cargo offer wins out, and they communicate their decision to Mr. Smith, informing him that an August sailing date is planned. The swift reply asks that 'Eliza' is first sailed to Folkstone Royal Navy docks in mid-July to have four cannons fitted and to have the 'cargo' loaded. Through June and July

William spends time at home with his wife, his own Eliza, and their young daughter of the same name – for once he spends more time at home than on his new ship. He worries out loud that he is being cruel, leaving them for this long voyage, but she will have none of it.

"I managed just fine when you were away privateering with Maxwell, and I'll be fine, honest."

"But you now have a child to take care of."

"The Chitty's have always been self-reliant and that goes for me too. My family are all around me and will give me any help that I might need. We made the decision to relocate to Buenos Aires and this voyage is the necessary first step – it makes perfect sense that you should go first, scout it out and get set up there. Father supports that plan. Don't worry – it will all work out."

"You are so strong, Eliza, and so sensible. Will you marry me?"

"Sorry, but I'm already married to a crazy Irishman that I love dearly."

They laugh and kiss and cuddle and then fuss over their daughter.

• • •

As the departing date for Buenos Aires draws near, Mr. Smith visits William again in Deal. He provides him with contact names and addresses in the independent government there, plus the name of a manager at the port of Buenos Aires who will accept the cargo. William is assured that he will be paid the agreed monies upon delivery of the cargo – in gold and silver, a generous payout which he is pleasantly surprised by. He is also provided with names and addresses of British diplomats and HMS naval commanders stationed in the region – to be contacted only in an emergency.

Mr. Smith continues – "The situation in the River Plate area is very fluid. The independent government is in control of Buenos Aires and now controls the smaller city of Colonia on the opposite bank of the Plate estuary. Montevideo, further east from Colonia, is firmly in the hands of the Spanish and they have a well-armed naval squadron based there under Jacinto Romarate, who is a very capable commander. The Spanish squadron have a blockade in place in the estuary near Montevideo and are trying to disrupt the water-borne trade that is the life blood of Buenos Aires, attempting to break the spirit of the independent patriots. You will have to find a way past this blockade but that should be quite easy on such a huge waterway. Earlier this year the independent government authorities created a small patriot naval force of their own to break the blockade, and to bring help to their land army further upriver who have been engaged in fighting against the Spanish Army. The Spanish squadron defeated the patriot squadron and either captured or destroyed all their ships. It is imperative that you get through to Buenos Aires with these urgently needed arms for the patriots, whom we are encouraging to assemble a new and better naval force to confront the Spanish."

• • •

The 'Eliza' sails back to Deal briefly, and William spends some final hours with his wife and daughter while food supplies are loaded. The goodbyes are very tearful, and the ship departs for Buenos Aires in August. They get a Royal Navy escort for a substantial part of the way and after that they must rely on a signal system to communicate with any Navy ship they may sight on their way south, plus they have four mounted cannons ready to defend against any hostile ships.

The remainder of the voyage is uneventful and by early November 'Eliza' is approaching the wide estuary of the River Plate. To save time, William makes do with the first pilot he can get, Francisco, and they are successful in finding a gap in the Spanish blockade. They get to within sight of Buenos Aires before disaster strikes. Francisco recommends that they follow a close-to-shore route in Barragan Bay and in the late evening the pilot runs 'Eliza' aground on a sand bank. She is stuck firm, and William gets furious with Francisco when he timidly suggests they should just wait for high tide to float the ship off the sand. William firmly says no – he is not willing to be a sitting duck waiting for the next tide – knowing as he does the 'sensitive cargo' they have on board.

Leaving his first mate, Jack, in command of the ship,

William takes the pilot with him in the longboat, and they are quickly able to row to the port to find help. Using Francisco as interpreter, they find his 'cargo contact' at the port, Senor Jose Lopez. Jose agrees to immediately send a flotilla of shallow-draft boats to the marooned ship, and in the darkness of night they begin to transfer the munitions cargo plus the four deck cannons ashore. They finish this task just before the clock strikes twelve noon on the following day, as three Spanish warships bear down on them. There is no alternative but to abandon 'Eliza' and William is inconsolable in the last rowboat to seek the safety of the shallow flats. The empty 'Eliza' is boarded by the Spanish, then is later pulled off the sandbank by one of their ships and confiscated for breaching their blockade.

While William is waiting to be paid for his cargo he complains bitterly to Senor Lopez about the loss of his ship, for he is now without a vessel to move forward with his merchant plans. It takes two days to get a decision from the local rebel government, but then Jose comes back with a plan that will allow William to earn extra money from his cargo. If he will undertake to transport overland the quarter portion of the weapons cargo bound for Chile, he will be able to triple his selling price for that portion. He agrees to do it even though he has no idea of the hardship that could be involved on such a trip.

A mule train must be assembled: William, plus guides plus some volunteers from his ship's crew spend the next two months traversing the Andes mountains to Chile where he sells his weapons at great profit. While there, he meets the leader of the Chilean independence movement, Bernardo O'Higgins. He is the son of Ambrose O'Higgins, originally of County Sligo, who was the former Viceroy of Peru – a meeting of these two young Irish daredevils takes place in the high altitude of the Andes.

By March 1812, William is back in Buenos Aires counting his riches. Adding together the monies from both sales, William is now getting ready to move ahead with his merchant plans. However, he is suddenly arrested while in possession of all this money and charged with illegally exporting cash. His money and his horses are confiscated, and he is imprisoned. Among his personal possessions he finds the address for Captain Green, the commander of the British naval force in the River Plate and he writes to him pleading for help. Green is decisive and gets William released by April, his money and horses are returned to him, and he gets an apology from the United Patriot government for good measure.

The stress of all of this has exhausted William. He contacts his American merchant friend, Pio White, who is appalled by his story and invites him to recuperate at his hacienda, while Pio searches for land and a ship for his Irish friend. In June William buys land in the Barracas area of Buenos Aires for his future home, on Pio's recommendation. In July the two men jointly purchase the schooner 'Industria' to begin a packet service carrying agricultural produce from Buenos

Aires to Colonia, returning with cured cowhides. Soon after that, a truce is signed between the Spanish government in Montevideo and the Patriot Authorities in Buenos Aires, which allows William to expand the ferry service to include Montevideo, and the expansion justifies the addition of two smaller vessels.

William buys out Pio's part of the business after a disagreement between them, and he is so confident about his prospects that he sends for his wife and two children to come from England to join him. Eliza had given birth to their second child in February, in England, a son she named William, for the absent father who has not seen or held his second child. Mrs. Eliza Brown bravely takes passage on a ship recommended by her father, Mr. Chitty – she and her two children arrive safely in Buenos Aires in time for Christmas 1812.

• • •

The Spanish Empire begins to recover its strength in the new year of 1813, after Napoleon is weakened by his disastrous invasion of Russia. King Ferdinand returns to the Spanish throne and the Spanish begin to steadily reinforce their garrison in Montevideo. Commander Romarate's Spanish naval forces take control of the strategically important Martin Garcia Island in the middle of the River Plate estuary, northwest of Buenos Aires, where the Uruguay and Parana rivers flow into the River Plate. This means that the Spanish fleet control both ends of the estuary. William Brown continues building up his packet service business, but his ships are being constantly harassed by the Spanish fleet, whose actions push him further to the point of wanting a naval offensive role against them.

His detailed knowledge of the intricate Plate waterway increases daily – he hones his master mariner skills as he himself sails a coaster carrying mostly munitions for the rebels – earning high fees and a growing reputation as a blockade runner. The new Spanish general commanding the area, Marshal Vigodet, goes after Brown's ship 'Industria' with a vengeance – on one occasion arresting the crew and forcing them to pave some streets in Montevideo. This aggressive behavior alarms the patriot government in Buenos Aires and rumors circulate that a large Spanish army under General Morillo is being readied to send to Montevideo, their objective being to recapture Colonia and Buenos Aires. As the year wears on, the Buenos Aires rebel patriot government sends an army led by General Carlos de Alvear to lay siege to Montevideo – knowing it will probably be ineffective because the Spanish can supply the city continuously by sea.

• • •

In November 1813 there is a change of government in Buenos Aires. A Triumvirate led by Antonio de Posadas comes to power – he becomes the Supreme Director, with Nicolas Rodriguez as Administrator and Juan Larrea as Secretary of War. They are quick to realize that they must break the Spanish blockade before Spain has time to send Morillo's Army, and for that they need a Navy, but the government has no money to fund it. They approach the wealthy Pio White and convince him to finance the formation of a new Navy, with help from independence veterans Gurruchaga and Echevarria. White buys a Russian registered 350-ton ship called 'Hercules' that is already outfitted with some cannons and Pio thinks it can be easily transformed into the flagship frigate of the New Navy. While more guns are added to 'Hercules' Pio follows on with more ship purchases to form a squadron. Next comes the most important question for the Triumvirate – who is going to command this New Navy? It boils down to a choice between three men – Stanislaus Courrande, a Frenchman who fought as a privateer against the British: American Benjamin Seaver, a very capable merchant seaman and close associate of Pio White: and the thirty-seven-year-old Irishman William Brown. William is well known to the Triumvirate as the operator of the packet service, as a blockade buster who successfully delivers munitions for the independence forces, and as a daring privateer who has already seized ships from Romarate's fleet.

Supreme Director Posadas makes his decision and offers William Brown the post of Commander of the New Navy on March 1, 1814, with the rank of Lieutenant Colonel, while the newly acquired ships are in the process of being refitted for war. William accepts the post and almost immediately a problem erupts because Captain Seaver has been assured of a Lieutenant Colonel rank by Pio White. Seaver states that he will refuse to accept orders from Brown, and he thinks he can run his separate 'Independent Navy' operation from his own battleship 'Julieta'. William Brown takes command of 'Hercules' and names it the flagship of the fleet, telling Seaver in a letter that "no ship of the squadron, under any pretext whatsoever will be allowed to leave port ahead of Hercules" – and he also writes to Larrea, telling him this standoff must be resolved immediately. Larrea clears up the situation in William's favor, leaving Seaver less than happy, but at least he concedes authority to William Brown as Commander.

While waiting for the ships to be readied, William compiles and distributes a book of signals to his captains, pulled together from his days in the Royal Navy. All fleet masters and navigators are being schooled to cope with the treacherous conditions that prevail in the Plate Estuary, with William Brown playing the role of the master teacher. Adding to his difficulties, William has crew members from many diverse nations, and he must meld them into one coherent group. Most of his officers are British, who acknowledge Commander Brown's Royal Navy credentials and experience, and he quickly gains their respect.

The improvised naval squadron that William has pieced together to represent the United Provinces is a mixed bag of untested ships, with crews from various nationalities and backgrounds – certainly untested in battle in the River Plate, and there has been no time to train. The assembled squadron comprises one frigate, one corvette, one brigantine, two schooners, one felucca and one sloop – with a total of 91 cannons, 415 sailors and 177 troops. Romarate's Brazilian squadron consists of three brigantines, one sloop, three gunboats, one landing craft and four minor vessels – with a total of 39 cannons, 430 troops, plus a powerful land-based gun battery on Martin Garcia Island that controls the river channel.

William knows that only three of his ships are fully battle ready, and he sets sail from Buenos Aires on March 8 with those three ships – towards Los Cerros de San Juan. These ships are his flagship 'Hercules', 350 tons with 200 crew and 32 guns: 'Zephir' a 220-ton frigate with 14 guns and a crew of 140: the brig 'Nancy', 120 tons with a crew of 80 and carrying 10 nine-pounder carronades, a recently invented artillery piece for close quarter fighting. Romarate is aboard his flagship, the brig 'Belen' with 12 guns, and he assumes that the United Provinces' ships are just on a reconnoitering mission – he orders his ships to withdraw to the fortified island of Martin Garcia, thereby handing over the initiative to Commander Brown. On March 10, Brown's flotilla is joined by the schooner 'Juliet' with Seaver in command, the schooner 'Fortunata', the felucca 'San Luis' and the gunboat 'Carmen'.

Commander Brown's squadron of seven ships heads for

Martin Garcia Island at dawn on March 11, keeping to the south of the sandbank named Santa Cena. Romarate positions his squadron of eight ships off the island harbor so that most of his ships can use their broadsides to fire on the approaching enemy, and he has the big land-based gun battery on Martin Garcia to support his ships – their cannons being manned by experienced gunners. 'Hercules' opens fire at 1p.m. with 'Julieta' following her lead. All the Spanish guns begin firing in response, including the shore battery, with the experienced Spanish gunners quickly showing their superiority. Casualties mount up quickly on 'Hercules', a Lieutenant and the pilot are killed – causing the ship to run aground on the sandbank. Captain Seaver on 'Julieta' is killed, also the captain of the marine troops that are aboard 'Hercules'. The rest of the patriot flotilla fails to follow their orders to standby the flagship, and instead they bear off to the southwest – giving Romarate what he thinks is the beginnings of an easy victory. Despite 'Hercules' grounded position she keeps up continuous fire on the Spanish till nightfall, while suffering heavy casualties. Commander Brown uses the cover of darkness to have himself rowed in turn to each of his ships and he outlines his plans for them. Three gunboats are sent around the sandbank to prepare to engage Romarate's ships at long range, while the 'Hercules' crew uses kedge anchors to turn the ship sufficiently so that she can fire full broadsides when dawn arrives – mostly at the shore batteries. The morning tide lifts 'Hercules' and she is moved back out of gun range in preparation for urgent repairs – from being hit by over 80 cannon shots.

William Brown's personal schooner 'Hope' then arrives and he sends her to Colonia with his casualties and to get reinforcements to replace them. Romarate is unwilling to pursue the damaged 'Hercules' and this gives Commander Brown valuable time for repairs and reorganization. By March 14 William has eight ships assembling south of the Palmas sandbank. He gathers a special force of 340 men from his combined ship's crews and leads them himself in the ships' rowboats under cover of darkness to the southeast corner of Martin Garcia Island – where they plan to assault the Spanish battery from the rear and take control of the island. Six of his ships have been ordered to proceed up the main channel and engage Romarate's ships to draw their attention away from the proposed island assault.

At 4 a.m. on March 15 the signal rockets are sent up, the bombardment begins, and the landing party goes ashore. They are spotted by the defenders and are pinned down by enemy musket fire. William is desperate to inspire his men to attack. He is just two days away from celebrating St. Patrick's Day and he decides to take a huge gamble. Inching his way to his piper and drummer he shouts at them above the noise.

"Irishmen are not going to allow anybody to stop them on St. Patrick's Day. Play "St. Patrick's Day in the Morning" as loud as you can – Now."

Once the music starts, William leads and urges his men

forward with loud shouts, and they overwhelm the gun battery forces of the island, while suffering only three casualties. Within a short time, his patriot gunners turn the Martin Garcia guns on Romarate's squadron and force them to retreat into the Canal del Infierno. William's ships pursue the Brazilians briefly, to push them towards the mouth of the Uruguay River. Then Commander Brown must consolidate his victory by securing the island and gathering his prisoners, which unfortunately allows the Spanish ships the time to slip away. The 'Hercules' limps to Colonia for repairs while Brown sends to Buenos Aires for more ammunition – secure in the knowledge that the threat of an attack on Colonia from Martin Garcia Island has been eliminated, and communication with the patriot army besieging Montevideo has been made easier.

Commander Brown assumes that Romarate has sent word overland to Montevideo and ordered more ships to sail from there to attack the patriots from the east – therefore he must prepare for that likely event. The Spanish ranking officer in Montevideo, Primo de Rivera, sends two barges of munitions to Romarate – then he leads six ships to attack the patriot fleet, but he soon loses confidence in that plan and goes back to Montevideo. Brown's ships must keep the Spanish fleet separated into two parts – each part being stuck at either end of the Plate Estuary. Once the emergency repairs to 'Hercules' are completed the patriot flotilla prepares to sail towards Buenos Aires on March 22 – minus the several vessels he sends to harass Romarate's squadron. These patriot vessels underestimate the firing power of the Spanish, who are lying in wait for the patriot flotilla, and defeat them in a three-hour artillery battle causing lots of casualties, while also suffering substantial ship damage themselves. Captain Nother of the patriot 'Trinidad' is killed, so are his next two replacements, and Captain Spiro of 'Carmen' gets killed as he tries to blow up his ship after it runs aground.

Knowing that his shore battery on Martin Garcia Island will prevent the Spanish from following him, William steers a course to Buenos Aires where he needs emergency repairs and supplies. On route there he is joined by several more patriot ships coming from the port, including what is left of Nother's flotilla. He orders most of these ships towards Montevideo, to cruise the estuary and keep a watch on the strong Spanish squadron there, and he then plays down the triumphant reception awaiting him in Buenos Aires. Instead, he concentrates on repairing and refitting the 'Hercules'. This takes several weeks and in late April 'Hercules' rejoins the squadron near Montevideo. Suggestions of a truce with the Spanish city governor, Vigodet, are rejected by Commander Brown, who sees it as an attempt to gain time for resupply and reinforcements.

By this stage the patriot fleet under Commander Brown consists of 'Hercules' with 36 guns under Captain Gibson: the 'Belfast' with 22 guns under Captain Russell: the 'Agreeable' with 15 guns under Captain Lantarea: the 'Cefiro' with 18 guns under Captain King: the 'Nancy' with 15 guns under Captain Lech: the 'Julieta' with 7 guns now under Captain McDougal: the 'Trinadad' with 14 guns under the recovered Captain Hubac, and the 'San Luis' with 3 guns under Captain Clark – 8 ships with 130 guns and 1,224 sailors. Commander Brown establishes contact with the land army besieging Montevideo, led by General Rondeau. Then he declares an official blockade which under international law gives him the right to stop, search and detain any ship trying to enter the port.

Montevideo is now besieged by land and sea – its population soon begins to suffer deprivation under city governor Vigodet, who still has his squadron of Spanish warships if he wants to use them for a naval break-out. Vigodet calls a Council of War and after an acrimonious debate they decide to add several armed merchant ships to their squadron and prepare their 1,400 sailors for a sortie. Primo de Rivera is against the plan, resigns his post citing ill health and is replaced by an experienced commander named Miguel Sierra. Then, a powerful Pampero blows through the area for a few days, halting all naval activity – after which the two sides line up for battle.

Commander Brown moves his ships closer to shore to maintain visual contact with the besieging patriot soldiers on land. During the night of May 13, Captain Gibson's lookouts spot signal rockets over Montevideo and get ready for the expected attack. At 7 a.m. on the March 14 the breakout Spanish squadron emerges from the morning mist – the

'Hiena' with 18 guns and flying Sierra's flag: the 'Mercurio' with 22 guns: the 'Neptuno' with 24 guns: the 'Corsario' with 8 guns: the 'San Carlos' with 8 guns: the 'Maria' with 4 guns: the 'Cisne' with 10 guns: the 'Fama' with two guns: the 'San Jose' with 16 guns: the ' Catalonia with 4 guns and 'La Podrida' with 2 guns – 13 ships in total with over 155 guns and 1,200 sailors. Spanish Commander Sierra leads the first division of four ships while Jose de Posadas of 'Neptuno' leads the second division. The Spanish squadron advances towards the patriot squadron – Commander Brown orders his ships to shorten sail, position themselves astern of his flagship and steer according to his signals – wanting to draw Sierra seaward so he could get windward of the Spanish squadron and cut off their retreat to Montevideo. Sierra's plan is to draw the patriots in under the heavy guns of the Cerro Fort which commands the northern part of Montevideo Bay.

Brown turns his squadron to port and 'Hercules' exchanges fire for thirty minutes with 'Mercurio' who is leading the port-hand line of the first division. The Spanish line falls into disarray – 'Paloma' is proving unmanageable from previous damage and 'Neptuno' has weight distribution issues that are multiplied by the action of the strong currents of the river. Suddenly the wind drops, and all the ships are becalmed. The Spanish lower their boats to tow the larger ships inshore and to the east, 'La Podrida' attacks the patriot 'San Luis' and captures two small boats that are with it, and then seeks shelter under the shore batteries when other patriot ships go towards her. A breeze at noon allows Brown to regroup and sail eastwards, causing Sierra to think they are withdrawing, and he gives chase. Fire is exchanged between several ships until darkness falls.

The two squadrons drift closer to each other during the next several hours and 'Hercules' manages to fire off two broadsides that inflict serious damage on the enemy ship 'Hiena', causing her to become unmanageable, forcing her and her sister ship 'Mercurio' to withdraw from the action. By dawn on May 15 there is no wind, and the patriot squadron is mostly in good order six miles offshore, other than 'Nancy' and 'Agreeable', who manage to reposition themselves with extra effort. The Spaniards are lying close together near the shore with Posadas in command. No action is possible that day and both squadrons anchor in sight of each other. When a Northwest breeze arises after dark, Posadas orders anchors raised and his ships move away to the Southwest. Brown cannot see what is happening, but he has a gut feeling that the enemy ships are moving; he orders sails to be hoisted, and they follow them, then he changes course to the Southeast.

Dawn breaks, showing that the Spaniards are still visible but are widely dispersed, and the patriot squadron is joined by another vessel, a shallow-draft sumaca, the 'Ytati'. Weak breezes continue and by mid-afternoon Commander Brown changes his flag to his fastest vessel, the 'Ytati'. They manage to maneuver it into a position to fire on an enemy brig, inflicting casualties, but draw a lot of return fire on themselves. Shortly afterwards a cannon recoil smashes into Commander Brown's leg. Even as they bring him to 'Hercules' for treatment he orders his ships to continue firing, and he insists that surgeon Campbell treats him on deck while he continues directing operations. At 6 p.m. a fresh breeze is quickly taken advantage of by Posadas and the patriot flotilla gives chase.

Brown's master mariner skills now come into play as he carries out a daring maneuver and sails between 'Neptuno' and 'San Jose', which throws the Spanish line of battle into confusion. 'San Jose' runs aground on a sandbank, 'Neptuno' hoists all sails to escape but is overtaken and captured by the patriot ship 'Belfast'. 'Hercules' blasts 'San Jose' with cannon fire and a boarding party is then able to seize her. The Spanish ship 'Paloma' comes within range of 'Cefiro' who pounds the ship and captures her. The patriot squadron by this stage has captured three Spanish ships, after having a day earlier put the Spanish flagship 'Hiena' out of action and forced 'Mercurio' into port.

A furious artillery duel breaks out between the two squadrons during the early hours of May 17 and the United Province patriots get the better of that exchange. One by one the Spanish ships break off engagement while Commander Brown holds his squadron together and keeps their prizes in formation. He chases the fleeing ships and cuts off the attempts of 'Cisne', 'Corsario' and 'Maria' to retreat to port. Those ships are so close to shore that some Spanish sailors swim to the city and tell the defenders of their terrible defeat. Soon afterwards 'Hercules' fires a 21-gun salute in celebration of their victory – quickly returned by the besieging patriot army. The patriot squadron is now able to blockade the city at close quarters, making its fall inevitable.

Finally, on June 24, Vigodet surrenders Montevideo. Soon afterwards Romarate surrenders in Arroyo de la China, as do the Royalists in Carmen de Patagones. The United Provinces take control of the entire Atlantic coast southward from La Plata Estuary, and Spain's colonial rule over much of South America ends.

This is all made possible because William Brown, the fiery thirty-seven-year-old Irish Commander of the patriot fleet wins the critical naval battle off Montevideo in May 1814.

CHAPTER SIX

EXPANDING REVOLUTION IN SOUTH AMERICA

Commander William Brown is celebrated for his great victory and is awarded the ship 'Hercules' as a gift in recognition of his service as the General-in-Chief of the Navy of the United Provinces. Personally, he is more pleased by the outpouring of gratitude from the ordinary people of Buenos Aires, and the fact that he can now go home to his wife and children. During his long absences Eliza gives all her attention to caring for the children and caring for her garden. Her frequent letters home to England are rewarded when she hears that her brother Walter Chitty is about to arrive in Buenos Aires along with her brother-in-law, Michael Brown. William is overjoyed to hear this news and wants nothing more than to spend some quiet time with all of them at his home, La Casa Amarilla. They pull out all the stops to welcome the visitors and the locals are happy to put on events to entertain their beloved Commander and his guests. After a rest, William plans to go back to his merchant shipping business.

Before long, the political factions within the United Provinces begin to argue among themselves, and disorder grows in the country. William has a problem with the influential American merchant, Pio White, who he thinks is attempting to undermine his authority as Commander of the Navy. White calls in support from ruling triumvirate members Larrea and Posadas, who are indebted to him for the financial support he provided to fund the navy. When William sees the confusion this is causing, he decides it is in his best interest to resign his position.

In his resignation letter to Larrea he writes –

"If abandoning my small business, my house, my wife and my family, risking my life all the time, so as to be able to do some small service to this country, is a reason why I seem to have made enemies, it is time for me to retire, whatever my intentions to help in any struggle against any future enemy."

He adds that he wants to see a quick and fair distribution of the prize monies owed to his officers and crew. Then he hires Michael and Walter into his merchant business and all three undertake commercial voyages which carry them away from Buenos Aires.

William's resignation is refused, and Larrea appoints him to the added position of harbor master of the fast-growing port of Buenos Aires. The government wants to turn the recent defensive war against the Spanish into a new offensive war: they want to achieve the complete expulsion of Spanish imperial forces from South America. William sympathizes with that objective – he must admit to himself that he has become quite the revolutionary during the war against the Spanish Empire. He agrees to go to the Banda Oriental (later to be Uruguay) in March to negotiate a common defense agreement with the de-facto leader, Artigas, and while there he succeeds in getting "an agreement of sorts" – the best that can be extracted out of the unpredictable Artigas.

Next, the United Provinces government declares a privateer war against Spanish seaborne trade – worldwide – and William is asked to plan a privateer cruise for his ships. He accepts, a letter of marque is issued September 1, 1815, and he begins preparations to send 'Hercules' under Captain Walter Chitty and 'Trinidad' under Captain Michael Brown into service in this new privateer venture. His plan is to them to sail south, around the treacherous Cape Horn and up the Pacific coast to raid Lima, Peru, the nerve center of Spanish rule on the Pacific coast, a city that is protected by the nearby heavily fortified port of Callao. He gets bales of leaflets printed to hand out to the ordinary people in Peru, and Chile and in the other territories – espousing the qualities of a local Republican government (using the newly independent United Provinces as a model): where a constitution guarantees the rights of its citizens over the corrupt imperial system of King Ferdinand of Spain.

Michael and Walter express their concerns about sailing round the notorious Cape Horn on the southern tip of South America – neither of the two, nor even William himself, have any sailing experience in these frigid southern waters. An accomplished United Provinces ship captain who had distinguished himself in the first navy venture, Frenchman Hipolito Bouchard, is planning a similar privateering cruise, and he offers to advise Walter and Michael.

"I have sailed round the Cape before. All of you are excellent sailors and even though the Cape is challenging and dangerous, I have every reason to believe that you will be just fine. I will be aboard 'Halcon', and Captain Russell in 'Constitucion' will sail alongside me – let's plan to meet up at the island of La Mocha, off the Chilean coast."

Walter and Michael are still apprehensive about the mission, until William decides that this expedition is of such importance that he must go along himself. He announces that he will go as Commander, much to the disappointment of his wife. Eliza pleads with him not to leave his family and his business for this dangerous adventure.

"My dear, you have been away so much. Surely it is time to stay home and operate your merchant business."

He tries to explain to her the importance of the expedition, but she holds her ground, using the children to help her case. Finally, he tells her that his mind is made up – he is sad to leave her and the children again, but this liberation mission is something that he must do.

She knows how stubborn he can be and meekly lets the matter drop. The government had given the expedition its full support to begin with, but when they become aware that William Brown himself is commanding one of the ships, they issue an order specifically forbidding Commander William Brown to be in command of a privateer cruise – saying he has unspecified "important duties" to carry out in Buenos Aires as Commander of the Navy. William is a very single-minded man, obstinate according to his wife, and unwilling to change his plans once his mind is made up – he informs the government that 'Hercules' is under the command of Michael Brown, saying nothing about his plans to also be aboard. The two ships sail to Colonia to take on provisions and then depart from the River Plate Estuary on October 21, 1815. To save face after the ships have sailed with William aboard, the Supreme Director of the government publicly authorizes Commander Brown to proceed with the cruise, but in internal government documents he writes that he will strip him of his Lieutenant Colonel rank for this insubordination.

• • •

Their voyage South begins with good weather and good progress. Soon, the landscape and the climate change as they near the polar region – the daylight begins to fade early and the vegetation along the coast gets sparse until it disappears completely. Penguins and seals are the only greeters of the passing ships, from the safety of the shore. The ships approach Cape Horn amid the floes of ice, the crews marveling at the white frozen landscape all around them. Rather suddenly the weather changes – drastically for the worse. Some of their sails are damaged by the fierce winds, the waves become as tall as the masts, causing the ships' bows to rise steeply and then plunge deep into the angry sea. Secured crates of provisions break loose and slide around the hold, the ships timbers creak with the increased strain.

The 'Trinidad' suffers damage to her steering, and Michael must take his chances by moving his ship off ahead into the open sea away from the rocks – her lantern soon disappears, and William is fearful she may be lost. 'Hercules' trudges on alone and enters the Straits of Magellan where she is buffeted about like a toy – the helmsman tries to steer towards a small cove for shelter, but the ferocious winds push the ship into a narrow channel between two huge rocks. They must hoist more sails to escape these rocks – the sails fill with wind immediately and hurl the ship forward, mercifully missing the large rocks but they end up stuck fast on some smaller rock shelf. Frantically the crew works to free 'Hercules', dumping cannons and provisions to lighten the ship – they manage to get her free but also realize that they have sustained a hole in the hull below the water line and are taking in water. While the crew pumps water from the hold, the helmsman manages to get the ship into a small bay.

They spend five days there repairing the hull – William

and Walter are consumed with the repair work, not allowing themselves time to dwell on whether Michael and the 'Trinidad' are lost. The exhausted crew members are allowed to go ashore in turns to walk around and that brings up another problem – desertion. Despite the desolate inhospitable landscape, there are increased murmurings by some crew members, preferring to take their chances on land rather than face the raging sea again. William doubles the guard but still loses six crew to desertion, two of them being sentries. He is certain that the deserters will die in this frigid land, and he does everything he can to entice them back – he delays the ship's departure; he fires a cannon three times. None of them return and before the ship departs, he orders that some food is to be stored on land between the rocks, plus two muskets and ammunition, blankets, a pan, a knife, a hatchet, tinder and a candle.

Then 'Hercules' gets under way and sails back into the Straits of Magellan, to continue their difficult passage – one that forces the helmsman to change course constantly to avoid huge walls of ice and rock that seem to appear before them out of nowhere. Eventually the channel opens up and a little further along the 'Trinidad' comes into view. There are tears of joy for William and Michael, and for both crews – they sail the final portion of the Straits together in the waning days of December and emerge safely into the Pacific Ocean.

After a review of their voyage plans, the two ships separate and begin searching for Spanish prizes for several weeks – with the rendezvous point remaining as La Mocha Island in mid-January 1816. William hopes that Bouchard will be there to greet them after a safe voyage. The 'Trinidad' captures a schooner on her route, the 'Hercules' finds no prize – but they arrive at Mocha within hours of each other and are happy to find the 'Halcon' waiting for them. Hipolito tells them the sad news of the loss of the 'Constitucion' during a fifteen-day storm off Tierra del Fuego.

"Captain Russell's ship was owned by the Chilean nationalists, and she was loaded with so many armaments that she was too low in the water. In the storm she was engulfed by the huge waves and we ourselves struggled so much that we were not able to help them – then suddenly she was gone. Chancellor Julian Uribe was aboard, along with our mutual good friend Captain Russell – may they all rest in peace.

My orders are to place my ship under your command – Commander-in-Chief, Sir."

William orders Bouchard and Michael (plus his prize) to harass Spanish shipping between Valparaiso and Callao, while he sails for Juan Fernandez Island to liberate Chilean patriots that are imprisoned there. As he nears the island violent storms force William to alter his course drastically, and must abandon his plan, he sails instead for Callao and Lima, in Peru. On route he captures the Spanish frigate 'Gobernadora' and when he meets Bouchard later in January, he finds that 'Halcon' has also captured a prize – and Michael shows up with his prize alongside his ship 'Trinidad'. Three more prizes are soon captured by their flotilla, so William decides to arm and man two of the six prizes. He then leads his squadron of five armed ships directly towards the forts guarding Callao, with all his ships flying the light blue and white ensign of the United Provinces.

On January 21, they anchor out of range of the fort's guns, then fire on and sink the Spanish frigate 'Fuente Hermosa' that night. Next day they attack the anchored Spanish ships in the bay, and the gunboats defending them – later withdrawing when darkness falls. They regroup and on Jan 27 William sends Walter Chitty to lead a crew in some of his ship's row-boats, their mission being to light fires on an island that is visible from the city – to spread anxiety among the local citizens while William sails 'Hercules' to attack the forts and gunboats again. Chitty captures a gunboat during his return from the island but is seriously wounded in the battle and is rowed to the 'Hercules' for urgent treatment by the ship's surgeon. The patriot squadron fires on the forts for hours before retreating to Lorenzo Island, and that night they capture the Spanish frigate 'Consecuencia' after a brief exchange of fire – finding several important Spanish officials aboard, including General Mendiburu, the governor of Guayaquil, a Spanish-controlled city further to the north.

The squadron and their prizes then sail north towards the Gulf of Guayaquil. At the mouth of the Guayas River, William sends the prisoners ashore from his prizes, in return for a supply of fresh fruit and vegetables, and a local pilot. They sail on towards Guayaquil, arriving on Feb 9. The first fort they encounter fires on their leading ship, the 'Trinidad', causing some damage. The action lasts for thirty minutes before a landing party from 'Halcon' storms the fort and captures it. William then elects to proceed upriver with only 'Trinidad' and its16 guns, and the schooner 'Crocodilo' with 6 guns, thinking this smaller force will make it easier to surprise the city.

After he opens fire on the next fort they encounter, the fort guns reply with heavy firepower and inflict serious damage on 'Trinidad'. The ship vigorously fires back, silencing the fort's cannons, and a landing party from 'Crocodilo' puts the surviving garrison to flight. An ebbing tide then causes 'Trinidad' to run aground very close to the city of Guayaquil, and William's landing party fails to follow his strict orders of protecting the grounded ship – after sacking the garrison they begin looting warehouses. These unfortunate grounding and looting incidents allow troops defending the city to regroup and make use of a stack of lumber sitting on the riverbank as cover, very close to the 'Trinidad'. Enemy soldiers bring the ship under heavy musket fire, killing and wounding dozens of the crew. William orders his colors lowered in surrender, but the Spanish continue firing, so he calls on the survivors to jump overboard with him and swim to their schooner, 'Crocodilo'. Only two men follow William's lead – both of those sailors are shot while in the water, arousing the plentiful alligators. William swims back to his ship to find that an enemy boarding party is systematically killing all the wounded and captured patriot crew members.

William grabs an axe and a lantern and rushes below deck to the powder magazine. He takes an enemy prisoner and sends him forward to tell the enemy commander that Commodore Brown, leader of the invading force, will blow up the ship immediately unless his men accept his surrender and stop the massacre of his crew. The man relays the message, and the commander stops the killing. When William is satisfied with the commander's good faith response, he wraps himself in a United Provinces flag and leads the surviving 48 crew members ashore to be taken prisoner. William is marched to Government House where under interrogation he identifies himself as an Admiral from the United Provinces. They are more curious than hostile towards him and he is brought to dine with a group of city officials.

His speech to the officials is an explanation of the aims of the insurgent movement in the United Provinces – a total surprise to his hosts, who declare that if they had known whom his ships represented, they would never have fired a shot. They allow him to write letters to Michael Brown and to Walter Chitty who are still anchored downstream at the captured fort. He asks them to send him clothes and some money – and, under duress from the officials he tells them to go home to Buenos Aires. Michael replies with a letter to the Spanish, suggesting an exchange of prisoners, which they agree to, but their terms are unacceptable to Michael. The patriot squadron then sails upstream and proceeds to bombard the city till a rudder on 'Halcon' is damaged and they withdraw. Bouchard returns to the harbor under a flag of truce, and they begin three days of negotiations. The patriot squadron maintains a blockade and threatens to renew the bombardment, and interestingly, the inhabitants watching this standoff begin to support the ideals of liberation that the patriots are preaching.

An agreement is reached – in exchange for Commander William Brown and the other prisoners, the patriots agree to give up four of their prizes, all their remaining prisoners, and hand over mail bags from Spain that they had confiscated and agree to cease all hostilities against Guayaquil. As soon as word of the agreement spreads among the inhabitants of the city a swarm of boats approach the patriot squadron wanting to purchase grain and other commodities from the prize cargos they have retained. William returns to his ship, and he writes a letter to the governor of Guayaquil thanking him for the good treatment he received while a prisoner. Meanwhile, Hipolito's ship 'Halcon' is in a very precarious condition – William decides to sail the squadron to the Galapagos Islands to carry out repairs in safety. While there the prize booty is shared, 70% to William and 30% to Hipolito Bouchard, who gets the captured ships 'Andaluz' and 'Consecuencia' for his share. Hipolito decides to refit 'Consecuencia' as a replacement for the badly damaged 'Halcon' and renames this new ship 'Argentina'.

Michael asks – "What does that name mean, Hipolito?"

He is happy to explain – "When Portuguese and Spanish shipwrecked sailors first showed up on these coasts, the natives helped them and gave them gifts made of silver. The sailors reasoned that there must be a lot of silver in the area – the Latin word for silver is Argentum. This led to the great river being named 'Rio de la Plata' in honor of this local silver. When we declared our independence from Spain as the United Provinces, I heard people in Buenos Aires trying to come up with a single name for the homeland – like how you fellows have 'Ireland'. A poet named Martin del Barco Centenera wrote a poem about Rio de la Plata and in that poem "Argentina" was the name he called the place. I liked it the first time I heard the name – it reminds me of home when I am far away at sea."

Shortly afterwards Hipolito decides to sail his two ships on a westerly cruise towards the Philippines, to continue disrupting Spanish commerce and spreading the freedom ideals of the United Provinces. William Brown sails to Buenaventura in Peru, which is controlled by Nationalists. He sends Dr. Handford and a rescued Cali insurgent off on an inland mission to New Granada (later Columbia), to incite a war of freedom against Spanish repression there, and to recount the important arrival of the patriot ships on the Pacific Coast. William sells the captured prizes, and all this money is stored aboard 'Hercules' – to be divided up between the state, his crew and himself, when they return home. William stays in port for weeks, waiting for Handford's return, while attempting repairs to make 'Halcon' seaworthy, but the effort is deemed a failure. They leave port when word comes of an approaching Spanish army led by General Morillo – he who had landed on the northeast coast (later Venezuela) in 1814 after abandoning his plan to land at the recently fallen Montevideo. Morillo had then rampaged across the continent towards the Spanish territory of Peru.

William reluctantly sails without Dr. Handford, he scuttles the hapless 'Halcon' after salvaging everything deemed to be of value, and sails back to Galapagos to allow his crew to rest before their perilous journey home. He is consumed with memories and visions of Eliza and their children. They have been alone in Buenos Aires for almost a year at this stage without any news of his whereabouts, unless the Gazeta de Buenos Aires has published reports of his exploits. The gash on the hull of 'Hercules' opens again, and they spend a full week repairing it to withstand the severe conditions they soon expect to face when rounding Cape Horn. They stock up on provisions and take dozens of live giant tortoises on board as food before setting sail for home. There is a huge stretch of ocean to be crossed before they get to Cape Horn and William must impose a strict diet to make their food supply last, catching what they can from the sea itself, and collecting rainwater during the squalls.

They enter the frigid waters of the Cape and make their way among the ice floes, some of which scrape along the sides of the ship, causing strange noises that drive some crew members to the edge of madness. They make it through to the Atlantic Ocean and sacrifice the last remaining tortoise in celebration of their safe arrival. William sets a course for the almost uninhabited Malvinas to seek food and water, but a ferocious storm prevents them from forward progress – they relent, and head for Rio de la Plata, not knowing what awaits them there.

It is mid-August 1816 when they meet the British brig 'Fanny' on passage from Montevideo to Falmouth. The captain agrees to sell them sacks of bread and tells William that the Portuguese are blockading the River Plate Estuary, and that Buenos Aires is consumed with anarchy. Brown calls his crew together for counsel – asking their opinions before formulating their best course of action, except for his brother Michael who is gravely ill with scurvy. He decides to head for the Brazilian port of Pernambuco (Recife), flying the Portuguese colors and they put Michael ashore to get treatment – passing him off as an English shipwreck victim while they secure urgently needed supplies. Without Michael, they head for the British Territory of the Lesser Antilles, to Bridgetown in Barbados, where William expects to receive fair and welcome treatment, and where he plans to undertake more repairs – after which he will assess whether to voyage on to Buenos Aires.

They arrive in Bridgetown harbor at the end of September, under the same Portuguese colors. The authorities suspect that 'Hercules' may be a pirate ship and send officers to inspect her privateering papers and cargo. They bring William ashore to the Customs House, where the governor reads the papers signed by the Supreme Director of the United Provinces. He shakes his head and states that His Gracious Majesty the King does not recognize this new state – he says Britain regards the province as a property of Spain and that the ship must leave after picking up supplies. While getting these supplies, William takes the opportunity of using the British postal system to send letters to Eliza in Buenos Aires, to the Chitty's in England, and to the Supreme Director in the United Provinces.

A Captain Stirling from the British frigate HMS 'Brazen' interrogates the crew of 'Hercules' in William's absence. Upon William's return he tells him that he personally knows Admiral Harvey, the British commander-in-chief for this region who is based in Antigua. He says that he is about to set sail for there and suggests that 'Hercules' should tag along, and he will be able to help William get his papers straightened out. The offer is accepted and the ships sail. After two days at sea Stirling sends an armed boarding party that surprises the exhausted crew of 'Hercules' – they arrest William and bring him to the 'Brazen'. Walter Chitty is ordered to follow close behind 'Brazen', with the armed boarding party making sure he does so. When they arrive in Antigua, William is arrested on Stirling's accusations of irregularities in his papers. Admiral Harvey cites an old forgotten British law which restricts all maritime trade east of the Cape of Good Hope and west of Cape Horn to ships belonging to the East India

Company. William is brought before the Vice-Admiralty Court of Antigua, which declares 'Hercules' and her cargo forfeit under this law. William's defense argument that he is acting under the license of a sovereign state is rejected.

To make matters worse, William falls ill with severe malaria and paralyzing rheumatism. He sends Walter Chitty to London as a passenger on another ship to begin the formal appeal process against the Antigua judgement. While Walter is on that voyage 'Hercules' and her cargo are sold at public auction for well below her real value, and none of the proceeds are given to William. By early March the appeal proceedings in London are under way and Walter Chitty writes to the United Provinces government advising them of the predicament that 'Hercules' is in, enclosing letters that William had sent with him. He informs the supreme director that William is coming to London to oversee the appeal process as soon as he is well enough – which he does in mid-April 1817 – penniless but resolute in his intentions. With help from the Chitty family, he pursues the appeal that Walter Chitty has set in motion. William also writes to the United Provinces envoy in Europe, Bernardino Rivadavia, in Paris, who already knows of William Brown and knows that he is an honorable man. Rivadavia is sympathetic to his predicament, and he responds promptly saying –

"I put it to you that you are required and duty-bound to return to Buenos Aires as soon as possible for the sake of your honor."

William decides to engage Hullet Brothers, who act as London agents for the United Provinces government, to prosecute the case in the Admiralty Court and attempt to recover 'Hercules'. He writes to the Supreme Director and informs him of his intention to return soon, saying in his letter –

"I am intending with truth and justice on my side, to give a satisfactory account of my conduct and operations."

In Buenos Aires the government has already suspended payment of William's wages to his wife Eliza, and then they refused her application for a visa to travel to England. She is devastated by this denial and writes to a friend describing her predicament –

"The government have no right to hold me, they know well that the service William is engaged in on their behalf is dangerous, and I know well how his former services were rewarded."

Eliza is resourceful as always and she manages to elude the government surveillance – she convinces the captain of the British frigate H.M.S Amphion to give her and her children passage to England. They arrive safely and join William in London. His appeal takes a long time but is partially successful in the end. The London Court decision is that on a technicality the court in Antigua had no jurisdiction in the case of William's ship, as the vessel was seized outside of Antigua. The Court orders that William should receive the sum raised by the sale of 'Hercules', including for her cargo and equipment. His triumph is short-lived when legal action is then filed against William by the Ambassador of the King of Spain. They are claiming the value of Spanish ships and cargo seized by 'Hercules' – on the grounds that William was acting under license from a state not recognized by Britain or Spain. This legal action results in more than half of the proceeds granted in the earlier court being awarded to Spain.

After the United Provinces government gets its share and the crew get their share, William Brown gets almost nothing.

• • •

William fulfills his promise to the Supreme Director and returns to Buenos Aires – alone. Three days after his arrival on October 23, 1818, he is arrested and charged with disobeying orders. The government prosecutors demand the death sentence, and he is confined in the military barracks of Aguerridos while this Court Martial takes place. The prosecution labels him as a pirate, while his defense counsel, Colonel Mariano Rolon, contends that although William had ignored an order, he had done so as the legally constituted Commander-in-Chief of the Navy – with a clear right to be consulted about operational policy.

He is found guilty of the charges – the verdict condemns William to be deprived of all naval rank and to forfeit to the state what remains of his personal share of the profits from the expedition, leaving him penniless, but at least he is allowed to hold on to his home.

The head of state in United Provinces at this time is General Rondeau, who had commanded the troops besieging Montevideo when William Brown won his great naval victory there. He has a lot of respect for William, and he pushes the government to have second thoughts about the verdict. On September 17, 1819, a decree is issued that restores William to his rank of Colonel, in command of the Navy, while declaring him to be henceforth retired from the service. William is still devastated by the trial verdict and to add to his misery he then comes down with typhoid. He is alone and in a bad way, but supportive friends named Mr. and Mrs. Reid take him to their home to nurse him back to health. On one of the days when he is deranged with fever, and not realizing that he is on the third floor, he falls from the balcony. Miraculously, he is not killed but breaks several bones including his femur. Again, his friends come together to help him, and they take turns caring for him for the full year that it takes him to recover. Once he can walk again these friends move William back to his estate in Barracas, where he begins a new life as a farmer.

Throughout these bad times that have lasted for almost four years, William has insisted that Eliza and the children stay in the comfort of England. Now that he is back in his home he finally relents and they return to Buenos Aires in 1822, escorted by his brother, Michael, whom William last saw when they left him in Brazil suffering from scurvy. Eliza again shows her mettle and takes over the management of the farm which allows the Brown brothers to seek an opportunity to get back into the merchant shipping business.

They buy the brig 'Hutton' and begin merchant trading with the West Indies, exporting mules and bringing back sugar and rum. William's original career plan was to be a merchant trader, and he revels in his return to fulfilling those dreams. Michael sees the joy in his brother's face – he is happy for him, but he feels obliged to ask the obvious question.

William – "When will the next crisis arrive? Enjoy this merchant hiatus while it lasts, because when that crisis comes, the leaders will be knocking on your door. They will want a proven leader to rebuild the Navy once more – and that leader is you."

"Naw. Michael, you're wrong, it's going to be peaceful sailing from now on."

CHAPTER SEVEN

WAR WITH THE EMPIRE OF BRAZIL

During the years that William Brown is tormented by his legal troubles arising from the seizure of 'Hercules', the political map in South America changes, much of that emanating from the revolutionary influences of the United Provinces.

General Jose San Martin marches his United Provinces army and his 'Granaderos a Caballo' (Regiment of Mounted Grenadiers), over the Andes into Chile and scores an important victory at the battle of Chacabuco in 1817. San Martin backs Bernardo O'Higgins to become governor of Chile, which declares its independence from Spain a year later. Royalist forces from the Viceroyalty of Peru threaten Santiago until April 1818, when San Martin inflicts a decisive defeat on the Royalist commander, General Mariano Osorio, at the Battle of Maipu which breaks the power of the Royalists. The Chileans and San Martin continue to press into Peru and fighting continues until victory at the Battle of Ayacucho in 1825 ends the Royalist threat there. Simon Bolivar and his independence forces have been gradually getting the better of the Spanish army led by General Morillo in the regions that will later become Venezuela and Columbia.

In the United Provinces region, a definitive declaration of independence from Spain is made in 1816 following The Congress of Tucuman and discussions begin on a constitution. The maritime exploration tradition begun by William Brown continues to develop – a United Province ship explores the previously unknown Antarctic Continent, and the frigate 'Heroina' visits the almost uninhabited Malvinas Islands and plants the country's blue and white ensign there. In 1823 a treaty of trade and friendship is signed with the old colonial power, Spain, opening a new era of trade and prosperity. The country then prepares to adopt a new constitution with the plan to drop the name United Provinces in favor of the new unofficial name of "Argentina" (it did not become the official name until 1860) – all of this while William and Michael Brown are out of the limelight and are rebuilding their merchant shipping business.

Mixed in with all of this 'progress' there are some serious political problems, chief among them being the continuous disorder in Banda Oriental. Portuguese troops who have been occupying part of the area since 1815 steadily extend their grip, and in 1820 the old independence warrior, Artigas, is finally driven out. That leads to King Joao of Portugal issuing a decree in 1821 incorporating Banda Oriental into his "Kingdom of Portugal, the Algarve and Brazil" – calling the new province "Provincia Cisplatina". In 1822 the situation gets even more complicated when Dom Pedro, Joao's eldest son, packs off the elderly King Joao to Portugal and proclaims himself Emperor of Brazil. Matters boil over when Argentine General Lavalle and a few dozen followers sail from Buenos Aires and land at Las Vacas in 1825, to proclaim Banda Oriental as a protectorate of Argentina.

As soon as news of this landing reaches Rio de Janeiro, Dom Pedro dispatches 1,200 troops to his provincial governor. He also sends a squadron of the Brazilian Navy to the area, commanded by Admiral Lobo, who anchors off Buenos Aires and Lobo sends a blunt note to the government in the city. Their demands are the recall of all Argentinian citizens who are helping General Lavalle, the punishment of those who had damaged their consulate in an attack, and a ban on sending supplies of war materials to the rebels in Banda Oriental.

The head of the Argentine government, General La Heras, vacillates while Admiral Lobo warns him that they will use force to get their demands met. La Heras sends troops to the west bank of the Uruguay River as a show of support for Lavalle, and Dom Pedro continues adding to the Brazilian forces in the area – resulting in an outbreak of fighting. On

October 25, the Buenos Aires government announces that Banda Oriental is being incorporated into Argentina. After some deliberation, Brazilian Emperor Dom Pedro answers Argentina with a formal Declaration of War against them on December 10, 1825.

General La Heras has been expecting this outcome, and he has been trying to put a naval force together to counter the Brazilian blockade of Buenos Aires that he assumes is coming. At this time Argentina has only two armed brigs in their Navy: 'Balcarce' and 'General Belgrano', and the armed launch 'Correntina', plus a dozen small gunboats. Meanwhile, a British naval officer named Captain Robert Ramsay has recently arrived In Buenos Aires to set up a Naval College there. The beleaguered government offers Ramsey the position of Colonel-in-Chief to command their Navy. He declines the offer, telling them that they already have a tried and trusted naval leader in their midst who is the most capable leader for their Navy in war – Commander William Brown.

The government is in a sticky situation caused by their earlier unjust treatment of William Brown. However, due to the Brazilian threat to the country they make an about-turn and offer Brown the Navy command in the waning days of 1825. Just like that, William is fully restored to favor, and he patriotically accepts the post, knowing that once again he will have to build their Navy from virtually nothing. His wife Eliza is wholly supportive of his decision and is full of pride that her husband is the man sought out by the government to save the country. Captain Ramsay visits William at his home to wish him well and pays him a supreme compliment by presenting him with the ornate sword that he himself used in all his naval campaigns. William graciously accepts the sword.

This time round, William makes sure his orders are clearly recorded on paper.

Those orders state – "That under his command are all the captains, officers, and crews of the warships, and leaving to his direction the changes and repairs that he considers necessary – and he alone is responsible for the operations to which they may be destined."

This time there are plenty of cannons, ammunition and other weapons available from storage since William captured them in his victory of 1814, and he immediately gets to work. A Privateer War is declared against all ships and property belonging to the Emperor of Brazil and his subjects. Michael Brown is pleased for his brother, but he does not want to be part of another Argentine war and has an emotional meeting with his brother.

"William, my family is in Britain, and they do not have any great desire to emigrate to Argentina, especially with the continuing turmoil. I have no stomach for getting involved in another war and I know that you are fully capable without me. As soon as I can find passage, I will sail home to Liverpool to be with my wife and children. I hope you are not disappointed in me."

"I totally understand, Michael, and I agree with your

decision. Likewise, please accept that I am fully committed to Argentina and will do my patriotic duty. Please visit Eliza and the children before you leave, and pass our fondest wishes to your family, and do keep an eye out for dear old Ireland."

The brothers have a long and tearful embrace, knowing that it is most probably their last farewell.

• • •

Commander William Brown decides that he needs to prepare a minimum of seven ships for his squadron and does so with great haste. They are the brigs 'Congreso Nacional': 'Independencia' and 'Republica Argentina': the schooners 'Sarandi': 'Pepa' and 'Rio de la Plata' – and a former Spanish frigate named 'Comercio' which he renames the '25 de Mayo' in honor of the date of the 1810 declaration of independence – and he designates her to be his flagship. He has just about enough ships to put a battle line in place, one that in total has150 cannons and 780 men – he adds some more power by commandeering three smaller vessels and several gunboats.

By January 13, 1826, Commander Brown hoists his flag temporarily on the 'Balcarce' (as '25 de Mayo' is not yet ready) and he sails out onto the Rio de la Plata. Arrayed against this tiny Argentinian flotilla is the much larger Brazilian fleet – 129 warships, 10 gunboats and thousands of seamen. The Brazilians carry 1,600 cannons, against 150 for the Argentines.

Admiral Lobo, the Brazilian commander, puts a naval blockade in place affecting the main Argentine ports in the estuary, and the lower Parana and Uruguay rivers – a blockade that he claims is so tight that even a bird cannot penetrate it. On January 13 William sails to the outport anchorage near Buenos Aires, known as Los Pozos, ordering each of his vessels to be ready at any moment to 'sortie' into the estuary. He shows his clear intention to engage the thirteen Brazilian blockading vessels, who decide to pull up anchors and head away to the southeast.

A quiet develops for a while – then two Brazilian sloops and a gunboat approach the Argentine shore and are challenged – the Argentines capture one enemy sloop and the gunboat. After another failed attempt to lure Brown's ships far out into the estuary, the opposing squadrons hunker down in place for a few weeks, keeping an eye on each other. The '25 de Mayo' finally joins the flotilla as William's flagship, along with three more refitted ships. Per his usual daring personality, Brown decides to directly challenge the enemy on February 9 and sights them off Colonia. Some maneuvering by both sides takes place and an hour of cannonade follows before the Brazilians break off to the southeast to reinforce their blockade, and William leads his squadron back to their anchorage at Los Pozos. While another lull in the action occurs, William leads his squadron to the outer roads and directs them through rigorous exercises – in particular, showing them how he wants the ships to take up formation in a line of battle. There is another maneuvering contest between the two naval forces on February 22 that ends in a stalemate.

On February 25, William puts on a surprise show of force in front of the harbor of Colonia, then he sends a messenger ashore politely requesting the surrender of all ships in port. The governor declines to surrender, and hostilities commence. William sails into the harbor and finds that all the enemy ships are aground. Both sides begin firing – the Argentine brig 'General Belgrano' is driven aground by a mistake of her helmsman and is severely battered by the enemy shore batteries. The crew escapes from the ship in row boats after throwing her heavy guns overboard, while their retreat is facilitated by covering fire from 'Balcarce'. In the rearguard action, Argentine Captain Ceretti is killed, before stormy weather ends the encounter.

William is angered by this setback and sends six gunboats, each with one 18-pounder gun, into the darkness of the night to set fire to the Brazilian ships. They succeed in burning the Brazilian flagship 'Real Pedro' but lose three gunboats and six men. The attack is still a success, the enemy ships are hemmed in by sea and by land – especially when General Lavalle arrives with 700 soldiers and a half dozen cannons. The Argentine flotilla bombards the port through March 13, until a large enemy squadron commanded by Brazilian Admiral Lobo arrives, and William is obliged to withdraw. The enemy squadron hopes to corner William's flotilla, but his detailed knowledge of the reefs, channels, sandbanks and currents enable him to escape. William's planning is also a factor – he had sent shallow-draft boats ahead during daylight to station themselves as guiding buoys along the escape channels. The Brazilians are bewildered by the ability of the Argentine flotilla to escape in the darkness.

Admiral Lobo loses the initiative and follows that with another fateful mistake – he withdraws the Brazilian garrison from Martin Garcia Island along with their supporting vessels. Immediately, Commander Brown replaces them with an Argentine garrison on the island and gives them a plentiful supply of artillery – knowing from experience that the island will control what vessels are able to move both upriver and downriver near the confluence of the Uruguay and Parana rivers into the Plate Estuary. William is well aware of the vastly superior number of ships at the disposal of the Brazilian Navy, and that a defeat of the entire enemy navy is extremely unlikely. His focus continues as before – to keep the shipping lanes to Buenos Aires open and stave off economic collapse. He also must keep supply lines open for General Lavalle in Banda Oriental, whose troops are fighting the Brazilians there.

• • •

Commander Brown wants to keep the enemy in a continual state of anxiety, and he achieves this by running sudden unexpected sorties to draw the Brazilian ships away from blockade duty. Early April brings an opportunity of this type – William leads his squadron out onto the river and sends two of his ships to blockade Colonia and to monitor enemy activity. The rest of his squadron heads downstream and he finds out from hailing a passing merchant ship that the Brazilian fleet is near Montevideo and has been joined by the powerful frigate 'Nitheroy'. In a continuing cat and mouse game, Brown makes attempts to capture 'Nitheroy' on April 9 and again on April11 but shifting winds scuttle his plans – he nevertheless captures three enemy ships, including a schooner.

Later, near Montevideo, William decides to sail '25 de Mayo' towards the main harbor entrance while flying French colors. When he sees a Brazilian sumaca he hoists Argentine colors and opens fire on the enemy ship. 'Nitheroy' hauls up her anchor and heads towards '25 de Mayo' along with four schooners. Brown is trying to draw the enemy frigate out to sea ahead of the slower supporting ships. This ploy leads to a two-hour cannonade between the two flagships, damaging both. 'Nitheroy' turns back to port at nightfall and William cannot give chase due to the damage sustained to his main mast – he has suffered eight seamen dead and twelve wounded, so he returns to Buenos Aires to regroup.

The Argentine fleet sets off on another search and destroy mission on April 26 – this time his seven-ship flotilla is aiming to eliminate 'Nitheroy' from the action. Both '25 de Mayo' and 'Nitheroy' run aground for a time during their engagement – which ends in stalemate. On May 5, when

William finds the Brazilians on blockade duty off Maldonado, he decides on a nighttime attack and finds seven enemy warships at anchor in the harbor. In the darkness they engage a ship they think is 'Nitheroy' but soon find that it is the 'Imperatriz', the largest frigate in the Brazilian fleet with 50 guns. The battle lasts seventy-five minutes and involves several ships from both sides. William decides to break off the action when he realizes the superior firepower present on the enemy side and he manages to safely escape from the Brazilian base with only three killed, three wounded and minor damage to his ships. The 'Imperatriz' is severely damaged in the engagement which results in her captain being killed, a seaman who is one of their most experienced officers. The attack is a huge morale boost for the Argentinian side and a bad blow to Brazilian morale. The result causes Admiral Lobo to be dismissed and be replaced by Admiral Guedes, who is immediately ordered by his angry Emperor to destroy the Argentine fleet.

On May 17, Admiral Guedes sends a 13-ship fleet to carry out the emperor's instructions, under the command of Captain Norton of 'Nitheroy'. The Argentine squadron sails to confront the enemy and over the following ten days the two fleets skirmish, and William realizes that they are up against a capable opponent in Captain Norton. On June 4, Norton receives fresh orders from the impatient emperor to make a frontal attack on the Argentine anchorage at Los Pozos. His fleet numbers have increased to 31, mounting 266 guns, against

Argentina's four ships with 60 cannons, plus six gunboats with one gun each. William places his flotilla across the narrow channel leading to Los Pozos – making the Brazilian ships approach one by one in a line, where only their bow guns can be fired at the Argentines. On June 11, the Brazilian ships sail down the channel towards Los Pozos. Their two leading ships must anchor when the channel gets too shallow – forcing Norton to move his flag to the 20-gun 'Itaparica' as he leads his attacking line. An audience of 12,000 Buenos Aires inhabitants (Portenos) watch the action unfold from the roofs of buildings in the city. When 'Itaparica' comes into cannon range Willian shouts orders to open fire. His gunners are fast and accurate, and Norton realizes that this plan cannot succeed – he orders his squadron to reverse their direction. This must be done while they are enveloped in the thick smoke from the gunbattle, and the Brazilians suffer more casualties during the process of their withdrawal. Brown shadows their withdrawal for four hours before returning to Los Pozos, where the Argentine citizens are celebrating wildly. They demand that Commander Brown comes ashore to be escorted to the city center, where he is congratulated by President Rivadavia (his old friend). There, he is crowned with a garland and presented with an embroidered flag – while four days of celebrations continue.

William gives the flag to the rector of the Colegio de Ciencias Morales, saying – "I would like you to show your students the flag that has saluted the feelings I hold for this country, distinguished in the civilized world, so that they may be encouraged in the performance of their duties and be moved to become forever the defenders of the freedom and independence of this generous and freedom loving nation".

• • •

Despite the Brazilian losses, Captain Norton can still maintain his blockade and he keeps his ships cruising the River Plate, ready to attack any Argentine ships coming from or going to Buenos Aires – and he is in place to intercept any Chilean ships that are rumored to be joining the Argentine fleet. Commander Brown knows the Chilean ships must pass the Brazilian blockade and he decides to undertake a risky surprise attack on the enemy to weaken their blockade.

He has 17 ships available since being joined by the privateer brig 'Oriental Argentina' and after nightfall on July 20 they leave their anchorage in silence. His plan is to pass between the Brazilian main body of larger ships and their lighter vanguard, then attack the vanguard and destroy several of these lighter ships. His flagship '25 de Mayo' sails between the two enemy groups and then opens fire. The Brazilians are quick to react and 'Nitheroy' heads straight for Brown's flagship. For an hour the '25 de Mayo' and her accompanying schooner 'Rio de la Plata' must battle the enemy group of ships surrounding them before they manage to break out in a show of great fighting skill and rejoin the rest of their squadron.

The battle resumes when Commander Brown gets his ships into formation. As always, he is ready to make daring offensive moves, and he tries a delicate maneuver to cut through the Brazilian battle line. If all his ships can follow him through, they will throw the enemy into confusion, but it is another risky operation. William's flagship '25 de Mayo' and his consort 'Rio de la Plata' under Captain Leonardo Rosales break through the Brazilian line, but the rest of the Argentine ships are prevented from following by the well-trained enemy gunners. Captain Norton can now concentrate his firepower on '25 de Mayo' and 'Rio de la Plata' as the rest of the Argentine line falls into disorder. William and Rosales are battered for three hours by five enemy ships. At that point Brazilian Captain Grenfell of 'Caboclo' hails Brown.

"Commander Brown, enough slaughter has taken place. I invite you to take tea in my cabin."

Brown's reply is blunt – "My ensign is nailed to my foremast; we will fight on."

William orders his stern gunners to contrate fire on 'Caboclo', and they succeed in forcing the enemy ship to retire to a safer distance after Grenfell's arm is shot off. William is bloodied when hit in the cheek by a wood splinter and his second-in-command, Lieutenant Espora, is wounded more severely in the ongoing battle. The '25 de Mayo' is heavily damaged – all her rigging is in shreds, her hull is full of holes and her rudder is wrecked – she becomes a floating hulk, while continuing to fight on. Amidst the firing, William has himself rowed to his brig 'Republica': boards her and makes her his flagship after giving Captain Clark a dressing down for failing to break the enemy line behind him and Captain Rosales.

Captain Norton now redirects his firing on the new flagship – as Commander Brown transmits signals to his squadron and brings his eight gunboats into the battle that have been laying off to the side. Six are directed to take station around '25 de Mayo' and fire on the enemy ships, while two more begin to tow the flagship towards land. The wounded Lieutenant Espora courageously directs this procedure and 'Sarandi' escorts the towing operation towards the Los Pozos anchorage. When the Brazilians try to follow her, Commander Brown thwarts them with fire from 'Republica' and several of his gunboats. The battle continues until the wind changes to the west and Captain Norton breaks off the engagement.

Commander Brown must acknowledge the battle loss in his report, despite serious damage inflicted on at least six Brazilian ships, including 'Nitheroy'. He lists his crew casualties at 53, and the shattered '25 de Mayo', saying – "we sought, we found, and we fought the Brazilian formation, but we could not overcome it."

• • •

The loss of his best ship and damage to the rest of his squadron means that William must for now concede at least temporary control of the River Plate to the Brazilian fleet while he takes stock of his situation. The people of Buenos Aires refuse to believe that the Argentine squadron has suffered a defeat, and William must word his report carefully to keep them on his side. News of the promised arrival of the Chilean ships is conflicting, and William Brown now elects to concentrate on the best option open to him – Privateering.

He plans to direct a privateering war against Brazilian trade and will attempt to break their morale – he writes to the government asking that his pay be sent to his wife Eliza during his upcoming absence from home port. In early August William sets off overland for Cabo Corrientes, some 170 miles south of the Plate Estuary, where the Chilean ships are expected to make landfall. He waits down south till early October – sees no sign of Chilean ships, so he returns to Buenos Aires to try and get the government to improve its political and financial backing of the Navy. On October 26, hearing of the arrival of the Chilean ship 'Chacabuco' at Cabo Corrientes, he heads south with his flotilla of three ships to rendezvous with her, using the swift "Sarandi' as his flagship. Contrary winds scatter his flotilla, two of his ships get sighted by the blockading enemy and must turn back to Los Pozos – leaving 'Sarandi' alone to meet 'Chacabuco' on October 30. At that meeting he is told of severe damage caused to the other two ships as they rounded Cape Horn, the 'Buenos Aires' and the 'Montevideo' – their attempted return to Chile or even their possible loss. Brown decides to proceed with his privateering cruise using his 'Sarandi' and the new arrival, 'Chacabuco'.

They stay well away from the Brazilian coast and sail north, avoiding the Brazilian ships he knows are searching for him, and in early November they are off Cape Frio, some seventy miles east of Rio de Janeiro. They soon take Brazilian prizes – 'Defensor Perpetuo' and 'Urania' – who don't know who their captors are, and they tell William that their information is that Argentine Commodore Brown is supposed to be blockading Pernambuco and has taken three Brazilian frigates. This gives William the idea of how he can spread rumors to draw the Brazilians away from blockade duty and destabilize their fleet. He puts prize crews on the captured ships, sends them off to a later rendezvous point, while he and 'Chacabuco' continue westward to cruise the area between Rio and Santos. Off Ilha Grande (south of Rio de Janeiro) they capture three Brazilian sumacas, transfer their cargos to 'Defensor', burn the two empty sumacas, and after cutting down the masts of the third one they transfer all their prisoners to that ship.

On November 20 the 'Sarandi' eludes a Brazilian frigate and takes another prize near Santos which William sends to Cabo Corrientes under a prize crew. They hail an American brig on November 25 and spread the fake news that Commodore Brown and the Chilean squadron are blockading Rio de Janeiro. Sailing onward to Santa Catalina and Rio Grande, they capture another prize and continue spreading contradictory rumors that Wiliam knows will disturb the Brazilian blockading fleet. 'Sarandi' chases the Brazilian Navy brig 'Estrela do Cabo' and shots are exchanged before the

Brazilian ship grounds on a dangerous shoal and breaks in two pieces shortly afterwards. He cruises off Rio Grando in early December while waiting to rendezvous with 'Chacabuco', taking 'Ezequiel' as another prize, transferring her cargo and sending her back into port with the Brazilian prisoners. Running short of food and water, he sends another prize to Buenos Aires and sails 'Sarandi' for Cabo Corrientes in hopes of meeting 'Chacabuco' – she does not show up there either. William finds out later that 'Chacabuco' had to run south to Carmen de Patagones to escape a powerful Brazilian fleet.

Without the planned rendezvous, and not knowing the fate of 'Chacabuco' at the time, Commander Brown decides to sail on to Buenos Aires, arriving there December 24 at midnight.

On Christmas Day, 1826, he fires a 21-gun salute to the city he had left three months earlier. Ironically it is also the one-year-old anniversary of the beginning of the war with Brazil.

Commander Brown is grateful for the Argentine victories to date, but he knows that the much larger Brazilian Navy will continue to press them and in time they will wear them down.

Can his superior knowledge of the River Plate Estuary keep them at bay until the world's big powers intervene – and compel both parties to accept a peace treaty that will guarantee an independent future for William Brown's adopted homeland of Argentina?

CHAPTER EIGHT

NAVIGATING THE BRAZIL WAR WHILE CIVIL WAR RAGES AT HOME

After a very brief visit with his family while his ship is resupplied, Commander William Brown must hoist his Argentine flag on December 26, 1826, because of the presence of a Brazilian naval force in the Uruguay River. He leads his small squadron out to engage the enemy.

• • •

At this same time the land war is also at a point of stalemate. Lavalle's guerilla forces hold some strongholds while the rest of Banda Oriental is occupied by the Brazilians. Another Argentine Army is laying in the valley of the Uruguay River along the western border of the Banda Oriental – in a holding pattern. Both sides have their agents trying to stir up separatist movement revolts in the provinces bordering the Banda Oriental. Within Argentinian political circles the leader, Rivadavia, is trying to keep some semblance of unity while the caudillos of the allied provinces are pushing to keep any central encroachment from disturbing their local power bases. The Brazilians are expecting a land offensive against Montevideo by the new Argentine general of land troops, Carlos Maria de Alvear. In their rush to upstage Alvear, the Brazilian high command tries to get the Argentinian provinces of Corrientes and Misiones to declare independence from Buenos Aires and align themselves with Brazil's new Cisplatina Province (Banda Oriental).

In support of this plan Brazil sends a fleet of naval vessels to the Uruguay River, under the command of Senna Pereira, a man who has friends and contacts there from his time with a Portuguese flotilla in an earlier campaign – with orders to stir up a rebellion in the region. William Brown's informers tell him that Pereira left Montevideo on December 10, 1826, with fifteen to twenty ships, to patrol the northwestern end of the Plate Estuary and prevent the landing of Argentinian troops or supplies in Banda Oriental. Later in December Pereira's fleet surrounds the Argentinian schooner 'Rio de la Plata' who is carrying troops across the estuary to Las Conchillas. They attack, and the 'Rio' battles them for two hours before being driven ashore, her captain is captured along with most of the troops aboard, but some do escape.

• • •

On this December 26, Commander Brown's Argentine flotilla of six ships and eight gunboats is attacked by seven ships of the Brazilian blockading squadron as soon as they clear the exit channel from Los Pozos. Their gunboats fire on the Brazilians and keep up the firing till the enemy sheers off at midnight, and then the Argentinian flotilla anchors off Martin Garcia Island. Next day they set out for the Uruguay River and this time they are confronted by a group of five Brazilian ships – Brown engages the enemy ships and chases them till the larger Brazilian fleet comes into view. The enemy fleet is on a course for the Uruguay River with Commander Brown's Argentine flotilla in pursuit, per his orders – "to pursue and destroy the enemy force so as to leave entirely free navigation on the Uruguay River and communication everywhere along the coast".

Brazilian commander Pereira forms his battle line in the middle of the narrow Yaguary Channel, where the Uruguay River joins with the Rio Negro and where there are many shallow areas. He thinks the commander of the Argentine flotilla is Tomas Espora but later is informed that their commander is indeed William Brown, news that unnerves him. Brown' ships arrive at the Yaguary Channel at nightfall on December 28, then William spends hours reconnoitering the enemy positions before withdrawing his flotilla a distance down the river to anchor.

There is no wind the next morning, the Brazilians stay at

anchor while Brown moves his Argentine gunboats forward, plus the shallow draft 'Sarandi' and another launch, and engages the enemy in an hour-long cannonade before pulling back. He then sends his second in command, Captain Coe, to speak with the enemy Commander, Pereira under a flag of truce, requesting his surrender. The Brazilian leader remains doubtful whether Brown is the opposing commander, and they refuse to let Captain Coe return, questioning the signature and the protocol of the request.

The Brazilians then send an officer to 'Sarandi' under a flag of truce to open negotiations, but all the while they are trying to ascertain if William Brown is the commander. Tomas Espora greets the Brazilian officer and tells him that if Coe is not freed within one hour the Argentines will open a full assault. While Pereira figures out what to do, a strong pampero storm blows up and stops all activity for the remainder of the day. When the storm eases, Commander Brown sends gunboats ahead to cannonade the enemy and tempt them out of their anchorage – they will not move. He then brings his Argentine flotilla down to the mouth of the Uruguay River and three days later the Brazilian ships proceed upstream, going all the way to Paysandu – Pereira is trying to show support for the sparce Brazilian ground forces along the river and he is trying to rally them.

Meanwhile, as the new year of 1827 dawns, Commander Brown decides to add fortifications to Martin Garcia Island and to set up two new gun battery sites on the Uruguay River, while awaiting the return of the Brazilians – who must come back downriver to access the Plate Estuary. The river batteries will bombard the enemy on their return south and William's plan is to intercept them in the vicinity of Martin Garcia Island, where they would be trapped between the island batteries and the Argentinian flotilla – and would be forced to fight a decisive battle. He sends a force of men to another small island to round up herds of cattle and sheep that the Brazilians had put ashore there for a food supply – depriving them of that resource.

Commander Brown holds a different viewpoint on the standoff situation than does his Minister for War, General de la Cruz, and they exchange terse correspondence. The General wants him to follow the Brazilians up the Uruguay River and defeat them there – a plan William knows from experience will not succeed. He half-heartedly agrees to chase them only when General de la Cruz turns the disagreement into a disobedience issue worthy of forcing his commander's resignation – it's an appeasement of sorts while Brown waits for Pereira's crews to get unsettled by the hostile attacks from native people along the riverbank. During this time Brown men continue to fortify Martin Garcia Island, and he puts Espora in charge of the island garrison. William sails 'Sarandi' to Buenos Aires in early January to get more supplies, meets there with Captain Rosales who is commanding a four-ship flotilla defending the city – then heads back upriver with hundreds of rockets and launchers removed from the wrecked hulk of the '25 de Mayo'.

There are rumors that the Brazilian Auxiliary Division has entered the Uruguay River with a fleet of eleven ships, and Commander Brown worries that they may attack Martin Garcia Island before the Argentine fortification projects are completed. Returning there with haste, Brown takes control of a five-ship flotilla and sets off in search of this phantom fleet, quickly finding out that the Brazilian Auxiliary fleet have indeed been heading to attack the island – until Commander Mariath's flagship 'Maceio' ran aground. Brown locates their fleet just after they have refloated 'Maceio' and engages them for over an hour in almost calm conditions, inflicting severe damage to the enemy flagship and to some of the accompanying vessels. Once a breeze comes up the Brazilians break off the action and sail towards Montevideo. Commander Brown then sails north on the Uruguay River to reconnoiter before slipping back down to their fortified island on January 21. While waiting there, the 'Sarandi' and other ships damaged in the action against Mariath are put under urgent repairs. Those repairs, and the island fortifications are complete by early February – they hoist the Argentine flag on their naval base and settle in to wait for the Brazilians to return.

• • •

The Brazilian ships had turned back south at the end of January and begun to make their way slowly back downriver to Arroyo de San Salvador, gathering the Brazilian ships he had stationed at points along the Uruguay on his earlier route upriver. William learns on February 7 that Pereira's flotilla is nearing the mouth of the Uruguay River – he gathers his captains in the cabin of 'Sarandi' for a council of war, then gives orders to weigh anchor. Struggling with unfavorable winds, his flagship and two other members of his flotilla reach the mouth of the river, where they are finally joined by his other vessels during that night. Early next morning the Brazilian ships are sighted coming down the river. William elects to drop further back downriver ahead of them.

Commander Pereira forms his ships in a line between the islands of Juncal and Solis – 18 warships with 63 guns and 750 men. His flagship is the165 ton schooner 'Oriental' with 8 guns. Brown divides his fleet into three divisions and gets them in line – with the 'Balcarce' division in the front: his flagship 'Sarandi' division in the center, and the 'Maldonado' division astern – 17 ships with 67 guns and 745 men. The two opposing forces are comparable in numbers, with the Brazilians having the edge on guns – they have thirty-four heavy guns, a mix of 24 pounders and 36 pounders, while the Argentinians have just eleven 24 pounders and no 36 pounders. Gradually the two battle lines move closer and closer to each other – at noon they are about 850 meters apart and parallel to each other across the current of the river. The wind dies down completely, and Pereira orders his ships to anchor.

A cannonade erupts between the two fleets and continues for an hour till a wind from the Southeast springs up

– giving William an advantage because he is downstream. He closes the range to 600 meters and forces the enemy schooner 'Januaria' to fall out of line. She is fired on by 'Balcarce', then by 'Sarandi' and then by three gunboats, suffering a lot of damage. Pereira sends a fireship to help her, but it suddenly explodes harmlessly, and the cannonade continues. The accurate firing of the Argentinian cannons forces more of the enemy ships out of their battle line. When the wind disappears again the entire battlefield is covered in thick smoke from the artillery. A sudden strong pampero storm blows in and causes all the ships to roll violently – the Argentine ship 'Balcarce' is barely saved from keeling over. As darkness falls, heavy rain pounds the combatants, and all ships are forced to hunker down – Brown takes the opportunity to feed his crews and do any repairs they can. When the wind eases, Commander Pereira tries to move his ships to a safer anchorage during the darkness – but in the confusion one of them loses her anchor and drifts into the Argentine line where she is captured.

By coincidence, this is the ship on which Captain Coe is being held prisoner (William Brown's flag captain who was taken prisoner during his visit to the enemy under a flag of truce). He is immediately freed and gives Commander Brown some valuable information on the enemy. On the morning of February 9, Pereira holds a meeting with his captains to plan for the battle ahead – they disagree on whether to fight at anchor or under sail. When a southeasterly breeze arises, Brown signals his Argentine fleet to immediately attack. As the Brazilians struggle to get into line, the Argentine ships come abreast of Solis Island and hit the Brazilians with heavy continuous cannon fire, throwing them into confusion. Some enemy ships hoist their sails to maneuver, and some try to re-anchor – all of which is taking place in a wind that is contrary for the Brazilians. Most of them are easy targets for the Argentine ships – who keep their formation, covering each other while maintaining heavy fire on the Brazilians.

Each enemy vessel is forced to fight on its own in the ongoing confusion, and Commander Brown orders his ships to concentrate their firing on the larger enemy warships – 'Oriental', 'Januaria' and 'Bertioga'. 'Januaria' loses her foremast yard and her bowsprit is damaged. When Pereira orders a gunboat to tow his flagship 'Oriental' out of the battle for emergency repairs, 'Balcarce' fires on the gunboat and drives it away. A further pounding from Argentine cannons brings down the 'Januaria' mainmast and shreds her rigging. Her captain gives orders to abandon ship, after spiking her guns and opening her seacocks. Argentinian heroes of the hour, Captain Segui and Captain Mason manage to get a boarding party onto the stricken 'Januaria'- they put out the fire, close the seacocks and get the captured prize ship towed out of the battle area. Captain Drummond on 'Maldonado' batters 'Bertioga', and after her mainmast is destroyed her captain strikes his colors.

The Argentines now concentrate on finishing off the flagship 'Oriental' and after several more broadsides they board her and find the wounded Commander Pereira, who surrenders by handing his sword to Captain Segui. The battle has been won by the Argentine fleet. Commander Brown transfers his flag to 'Balcarce' and sends Captain Coe in 'Sarandi' along with three gunboats to pursue the remains of the Brazilian fleet who are trying to flee. On 'Balcarce' the crew celebrates the victory, and Captain Segui turns to Commander Brown.

"Sir, here is the sword of Brazilian Commander Senna Pereira – a special prize for your great victory."

Brown waves him away – "You keep this sword, Captain – as proof of how well you conducted yourself in battle today. But this victory is only a partial one. Many enemy ships are trying to slip away and must be captured to complete our victory."

The next day Commander Brown sends seven captured prizes to Martin Garcia Island along with some of his own ships that need repairs, while he transfers his flag to 'Maldonado' and sets out with his remaining gunboats to prevent scattered ships of the defeated Brazilian fleet from escaping. Captain Rosales sends two ships from Buenos Aires to help, and they fight another night skirmish with the fugitive Brazilian ships, pushing them back upriver. Brown then pursues five fugitive ships commanded by First Lieutenant de Souza (the senior surviving officer of Pereira's fleet) – to the mouth of the Gualeguaychu.

There, he finds that many of the enemy crews have surrendered themselves to the local authorities, but the fugitive ships have continued up the Uruguay River. He follows them all the way to Campichuelo where he seizes the five ships – and sails them back downriver to Martin Garcia Island to add them to the previously captured prizes. Repairs to his own ships continue nonstop, and to the eleven captured Brazilian prizes, which he wants to add to the Argentine Navy fleet.

By February 23, Commander Brown sails his expanded naval fleet towards Buenos Aires, stopping at Las Conchillas at nightfall. A fleet of ten Brazilian ships approaches next morning, and William Brown leads a 27-ship flotilla out to engage them near the Quilmes promontory. The battle begins in the afternoon and continues till nightfall, when five schooners arrive to reinforce the Brazilians. Brown signals his gunboats to engage the newcomers. An accurate Argentine cannonball hits the powder magazine of the Brazilian schooner '2 de Dezembro'. The ship is destroyed in the explosion, killing 117 of the 120 crew, including Captain Pedro de Carvalho, who had been the captain of 'Januaria' in the Battle of Juncal. After this traumatic explosion the two sides disengage.

Commander Brown sails on to Buenos Aires, arriving next morning to an ecstatic welcome.

That day, February 25, Commander William Brown is literally carried to the citadel on the backs of the citizens, where he is congratulated by government representatives amid wild celebrations. Later that night he attempts to take a quiet carriage to his home, Casa Amarilla, where he has spent just one night in the previous four months. Large crowds meet his carriage, shouting his name and they insist on carrying him the last thousand yards to his front door. The Argentine Congress later votes him an award of 20,000 pesos in recognition of his great victory, and each crew member involved is awarded two months extra pay. The Congress also decrees to have an inscribed shield of honor badge made to commemorate the "Juncal" victory – gold for Commander Brown, silver for his officers and brass for the rest of the crew members involved.

In the Juncal Island campaign Commander William Brown's Argentinian flotilla succeeds in eliminating an entire division of the numerically superior Brazilian Navy – they capture11 enemy vessels that are quickly incorporated into the Argentinian Navy, destroy at least 4 more enemy ships, and force several enemy vessels to flee in all directions trying to escape capture. The campaign liberates the area of the Parana River delta, the Uruguay River, and the western end of the River Plate Estuary from Brazilian military and political influence, clearing the way for the Argentinian land army to move into Provincia Cisplatina (Banda Oriental), while giving a much-needed boost to Argentine morale.

• • •

The victory is made possible by William Brown's skill as a commander, his expertise in navigating the difficult River Plate Estuary waters, the accuracy of his gunners that he personally trained – and especially because of his unflinching bravery and his trust in the abilities of his crews.

• • •

Now, the demoralized Brazilian Navy decides to switch their attention further south, aiming to wipe out the Argentinian privateer base in Carmen de Patagones. They send four warships to the area near the mouth of the Rio Negro, where they are fired on by the battery at the Argentine fort, forcing one ship aground. The Brazilians then put a large landing party ashore, where they are soon met by Argentinian forces made up of troops sent down by Rivadavia, local seamen and freed negro slaves, who quickly defeat the Brazilians. Three of the enemy ships are captured, one is destroyed, and over a hundred non-Brazilian crew members change allegiance and agree to serve with the Argentine privateers. William Brown gets much credit for this victory because of the inspiration that his actions provided to the Argentinian forces.

• • •

In March, Britain begins to bring political pressure on both sides to make peace. Rivadavia is not inclined to make any concessions in this climate of victory, other than to allow Banda Oriental to become an independent country. Senor Garcia, the Argentine envoy in Rio de Janeiro, initials a treaty there under pressure from the British Ambassador, but without having any authority to do so. This treaty gives Banda Oriental to Brazil, also gives them the strategic Martin Garcia Island in the estuary, and even offers them some political leverage in the Argentine provinces on the right bank of the Uruguay River. Rivadavia is appalled. He publicly repudiates the treaty, but because he is perceived to have allowed his envoy to do this, he is forced to resign. He issues a departing proclamation that is very supportive of the Argentine Navy and praises Commander William Brown in particular –

"On abandoning public life in which it is no longer possible for me to be of use to the Fatherland, allow me to thank you for the days of glory with which you marked my period in office. The terror that the Argentine flag inspires in those who have dared to call themselves masters of the River Plate is due to you and your unconquerable Admiral."

Rivadavia is replaced as head of state by General Dorrego, and the war continues.

During this upheaval Commander Brown concentrates on his main duties – the protection of the Argentine coast, keeping supply communication links open for their forces who are fighting Brazil in Banda Oriental across the estuary, weakening the Brazilian blockade that is trying to choke the Argentine economy, and a continuation of attacks on Brazilian seaborne trade. The Minister of War and Marine asks Brown to do another cruise along the Brazilian coast to harass Brazilian merchant shipping, which he agrees to do.

In April, four ships set out in the late evening from Los Pozos, including Commander Brown's flagship, 'Sarandi' and they sail through the night. The following day they are sighted and chased by Brazilian ships on blockade duty. Hit by difficult winds, two of the Argentine ships, 'Republica' and 'Independencia' run aground on a sandbank off Santiago Point. They remain stuck fast through the night, while 'Sarandi' with William Brown aboard, and 'Congreso' anchor nearby.

Next day the Brazilian ships form into a battle line, and they cannonade the grounded ships all day: the Argentine ships fight back and are helped in the fight by their two sister ships. Substantial damage is suffered by both sides. Another night of refloating attempts fails to get the two stuck vessels off the bank, and by morning 18 more Brazilian ships arrive and begin pounding the Argentine vessels. The battle rages all day, with the Argentines giving as good as they are getting. The stranded ships are running low on gunpowder and Captain Drummond of 'Independencia' has himself rowed over to the flagship 'Sarandi' to get supplies. As he is climbing back down to his boat, he is hit in the thigh by a musket ball which severs a main artery. He is immediately carried onto 'Sarandi' where the surgeon struggles to stem the flow of blood with a tourniquet – all the while the battle rages on around them.

Commander Brown's men recover what supplies they can from the two stranded ships and Brown gives the order to set fire to them and abandon ship. A Brazilian boarding party gets there before the tasks are accomplished on the second ship, and the remainder of the Argentine crew of that ship are captured.

Darkness causes a lull in the battle. Commander Brown weighs anchor: 'Sarandi' fights her way out and he sets sail for home base, while the wounded Captain Drummond is comforted by his friend, Captain Coe. When his condition worsens significantly, William enters the cabin and relieves Coe. He kneels over Francis (Pancho) Drummond, the handsome young Scot who is engaged to William's own daughter Eliza. He embraces the young man and speaks to him in a voice full of emotion.

"Pancho, it is me, William."

The lad forces his eyes open despite the pain and exhaustion from loss of blood.

"Admiral, thank you. I die doing my duty. Give my watch to my mother, and my ring to Eliza."

"Yes, my son, you have done your duty. I will do as you ask."

William holds the boy's hand as he draws his last breaths, then leans over and kisses his forehead.

• • •

The Battle of Monte Santiago is over and is a sad loss for Argentina as well as a personal loss for William Brown. The toll is 62 dead (including Captain Drumond and some other officers), 26 are wounded (including Captain Granville who lost an arm and Wiliam himself who suffered cheek and shoulder injuries), 65 are taken prisoner of whom many are wounded, two ships are lost and the remaining two are severely damaged and taking on water. Rumors are sweeping Buenos Aires that Commander Brown has not only lost the battle but has himself succumbed to the Brazilians. The crowds are ecstatic when they find that he is alive but fall silent when the body of Captain Francis Drummond is carried ashore. His funeral cortege is attended by the government leaders, his comrades-in-arms and thousands of citizens – a cannon fires every fifteen minutes in his honor. William's daughter, Eliza Brown, is inconsolable as she weeps and presses Pancho Drummond's ring to her breast.

• • •

The War continues, and after a few weeks of recovery from his wounds, Commander Brown is back on duty, overseeing repairs to the damaged ships and the fitting out of new additions to the fleet. In a June cruise he captures seven prizes and continues to harass enemy trade and their ability to supply their ground troops. Sorties continue through the months of July and August, including the capture of the Brazilian privateer schooner 'Maria Treesa' which is added to the Argentine fleet. In late September the Argentine flotilla sails east from Martin Garcia Island, along the Banda Oriental coast, past Colonia and on to Montevideo, bombarding Brazilian bases along the way and destroying many enemy vessels – then returning safely to their island base.

On December 27, Commander Brown is aboard his flotilla at the Los Pozos anchorage, when his second-in-command knocks on his cabin door and requests to speak with him.

"Of course, come in Captain Sanchez. What's on your mind?"

"Sir, I have just received a letter from your wife, asking me to personally relay some very sad news to you. Your daughter, Eliza, has perished in a drowning accident – please accept my sincere sympathy."

The news hits William very hard – he slumps into his chair and buries his face in his hands.

"Please prepare my boat for immediate departure."

"Yes Sir."

Alone now, William cries for several minutes before he gathers himself, grabs some personal items and heads for the boat. Captain Sanchez is waiting there with the rowing crew.

"Captain, take control while I am away. Keep me abreast of any developments and don't hesitate to contact me in the event of anything urgent."

"Yes Sir."

On arrival home, William is met by his distraught wife and their surviving children – they and the rest of their extended family are numbed with grief. His eighteen-year-old daughter lies in the next room in a coffin, so beautiful that she seems asleep until he kisses her cold forehead – he then breaks down in tears and is comforted by his children and the attending Priest. Eliza had gone to the Balizas Canal with a younger sibling to bathe, and shortly afterwards disappeared under the water. Her sister found her on the bottom and tried unsuccessfully to revive her. Some believe it was an accident, and some think she committed suicide – for it is well known that she had been consumed by sorrow and pain since the death of her beloved Pancho Drummond.

The Brown family bury their young and beautiful Eliza in the Catholic cemetery, next door to the Protestant cemetery that holds the tomb of her fiancé, Pancho – ending the very sad year of 1827.

• • •

William Brown's wife, Elizabeth, is his rock during this very difficult time for the family – never complaining about the heavy toll that his patriotic service to the country is taking on all of them.

Commander William Brown longs for the Brazilian War to end but he does not have the power to achieve that result on his own – he will do his duty, his Navy will eke out every victory they can, while he prays for a just peace and for the souls of Pancho and Eliza, who visit him often in his dreams.

CHAPTER NINE

INTERVENTION BY WORLD POWERS – ROBBERY OF THE SQUADRON

William Brown spends a few extra days at home to grieve alongside his family – the war with Brazil continues and in the early days of the new year of 1828, he is back at Los Pozos commanding his fleet. His flagship 'Sarandi' leads a flotilla of twelve vessels in January that captures an enemy privateer and a coaster off Colonia. On their return to port, they are attacked by a large Brazilian squadron – a major skirmish ensues from which the Argentines escape, but to achieve that escape they must abandon their prizes that are slowing them down. Being always short of ships, William gets government approval to send Captain Fournier in the ship 'Juncal' on a mission to the east coast of the United States of America to acquire more ships for their Navy. 'Sarandi' and two other ships escort 'Juncal' past the Brazilian blockade, after which Fournier sets a course for Savannah, Georgia. The returning Argentine flotilla is attacked by sixteen Brazilian ships but William's superior knowledge of the channels and sandbanks off Rio Santiago allows them to escape and return safely to base. Sadly, the 'Juncal' is unable to complete her mission – she is wrecked in a storm off the West Indies and sinks with loss of all aboard.

The Argentine Navy continues to fight a rearguard action from February through August of 1828, giving as good as they get – their survival being primarily due to the leadership of Commander William Brown. His constant daring raids, frequent victories and his privateer attacks on the Brazilian merchant fleet takes a toll on the Brazilian economy. The Brazilian Emperor is under pressure from influential sectors of the country to seek a peace – his merchant ship captains; Brazil's wealthy classes who are both suffering these losses – and from the major world powers, Britain and the United States. On August 31 General Balcarce of Argentina signs preliminary peace terms with Brazil in Rio de Janeiro and by September 11 Argentine Colonel O'Brien carries the peace term documents to Buenos Aires. Then, on September 16, Commander William Brown sails out in 'Sarandi' to escort home the Argentine delegation returning from Rio de Janeiro – greeting them with a 21-gun salute. A week later he sails again, in 'Maldonado' to greet the Brazilian frigate 'Nitheroy' under the command of his old foe, Captain Norton. They both hoist white flags, then fly each other's ensigns on their masts, and finally the two flagships exchange blank broadsides in salute.

On October 4 the Argentine government selects William Brown, whom they describe as the hero and keystone of the Republic, along with Domingo Azcuenaga, an eighty-one-year-old veteran of the original independence movement, to have the honor of signing the formal peace document with Brazil. The two men embark for Montevideo, where the signing ceremony is to take place. The peace terms are a compromise between the two combatants. Banda Oriental joins neither country, instead they both renounce their claims to the territory, and it becomes the independent 'Republic of Uruguay' – bowing to pressure from Britain who has strong interests there. Brazil drops its claim to Martin Garcia Island, which Argentina retains but agrees to demilitarize the island, and Argentina gives up its claims to Rio Grande do Sul in Brazil. William Brown is satisfied with the outcome other than the demilitarization of Martin Garcia, but he consoles himself with the fact that it remains Argentinian territory.

His tiny Argentine Navy has foiled the expansion plans of imperial Brazil, who has a Navy fleet that vastly outnumbers that of Argentina. Brazil's Navy will no longer to be a threat to William Brown's beloved adopted homeland.

• • •

In this same month the Argentine government finally bestows upon Commander William Brown the official rank he so richly deserves and gives him a title by which he is already referred to by the people. On October 19 General Juan Ramon Balcarce, Minister of War and Naval Affairs, officially promotes fifty-one-year-old Commander Brown to the most elevated rank on their military scale – Brigadier-General of the Navy, corresponding to the European rank of Rear-Admiral.

Admiral Brown modestly accepts this honor, saying quietly "I do not deserve it." His red hair is turning gray, but he is in good overall health despite the hardship of years at sea, and his many battle wounds, including lameness from when his leg was shattered by the recoil of a cannon. Now that the war against Brazil is over, he believes he is no longer needed and asks to be removed from active service.

His letter of resignation includes the following extract -

"If, on another occasion, I am to be recalled, I will hurry with the greatest rejoicing to fight once more with such honorable companions and brave comrades. Meanwhile, I desire to enjoy the pleasures of my homeland as a private citizen, and to educate my children in a way that is infused with the feelings I hold for this country, so they may some day be able to bring more honor to their father."

His devoted wife Eliza Brown welcomes him home after so many difficult and lonely years for her, when she had to manage their family on her own. She has become an excellent farm manager and has acquired expertise on poultry and plants, helped by her children and some hired workers. The farm comprises the acreage around their home and estate in Barracas and they have enlarged their holdings by acquiring another small estate at Quilmes.

The government does not accept Admiral Brown's resignation, saying there is much still to do. In the weeks after the end of the war, Brown's fleet is busy bringing home their troops from Uruguay, and in November General Lavalle, commander of the First Division of the Argentine army arrives home in Buenos Aires. The old animosity between the unitarians and the federalists soon flares up again. The head of state, General Dorrego, believes in a unitary centralized state and leads an army into the interior to restore order in areas of the country where the authority of the central government has been challenged. Lavalle believes a loose federal or confederal form of government is the best way forward for the country.

While Dorrego is away on this military campaign, General Lavalle leads an armed coup on December 1 that deposes Dorrego as governor of Buenos Aires Province. William Brown takes no part in the coup, which marks the beginning of a period of civil war that he is ashamed of – he does not want to take sides, and he hopes that the situation can be resolved, and that a national unity government can be formed. Dorrego is worshipped by the gauchos in the countryside, and he consolidates his forces there. William writes to Dorrego and to the rising federalist leader, Manuel Rosas, asking them both to accept the new situation and to avoid any actions that might lead to a bloody conflict. General Lavalle wants to lead his forces to seek out his opponent in the countryside, and he summons William Brown, the most popular man in the country, to a meeting with him.

"Admiral Brown, I will be away for some time, and I can think of nobody better than you to take on the role of Governor of Buenos Aires, at least temporarily."

"Sir, I know this is a great honor, but I do not think I am the person for that job – surely there are people more deserving than me."

"Nonsense, there is nobody more deserving that you, the man who has won the most important naval victories, without which Argentina would not exist. My dear Admiral, I know you are a patriot, and it is your patriotic duty to take on the role of Governor Delegate – I have heard from the people on this, and they respectfully demand that you accept. They are your people, and you cannot let them down. Tell me that you will do it."

"Please, give me a few days to consider how I can serve my people in this role, I will give you an answer by the December 16."

On that promised date Admiral William Brown accepts Lavelle's offer and becomes the Governor Delegate of Buenos Aires.

• • •

William's first action as Governor is the maintenance of order, and when he moves to the seat of government, he brings 200 able seamen from his old ranks with him as a guarding force. He forms another contingent of citizens to help defend the city, and he organizes a flotilla of vessels under his naval subordinate, Captain Rosales, to operate in the upcountry Parana River area. Next, he cancels all privateering licenses issued during the Brazilian War because they are being used by some captains to cover acts of piracy. Free trade, both internal and external, is thus encouraged – something that is sorely needed to bring money into the treasury to pay local garrisons, crewmen in the new flotilla, government officials – and to cover the costs of reinforcements and guns that Lavalle is demanding. The only legal tender in Buenos Aires Province is coinage, and it is in very short supply – Governor Brown issues a decree authorizing the use of paper banknotes as legal currency.

When Governor Brown hears that General Lavalle's forces have captured his opponent, Dorrego, he appeals to him to spare his life and to send the captive into exile in the United States – he urges both men to settle their personal disagreements. As soon as he learns that Dorrego has been executed without a trial, he tenders his resignation to Lavalle, who refuses to accept it. William is disgusted by the killing of Dorrego but feels he must continue to do the work of the people in these times of civil war and confusion – he stays on the job and completes important work in the fields of public health, university education and the administration of justice. He oversees appointments of doctors for public hospitals and organizes a campaign of vaccination against smallpox.

• • •

The two opposing armies continue their civil war into the new year of 1829. In February, the other 'pater patriae', General San Martin, sails into Buenos Aires from his self-imposed exile, in response to an appeal from friends to try to broker a peace between the two warring sides. Governor Brown sends Tomas Espora to visit San Martin's ship, to present the Governor's greetings and to invite him to come ashore. After learning the latest news from Espora and from other sources, the General quickly sees that the two opposing armies are determined to fight it out and he refuses to be drawn into the fray – he decides not to come ashore.

However, he writes a letter to Governor Brown in the presence of Espora who carries it back

"I am sorry that I have not had the honor of meeting you, but as a son of this nation, you will always merit an eternal recognition for the service you have given."

San Martin's ship soon departs for Europe, where he will spend the rest of his life in exile. In April, Governor Brown proposes a truce between the two sides, so that the people can vote on whether they want to be ruled by Unitarians or by

Federalists. His proposal is ignored, so he refuses to take any further part in the politics of the Civil War – after 148 days as governor he sends a second letter of resignation to General Lavalle.

Part of William's letter reads –

"On different occasions I have already indicated to you my ardent wish to leave the position to which you have done the honor of appointing me. I took this up for the sole reason of not shirking a sacrifice on behalf of the country to which I owe so much – as a temporary position to bring tranquility to the country. When necessary to fight the enemies of the Republic I have done my duty. Now I must give up these responsibilities and return to civilian life."

In May his resignation is accepted.

Events soon turn against General Lavalle, who is defeated at Puente de Marquez by the federalist forces led by Manuel Rosas. Two naval vessels are captured by the federalists in May, and they advance on Buenos Aires, and William's one-time flagship 'Maldonado' is captured. Rosas persuades a French squadron in the Estuary to attack an Argentine flotilla, on the grounds that they are obstructing international commerce, and the French seize several Argentinian ships. Fighting between the two land armies takes place at the edge of the city, near William Brown's own residence, but his property is not damaged. By the end of August, the federalists are closing in on victory, and Rosas becomes Governor of Buenos

Aires in December. During this period of Argentine military weakness, Britain sends an expeditionary force that expels the small group of Argentine officials on the Malvinas Islands – they occupy the islands that they would later rename The Falkland Islands.

• • •

As the new year of1830 begins, Mrs. Eliza Brown decides to visit family in England, and she takes her sons William and Eduardo with her. They visit for several months and on their return voyage they are shipwrecked off the Brazilian coast, but all three of them are rescued and get home to Buenos Aires safely. Although he is now retired, Admiral Brown retains the title of Commander-in-Chief of the Navy. In that capacity he attends the official ceremony when Manuel Rosas is installed as Governor of Buenos Aires and he also attends a state funeral for the late leader, Dorrego. Governor Rosas tries to court favor from Admiral Brown and encourages him to sign a document supporting a move to grant Rosas extraordinary powers – William refuses to sign it and instead he concentrates on his merchant activities in Colonia during these years.

The Brown family visits Montevideo in 1834 on the occasion of the marriage of their daughter, Martina, to a business merchant there. William's own merchant business continues to prosper during the late 1830's – he breeds mules on his farm and exports them to the Caribbean. The regime of Governor

Rosas becomes more and more dictatorial, and Rosas abolishes the National Bank. That action has little effect on William Brown's business – he continues to keep Rosas at arm's length while not being on bad terms with him.

• • •

During his prior service as Governor of Buenos Aires, one of the decrees introduced by William Brown dealt with foreign nationals – directing that they are expected to perform military service.

In 1837, the French Consul decides to take exception to this arrangement. When his protests are ignored, he demands to be given his passport and he moves to Montevideo – an act that Governor Rosas views as provocation, being that Montevideo is home to Unitarian exiles from Argentina. The French Government escalates the disagreement by sending a naval squadron in March 1838 to blockade the River Plate Estuary. Shortly after this, Admiral Brown is riding his horse along the estuary shore one day when he witnesses French ships capturing two Argentine feluccas. He is enraged and rushes home, where he pens a letter to Governor Rosas, denouncing the French aggression, and adding the following – "it is my patriotic wish to accept whatever service is required from me in order to save the dignity of the nation."

Rosas does not respond immediately, and William does

not pursue the offer any further. In July William goes to Montevideo to visit his newly born grandchild. While there he learns that the French have attacked and captured Martin Garcia Island from the Argentine defenders, a place dear to his heart. He is persuaded by his son-in-law to offer his services to Uruguay, and President Oribe of Uruguay issues a decree naming William Brown as the head of their Navy. The French immediately denounce the appointment as an act of aggression and declare a blockade of Montevideo.

Then, Uruguayan General Rivera, with secret backing from the French, launches a coup and overthrows President Oribe. Because of these events Admiral Brown considers his offer to Uruguay to be null and void – he returns to Buenos Aires without fanfare, before French Admiral Leblanc can close the port of Montevideo with his French fleet. In January 1839 a new formidable French squadron under Admiral Mackau, appears in Argentinian waters. Then, a local conspiracy to overthrow Governor Rosas is foiled, at a time when ousted General Lavalle assemblies a strong Unitarian army, with help from General Rivera in Uruguay. French approval and interference are suspected when Lavalle declares war on Rosas. William Brown, and many Argentinians swallow their dislike for Rosas and rally round him to protect the national sovereignty of their country from foreign powers. The situation is defused when French Admiral Mackau takes steps to lift the blockade of Buenos Aires and other ports, evacuates Martin Garcia Island and severs relations with both Lavalle and Rivera. He conducts a cordial meeting with Rosas and all the French ships then sail for home, beginning a spell of peacefulness during which William Brown concentrates on his merchant business.

1841 begins with more trouble for Governor Rosas – Britain and France together demand new trading policies from Argentina that are favorable to both countries for the benefit of their merchant shipping and commercial interests. Rivera continues helping the Unitarian army in exile, who begin actions to entice some of the smaller and more distant Argentine provinces away from the control of the central government in Buenos Aires. Economic conditions in Argentina deteriorate rapidly and people begin to emigrate, especially to Bolivia. Rosas becomes so worried by the rhetoric coming from Brazil, that he now fears an intervention by them in Argentina's affairs. These combined issues persuade him to drop his objections to bringing Admiral William Brown out of retirement.

• • •

On February 2, 1841, he names Admiral Don Guillermo Brown to be head of the Argentine Navy for the third time, at the age of sixty-four. Once again, Commander Brown will have to conjure up some creative magic before the Navy can be led into action.

William complains to his wife Eliza –

"My Argentine Navy has only 107 officers and men, only four or five seaworthy ships with 10 guns between them. Sadly, Tomas Espora is dead and some of the old guard like Coe, have thrown in with Uruguay – what am I to do?"

Eliza dismisses his concerns – "This is no different than the previous two times that you have led the Navy – trust your judgement, trust in the Lord and you will find a way to raise your Navy from the ashes."

The Admiral personally scours the docks and the shorelines around Buenos Aires, looking for good recruits and lost cannons. Within a few weeks he has five ships ready to defend their coastline. Pancho Drummond and Tomas Espora are dead, but William has experienced officers from previous campaigns at his side – Irishman Juan King, Francisco Segui, Nicholas Jorge and Alsogaray, plus a full complement of junior officers that includes his own son, Eduardo. Admiral Brown hoists his flag on 'Belgrano' when the Uruguayan Navy under Captain Coe (his former flag-captain) appears off Buenos Aires with a flotilla of ships. Captain Coe sails away before any engagement can occur. On March 30 Commander Brown chases lurking Uruguayan ships from the Colonia area back to Montevideo. He imposes a blockade and uses the following weeks of blockade patrol to train his new crews and to finetune his ships, while his shipwrights are working day and night to outfit more ships to add to his fleet.

It is late May 1841 when Admiral Brown readies for his first naval battle since 1828 – this time against Captain Coe and the Uruguay squadron, a few miles south of Montevideo. The wily Admiral forces the Uruguayan schooner 'Montevideana' aground, and she is destroyed. The crew of the small enemy schooner 'Palmer' breaks into mutiny, and under her Irish Captain, Malcolm Shannon, they join the Argentine fleet. Captain Coe breaks off the engagement and sails his remaining ships back into Montevideo. As a result of the battle, the Argentine squadron have some damaged ships to repair, and they are very short of men – they return to their anchorage, and Admiral Brown sends some officers ashore to recruit more seamen.

Unfortunately, the earlier treaty signed with French Admiral Mackau prevents Argentina from impressing foreign sailors into their Navy, and William's officers only manage to sign sixteen men. Brown therefore decides to idle the smallest ships and transfer their crews to fill out the muster rolls of the larger ones. In July there is a small skirmish with the Uruguayan fleet and in early August Brown has his second battle with Coe in the Plate Estuary, where Argentina has seven ships to Uruguay's five. The Argentine captains do not follow Admiral Brown's orders correctly and his flagship 'Belgrano' ends up doing most of the fighting to secure a victory in the battle. He forces Coe's ships back into port and sinks the schooner 'Rivera'. The Argentine flotilla then returns to their anchorage to pick up fresh supplies after an outbreak of sickness caused by rotten meat. William appeals directly to Governor Rosas to get the supply issue resolved and to free up money for repairs – thereby allowing Captain Coe and the Uruguayans to have temporary free reign on the River Plate Estuary.

By mid-November the Argentine squadron of seven ships is back patrolling the river. Coe comes out to challenge them in December with four ships, and their third battle begins some fifteen miles southeast of Montevideo. The cannonade lasts for several hours, till the Uruguayan ships run low on ammunition, and Coe tries to disengage, but his brig 'Cagancha' falters and Admiral Brown sees an opportunity.

While keeping up their cannon fire he leads the Argentine squadron through the enemy line, cutting off 'Cagancha' from her consorts. She then changes course repeatedly and tries to find refuge in Montevideo. A fresh breeze comes up and William signals his squadron to split into two groups – he orders three ships to continue to pursue 'Cagancha' while he himself leads the other four ships towards the Montevideo roads to intercept the bulk of the Uruguayan squadron when they try to re-enter the harbor. After more damaging hits on 'Cagancha', her captain, Beazley, strikes her colors and the captured Uruguayan ship is towed to Buenos Aires. Meanwhile, contrary winds and a shortage of ammunition conspires against Brown, and that allows Coe to make port. Another minor battle in December shakes the morale of the Uruguayan Navy even further – after which they stay in port a long time, allowing the Argentine fleet to cruise unchallenged up and down the River Plate Estuary.

Admiral Brown uses this time to reinforce the flotillas he had earlier sent up the Parana and Uruguay Rivers – in a mission to support the federalist army of the ex-Uruguayan leader, General Oribe. In January 1842, Brown sends two ships westward under Captain Segui and Captain Jorge to support the land troops deployment of Governor Rosas. In February, he adds 'Chacabuco' and 'Republicano' to his fleet, then the repaired 'Cagancha' is added and renamed as 'Echague'.

• • •

On June 23, the Uruguayan schooner 'Libertad' along with a brig and a lugger, sails upriver from Montevideo, under the command of Captain Giuseppe Garibaldi, an Italian – heading for the rebel province of Corrientes to strike Governor Rosas' forces unexpectedly. Cannon fire from the Argentine fort on Martin Garcia Island alerts Admiral Brown that something is afoot, and his squadron leaves the anchorage immediately. 'Belgrano' runs aground twice before Brown decides she is unsuitable for upriver warfare – he changes his flag to the shallow draft vessel 'Echague' and moves at full speed up the Parana River. Garibaldi's flotilla is well ahead of him, arriving at La Bajada (Parana) on July 19, where he forces his way past Segui's blockade and is joined by three rebel ships from breakaway Corrientes province. They continue as far as Costa Brava, on the border between the provinces of Corrientes and Entre Rios, where they are forced to stop because of a drastic fall in river depth.

Admiral Brown's pursuit continues relentlessly, via sails and oars – he possesses great stamina for his age. He rendezvous' with Segui's squadron and commandeers three vessels from him to increase the strength of his own flotilla to eight ships, with 450 men and 50 guns. By August 14 they have almost caught up to Garibaldi's flotilla when the wind suddenly drops at nightfall, and Brown orders his ships to anchor where they are. The battle begins at sunrise, first between both sets of marines, because the Argentine ships cannot get close enough to effectively engage the enemy with cannons. Brown halts the action at 4 p.m. and decides to feed all his crews, during which time he has himself rowed from ship to ship to encourage his men – stopping to accept an invitation from Captain Donati of 'Americano' to eat a meal on his poop deck. During the meal an enemy cannonball slams into the riverbank nearby, showering their food with mud spatters.

The Admiral is unperturbed by the incident, and he comments quietly to Donati.

"Captain, the enemy have sent us salt for our meal."

The battle begins in earnest as night falls. Garibaldi sends two fireships down on the current, trying to disrupt the Argentine formation. Both are intercepted and guided to the side of the river to burn out. When dawn breaks on August 16, the Admiral has his ships in perfect position. Using what little available wind, and their oars, he pushes the attack. The accuracy of the Argentine gunners makes short work of the Uruguayan squadron – reducing them to riddled hulks.

Garibaldi manages to get ashore and can escape overland with his marines – Admiral Brown elects to not risk his men with a pursuit over such difficult terrain. Brown moves among his victorious seamen and awards Lieutenant Cordero for his brave actions – giving him the ornate sword taken from the dead body of Garibaldi's second-in-command. Six schooners, a passenger ship and two fireships are captured, dozens of prisoners are taken, and a large quantity of gunpowder is recovered.

On August 17 Admiral Brown places the river force under the command of Captain Pinedo and sails back to Buenos Aires in '9 de Julio' where he receives another hero's welcome. He doesn't rest on his laurels, but instead he sets a plan in motion to improve his squadron. By late September he has eleven sea-going warships plus a significant number of armed smaller vessels – with a total of 150 guns and 1600 sailors. His Argentine deep-sea squadron can sail the Plate Estuary unchallenged, and his Argentine privateers in the Atlantic are harrying enemy merchant shipping on route to the Uruguay ports of Montevideo and Maldonado. In January 1843 General Oribe's army defeats General Rivera – and preparations begin for a full land invasion of Uruguay and a full blockade of Montevideo. William leaves Los Pozos with four ships to tighten the blockade of Montevideo while Oribe's army tightens its siege on land. Captain Pinedo captures Mercedes on the Rio Negro, the enemy's final river port, thereby opening the trade routes all the way up the Parana River to Paraguay.

Then Captain Pinedo sails his 22-ship flotilla to Colonia and lands 2,000 troops ashore to join Oribe's army for the march on Montevideo.

• • •

Coincidently, the large British frigate HMS Alfred under Commodore Purvis, commander of British naval forces in the South Atlantic, arrives in the River Plate Estuary and begins harassing Admiral Brown's Argentine flotilla. Purvis sends him a condescending note addressed to "Mr. Brown", ordering him, as a British subject, to take no more part in this conflict. William does not reply and sails to Buenos Aires to discuss this demand in the full knowledge that he had never taken Argentine citizenship. Purvis' note is ignored, and Brown goes back to blockade duty, now with seven ships in his squadron. In April Purvis sends another note to the Admiral, informing him that any British subject interfering with any British ship near the coast of Uruguay will be deemed guilty of piracy, with the obvious implication that such punishment will be death by hanging.

Commodore Purvis then proceeds to break the Argentine blockade (which had been imposed according to international law), by escorting a British merchant ship into the port of Montevideo. The British commander also puts pressure on the French ships in the estuary to change their stance from recognizing the Argentine blockade to denouncing it. The next note from Purvis is addressed to 'Commodore Brown' and orders him to return control of a small island to Uruguay – one that the Argentines had recently captured. Governor Rosas' orders to Admiral Brown are to avoid hostile incidents with the major powers – so he cedes control of the island to Uruguay. Even with these interferences, the blockade is causing great hardship in Montevideo.

Purvis keeps up the harassment – he boards Admiral Brown's Argentine flagship 'Belgrano' on one occasion to personally protest the positioning of the Argentine ship. Admiral Brown listens to his protest and then says, without giving Purvis the courtesy of any title –

"Sir, you have said your piece. Now it is time for us to get on with our naval duties. My officer is ready to escort you to your boat."

Just after this confrontation, HMS 'Alfred' fires on 'Echague' and '9 de Julio' to prevent them from sailing to Maldonado, on blockade duty. William realizes that his hands are tied by Governor Rosas' orders and that this kind of foreign interference means that the blockade cannot be fully enforced. He finds other ways to support General Oribe's army that the British are not able to see or affect. Governor Rosas is getting squeezed by the major powers who all want a slice of the potential trade and money from South America, and Rosas' own very survival is in question – a situation that pushes him to make rash decisions. In mid-May he orders the blockade squadron back to Buenos Aires and then he vacillates for a month before ordering the Argentine ships back to sea once again to patrol the area around Montevideo.

Meanwhile, Garibaldi is back in Montevideo, and he organizes a scheme to get urgent supplies for the city – using fast small craft that hug the coast and move at night. Admiral Brown uses similar vessels to apprehend these 'mosquito' craft, and several armed encounters occur. The land war becomes vicious and there are some shameful acts when both sides murder a significant number of prisoners – a part of Civil War that disgusts William Brown, because he is a man who continues to treat all his prisoners with proper dignity. He decides to tighten the blockade as the year end approaches. In a joint operation with Oribe's land forces they succeed in subduing the port of Maldonado, only to lose control of it again when their garrison is surprised by Rivera's forces on December 31. On January 2, 1844, two of William's ships, '9 de Julio' and 'Echague' stage a surprise attack on Maldonado and recapture the port – then they succeed in repulsing Rivera's troops when they mount a counterattack.

• • •

By this stage the Argentine Merchant Navy has grown to some 880 ships, a tribute to Admiral Brown's ability to keep the river and the greater estuary area free of hostile privateers. Neighboring forces and those of other naval powers continue to interfere with and challenge the Argentine dominance in the Rio de la Plata as the year of 1844 progresses. By July, Brazil openly supports Uruguay against Argentina, and Chile then occupies Argentine land down south along the Magellan Straits, causing friction between these neighbors who had previously been allies. William replaces the worn-out 'Belgrano' with the brig 'San Martin', naming her in honor of the founding general of the Argentine Army.

While Admiral Brown is ashore, the commander of the U.S. frigate 'Congress' seizes some Argentine ships on the pretext that they are interfering with Uruguayan fishing vessels – he then orders and succeeds in having the Argentine naval ensign hauled down. This is a flagrant violation of the Monroe Doctrine, under which the US was to help Argentina to rid her waters of aggressive European warships. During December, Admiral Brown is aboard his new flagship 'San Martin', at sea and in charge of the blockade. When he hears that Garibaldi has put together another Uruguayan fleet to challenge Argentina, Brown asks Rosas for the newly refitted ships 'Federal' and 'Maipu' to strengthen his flotilla. Both are sent immediately, and Garibaldi decides to stay in port.

In January of 1845, Governor Rosas orders that the blockade to be applied with equal severity to ships of all nationalities, and he declares that no ship which calls at Montevideo will be allowed entry into the port of Buenos Aires. This quickly starves Montevideo of merchant shipping. General Rivera's land forces suffer a resounding defeat to General Oribe's attackers in February, and Admiral Brown receives orders to begin a daily bombardment of Montevideo, to push Uruguay towards full defeat.

Behind the scenes, the foreign major powers are pressuring Governor Rosas, and by April there are 28 foreign warships in the River Plate estuary in a show of force, with 360 guns and 4,800 men. The French and British diplomatic representatives withdraw from Buenos Aires, and both fleets send armed landing parties into Montevideo to reinforce its defense against Argentina's blockade. These same foreign powers order General Oribe to cease hostilities and they declare their own blockade of all the Uruguayan ports under his control.

Out of the blue, in mid-July, Governor Rosas orders Admiral Brown to lift the blockade of Montevideo and to return to Buenos Aires. Unfortunately, Brown is still under strict instructions to avoid using force against the foreign powers – an order that puts him in a dreadful predicament when he is informed by the French and British commanders that his Argentine squadron "is detained".

On July 31 the French and British agree that the Argentinian squadron can return to Buenos Aires after Admiral Brown hands over any French and British subjects in his crews. He responds, asking to postpone the handing over till the ships reach home base. Receiving no reply by the afternoon of August 2 he gives orders for his ships to proceed to Buenos Aires. French warships open fire as soon as the

Argentine ships begin to move – leaving Admiral Brown no option but to strike his colors and surrender – the saddest moment of his distinguished naval career.

This surrender becomes known in Argentine history as "the Robbery of the Squadron" – the surrendered Argentine ships are shared out between the French and British squadrons. Admiral Brown and his officers are held prisoner until they sign a declaration stating that they will take no further part in the war against Uruguay. This is completely illegal in Admiral Brown's mind, and he makes it clear to their respective government representatives that he is not obligated to keep a promise that is extracted by 'force majeure'. The Buenos Aires crowds still turn out in large numbers to greet their hero on his return to the city. Notably absent is Governor Rosas, who bears the responsibility for the humiliation of his Navy, and his gallant Admiral, while he himself is cutting deals to hold on to power.

• • •

Admiral William Brown goes home to Casa Amarilla. He is not recalled to service. The citizens of Buenos Aires, who now include William Brown, must watch as the end game unfolds – mounting foreign pressure on Governor Rosas, the slow collapse of his power base and his ultimate fall. After the fall of Rosas, many of Wiliam's fellow naval officers are dismissed.

Admiral Brown is allowed to retain his rank in his unofficial retirement, for reasons stated as follows –

"On account of your former loyal services to the Argentine Republic at the most solemn stages of your career."

Admiral William Brown is a proud man, a man of the people and a man who has won great naval victories for Argentina. He is humiliated by his forced surrender, having never been defeated in battle.

Despite all of this he continues to be treated with immense respect – he is revered by people of all political opinions and is universally the hero of the Portenos.

CHAPTER TEN

RETIREMENT AND PILGRIMAGE TO FAMINE IRELAND

Admiral Brown is sixty-eight years old when this "Robbery of the Squadron" incident causes him to be unofficially retired from the Argentinian Navy. At that time, he is still in reasonably good health, despite his battle wounds and his fall from the house balcony during his prime fighting years.

As he did in previous life setbacks, William retreats to his Casa Amarilla, his haven, and there he busies himself with farming activities and with his grandchildren. He reads the shipping news in the British Packet and in the Mercantile Gazette, which encourages him to spend time looking out to sea with his long spyglass. There are some warehouses in Colonia that he still has a commercial interest in, and he makes visits there, plus to Montevideo to see his daughter Martina and her family. His naval subordinates and other seafaring acquaintances are frequent visitors to Casa Amarilla to enjoy his hospitality and friendship.

Despite his peculiar childhood in Ireland and early departure from the land of his birth, William Brown has maintained an interest in Irish patriotic attempts to break the British stranglehold over the Irish people and their culture. From the early 1820's he has been an admirer of Daniel O' Connell's movement for Irish Catholic Emancipation and sent money to 'The Liberator' several times. Through his Irish-born confessor in Buenos Aires, Father Fahy, he learns of the devastating famine gripping Ireland during the 1840's. William has not set foot in Ireland since his fleeting visit in 1818 during the 'Hercules' court case, when unfortunately, he had to leave Dublin shortly after his arrival there, to deal with urgent court matters. Even at the age of seventy, he has not lost his willingness to be decisive, he now makes a snap decision to visit his homeland after hearing Fr. Fahey's accounts of how the terrible famine has been affecting Brown's home area of County Mayo.

By visiting the country William hopes to inspire the people of Ireland in general, his own County Mayo in particular, and he wants to render any assistance he can during this disastrous time.

In July of 1847 he departs from Buenos Aires on 'La Ninfa' in the company of his daughter Martina, bound for Liverpool. They stay a few days with Rose Brennan, with whom he has had sporadic contact in recent years and who is a relative of his deceased sister, Mary Brown. His brother Michael had also settled in Liverpool after leaving Buenos Aires and he continued to reside there until his death some years before the famine.

The Argentinian guests spend several hours with Michael's widow, Margaret, and meet two of his children, Sarah and John Michael. Then they cross to Dublin on a ferry and travel west by horse-drawn coach, via Athlone and Boyle – finally taking a Bianconi coach to Ballina, County Mayo. This Ireland visit is at a time in 1847 when the effects of the famine are plain to be seen all along the way. William sees first-hand the starving Irish wandering along the roads, gaunt figures foraging in the fields, and sadly he also sees the dead bodies strewn along the roadside as the carriage heads west – he is profoundly shocked.

In the town of Ballina, the population has exploded with the influx of thousands of starving people from the surrounding area, who are seeking relief outside the overflowing workhouse. He visits his nearby hometown of Foxford – a tiny village of 700 people on the banks of the River Moy that has changed little since he lived there as a child. The local relief center is too overwhelmed to spend time talking with the visitors and warns them of the prevalence of the 'famine fever' – typhus. The relief committee is happy to accept his money donation, and the local priest blesses William and Martina, and gives them sets of locally made rosary beads.

William can plainly see that Ireland is on her knees and is too preoccupied with basic survival to be concerned with the ideals of freedom fighting – there is no point in telling starving people the story of how South America won their liberation battle. William asks Martina to sit with him beside the banks of the flowing River Moy and he points out the distant Ox Mountains where the river rises – then he dips his hands into the cold clear water. Despondently, and feeling somewhat ill by this stage, William quickly leaves for Dublin and returns to Liverpool with mostly sad memories.

After another visit to see Margaret Brown and another short stay with Rose, they board a ship bound for Montevideo. Martina's husband and her young son, William, welcome them home, and Admiral Brown has plans to seek out his erstwhile enemy, Giuseppi Garibaldi, who is living in the city. It turns out that Garibaldi seeks him out when he hears that the Admiral is in town. The two heroes meet, embrace, and William spends several hours talking to the Italian and his Brazilian wife, Anita.

• • •

William then returns to Buenos Aires and to his quiet farm life with his wife Eliza at Casa Amarilla, where his son Eduardo oversees a crew of farm workers that are eking out a small profit. One day while William is out working in his fields a carriage arrives at his house. Out steps a man in a starched uniform adorned with medals – none other than the head of the Brazilian Navy, Admiral John Pascoe Grenfell. The

Brazilian insists on walking alongside Eliza to find William in the field after she tells him that he is out sowing crops. William recognizes the approaching uniformed gentleman, mainly from the one empty sleeve. When they are a few meters away from each other the two old men stand still for many seconds and gaze at each other, then approach and embrace. The heroes then walk back to the house together – one man in a splendid uniform and the other in simple farm clothes, and Eliza Brown prepares tea for them in the modest reception room of their home.

Admiral Grenfell speaks – "I still remember when the frigate '25 de Mayo' crashed through our formation and then held out under fire from twenty-three of our ships. You turned down my invitation to take tea with me and then almost blasted me out of the water with your Argentine gunners."

William's wrinkled face beams as the memories flood back.

"Thankfully you survived, and I am so grateful that you have come back to visit me. I now invite you to take that tea with me in quieter times than the heat of battle. Forgive me for being in my humble farming clothes."

They both laugh, take tea and settle into comfortable chairs for a long chat.

In 1854 William hears of the death in the United States of General Carlos Maria de Alvear, his comrade from the Spanish and Brazilian wars. The General had served as Argentine Ambassador to the US, and later decided to remain there as an exile. William learns that the General's remains are coming to Buenos Aires on the 'Rio Bamba'. He asks permission from the government to be allowed to go on board the ship in the La Plata Estuary, and to accompany his friend on the very waters on which they had served together with such distinction. Not only is Admiral Brown accorded this privilege, but he is also given command of the ship for this final part of the voyage.

William's gesture brings an outpouring of emotional appreciation for both the deceased General and for the Admiral himself from the Portenos, and from their government leaders. Several eulogies for Alvear are given prominence in the newspapers and Admiral Brown is praised for his devotion to his friends. William is further praised as the defender of the nation where he chose to live, and readers are reminded that this 'foreigner' deserves just as much merit as any of the heroes that were born in Argentina.

In December of 1856 personal tragedy strikes Admiral Brown's family once again when his son Eduardo is killed in a freak accident on the farm. Edwardo's death takes a tremendous toll on William, and his own health declines from that point forward. His doctor prescribes total rest for the Admiral – Eliza persuades their two children living nearby, Martina and Guillermo, to take turns spending special time with their father. William's confessor, Father Fahy, introduces William to the journalist and local rising political star, Bartolome Mitre, who is Minister of War for Buenos Aires at this time when the home province is in temporary separation from the rest of the Argentine federation. The two men become fast friends, and Mitre works hard to persuade William to write his memoirs, as they often sit together admiring the view of Rio de la Plata from Casa Amarilla.

Wiliam responds to Mitre's request after a few minutes gazing out at the vast estuary –

"I am not a man that is drawn to writing about myself. My life before Argentina is of no importance, and even here in Buenos Aires the only events that deserve to be remembered are our victories during the Spanish and Brazilian wars."

"My dear Admiral, you are being far too modest. You are the person that is dearest to the hearts of the Portenos, and they want to hear your story in your own words. Promise me you will write up your Memorias of the campaigns of liberation and of your great naval victories."

"Soon – very soon, I will send you my Memorias."

William keeps his promise – he knows that his time is not long, and he has always been a man to finish his tasks. His Memorias are a simple chronicle of events where Brown himself is just another character in the story of liberty. They cover the period from 1813 to 1828, nothing about his early life in Ireland and nothing about the Argentine Civil War that William wants only to forget. He has kind words for the brave men that fought under his command – like Drummond, King, Rosales, Sequi and

Espora. William sends a note to Bartolome along with the handwritten Memorias –

'I was determined to complete these notes for you before undertaking the long voyage to the dark seas of death.'

On March 3, 1857, one of William's former officers, Alejandro Muratura, is seated next to Admiral Brown's bed, talking with the resting Admiral. It is noon and the officer stands up to leave, when the Admiral tugs his sleeve.

"Dear Jose, the time has come when I must move to a new anchorage. But don't worry, I have my pilot already on board."

With that, Admiral William Brown draws his last breath at eighty years of age.

• • •

William's wife Eliza, Father Fahy, his daughter Martina and son Guillermo were in an adjoining room, and they came immediately to his bedside. The doctor was summoned, and he confirmed the Admiral's death. Father Fahy sent a letter by courier to the Governor of Buenos Aires, Dr. Obligado, part of which included the following –

"William Brown was a Christian whose faith impiety could not break; a patriot whose integrity corruption could not buy; a hero whom danger never succeeded in overcoming."

The Governor issued a decree ordering official government condolences to be presented to Admiral William Brown's widow and family, they appointed a naval guard of honor to watch over his coffin and named a commission under the Minister of War to organize a state funeral. The dining room at Casa Amarilla was turned into a funeral chapel where William Brown was laid out in his resplendent Admiral's dress uniform His coffin was draped with the Argentine national flag, plus the flag from the Battle of Los Pozos, and his ornamental sword lay beside him. Soon, a constant stream of people began to file past the coffin to gaze one last time on their hero – peasants, friends, political dignitaries from near and far, religious clerics of all denominations, members of the Army and Navy. When the lid was placed on the coffin the inscription on it summed up this Irishman from County Mayo, a modest man who was loved by all Argentinians –

"REMAINS OF ARGENTINE ALMIRANTE DON GUILLERMO BROWN"

A huge funeral cortege made its way to the Catholic Chapel on March 4, where Father Fahy presided over the funeral service, followed by a massive procession to Recoleta Cemetery. The Argentine fleet fired seventeen broadside salutes, one every quarter of an hour. At the graveside the family were joined by the Governor, all the government ministers, generals from the Army and officers from the Navy – among them being Francisco Sequi, the hero of the Battle of Juncal.

Bartolome Mitre, Minister of War, delivered the stirring graveside oration, which included these words -

"Admiral Brown, alive, standing on the quarterdeck of his ship, was worth as much as a fleet to us –

If some day, new dangers threaten the shores of our Argentine fatherland, and we should find ourselves obliged to confide to our floating timbers the banner of May – the conquering breath of the old Admiral will swell our sails, his ghost will grab our helm in the midst of the tempest and his warlike figure will be seen to stand on the top deck of our ships, guiding us through the thickness of the cannon smoke and the din of the grappling shouts.

Farewell, good and noble Admiral of the Fatherhood of the Argentine people; farewell.

The shades of your esteemed dead comrades will rise to receive you in the mysterious mansion of death, and while they salute you with palms in their hands, the people of Buenos Aires are weeping for the death of their illustrious Admiral."

The capital of the Argentine federation at the time of Admiral Brown's death was located at the city of Parana, where President Jose de Urquiza led funeral honors for "the hero of the Argentine naval glories."

The journal 'Nacional' published a eulogy entitled 'Rivadavia y Brown' in which William Brown was directly linked with the great Argentine statesman, Bernardino Rivadavia.

The Nacional wrote –

"Brown belonged to a class of leader who saw it as their duty not to discuss the orders of his government, but to obey them within the limits imposed by military honor and the dignity of men. Bernardino Rivadavia was the most complete personification of liberty and progress in the Rio de la Plata, and Admiral Brown was the symbol of the glory of the Rio de la Plata.'

THE END

EPILOGUE

Admiral William Brown was not a wealthy man, despite his national fame. He and Elizabeth were blessed with nine children – William: Eliza: Juan: Ignacio: Eduardo: Martina: Miguel: Patricio and Pedro. Joy and sorrow visited the family, and three of their children died very young.

Upon his death, William left substantial debts behind, and he died without making a will. His widow, Elizabeth Brown, had to sell off some of their land to repay debts and cover the cost to erect a modest gravestone for her husband. When Elizabeth died, the family could not bury her alongside her husband because non-Catholic burials were not allowed in Recoleta Cemetery – she was laid to rest in Cementerio de Victoria.

Years later a new monument was built at William's grave, a single Corinthian Column topped by the model of a ship with wind-blown sails. The Admiral's ashes are conserved at the grave in a bronze urn cast from cannons of ships he commanded. The monument was painted green in honor of his Irish birth and in 1946 it was declared a National Historic Monument.

Casa Amarilla was sold by the family, then fell into disrepair and was eventually demolished. The site later housed a fuel depot, a tram terminus and a potato market. In 1983, to commemorate the 206th anniversary of Admiral Brown's birth, a replica of Casa Amarilla was built on the street in Buenos Aires that was named in his honor – Avenida Almirante Brown. It houses the Department of Naval Historic Studies, the Brownian Institute, and a library / museum dedicated to Admiral Brown and the Argentine Navy. The museum holds the original sword worn by Admiral Brown – a replica of the sword is worn by all Admirals of the Argentina Navy.

Almirante Guillermo Brown is still revered as a national hero in Argentina, where there are hundreds of monuments in his honor, and streets all over the country are named for him.

In Ireland, there is a monument to him in Foxford, County Mayo, the town of his birth, and another in the capital city of Dublin, on a quay alongside the River Liffey.

Every year the Irish national rugby team plays the Argentina national team in a match for the Admiral Brown Cup.

• • •

SECOND AUTHOR NOTE

As mentioned in the Prologue of this book, information on the childhood years of both John Barry and William Brown is scarce and therefore their early lives are open to interpretation.

This is particularly so in the case of William Brown. Many historians and commentators have accepted the story path that William went to Philadelphia with his father as a young child. As that story goes, not long after their arrival in America his father was struck down by yellow fever. The orphaned child wandered the docks until he was taken pity on by a ship captain who brought him aboard his vessel, fed him and then gave him a job as a cabin boy on the ship. His ensuing merchant shipping career took off from there and he eventually moved to Buenos Aires and found his calling there. From my study of the historical facts, this story is too simplistic and does not support William Brown's arrival in South America or explain how he acquired such great naval skills that allowed him to build a Navy for Argentina on three separate occasions.

William Brown's life from the time of his arrival in Buenos Aires and his later naval career is corroborated by multiple historical records and documents – which I have made use of. He never divulged any specific details about his early life and stated publicly that he regarded that story as being unimportant.

I researched the likely pathways that could explain his later expertise in naval warfare and his organizational ability to create three Argentine Navies from scratch, during his extraordinary career. He needed to have significant formal training to enable him to do this and the most obvious source of that training at the time was the British Royal Navy. Furthermore, when he was Commander of the Argentine Navy, he had several ex-Royal Navy officers on his ships who had total confidence and respect for him. A child from a peasant Catholic family with little or no education and who spoke very little English, had no route into the Royal Navy in William Brown's lifetime. This and other circumstantial evidence led me to search for a plausible pathway for William to enter the Royal Navy – via the patronage route of somebody important enough to open doors for the young boy.

The Irish aristocracy during William Brown's early years were related by blood and marriage to the very top of British society, including Army Generals and Navy Admirals. Society being what it was, many of these aristocrats fathered illegitimate children and history has lots of examples of these children doing very well for themselves when given the opportunity. The narrative thread I chose has the real-life historical figures to support this route for William to enter the Royal Navy and once he was there his natural ability enabled him to learn and progress. His reluctance to talk openly about his early years also supports this narrative, as illegitimacy was kept hidden by all of Irish society.

His early-life story is of minor significance to the overall story of this great man, and I respectfully ask forgiveness from any readers who prefer a different beginning.

• • •

I hope you have enjoyed this book and will explore my other titles.

My website at www.MichaelGerardAuthor.com has more information about me, my books, and links to where they can be purchased – all are in print, e-book and audio editions.

RESEARCH SOURCES, REFERENCES, INSPIRATIONS, ACKNOWLEDGEMENTS

Part One –

Gallant John Barry by William Bell Clark (1938)

Story of Commander John Barry by Martin Griffin (1908)

Commodore John Barry by J Gurn (1933)

J Fenimore Cooper's History of the Navy of the United States – USNI

How the Irish won the American Revolution by Philip Thomas Tucker

John Barry Papers – Library of Congress

Richard Dale Papers – Library of Congress

John Hancock Papers – Library of Congress

A Naval History of the American Revolution by Gardner Allen (1913)

The Life of Commodore Barry by J Brown & J Kessler (1813)

Patriots of the American Revolution by Richard Dorson (1953)

John Barry Fighting Irishman – American History Illustrated

America's Maritime Heritage – Naval Institute Press
Ireland in the Empire by Francis James (1973)
Naval Records of the American Revolution – Government Printing Office
Commodore John Barry by William Meany (1911)
Stodder's War by Michael Palmer (1987)
Robert Morris Forgotten Patriot by Eleanor Young (1950)
Benjamin Rush Papers – Library of Congress
George Washington Papers – Library of Congress
Mrs. John Barry: A Patriot in her own Right by Peg Pappalardo
John Barry: American Hero in the age of Sail by Tom McGrath
The National Maritime Museum of Ireland – Library Archives
Joshua Humphreys Papers – War Department Papers
Who Built the first United States Navy by Colonel Humphreys
County Wexford Library Archives – Local Studies
John Barry: A Most Fervent Patriot by William Morgan
Barry-Hayes Papers – Independence Seaport Museum
Richard Sommers Papers – Gloucester Co Historical Society
John Adams and the creation of the American Navy by William Anderson
Ships and Seamen of the American Revolution by Jack Coggins
The Great Age of Sail by Edita Lausanne

Part Two –
Admiral William Brown: Master of the River Plate by Thomas Hudson
The English in South America by Michael Mulhall
Argentina 1516 to 1987 by David Rock
The Admiral from Mayo by John de Coursey Ireland
Almirante Brown by Captain Ratto
The Story of the Irish in Argentina by Mario Belgrano
Admiral William Brown: Liberator of the South Atlantic by Marcos Aguinis
Great Britain and Argentina by Gallo
Life of Richard Earl Howe by J Barrow
Campanas Navales de la Republica Argentina by Angel Justiniano
Spanish American Revolutions by J Lynch
The Royal Navy by Laird Clowes
Enciclopedia General del Mar – Ediciones Garriga by Jose Martinez Hidalgo
English Invasion of the River Plate in 1806 by A Kraft
Las Memorias del Almirante Brown – Academia Nacional
Commissioned Officers of the Royal Navy – British National Maritime Museum
A History of the King's Serjeants at law in Ireland
British Newspaper Archives from Eighteenth Century
Collier's Artillery Encyclopedia Vol 2

MEET THE AUTHOR

Michael Gerard was born in Kilkelly, Co Mayo in Ireland. Having the inclination to roam he left Ireland in the late 1970's. After career stints in other European countries and in South Africa he settled in America in 1985 and calls Beaufort SC home. He is a working author – he and his family run a processing machinery business based in SC. History and writing are two of his passions and they have come together as his writing career has blossomed alongside his busy 8-to-5-day job. His mission is to make Irish history interesting and enjoyable to the average reader by highlighting real people from that rich history who have made an impact on Ireland itself and the world at large. One of his delights from researching his own books is the knowledge gained in the process, a pleasurable chore that usually leads him to finding new subjects for his future writing. 'The Irish Admiralty' is a book that is a shining example of the Irish spirit at its best, in the personage of Commodore John Barry and Admiral William Brown. Both men rose from humble beginnings in Ireland of the 1700's to become celebrated naval heroes in their adopted countries of

The United States of America and The Republic of Argentina respectively.

This is Michael Gerard's fourth published novel.

See Author's website www.MichaelGerardAuthor.com for more details and links to purchase his books – either online or from your favorite bookstore. Readers are encouraged to post reviews and spread the good news.

Follow him on X – @MgerardK and on Facebook – MichaelGerard-Author

www.ingramcontent.com/pod-product-compliance
Lightning Source LLC
Chambersburg PA
CBHW020943310726
48980CB00001B/29

9798992351422